SENSUOUS SEDUCTION

Kalida could feel the tension in Deuce's body as he balanced himself over her, waiting, seeing everything she could not hide. It was all in her face—the wonder of her response to his kiss and her determination not to give in to it.

His lips touched hers lightly. "Marry me," he whispered.

"I don't want to," she said succinctly.

"That hardly matters," he answered. "All you have to do is admit"—his lips descended to her traitorous mouth—"that I can make you want me."

Suddenly she wanted to pull closer instead of thrust him away, wanted to feel his hands upon her heated skin, caressing her, enflaming her.

He was expertly ensnaring her in the trap he had laid for her, and she was becoming his willing victim. . . .

Reckless Desire

THEA DEVINE

ZEBRA BOOKS
KENSINGTON PUBLISHING CORP.

ZEBRA BOOKS

are published by

Kensington Publishing Corp.
475 Park Avenue South
New York, NY 10016

First printing: January, 1988

Printed in the United States of America

My eternal gratitude to
Page Cuddy,
and to Carin Cohen for her
unerring sensitivity.

This one is for my children,
Michael and Thomas,
and for John, my friend, my love,
my husband.

Prologue

May, 1873

She didn't understand why Ellie had tried all the week long to put off their plans for returning home for just another day.

"Papa is expecting us today," she pointed out adamantly as she and Ellie packed clothes and schoolbooks, and she tried very hard not to act as if she had just been let out of jail.

"Kalida, what harm will waiting one more day do?" Ellie asked reasonably. She was beginning to resent Kalida's stubbornness and the fact that the onus of dissuading her imminent return was on *her* shoulders and not Hal Ryland's, where it so squarely belonged. His letter still crackled in her pocket where she kept it every moment lest the curious Kalida discover it—and her perfidy.

The point in fact was her father did not want her to return home as scheduled. Her father didn't want her to know the ranch was—again—in almighty trouble and that he was depending on Deuce Cavender's wealth, bounty, and good business sense to salvage his winter.

And he especially didn't want her to be aware of the fact that her own beloved pony was in the string of horses he was selling to Deuce.

7

"*I* am going home today," Kalida stated, "even if I have to go by myself. I'll—I'll ride, that's all. You can send the rest of the stuff later. And then," she added slyly, "you won't even have to make the trip from town." Her finely shaped black brows lifted in a show of innocence, as though to say she didn't mean anything by that simple statement, but her cobalt eyes, glimmering with mischief, betrayed her.

Ellie turned away, biting back a comment and shuttering her feelings behind her opaque black gaze. Kalida could very well ride back home without her, she thought, assessing Kalida's threat. Kalida could do too damned much for a fifteen-year-old girl. She ran the Ryland ranch, had done so for a year or more. Had taken to it like she had been born on the Montana plains, while her sickly mother wasted away from the unendurable hardships.

She could ride and rope with the best cowhand, and someone had taught her to shoot straight as an arrow with a rifle. She could cook and tend to the house, she raised the garden and looked after the ponies, and if Hal didn't have her, he would have sold out two years ago.

Kalida Ryland did not need Ellie Dean.

"All right, Kalida," she said resignedly, "we'll make the trip today."

All it required was hiring the wagon and team. Kalida handled the reins with relish, and they arrived at the Ryland ranch in the late afternoon, after a wearing day long trip.

As they pulled up to the house they found a crowd of men hanging over the barn corral fence watching one man on horseback within who seemed to be cutting horses. Kalida leapt from the wagon and catapulted herself onto the fence. She knew the rider. He was Deuce Cavender, their wealthy, powerful neighbor to the east—if an autocrat like him could be characterized as a neighbor. She had always been of the opinion that he had been trying to drive them out; he wanted the prime Ryland range, and he wanted control of all southern Montana if he could get it. He wanted, she thought, to be king of all he surveyed.

She could abstractly admire the ramrod straight posture of his that sat his mount as if he were royalty, the flexing control of his muscular thighs that moved the horse effortlessly to his will as he circled his prey, stalked it mercilessly, and ultimately captured it.

She hated him.

She sensed Ellie behind her. "What's *he* doing here?" she hissed under the applause and catcalls of the men who were obviously Sweetland ranch hands.

"He's cutting out horses," Ellie said mildly, her bright dark gaze on Deuce Cavender's broad shoulders as he worked the lariat.

"Why?" Kalida demanded sharply. "Where's Papa?"

"I don't know; he's not expecting us today," Ellie evaded, turning her head to search for Hal Ryland's distinctive white mane. Obviously, he could not bear to be a part of this. She did not know whether to stay with Kalida or to search him out.

"Malca's in with the string that he's cutting," Kalida whispered suddenly. She turned on Ellie. "What is going on? What has Papa done?" Her eyes shot back to Deuce Cavender and a frown punctuated her troubled expression. She knew. She already knew.

"Papa sold the horses," she said in a unequivocal voice. She watched Ellie's face, which instantly registered the truth of her statement. "Things are *that* bad?" she demanded in disbelief. Ellie nodded, her heart sinking.

"*So* bad that even Malca has to go?" Kalida pressed, with a note in her voice that Ellie knew boded trouble.

"Yes." How could she lie—now?

"Oh God . . ." The moan came from deep in her soul; Kalida turned to the corral again, watching as one of

Cavender's cowhands released the next quarter horse for testing and came still nearer to bringing Malca into the ring.

That Papa would give up Malca! She couldn't bear it. She had so little else but her indomitable strength of will and sense of adventure. And Malca, her freedom.

"He won't have him," she ground out suddenly, clenching her fists. She began climbing down the fence, only to feel Ellie's ineffectually restraining hand.

"Don't," Ellie begged. "Don't do anything foolish. Don't embarrass your father."

"That damned Deuce Cavender doesn't *need* Malca—and I do," Kalida said stonily, allowing herself to be detained for just that moment.

"Kalida, you can't—they have a contract—"

"I don't care," Kalida raged. "Damn him, damn him! Do you think he doesn't know that's *my* horse? Do you think that cowboy king cares about anything or anyone? I'll tell you what I know, Ellie, I'll tell you what I've learned already after two years' living in this godforsaken country: You take what you want, and everyone else be damned. And I'm going to take back my horse."

She wrenched away from Ellie and darted toward the barn, the only sure way to obscure herself and her intent. Ellie watched her until she could no longer see her midnight black hair, and then she turned and ran for the house.

Kalida caught Ellie's movement and was glad she was out of the way. By the time she scared up Papa, Kalida knew she would have accomplished her ends: All she had to do was jump Malca and get him over the corral fence.

Tricky. But not impossible. And her determination was fired up and intense, licked with white hot flames of hatred for the man who would use her Papa so. She darted into the barn, the fastest way to reach the corral side where Malca was gated. And the quickest way to arm herself should someone try to stop her. Papa always kept a gun buried in the stall nearest the doorway. And right then Kalida knew she would kill anyone who tried to stop her.

She foraged for the firearm, tucked it in her skirt, and ran for the corral door, flattening herself against the outside wall as she exited; she was in luck, for that perpendicular wall was deep in shadow. She watched the horses milling and the cowboys refocus their attention on Deuce Cavender who had, wonder of wonders, just then rejected one of the quarter horses in the string. A murmur swept the onlookers, and under the cover of that, Kalida took her chance and whistled shrilly. She was rewarded by the pricking of Malca's neat ears. Another whistle and the beautiful bay stallion lifted his head and turned toward the sound.

Kalida waited. It was almost as if time were suspended and she and the horse were moving in minuscule increments of motion.

Malca's curiosity propelled him to the edge of the herd of horses. Another whistle, now faint, had him trotting effortlessly to the side of the barn where, recognizing his mistress, he tensely waited to see just what Kalida would do.

Kalida waited. The noise around her rose and abated. When she was sure that all attention was fixed again on the corral ring, she jacked herself onto the fence and in a vaulting motion hurled herself onto Malca's back and spurred him toward the rear fence.

She heard the shouts behind her and the wind rushing in her ears. She felt her triumph rise into the wind. She had opposed and defeated the mighty Deuce Cavender.

She twisted her body and grabbed the gun as she became aware of hoofbeats behind her. The king, riding to battle, determined not to lose a dollar of his investment, she thought angrily, lifting the pistol and taking

11

careful aim. She had one shot, one shot only; she risked scaring Malca and throwing herself. She risked that she might kill Deuce Cavender. She didn't care. She squeezed the trigger; the resultant roar jarred Malca's smooth gait and he almost stumbled.

And he caught himself just in time. The back fence rushed toward them. She tossed the gun to free her hands and grabbed onto Malca's mane as she urged him onward, then smoothly up and over the back fence.

In the distance, in the stunned silence, the gaping audience watched her receding figure.

Behind her, Deuce Cavender lay on the ground holding his grazed shoulder, a grim smile on his firm lips, his gray eyes hard and stone cold.

One

May, 1880

"He *what?*"

Kalida whirled on her father, her eyes a blazing cobalt shock of amazement.

"Must I recount the whole bald conversation?" her father asked her gently. "Dear Kalida, it is not impossible to understand that he wants to marry. And he wants *you.*"

"Nonsense," she snapped, wheeling away from him and turning her gaze out the window once again.

Hal Ryland smiled to himself. Kalida had strong feelings—about everything, he thought with a slight touch of humor.

"On the other hand," Kalida added suddenly, turning to face her father, "I'm the only available woman around for miles. That's probably it. And I come from a respectable family. I'm a veritable treasure, aren't I? You can tell Deuce Cavender I'm not interested."

"Now you're talking nonsense," her father said mildly. He settled himself in his rocking chair, preparing to do a subtle kind of battle with his daughter in order to achieve his ends. He went on. "We are talking a kind of give and take here, Kalida."

"You give, he takes," Kalida interjected, leaning her slender body against the window sill. "As he's always taken," she added almost to herself.

"Kalida, believe me when I say he is determined to marry you."

"He's crazy; I hate him, and he knows it."

"Yes. Rest assured, he is prepared to overlook a certain amount of antipathy; but, my dear, *you* are not considering the advantages to be gained by this marriage."

"There couldn't be any," Kalida stated. "At least any that I would consider."

"My dear." Here was her father at his most conciliating. She waited, her interest piqued. "Think of it—mistress of Sweetland. You'd share his wealth and power. You'd have everything you could possibly want."

"And Deuce would have a housekeeper and someone to share his bed while he goes his own usual way," Kalida finished. "That's what he wants, Papa. And that's all I'd get and I won't settle for that, I'll tell you, when I've been my own mistress all these years."

"You don't know that," her father said.

"Papa, you're more naive than I am. Do you really think someone like Deuce Cavender could give in to 'the finer feelings'? Do you think he could love me? Or I him?"

"Oh—love, piffle," Ryland snorted.

Kalida grimaced. There was something more. "Tell me the rest, Papa," she invited, her voice on the edge of sarcasm.

"There is no rest. The man wants you, always has, only you've been too pigheaded to see it. You could be living in the lap of luxury, my girl. You'd manage Sweetland as admirably as you do us here, and you'd manage Deuce Cavender too, I'll warrant. There's nothing wrong with it, and I couldn't wish more for my daughter than a union with a man like Cavender. Tell me what could be better, just tell me. All that wealth—and Sweetland too! Really, Kalida!" Damn, he thought. He had let his emotions run away with him; he wondered if he had gone too far. He looked at Kalida's stony face and rather thought he had.

"You want to get rid of me," she said tightly.

"Do I really," her father said pitifully, "with you the image of your mother? But God, Kalida, you want a life of your own. You'll only wind up taking care of me eventually. And you would be giving up the joy of having your own family, your own home. It's unnatural."

"I think Deuce Cavender's wanting to marry me is unnatural," Kalida said abruptly, moved not one whit by her father's diatribe. She had never yearned for her own home and family. Ryland ranch was her home, would be her home forever as far as she was concerned, and that was the end of it.

Or was it?

She watched her father's face working strangely. It was almost as if he had something more to say and was warring with himself as to whether he should speak.

He began hesitantly. "He—he has asked my permission to propose—"

"Just like that?" Kalida's voice shot out in exasperation.

"And I said yes. And, Kalida, you will listen, and you will not play tricks, and you will make the right decision." His voice was rock hard now with some determination she knew nothing about.

She faced him down. "Why?" Her voice was as flat and hard as his. Now they were coming to the hidden currents that she had been sensing all along. Yet she could see how reluctant he was to tell her anything. He had expected, she thought in wonderment, that she would leap gratefully on the idea of marrying Deuce Cavender! Incredible! So she waited.

And finally Hal Ryland pulled himself together and

acknowledged silently that there was no way to hide the truth of his exchange with Cavender from his daughter. "It's quite simple," he said gently. "Do sit down, Kalida, and stop looking like some wild avenging angel. It's nothing cataclysmic." He watched with fond eyes as she warily took a seat nearby. "It's a trade of sorts, my dear. I want to get in the syndicate; he wants you. A bargain with no promises, no demands. Just the suggestion that since I am interested in the one and he is interested in you . . ."

Kalida was dumbfounded. Her loving, good-natured, slightly scattered-brained father was telling her that he would willingly trade her for a place in the Sweetland cattle syndicate! It was mind-boggling. She couldn't believe it, yet as she looked at his slightly apologetic expression, she did believe it. She believed that he wanted that place and his piece of the Santa Linaria breed that Sweetland was famous for. That he wanted a lot more than he had ever let on to her. Further, to her, as she thought about it, it was obvious that this might be his last chance. He had tried to buy in before, and Deuce Cavender had baldly rejected his offer; he hadn't wanted Hal Ryland's money. It was even conceivable that Cavender hadn't wanted her, but that her father had used the last card he had—perhaps to bluff Cavender.

But no, she couldn't believe that, even of her father; he was not avaricious. He was kind and ambitious, and he loved running the ranch and the comradery of the roundup and the cutting out of the herd and driving them across the Bozeman Trail to Mingusville or Medora. He loved the wheeling and dealing with the newly incorporated meat processors, and he loved preparing his advantageous reports to his own shareholders, a small consortium of friends who had financed the ranching operation to give themselves an outlet for their own burgeoning rail, overland, and meat processing businesses.

Though he was not a ranchman born and bred like Deuce Cavender, he was successful, and she could not understand why buying into the Sweetland syndicate was so seemingly urgent that he would use anything at hand — even her — to accomplish that end.

It was almost as if he were following her thoughts. "I need the Santa Linaria. This is going to be a down year for us because of the aborted drive from Texas. We didn't get the infusion of new blood that we need. Santa Linaria will be like a shot in the arm to the herd, do you understand? The breed is tough, resilient. They need very little water; they feed on any kind of roughage, so feed costs are reduced; they don't need the same kind of coddling. And from that we get more meat, and leaner meat for processing. And if we can breed them up with our tall horns, we'll have something else, I'll tell you. It could revolutionize the market." He stopped abruptly at the expression on her face.

"It's that desperate?" she asked gently.

"We'll go under this year if we don't buy in," he said plainly.

She was silent, so silent for such a long time. He wondered what she was feeling. He himself did not at all consider he was sacrificing her; if anything, he had made a good bargain for both of them. There wasn't a man around for a hundred miles that could care for her or give her the things that Cavender could. Moreover, Cavender *wanted* her. It was nothing he had said or given away. It was just his rank determination, on the cutting edge of what he knew would be disaster for Hal Ryland, to have her in just this way. Ryland admired it, even in his desperation.

Kalida drew in a harsh breath. "I hate him," she ground out. "Oh, I thought I hated that man before, but it's nothing to how I feel now, for how he has forced you to

17

your knees, to have you beg for one stinking share in his wretched syndicate. He could have done it without bargaining for me. Just like he could have kept Malca back, all those years ago. But he didn't — he didn't; he needs to abuse his power. He needs to step on people. He doesn't want anyone to succeed but himself. Well, that's fine, Papa. And yes, I know you think it's not a bad bargain for me. I know you have my best interests at heart, and in fact, if I were any other kind of woman, this proposal *would* be heaven-sent, despite the strings.

"But not me, Papa. I'm going to fight him. I'm going to thwart him."

"Kalida . . ." Her father knew there was a tinge of urgency in his voice, but he couldn't help it. She was so damned stubborn! She hated Deuce so much! And now, instead of playing on her sympathy and her desire to help *him,* he had turned her against Cavender. He felt a moment of impotence, a helplessness to stop the waves of anger that convulsed her.

Her young-old eyes swept over him compassionately. "I understand it all, Papa. You promised him, didn't you? You told him you would convince me to accept his proposal. Yes, I see you did. What else could you do?" She slammed her fist down on the flat arm of the chair she sat in. "Oh, the bastard. It's just like him. Just what you'd expect." Her face hardened and her blazing eyes narrowed as she paused a moment for thought. Her firm, lovely mouth worked into a vindictive line, and she lifted her square, determined chin.

"All right." She came to a decision. "Bear with me, Papa. Please. I'm going to get out of it. I'm going to foil him. I don't care about going under, I don't. We'll save the herd somehow, I promise you, even if I have to drive them to Texas myself; but, Papa, I will not marry Deuce Cavender, to save you — or even if I had to save myself. I'd die first. I'd — "

Her father's distress communicated itself to her through her white hot anger. Her voice softened. "I'll get out of it with honor, Papa. I promise I will. I promise."

Two

Deuce Cavender reined in just by the Ryland ranch porch, swung his legs over the pommel of his saddle, and contemplated the unlikely picture of Kalida Ryland demurely awaiting his arrival.

His finely cut lips twisted in sardonic amusement. So the old man had only just told her. Look at how she slumped down in that porch rocker, as if this ungraciousness could fool anyone who had watched her grow up for these past seven years. Nor had she made any concession to the occasion. She was dressed just as usual in a crisp white shirt that was tucked into her heavy dark canvas skirt, and her dusty brown boots. A tan flat-crowned hat was slung carelessly over the back of the rush woven rocker.

He waited as she pointedly ignored his presence, and finally the taut silence impelled her to lift her finely modeled head, which was enhanced by the way she had pulled back her midnight black hair into a braid that lay close to the nape of her neck and down her back. Her perfectly shaped black brows contracted over her narrowed blue eyes, and her lids lowered speculatively, shading her animosity behind a thick fringe of spiky black lashes.

His cool gray eyes assessed this rebelliousness, and his mirthless smile disappeared abruptly. "I am overwhelmed by your enthusiastic welcome," he remarked as he dismounted and removed his hat. "Good morning, Kalida."

Her jolting blue eyes attacked him. "A morning like any other, *Mr.* Cavender," she said pointedly as he propped one expensively booted foot on the porch steps and continued to regard her in that muscular see-all, know-all exasperatingly *dominating* way. "You could have saved yourself a trip," she added ungraciously, just as her father sauntered out of the house with a coffee cup in his hand and a determination to make things appear as normal as possible.

He was impeccably dressed as usual, and in a suit rather than the working gear he tended to wear more often than not. His open bluff face was more genial than usual, with its warm ready smile, but his blue eyes—paler than Kalida's, and as sharp—pinpointed everything to a nicety and missed nothing. He exuded a kind of strength this morning, as though he were sure that Kalida's avowed threat had no bearing on the ultimate outcome of the morning. Cavender's own strength assured that. And since Cavender was certain to overcome Kalida's objections, Hal Ryland could foresee nothing but a fortuitous aftermath for all concerned to what seemed to be an oncoming collision of wills.

He was able, therefore, to greet Cavender heartily and invite him to have some coffee. That offer was refused and they sat instead on the porch chatting about the state of the cattle market for a few moments while Kalida itched to claw Deuce Cavender's dark, rawboned face. His cool gaze grazed her from time to time, and she felt exposed, naked under those piercing gray eyes, resentful that he saw so much and thought he knew everything.

Kalida looked at her father pleadingly, but all his attention was focused on Deuce Cavender. Ryland was ignoring her and expecting her to be cooperative in the face of this unexpected arrangement between him and Cavender. She saw a muscle twitching in her father's jawline; the pretense was wearing. All of them knew why Deuce was here and what she was supposed to do.

Finally her father said, "It's time to saddle up, Kalida," and in his voice was none of the warmth with which he had spoken to her enemy. Now she was the enemy, the barrier to his express wishes. She hadn't thought he would be quite that adamant once he knew how much she detested the idea.

She felt as though she had no choice in the matter of riding out with Cavender. But that didn't mean she didn't have a plan. She had hoped she wouldn't need plots and devices, but it was obvious that Cavender's hold over her father was very strong. Well, so was she.

She bolted to her feet and strode across the corral purposefully, and when she reappeared, she was mounted sidesaddle. She expertly maneuvered her mount right up next to her gaping father, her hard expression warning him not to say a word.

"But Kalida—" he protested before he noticed. Kalida *never* rode sidesaddle. Then his mouth snapped shut as she interjected, "It's a genteel occasion, Papa; I'm pretending to be a lady, to suit the circumstances." Her voice for all its thick layer of sarcasm held a trace of bitterness.

She looked at Deuce Cavender, who had remounted and was waiting for her with a faint air of impatience. "Let's go."

She wheeled Malca around and cantered down the long dirt track into the pasture before she broke into a trot. He followed a little behind, letting her have her head for several hundred yards before he spurred his horse and raced after her.

He had to admire the fact that she fully intended to keep a distance between them, physically and mentally.

22

He did not underestimate her one whit. But he was as determined as she. He tracked her erratic weaving patiently until she led him through the northern acreage of the ranch.

This was the prime grazing land, and it was dotted here and there with small fenced-in corrals, empty now that the cattle were up in winter pasture.

She whipped around these, leading him in what looked like figure eights around the corrals. He was utterly puzzled as to her intent and feeling exasperated because Ryland had led him to believe that she would be receptive to what he had to say this morning.

But she was racing the wind around and down the field almost crazily, and he pulled up and eased down on his mount. He was not going to chase her; she obviously had something up her sleeve. He watched curiously as she primed Malca to jump one of the downed fence rails at the entry of the nearest corral.

He watched in admiration as her foot seemingly caught and she slid with a thud from her horse onto the dirt floor of the corral. What a delicious ploy; she was playing coy before she submitted to the inevitable.

He waited, but she did not move as he had fully expected her to. Damn, he thought; he had no time for these games. Irritated, he dismounted, tethered his horse to one of the fence rails, and climbed into the corral.

Kalida had still not moved, and she looked curiously young and defenseless stretched out in the dust. Warily he knelt beside her and touched the smooth skin of her face. She was warm and her color was good; the pulse at her neck throbbed strongly against his palm as he gently examined her head for bruises.

God, she was beautiful, he thought almost abstractedly. And damned strong willed. And heavy. He lifted the upper part of her torso onto his knees so that her head rested against his thigh and her lustrous black braid

23

snaked down his leg and curled around his calf with an unerring possessiveness. He lifted it, feeling its weight, staring down at her perfectly featured face, hard put to tell if she really were unconscious. Beneath that flawless face was an intelligence that was very capable of deceit, he thought. And he wanted it, no matter what the cost or the price.

He shifted her weight slightly, and as he did he noticed the barest flutter of her thick fringed mink-black lashes. So his assessment was right on the mark: This *was* a trick, and somehow she was planning to avoid hearing his proposal or to reject it in some decidedly picturesque way. The thought piqued his sense of humor. He was holding her in his arms and she still was giving nothing away. Lucky he was so sharp-eyed. But she must be tingling to know what he was going to do with her now, and she could not open her eyes to see, nor could she ask.

It was very unlikely she was injured; she was pretending for her own purposes to outwit her father somehow — and him. It was rather ironic that to accomplish this she had allowed herself to be at his mercy.

What was she counting on?

He considered her unusually tranquil face. At his mercy. God; marrying her would not be a business arrangement. He was half in love with her willful, all-fired stubbornness already, and the tenacity with which she carried her hatred for him. And now she not only hated what he was, she hated the fact that he had power over her father that her father did not even understand. And he knew she hated the fact he was rich and landed and had known every woman from Sweetland to the Judith Mountains, and she had made it quite plain she was not going to be another one of them.

And he was equally determined to have her. To discover the delights hidden deep within her, beneath those forbidding canvas skirts. To love her within an inch of her life.

24

To be the only one to taste those firm, perfect lips.

To kiss her until she begged for mercy—now.

And as he thought it, he lifted her tightly against his chest and bent his head so that his mouth slanted across hers, just touching. He could feel the swell of her right breast just beneath his arm and the warmth of her breath against his lips, and the wave of desire that jolted through him was breathtaking. He gave into it; his mouth covered hers softly, touching, exploring the contours of her lips gently with his tongue. It was not enough. Hadn't he known that? He wanted her warm and willing beneath him, giving, wanting him. And she lay as limp as a marionette, unaware of consuming fires and the depths of his desire. He groaned in frustration and lifted his head. Nothing had changed. He had not roused the sleeping princess.

Damn, he would awaken her, by God. "Princess Kalida," he murmured against her lips, and it sounded impossibly exotic and desirable. His mouth claimed hers again, invading this time, abrasive and intent, and his supporting arm moved so his large warm hand cradled her breast gently, but aching with a need to undress and explore.

She knew she couldn't take much more; it took every ounce of her will not to lift her hands and shove him away from her. She had to play it through the way she had planned, but the audacity of him! The snake! How could she keep still and not bite him with the viciousness she felt about the way he was making her feel. She wanted none of this from him; but her treacherous body was saying otherwise. Her response astounded her. She hated him!

She let herself stir—just a movement, and then another, and then she twisted her body against his encroaching hand and was shocked by the sense of his fingers brushing against her nipple.

Her eyes shot open to find his face not an inch from hers and his eyes cold and mocking.

"Get your hands off me," she hissed, perfectly aware of how inadequate her anger was and that he could and would do whatever he wanted and there was little she could do to prevent it. And indeed, his rock solid arm tightened around her and she could feel him lifting her closer yet to him until once again his mouth was touching hers and she could not prevent the words that inevitably followed. "Marry me." A whisper. A statement.

She pushed against the cliff wall of his chest. "No!" She felt desperate suddenly, and helpless. Even though he held her close and fast, she felt as though he were stalking her mercilessly.

"Marry me." His lips brushed hers and she shuddered. He felt it clear through to the core of his body. "Kalida . . ."

"I won't!" She compressed her mutinous lips. "You're crazy!" He had to be; there was something inexorable about the expression in his eyes, something a touch primitive in his face.

"I am," he agreed huskily. "I'm glad you know it." His mouth crushed down on hers remorselessly. His hunger for her had to convince her if nothing else would. If she sensed it, or felt it as his tongue plundered the tender, untried recesses of her mouth, tasting, feeling, urging. There wasn't nearly enough time. "Marry me."

She heard the words somewhere in the back of her mind as she was trying to sort out the sensations she was feeling, and the betrayal of her body, and her wanton tongue that welcomed his with a shocking eagerness. "Never!" She barely breathed the words before he enslaved her mouth again, all hunger and voluptuous heat that enthralled her, unwilling as she was.

"Yes, oh yes, Kalida." His lips grazed hers now and she felt bereft. "Say yes." He nipped at her lower lip emphatically and drew it between his teeth to nibble at it.

"No . . ." Her resolve was melting fast at both the sensation of being held immobilized and being feasted upon. Her flailing hands were utterly useless against his iron solid body. He didn't even feel them. And she was feeling too much.

"I want you." The merest whisper of his most intense desire propelled her senses into a semblance of reality.

"You want a housekeeper," she snapped, pushing at him and catching him off guard so that his body slanted backward. Immediately she wriggled away and sat glaring at him. He sent her a mocking grimace and sat up, leaning his elbows on his knees.

"So now, Kalida . . ." His deep voice was harsh, unrelenting.

"You have a world of women to choose from," she said. "I want to go back to *my* world."

"Hell," he swore, and jacked himself up in one fluid motion. He reached for her hand and pulled her to her feet hard against his whipcord body. He held her arm against his chest in a grip like a vise, and her balled-up fist could not even attack him.

Her cobalt eyes darkened to dangerous navy. "Don't say a word," she grated as she tried unsuccessfully to wrench away.

"We're not finished, you and I," he promised harshly in a voice thick with some unidentifiable emotion. "Now that I've tasted you, my willful Kalida, no one else will have you. Take it as truth. You'll marry me . . . and nothing else enters into it." He loosened his grip on her arm abruptly, and as he released her, she saw her chance.

She breathed a sigh of relief—and crumpled to the ground.

She didn't expect him to slap her face so unsympatheti-

27

cally. "Damn it, Kalida; stop your nonsense."

She smacked away his hand. "My legs gave out." She opened her eyes and looked up at him hunkered beside her appealingly. His expression was dark and skeptical. "I promise you."

"I don't believe you," he said bluntly. "Get up."

She made a show of trying. "I can't."

"Kalida." The tone brooked no argument.

"I *can't*." Her own voice was gritty with impatience.

"I wonder why I'm not convinced," he said, swinging his rangy body upright.

She panicked as he began to walk away. "Don't leave me here! Deuce!"

He ignored her and went for his horse, untethering him and leading him carefully over the crosspieces into the corral.

"I'll take you back to Papa," he said stonily. With one swoop, he lifted her up in his arms. And stopped in mid-motion. They were face to face, her beguiling blue eyes battering against his glittering gray ones. Her expression for the first time seemed unguarded, but he didn't trust that. It was the way she was looking at him, without the barrier of her hatred, her lips parted invitingly and nothing between them — nothing but the strength of his desire.

The moment hung, suspended by his fascination with the possibilities of a future moment like this and by her own enveloping sense of him holding her, that again she was at his mercy. Only this time his face was not so forbidding; his eyes were still wary, but his mouth had softened and there was a wry curve to his lips that dented his lean left cheek. That bare hint of a smile alleviated the raw cast of his features, made the dark, thick drawn brows look less menacing.

But he didn't trust her. The self-mockery of that brief smile was evident to her. In an instant, he pressed his lips into their usual inflexible line and his eyes darkened to charcoal as they slid down to rest his gaze on her lips.

There was another beat of a tense moment and she thought he might kiss her again, but instead he suddenly heaved her up and slung her across his saddle; and then, to her dismay, he mounted up behind her, leaving her with her head hanging over one side and her feet dangling from the other.

"Deuce Cavender, you let me down from here!" Her anger and frustration positively grated through her voice. She certainly hadn't expected him to ride; she could have borne the humiliation of being returned home like a sack of wheat if he weren't so casually riding up there behind her.

"If you can't stand up, how can you possibly sit?" he asked reasonably, somewhat entertained by the sight of her wriggling rump and flailing arms. He absolutely admired the fact that she carried out the effect by consciously not moving her legs.

"I am not pretending," she hissed through clenched teeth.

"Of course not. I really am taking this as seriously as you are," he said conciliatingly as he urged his horse over the crosspieces of the fence and into the pasture. "You need to get home as fast and as expediently as possible. And this is what we are doing." He spurred his mount into a brisk trot and waited for her next protest.

But none came. She knew when she was licked, and she knew that in order to carry forward with her plan everything had to appear as legitimate as possible. Her body went limp, one hand grasping the calf of his leg and the other the saddle riggings, and she didn't say another word until he reined in at the Ryland house where, as she could have predicted, her father was waiting for her to return with the news he expected.

His handsome face was a study as he leapt down the

steps and confronted Deuce. "What happened?"

"She had an accident," Deuce said briefly, his expression mirroring the same disbelief as Hal Ryland's. He dismounted and impersonally lifted Kalida into his arms. Her eyes were glazed with loathing.

"My God," her father muttered as he followed Deuce into the house. "My God." He motioned Deuce to a small room behind the living area of the rough two-story ranch house. There was a bed, a washstand, and a wardrobe in there, all plainly made of unvarnished, unadorned oak. Deuce unceremoniously dumped Kalida onto the bed and stood looking at her with that same skeptical expression, while she directed her now frustrated, tear-filled gaze at her obviously discomposed father.

"All right now, what happened?" he growled, at a loss himself to account for the stubbornness of his daughter and this new wrinkle that did not bode well for his plans.

"She had an accident," Deuce repeated expressionlessly, folding his arms across his chest and waiting.

Like some bird of prey, Kalida thought venomously.

"So?" Ryland asked hoarsely.

"She collapsed," Deuce amplified unhelpfully.

"Papa . . ."

"This is crazy," her father exploded. "She's never had a riding accident in her life." He turned to the pitiful figure of his daughter cowering in the bed. "Never! Kalida, what on earth is going on here?"

Kalida shrank against the pillows. She had known his reaction would be strong, but she never thought he would have no sympathy for her whatsoever, that his scheme would be more important than her health. She knew at that instant she would have to play the moment to the hilt and play it only to her father, for Deuce would never believe it.

It didn't matter. She only needed her father's credulity; if he would just send Deuce away, she could convince him of the rest, she knew she could.

"It's my legs," she said piteously. "My foot caught and I fell off of Malca. I landed wrong, and when I tried to stand, I couldn't; my legs felt boneless, Papa. I felt like . . . I couldn't walk." She lifted her overflowing eyes to her father. "Papa, I don't think I can walk!"

Three

"Papa, Deuce Cavender is insane to insist on marrying someone who might never be able to fulfill her wifely duties!"

Hal Ryland shrugged and pulled a chair over to Kalida's bedside. "I put it to him as plainly as possible," he said reasonably. "He doesn't seem to see any obstacle to his marrying you."

Kalida slammed her fist into her blanket in frustration. "You told him what the doctor said?"

"As well as I understood it, yes. And believe me, it did not seem to worry him." Ryland leaned forward in his chair. "I've been thinking a lot about this, Kalida. I want you to promise me this isn't some trick on your part to get out of accepting Deuce's proposal."

"Papa!" She put just the right amount of indignation in her tone, she thought; amazing how well one could act when one was up against threatening circumstances. She hadn't known she had it in her. Her father, however, seemed convinced.

He went on. "I've been worried ever since you swore you would find a way to circumvent him."

"Well, I'd hardly choose to do something that might immobilize me for life, would I?" Kalida asked. And indeed, the perfection of the plan, it had seemed to her when she conceived it, was that it was so unlikely. "You told him the doctor was convinced my mind was playing some trick my body accepted and that he couldn't be sure when or if I would regain the use of my legs?"

"Exactly. It didn't seem to faze him."

"He's a fool," she muttered. And so damned determined. He would never stand to lose something once he set his sights on obtaining it.

"He hasn't withdrawn his proposal," her father went on, watching her pale face and the cobalt eyes blazing so unnaturally navy. "And I don't need him any less than I did yesterday, my dear Kalida. I won't go back on my promise. And that should be the end of it."

"That is not the end of it," Kalida threw back obstinately, crossing her arms over her heaving chest in irritation. Why her father would not consider her wishes was beyond her. "I do not see what Deuce stands to gain from your 'deal' anyway. He doesn't need Ryland ranch. He doesn't need you. He surely doesn't need me."

"He wants the deal," Hal Ryland said, as if that put the final period on it. "And I want the deal."

"You want the damned Santa Linaria," Kalida contradicted boldly, "and it's just possible you want to get rid of me." And hadn't they been over this same ground for a week or more? And he had done nothing, since the doctor had come, but repeat that everything was still the same and she had no choice: She must help him, she must marry Deuce Cavender, and she could do worse. She had the distinct feeling there was something more to it, but all her incisive questioning of her father brought her to nothing. The fact remained her father would go bankrupt if she didn't marry Deuce because she was his passport into the syndicate that would save his herd and his own consortium. If she didn't, he would be in court with his backers for the rest of his life.

And every time she insisted he must want to be rid of her she felt a small pang of satisfaction that he had no answer for that: It stopped him cold, but it did not ultimately lessen his insistence that Deuce wanted the whole package—Kalida Ryland and her father, in exchange for a share in the Sweetland syndicate.

It made no sense any way she attacked it. Deuce seemingly gained nothing: rangeland he didn't need, a wife he didn't love, another partner he couldn't possibly want.

She turned her head toward the window as her father sat silent once again. The window overlooked the rear garden, which she herself tended lovingly every spring and summer, the huge barn and corrals, the cow pens beyond that, and the mountains looming far in the distance. Spring was approaching now and the turf was exploding into fresh green tufts all over the fields; it made her happy just to look at it.

If only she could stay here and nurse her garden and her ponies, she surely would be content.

She turned to her father once again. "Well, you can mumbo jumbo all you want about Deuce's overwhelming desire to marry me and make you one of his partners, but I tell you, Papa, he will not like supporting a disabled wife and that should be the end of it."

"That's his lookout," her father said in a deceptively bland tone of voice.

Kalida looked at her father sharply.

"The doctor said your legs felt fine, my dear, and that there was no reason you couldn't walk. I believe you will when you want to. So there's no reason to keep Deuce waiting. None whatsoever." He stood up abruptly. "And he thinks so too."

She was so tired from talking with her father that she

found it was easy to settle in for a brief rest before dinner. His words had chilled her; she was beginning to feel as penned in as one of his steers. She didn't want to think about it any more. The only consolation she had was that Deuce had not come around for the past week. Thank God. Another day's respite. Just another day.

She hovered on the edge of consciousness. Her plan would work—she'd make it work; she wouldn't think about it. Just this minute she didn't have to . . . she didn't . . .

She heard the door of the room open and a light footfall enter and stop at her bedside.

A cool hand touched her brow and smoothed back the tangle of hair against her temples. And then a low voice murmured, "Kalida? Kalida dear?"

She knew that voice! Ellie Dean! What was *she* doing here? Kalida tensed beneath her light blanket.

"Are you sleeping, I wonder?" Ellie's disembodied voice whispered. "Oh, Kalida, I had to come when your father sent for me. Yes, my dear, I'm here to help you. And I'm here to congratulate you; that was very well done, Kalida. Very well done indeed. We'll see where it gets you though, won't we? We'll just see. You don't know how determined your father is. As am I. I hope you're awake, my dear. I hope you know how I admire you and the flair with which you pulled this off. But now you need my help and care again; so we're one big happy family once more, my dear. I'll be staying for a while to help with . . . things. With you. I wish you sweet dreams, my dear. You really are quite unexpected. But you'll give in to your father's wishes eventually. I really think you will. . . ." The footsteps receded suddenly, and the door closed softly.

Kalida lay still, holding herself tightly. For all she knew, Ellie was still in the room; she was that devious.

She could picture Ellie in her mind's eye. A figure always dressed in unrelieved black, moving silently, spare

35

and unadorned. She was brittle, but she had been kind to Kalida that year in Bozeman, setting aside her own problems to provide a family atmosphere for her. She had a young woman's face surrounded by an old woman's dress and hair, and she was a woman, Kalida always sensed, playing a waiting game, as if she had hoped to win Hal Ryland's appreciation and indebtedness to her, if not his love.

Ellie Dean had come to the Ryland ranch that summer to be housekeeper and companion to Kalida, thinking she would run the house, the child, and the bereaved husband and finding instead that they all were in direct opposition to everything she wanted. The child, she found, could manage everything deftly by herself and had no need of Ellie's well-meaning but rigid interference. They were instant enemies, once they reached the ranch, both after Hal Ryland's affection, chained by his expressed desire to have both of them there and *happy*. Ellie had stayed for a long time, living on hope and gritted teeth, but at last, in the winter '76, she gave up and left.

Kalida was eighteen and the situation had degenerated into two women clashing for power. Ellie had no desire to be a parent. And it had become obvious that Hal Ryland would never see her as more than a substitute mother for Kalida.

But now . . .

More complications. Kalida heaved a sigh. How could it matter when she was in so deep already? Ellie Dean's presence could not change matters. Except, from what she had said, she was on Papa's side. Kalida closed her eyes, contemplating this new wrinkle. Did her father really think Ellie could influence her? How desperate was Papa anyway? So frantic to save the ranch he would use any means to convince her?

* * *

A hard thumping at her door startled her into wakefulness. It was dark out. There was no light except the thin rim she could see just slipping through the crack above the door. It took her a moment to acclimate herself; she must have fallen asleep. "Who is it?" she finally called, pulling her cover tightly around her.

The door opened a crack and a dark silhouette appeared at the door. "You're awake, my dear?"

Papa. "Yes, you did a thorough job of that. Can I have a light?"

"Deuce is here," her father announced, putting into his voice a kind of benign approval of this unexpected appearance.

"No," she said flatly.

"Oh, Kalida," her father said reproachfully. "If you are going to be bedridden for any length of time, you'll have to receive him exactly as you look tonight."

"I don't want to see him."

"Of course you will."

"I am not ready to receive him."

"But he's ready to see you," her father said unyieldingly.

"How condescending of him," Kalida snapped. And how nice of her father. Not only had she just awakened, but she hadn't eaten for hours and she wouldn't have a chance to wash, put on a wrapper, or comb her hair. She did not like her father very much at that moment.

But as Deuce stalked in with a kerosene lamp in his hand, she doubted very much whether her father could have deterred him at all.

The lamp went down on the washstand with a dangerous thump and the door swung shut behind her father with a savage shove. It was obvious what kind of mood Deuce Cavender was in. For some reason, the thought calmed her rather than upset her.

"Good evening, Deuce," she said in her most serene

37

voice. Thank heaven he hadn't been looking at her! The forbidding face he turned to her might have compelled her to jump out the window rather than face his wrath.

And he hadn't even dressed to pay her this informal call; he looked as if he had just come in from the pasture, with his wrinkled plaid flannel shirt that looked like it would tear if he flexed one muscle and his lean, trail-dusty denims that were tucked into equally grimy, well-worn boots. He was sliding out of a decrepit leather jacket with his usual brisk, impatient movements, throwing it across the narrow expanse of the room, in a barely controlled, violent movement, onto a small chair that stood next to the wardrobe.

"What the hell are you trying to pull?" he demanded suddenly. He loomed over her threateningly, and she knew in that moment she had to face him down. She could not allow him to scare her or to bully her.

"How can I pull anything while I'm confined to bed?" she retorted tartly.

He shot her a cynical look. "You're up to something."

"You know everything," she rejoined cryptically.

His face visibly hardened. "I know nothing," he contradicted roughly. "But I do know this"—he pointed a sweeping hand to her prone figure—"is meaningless."

"Not to me."

"It makes no difference to us."

"God, you're crazy. I won't listen to you," she burst out in frustration. "There is no 'us.'"

"You obviously weren't listening that day. There is an 'us,' Kalida. Make no mistake about that."

He loomed over her bed suddenly and leaned his body over hers, placing one work-roughened hand on either side of her body, effectively trapping her so that she couldn't move. "There is an 'us,' Kalida," he reiterated softly, "because I want there to be. Your father needs me, yes, and you'll be his obedient daughter and rescue him,

38

yes. But it's only possible because *I* want you."

"You'll never have me," she spat at his passion-darkened gray eyes. "Never!"

He pushed himself away from her abruptly and wheeled to look at her in that uncomfortable, speculative *male* way she so despised. "That's good, Kalida. You said that with real venom in your voice, and I believe you really mean it. But I want you to believe that I mean what I'm telling you, too. I want you, and this so-called disability makes no difference to me."

"I don't see how it can't," Kalida retorted. "After all, you want the perfect consort for the 'king' of Sweetland, do you not? Unless you intend to wheel me down the aisle in my bed?"

"It's you who doesn't understand," Deuce retaliated with that barely controlled impatience. With a sudden movement, he whipped the skimpy cover down over the low footboard of the bed, exposing her legs, which were partially sheathed in her equally thin nightgown.

His eyes glittered as they followed the slightly splayed line of her limbs from her bare feet up to the thin crush of material at the juncture of her thighs. His hand reached out, enfolded her ankle, and then moved up, slowly and tensely, from the back of her calf to the edge of her nightgown. The tension of keeping her legs limp and ignoring the heated sense of his huge hand on her body almost made her scream hysterically.

"When we make love—" he said softly, and she interposed, "Never," in a gritty voice filled with loathing and dismay. He went on, his hand still hovering at the edge of her gown, brushing the hem upwards just a bare inch at a time. "When we make love, I need only"—he gently pushed her legs apart, and before she had any notion of what he meant to do, Deuce climbed onto the bed and straddled her thighs, carefully insuring that she did not take his full weight—"make this little adjustment and"—

39

he braced himself on his knees—"nothing is hindered by your . . . incapacity."

"Like a horse," she muttered, refusing to look at him, refusing even to concede that he could mount her as easily as that.

"An unbroken filly," he agreed in an odd voice, shifting forward onto his hands so that she had to look into his eyes. "Now, Kalida . . ." His mouth swept down on hers unexpectedly, pressuring and then releasing her unwilling lips in a hard and demanding caress. "We'll invent all manner of new ways to accommodate you," he murmured, and he assaulted her lips again, his hand this time reaching to cup the stubborn line of her chin so that she could not pull away.

His mouth was hot and relentless; he was so strong and fierce that she had no reserves to put up against him. He plundered and he took, and she was forced to give unwillingly and she hated it. She hated him kissing her like that again, draining her will with his consuming, exquisite skill. Her hands reached up to him to protest, to beat him away; they grasped his hard muscled arms and they bit deeply into his skin as he explored every inch of her mouth. And she let him. She couldn't believe, even as it was happening, that she let him; that, as he reached for her again and again, she wanted it; that her will to oppose him was suborned to this insane sensual onslaught.

She was dizzy with it when she could finally tear her mouth away and lick her wounds; her lips were swollen with the taste of him, his own lips were hardly an inch away, and he was watching her every movement.

"There is no impediment." His voice was low and just slightly mocking. "Don't challenge me on it again."

She could feel the tension in his body as he balanced himself over her, waiting, seeing everything she could not hide. It was all in her face—the wonder of her response to

40

his kiss and her determination not to give in to it.

And he knew he couldn't allow her even that much time to explore her feelings because she wouldn't, or couldn't, acknowledge them. His lips touched hers lightly. "Marry me," he whispered.

"I don't want to," she said succinctly.

"That hardly matters," he answered in a flat, expressionless voice, rearing back slightly at the bluntness of her words. "All you have to do is say yes."

"What a farce," she snorted. "I am to pretend that this whole thing isn't arranged and I really have some say in the matter?"

"Oh no," he said, grasping her chin once again and eyeing her resistant lips, "all you have to do is admit"— his lips descended to her traitorous mouth—"that I can make you want me," and again he kissed her, playing with her emotions and her overwhelming desire to respond to him.

For there suddenly was a point at which she wanted solely to pull him closer instead of thrust him away, a point at which she became desperate to feel the heat and weight of his lean body, a point at which she wanted to feel his hands on her. It was so insane to her, and yet such a deprivation that he refused to do anything more than deliberately and intentionally seduce her mouth and not touch her anywhere else.

She felt like she wanted to strip away all encumbrances and reveal all secrets, and this minuscule sane self that was trying to hold on to reality kept pushing before her the notion of how well Deuce was putting his vaunted experience to good use. He was expertly ensnaring her in the trap that both he and her father had laid for her, and he was becoming, by virtue of merely succumbing to his ated kisses, his willing victim.

Somehow that notion got through to her, through the ving haze of desire that utterly beclouded her reason.

41

And yet, though he did not do more than kiss her, her whole body felt as though it had stiffened and opened for him, and that she was giving him all that he wanted.

But she couldn't, not yet, pull away from him, and she told herself it was because she wanted to fully explore the sensations he was creating within her and to see what he would do next—if he would do anything next.

And she wondered if he were feeling the same galvanic awareness as she.

But what if he weren't?

That dashing thought stopped her cold, and she pulled away from him violently.

"Kalida . . ." The caressing sound of his voice uttering her name was a mere breath between them.

"No . . ." She didn't know whether she whispered the word or merely formed it with her lips, but his mouth closed over hers again, softly, caressingly, tasting her. He knew, she thought, bedazzled by this new set of tantalizing sensations; he knew exactly what he was doing to her. And exactly what more to do, for she felt his hand move next from its inflexible hold of her chin down her neck and across the flat of her chest to the swell of her breasts beneath the flimsy nightgown. And she could feel her nipples swollen against the thin material that rasped against their tautness, could feel her desire balloon as his hand came closer and closer to touching one of them.

Oh, but which?

She felt the breath of his words against her lips, hardly audible, intensely enthralling. "I want you, Kalida. Listen to your body's response, feel it, Kalida. I do that to you, no one else. No one." He delved into her mouth again as his hand slid down still further and cupped her left breast. "Say it, Kalida." Did she imagine the words' "Kalida, say it."

"No," she groaned, summoning up the last ounce strength she had to resist him.

"Yes." He bit at the thinned line of her lips. "Kiss me, Kalida."

She shook her head mutely, knowing full well that would not discourage him. His mouth hovered just above hers, and his ever-darkening gray eyes were watchfully focused on her lips. She could barely breathe with the strain of sustaining her refusal and not letting the awareness of his hand on her body affect her.

But it was affecting her. It was impossible not to feel the stressed encompassing heat of his fingers holding her breast, impossible to ignore what it made her feel. She burned with resentment that her own body was about to betray her to him.

"Kalida!"

"No!" She had to answer the insistence in his voice.

"Yes!" His lips were right on hers as she tried to deny him, and he thrust his tongue into the recesses of her mouth again with an unabated hunger that was stunning to her and breached her defenses.

He knew it. "I'm showing you," he murmured against her lips, "over and over how much I want you."

"I don't see that," she whispered, but she saw it all too well.

"You feel it," he contradicted in the softest of all-knowing voices, and almost as if to put the final burden of proof on her, he shifted his position slightly to free his left hand to surround her right breast with that same electric warmth.

He could just see her face in the dim lamplight that the bulk of his body was now blocking, and it reflected shock first, then a kind of hectic strain as if within herself her feelings were warring.

"Deuce—" Her voice was hoarse, a mere pleading croak.

"Your body says yes," he answered her, and her hands flew to his wrists as she sensed him about to move, about

43

to shatter her sensibilities with just one flick of one finger.

"Don't—" Pure begging now; she did not want to feel what she knew he could make her feel. "Not like this, not—"

"Yes." His voice was so low and adamant. "Yes, Kalida, because you'll know only I can make you feel this way; and that's what I want—that's all that I want. . . ." Now his mouth firmed into that inflexible line she despised, and her whole body arched forward instead of caving in at what she knew was coming; it was almost as if, in spite of her protestations, she wanted it, and a part of her was standing, disembodied, watching in fascination as his hands cupped the weight of each breast and then moved very slowly forward, and still forward until just the thumb and forefinger of each hand was touching each taut, protruding fabric-covered tip.

And then, firmly and gently, he squeezed each rigid nipple and watched her response with great satisfaction. A cascade of pure pleasure rioted through her veins, reflected in her eyes and in the great huge moan he captured in his mouth and felt right through to the core of his body.

She couldn't believe the incandescent sensations that pulsated through her whole body by just his contracting his fingers in that way. She felt weightless and liquid as he kept up the pressure of both his fingers and his mouth on hers, urgent and gentle all at once, and then his voice, moving the words against her passion-swollen lips, "Now, Kalida," punctuated again and again with the ruthless captivation of her lips that underscored what he was doing with his hands. "Now tell me," once more against her lips, and she couldn't deny it when her body was so blatantly demanding his caresses.

"I feel it," she whispered, wholly under his spell, her body writhing at just the thought of how he was touching her.

"From me," he rasped, holding her now without moving.

She pulled in her breath as her imagination supplied the sense of the movement. He held her hostage in that suspended moment. "From you," she whispered shakily.

"You will marry me."

A husky statement. She could give in, and she would have all she desired. And yet . . . She hesitated. "I—"

"For this." He knew just when to apply pressure. "Say yes."

"Deuce—"

"Your legs don't matter, Kalida." His voice was rough with frustration at her refusal to agree. "This matters." His fingers tightened still again. "And this matters." His mouth covered hers and his tongue thrust against hers demandingly; she met it with an equal urgency of her own that was compounded by the sense of the taste of him and the insane pleasure she felt from his expert manipulation of her nipples.

Expert . . . She just had time to think before his harsh voice was demanding a reply from her again. "Kalida . . ." And there was a faint warning tone now; even as it caressed her name, it spoke of patience dwindling, of her last chance to capitulate willingly, to have all he was promising her.

Did she want it? If she really had no choice about it?

And as if he felt her indecision, he moved his thumb against each taut peak simultaneously, pushing each, pressing, playing, driving her to the brink of . . . what?

"This matters," he repeated hoarsely. "You want this, Kalida, and you want me, Nothing else, and no one else."

God, she should be fighting him, she thought dimly, and instead she was in thrall with his words and his devastating hands. He had no right to do this to her, to make her mindless and awash in such sensations that her reason became a dull haze of pleasure; she could never win against this, not this kind of assault, this overwhelming otherness in her she had never known existed.

Oh, but she had to keep trying. She could not give in to him because her body was weak and her sanity was willing to surrender to her body's betrayal.

No. And no.

"Kalida," he growled, surrendering her breasts suddenly and moving his hands down her body to her hips. She felt him pulling her downward as easily as if she had been a rag doll, and it was then she began to fight him, using her hands, twisting her body. Forgetting her legs were supposed to be immobile, she almost raised her knees to savage him in the place he would feel it most. But he was too fast, too strong for her. He grabbed her hands first, pulling them up over her head, and he maneuvered his body down on hers ruthlessly, using his long muscular legs to cover and imprison hers, his body and his mouth to subdue her totally. He had no caution now as to how she bore his weight; he pressed himself against her as if he wanted to imprint himself on her body, to make her feel him, the length of him, the rock hard maleness of him, in this ageless primitive way. To conquer her, with his immovable masculinity and with the dominance of his ravaging tongue.

Her protesting body arched against his, and his huge, hot right hand grasped it and ruthlessly pulled her tighter against him, cupping her buttocks and moving harshly up the line of her back to feel the curve of her outthrust breast and finally to surround her neck and jaw, feeling in all of his exploration the movement of her body, the response, the intensity of her protest and her obstinate surrender.

And it was unbearable to her, how he could overpower her and ravish her senses so that she lost all control. If anything, she hated him the more for it, for how he was making her submit to him, making her body demand his hands on it, feeling it, learning it in a way that should have been repulsive to her. But it wasn't. And she had to guard against that. She had to.

It was impossible without her legs, without being able to flee from him, literally and figuratively. Everything within her reached for the sensations he evoked. If only she could just lay still and command her treacherous mouth and body to lay quiescent. If only he hadn't touched her breasts in that way that made her long for more. If only he weren't so strong and so damned determined.

He felt the change in her. It was like she had been doused with cold water. Her heat evaporated and her body calmed under his hands, not seeking anymore, not participating.

He pulled away from her avid mouth to gaze into her glazed, half-closed eyes. Her lips were bruised and swollen from his onslaught, and her body still curved toward him, the gown wrinkled and hiked up around her hips, her breasts still taut with desire and invitation.

His own eyes reflected that passion and appeal, she perceived. She affected him, and she felt a curious little wave of both triumph and denial. She did not want him to have feelings for her in any way. And yet, if she were bound to him, as he and her father were so determined she would be, it would be so much easier for her if . . .

But she wouldn't think that far.

"Beautiful Kalida," he whispered suddenly, moving his thumb over her raw lips with a kind of tender possessiveness.

Her lids flickered at his touch, his fingers were magic, she thought abstractedly, and then she was aware that he had lifted himself from her body and stood looking down at her with a deep sense of satisfaction reflected in his face.

She was like a pagan princess lying there, her hair in wild animal disarray, her gown exposing the line of her long bare legs, her breasts outlined fully and tightly against the crumpled nightgown. She had to throw her head back to look at him, and her expression had turned into hard, unremitting loathing that curiously enhanced her bruised lips and the glittering navy of her resentful eyes. "Leaving now?" she demanded throatily, filled with that insane disappointment at the removal of his hands and body from hers. God, she only wanted to challenge him. Why was she so angry?

"You've had enough . . . tonight," he said with a touch of amusement. He moved to the door. "Sweet dreams, Kalida. Only think what awaits you in our marriage bed." He opened the door and turned to look at her taut face.

"If that was a sample, it doesn't bear thinking about," she tossed back insolently to protect herself.

His reaction was instant and violent. She smiled in rueful satisfaction at the earsplitting sound of the door crashing shut behind him.

Four

Naive fool, she castigated herself endlessly through the long, sleepless night. Stupid fool to think she could will away the disastrous effect of her body's memory of his hands on her. Crazy fool to have denied it to his face.

She would never learn. She had provoked him the way she had ever since she had known him, at first in her childlike ways, by ruining dinner, say, if her father had invited him, or by chasing off his stallion so he had to walk home; or by snubbing him when he spoke to her, or by running away. By taking back Malca, and by paying him for him, penny by penny, over the course of two years; or by refusing to be civil to him on social occasions with the neighbors. Oh, she'd been a spiteful little witch, and that same hostility festered in her treatment of him to this day.

And so why, she wondered, as she stared dismally out the window, did he keep insisting he wanted to marry her? He must have a purpose. There was some other reason underpinning his proposal, something other than Papa's desire to buy into Sweetland. There *had* to be, otherwise nothing made sense. She was as sure of that as she was sure she was stuck in her narrow bed and walls-closing-in room until such time as she decided to put paid to her little scheme and confess the truth. Which she was sure Deuce knew anyway.

Damn it. Papa still believed her. He had no reason not to; everything would work out to his satisfaction since Deuce saw no detriment to their union. And, if she were truly pragmatic as indeed her papa was, she would have to admit he was right: There was nothing objectionable in her marrying Deuce Cavender. Another woman might envy her. And Deuce himself had taught her, to her great regret, how easily she could be made to desire the very thing she disdained.

He was due, in fact, this afternoon, Papa had already announced. So, in spite of her protestations and provocations, he would come and he would press his seduction further.

It was a little like being lifted into a tornado: He overtook her, stormed her defenses, and made her, in spite of her own will and desire, totally his.

The very thought made her nipples peak, and she groaned. Relentless, that was what he was. How could she begin to know such a man when she had despised him for this very trait for as long as she had known him?

And yet, his hands . . . his knowing, skillful hands. Hands that had caressed many women and knew just how to touch her. She hated being at the mercy of those hands and that unyielding male domination. And she hated herself for concocting a scheme that would keep her just within their reach.

And now, her sole occupation was waiting . . . and thinking. Another hour of it, and she was sure she would give it all up. But she changed her mind instantly when Ellie Dean opened the door and entered carrying a tray.

There was something very different about Ellie, although her voice, as she murmured, "Good morning, Kalida," possessed the same dry, noncommittal tone that Ellie had always used with her.

"Ellie. What a nice surprise." What an understatement that was! Kalida took the tray and set it on her thighs, and then looked into Ellie's opaque black eyes. She could read nothing there, and Ellie's expression was benign, almost pleasant, as if she had nothing better or more rewarding in life to do but serve Kalida her breakfast.

Apart from that, the only discernible difference about her was her mode of dress. Gone was the stark black mourning she used to affect, and in its place she wore soft dove-gray trimmed with ivory lace and charcoal velvet. Her hair was no longer pulled back in a severe bun; rather, it was obvious she had taken some pains with it, and it framed her face neatly, divided with a center part and rolled fashionably over each ear, which now sported a silvery earring.

Her smile was just as detached and impersonal as it ever had been, but Kalida's sense that something had changed persisted as Ellie lingered a moment, fussing over the bed cover and pulling down the sheets at the foot of the bed as if she were waiting for Kalida to comment on what she was doing.

Finally she looked up at Kalida and threw her a rueful little smile. "Well, Deuce is coming in a little while, you know."

"You can hardly do much to make this place presentable," Kalida responded dryly in kind. "He's seen it before, at any rate. And me."

"Oh yes," Ellie said thoughtfully. "And you. He *is* rather charged up about marrying you." Her tone now was insinuatingly pensive. Kalida instantly became wary as Ellie went on. "It's a wonder he ever forgave you all those little tricks you used to play. Well, you never would let your papa get close to him, and look where it's got him now. If you had just been a little more bending, Deuce probably would have allowed your father to buy in the syndicate sooner and you wouldn't be in this predicament."

Kalida was jolted by her words, and she shoved her tray away violently, remembering just in time she could not stand up to vent her indignation. "That isn't true, and besides, I hardly think a few snubs from me set Deuce against Papa for life."

"Snubs? Really, Kalida. Snubs. Ever since that incident with Malca, you've had it in for Deuce and you've always been trying in your little way to cut him down to size. And you've messed things up for your father in the bargain."

Kalida stopped her restless movement, attentive suddenly to Ellie's words. No, not Ellie's words — her father's words, the things he would never say to her. The things he needed to say to convince her to marry Deuce and wouldn't say because he would never want to hurt her feelings. But Ellie, who had always been her father's partisan, would never hesitate to do just that.

The errant thought occurred to her that it was Ellie who would not mind getting rid of her. But then, that was ridiculous. This was the first time her father had seen Ellie in years, and he had obviously appealed to her as an old, trusted friend.

And he was probably paying for her nursing services, Kalida's ungovernable inner voice added with a touch of malice.

"Thank you so much for setting things straight for me," she said to Ellie, the animosity patent in her voice.

Ellie ignored it. She held out her hand. "Come, we want to make you provocatively presentable for his visit this afternoon."

"He already finds me provocative just as I am," Kalida retorted pettishly. Well, she couldn't help it. This new, pretentious Ellie was even more dislikable than the mousy widow. And further, she had no business lecturing Kalida.

Ellie shrugged. "I thought you might want to dress and do your hair."

"Don't be silly. Why would I want to dress if it's more to the point for me to remain as I am?"

"Kalida, you're impossible. And you always have been. I wish him luck with you. I don't think Deuce knows a whit what he's getting into with you."

A faint smile drifted across Kalida's lips. "Yes, he does," she said softly. "Oh yes, he does."

Yes indeed, Kalida thought, holding up the mirror her father had thoughtfully provided her with, she did have to think about the things that Ellie Dean had said. The "if she hadn'ts" and the "would he haves"; the past did have an impact on the present. She pursed her lips at her reflection. She looked hellish, with her hair in an ebony tangle from her restless night and her eyes flashing with a cobalt intensity that was almost unnatural in color.

She had to assess Ellie's words. Why had Ellie said them, and why not her father?

She tossed her head; how could he? They were hateful words that put an onus of guilt on her she did not need, as well as the burden of her father's failure.

Kalida felt torn and trapped, and she ran a futile hand through her tumbling curls in an effort to calm herself, not to avoid the ultimate conclusion she had to reach.

She had to marry Deuce to atone for her father's lack of success.

For her father's failure. To save her father.

The words reverberated within her, and she knew she had no choice now. Because it was just possible it was her fault and her failure and she had to do anything possible to make it up to her father—even if it meant sacrificing

53

herself to Deuce Cavender.

She wasn't ready for him when the door thrust open and he appeared in its threshold, tall and forbidding, positively filling the door frame, burning her with the flashing intensity of his smoky gray eyes as they scorched over every line of her body.

Her hands dropped the mirror and involuntarily grabbed the cover and pulled it up over her breasts. So much for her brave words to Ellie, she thought sourly, not expecting at all what happened next. She found herself being unceremoniously hoisted up from her bed into Deuce's brawny arms as she made a futile clutch at her blanket, which slid smoothly off her legs and onto the floor.

He lifted her easily against his hard flannel-shirted chest, and the shock of his huge warm hands on her body shot right through the thin muslin gown she wore. A fine tremor shook her whole body as she met his mocking eyes and sardonic expression.

"Don't get hysterical," he advised in that hateful, caustic tone. His grip around her legs and midriff tightened, and she balled her fists to keep from pounding them into his face.

They were eye to eye as he held her there, unmoving for that brief moment. She could see every fine line radiating from his eyes, every miniscule scar he carried from every encounter with every animal he had ever tamed, the perfect shape of his thick, perpetually drawn brows, the satiric twist of his firm lips that immediately raised her hackles. She couldn't find a particle of kindness in that face, only arrogance. And desire. It warmed his eyes, smoking them into blazing charcoal as they sought her lips, rested there, and contemplated them with such leisurely intent that she could have screamed from the tension.

"Put your arms around me," he said suddenly, and his voice was like a whiplash.

"What for?" she asked, her tone equally flat and harsh to show him she was taking no nonsense from him either. She felt peculiarly helpless swung up in the air like that and enfolded against the rock hard wall of his uncompromising chest. She couldn't move her legs, though how she had managed to remember that she would never know. She couldn't hit him; well, she could, but she was sure the consequences would be worse than her not having hit him. And she didn't know quite what to do except that the last thing she wanted to do was embrace him.

However, his answer to her question caught her completely off guard. "I want to feel your arms around me," he murmured in a totally different tone of voice.

"You're mad," she said bluntly. "And now that you've shown me how big and strong you are, you can put me down."

"Yes, I am big and strong," he agreed mockingly. "You can't fight me; you'd be much better off doing whatever I wish. What*ever* I wish," he emphasized meaningfully, his eyes sliding to her mouth again. "Put your arms around me."

"I'd sooner hold a snake," she snapped, obstinately crossing her arms over her chest as best she could.

"Kalida, Kalida," he sighed despairingly, and then his voice deepened. "Hold *me*, Kalida."

"Deuce—" she protested futilely.

"Hell," he swore vehemently, lowering his head, forestalling whatever words would have followed by crashing his mouth down on hers and taking her lips and her senses by storm.

Oh God, she groaned silently; it wasn't fair. It was abominably unjust that he could do this to her, that she wanted to be enslaved by his mouth; she wanted desperately to pull away, to show him that she did not want his kisses at all. But her body did; if she hadn't learned that yesterday, she was having it reinforced right now. She was pulling herself up against him, and he did not have to ask again to feel her arms around him. It was the only way for her to pull him closer, to taste him fully, to feel his heat against her body. Her hands, of their own volition, twisted into his thick dark hair and around his taut shoulders, flexing against him almost in concert with the degree of passion she was feeling.

He knew it.

It was the thing that got to her everytime, at the height of her bedazzlement, when she was at the moment of letting go totally; she remembered he knew it, he knew her. He had known many women; this wasn't a romance. His seduction of her was as practiced and purposeful as everything else he did. He was turning her into a fool and a willing victim, and some little remnant of pride forbade that. Just that little particle of skepticism doused the sensual fire raging within her. Just right, and just in time.

He sensed that and pulled away from her. His eyes gleamed, all-wise to her; it was unnerving the way he seemed to know everything. She licked her lips nervously, and his eyes held the movement.

And then, without saying another word, he turned, still holding her, kicked open the door, and carried her into the main living room.

"Ah, there you are," her father said with obvious satisfaction evident in his voice.

"Indeed? Where am I?" Kalida asked tartly to cover the wave of heat that suffused her body. Of course her father knew what was going on, and look at how he fully approved. It was galling. And worse still, Ellie Dean was in the room with him, but at a nod from Ryland, she disappeared out the door to the porch, reappearing in an instant with a chair that she rolled in through the door.

"What is this?" Kalida demanded as Ellie pushed it right up to where Deuce stood holding her.

"For you," Ellie said sweetly. "Deuce and your father rigged it up for you so you wouldn't be chained to the bed. It's an—um, invalid chair, I guess you would call it."

"It surely will go more easily down the church aisle," Deuce commented in an undertone as he lowered her into it.

"Get that notion out of your head," she whispered back fiercely.

"Get it out of yours," he shot back, his hands biting into her shoulders as he settled her against the back of the chair. His hands moved softly up to encircle her neck, and then her head, his thumbs lifting her chin so that her defiant eyes could not avoid his. A faintly jeering smile played across his lips. "Your objections have no weight, Kalida; I have made you mobile."

He met her lightning-bolt gaze blandly. She looked like a gorgeous trapped creature sitting there helpless in her wheeled chair, her eyes blazing, her midnight mane like some wild disheveled halo around her perfect face.

And then she began to laugh. It *was* funny, perfectly hilarious that Deuce should have found some way around all her machinations. Funny, and typical of the obsessiveness of his nature once he went after something. She looked at her father, who was smiling broadly, then at Deuce, who looked irate, and then she abruptly stopped. The question still remained: Why?

"Well, now you can join us for the noon meal," her father was saying jovially, moving toward her to take the back spindles of the chair in hand to push it. Deuce beat him to it.

"I would imagine, since Kalida has been cooped up for a couple of days, that she would like to go for a walk," he interposed meaningfully, grasping the back of the chair and giving it a forceful push.

57

"I would not," Kalida contradicted.

"Yes, fresh air is necessary to maintain the health of the invalid," Deuce said serenely, shoving the chair forward once again. Kalida grabbed the arms and shut her mouth. She would not have put it past him to push the damned chair down the porch steps and let her fend for herself as best she could.

She bristled with antagonism as he tilted the chair back and lowered it from the porch a bumpy step at a time.

The fresh crisp air hit her hot body like icy water. She wrapped her arms around her breasts and shivered.

Deuce, however, did not notice—or was pretending he did not notice. He pushed the chair briskly down the dirt path that led to the back of the house and the stables. Straight ahead of her she saw Malca ambling aimlessly in the corral, and she shot a suspicious glance up at Deuce.

"Why this?" she demanded. "Why now?"

He pulled the chair to an abrupt halt and hunkered down next to her. "Look at him. I want you to look at him, and I want you to know how much you are going to miss him if you keep up with this absurd deception."

"*What* are you talking about?"

"Your little ruse that backfired." He motioned at her legs.

"Now I truly don't know what you're talking about," she hedged, reaching out her hand to touch Malca's velvety nuzzle as he poked it through the fence.

"Look, Miss Innocent, it was a good try. I applaud you. You really had your daddy going. Not me. But your daddy, yes. You had him just where you wanted him because he was scared as hell I wouldn't want you—just as you were cussedly sure I wouldn't want a disabled wife. Interesting idea, Kalida; it took a lot of guts for you to oppose me. And now you've learned the hardest lesson. You can't do it."

"You arrogant bastard," she spat out, swiping at him

with her free hand.

He caught it and held it tightly, so tightly she felt manacled. "All right, keep up your useless pretense if you have to, Kalida. It's kind of fun watching you figure out how to outwit me. But you'd better understand this: Nothing you dream up is going to prevent my having you. When you finally accept that, we'll be fine."

She turned to face him slowly, her face mirroring disbelief at his utter presumption. "Why?" she shot at him.

"Why what?"

"Why do you want to marry me?"

"Trust me, I do."

"I don't trust you, and I don't."

He shrugged. "Nonetheless . . . you will marry me."

"We'll see whether I will or I won't," Kalida said sharply.

He smiled maddeningly. "Your father needs me, Kalida; I presume that's enough reason—for now."

She jerked her eyes away. It was, damn it, damn him; feelings didn't enter into it. It was a business arrangement, purely a barter to save her father, his holdings, his reputation. She might have known Deuce wouldn't pretend otherwise. "Take me back to the house," she said in a strangled voice.

She felt his hand take her chin and force her eyes back to his. The maddeningly provoking smile skimmed his lips again. "I'm going to kiss you, Kalida. I swear it's the only way to keep you in line. I just wonder which urge in you is the strongest, the one to run away"—he leaned toward her and his lips touched hers again—"or the one to give in." His mouth closed over hers now with devastating intention, but this time, this time she struggled, she pushed against him with all her heart and might, and all her hate, swatting at his hands as they began to course their way down her shoulders to her breasts. Her sense of helplessness lent her uncommon strength, and suddenly, with one muscular shove, she thrust his body away from her with such force that he wound up on his back in the dust at her feet.

Her faint thrill of triumph was short-lived; the expression in his eyes was not to be reckoned with as he eased himself upright. "Damn hell, Kalida, you better take what I say seriously," he warned as he positioned himself behind her chair.

"I am not going to marry you," she snapped out obstinately.

"You're not, you're not. Always what you're not," Deuce growled, pushing the chair forward roughly. "You're not going to obey your father, you're not going to pay attention to me, you're not going to walk. Well, we'll see about that, Miss Uppity Ryland." He shoved the chair again in his growing anger. "We'll just see what you're *not* going to do anymore."

He barreled her chair past the corral, but then, instead of turning toward the house, he swerved it in the direction of the barn.

"Where are you taking me?" Kalida demanded, her tone both angry and wary. He was going crazy, she was sure of it, and she weighed very seriously the notion of flinging herself out of her seat. But suddenly he jolted the chair to a stop, and before she could stop him, he heaved her up over his shoulder and carried her down to the barn while she beat her fists futilely against his canyon wall of a back.

She couldn't see where he was taking her, so she was utterly shocked when he abruptly swung her down and dropped her unceremoniously into one of the watering troughs.

Kalida flailed around ineffectually as she tried to get her bearings and pull herself upright, sputtering and cursing at him as she did, remembering with a shattering start that sent her heart careening to her toes that she must not move her legs, aware he was watching her every movement, and trying with all that to think of something equally humiliating to pay him back.

Finally she shifted herself into a sitting position and pushed the sodden masses of hair out of her streaming eyes. "I won't swim for you either," she spat through clenched teeth as, with both hands, she agitated the water and then dashed it into the smug face that leaned over her.

"You may yet crawl to me," Deuce retorted in a grating tone of voice that had no humor in it whatsoever. He was awed by her determination to continue portraying the invalid. He could not tell from the motion and commotion when he tossed her into the water whether her arms were moving or her legs, and by the time she had calmed down, her resolve was back in place and his experiment had obviously failed. Nonetheless, drowned as she was, she looked utterly beguiling. Her sopping nightgown looked like it was pasted to her skin, and everything beneath was totally visible.

His eyes explored the lush lines of her exposed upper torso as she sat indignantly waiting him out, her breasts heaving and her eyes blazing deep navy-blue. Or did they close slightly as his eyes rested on the peaked nipples that thrust out from the wet gown as though she were totally naked? She reacted, he sensed that, and she would not move. She had won the round; instinct had not made her lift herself up and out of peril; at this point, his growing desire was more a peril than anything else and even the chill that coursed through his body was no drawback to that.

With a brisk motion he hoisted her protestingly into his arms and stalked back up to the house, carrying her like some primitive man who has seized his woman at the moment and meant to make the most of it.

61

He pushed his way into the partially closed door, fully expecting to be waylaid by a wrathful father, but the house was suspiciously empty. Good, he thought grimly, bearing Kalida into her bedroom and shoving the door closed behind him with his foot.

He looked into Kalida's flushed face. "Back to the beginning of the story, Kalida."

"There is no beginning of this story," she shot back, wriggling in his tenacious grasp.

"Stubborn witch," he growled, and dumped her again on the bed. "Take off your nightgown."

She struggled with the remnants of her self-control. "I know enough to do that, if you'd only just remove your obnoxious presence."

He sent her a sardonic glance and then calmly began removing his shirt.

"Deuce, damn it — "

"I'm soaked through too," he pointed out reasonably as he discarded the shirt and began unbuckling his belt.

"I'll scream," Kalida threatened, scrabbling for her cover, rather unnerved by the sight of his massively broad, matted chest. He reached for the blanket first and pulled it well out of her reach.

Still leaning over the foot of the bed, he said calmly, "Your papa would just love to catch me in here with you like this. It kind of removes all the constraints, don't you think? Naturally, I'd be a gentleman about the whole thing. But you can be sure everyone would know about it. So, don't threaten me, Kalida, and just take off your gown."

"What are you going to do?" she demanded, rather dismayed by the scenario he had just outlined.

The look in his eyes almost sent her over the edge; they said, You remember what I can do. But all he said was, "Warm you up." And she shivered at all that those three little words implied.

He whipped his belt off his narrow hips and draped it over the footboard, and then stood looking at her. His muscles rippled as he moved his arms, and he filled her dazed eyes and senses with his sensuality. And she couldn't run away from him; she couldn't allow herself to move.

He moved, and she felt as irrevocably stalked as if she were his prey as he came to the side of the bed and bent over her. She was assaulted by the heat of his body and the alluring animal scent of his nakedness. He was so inescapably *male*, and she reacted to the menace in him. "You're trembling," he murmured. "Cold—or scared?"

"Of you?" she scoffed, forcing herself to look right into his eyes, to be enveloped by the smoking desire that burned there.

"I wonder what you're planning to do now?" he said conversationally as his weight depressed the side of the bed.

"Your scare tactics are not working," Kalida snapped.

But he completely ignored that and put out a hand to touch her. "I hope you have towels," he said, moving his hand from the damply curling hair around her hectically flushed cheeks to her neck. "Where do you keep them?"

She sent him a rebellious glare. He immediately made for the washstand where, in one of the narrow drawers, he found a length of rough cotton toweling that he draped around his neck.

"Now," he said suddenly, and the crackling sound of the word was like a gunshot. He came to the bed in two strides, his hand reaching for the front of her gown, her own hands immediately coming up to push at his. The force of both opposing strengths instantly tore her gown down the front like thin paper.

He pulled at the flimsy material and it peeled away from her body like wet wallpaper; her back stiffened up and she sat there regally, resentful and naked, with the long sleeves of her gown sliding provocatively off her shoulders.

He smiled sourly, sat down at the foot of the bed, and began briskly rubbing her legs with the towel, working it upward and still further upward, coming closer and closer to her femininity with his hot hands and sensual movements.

"Your muscles are tense," he commented in an almost natural voice, but it was betrayed by a faint ragged edge to it. His hands encircled and stroked her nerveless limbs, coming closer and closer to the heart of her desire.

"Nonsense," she denied briskly, but her voice was throaty with the sense of what he was doing to her. She could not, this time, meet his glowing gaze. Her eyes focused instead on his hands, on her stiff legs, on her billowing breasts that seemed to thrust out at him of their own volition and peak tighter and tighter with every movement he made.

"You're warmer now." He draped the towel across her thighs and pulled her against him to slide the sleeves of her torn gown down from her shoulders. The taut tips of her breasts grazed the rough, matted hair on his chest, and a chord sounded deep within her as he shoved the remnants of her nightgown onto the floor and just held her against him with her nipples just barely touching him.

It was a gorgeously erotic moment. She was aware as she never had been in her life of her breasts and the power of their enticement, of his hard masculinity reaching out to her—no, demanding her. Of her nakedness and her desire. Of passion just below the surface, just waiting for the moment, the man.

But not him, everything in her screamed, even as she felt a deep yearning to feel his body wholly against hers once again.

And almost as if he had divined her desire, he shifted her body slightly and she found herself on his lap, her bottom pressed hard against his towering manhood, her breasts crushed tightly against his bare chest, his rock solid arms enfolding her in such a way that she could not pull free. "You're deliciously warm now, Kalida. No, don't move. Don't talk. I don't care what your game is, I want you here just like this—naked and warm in my arms. And willing, Kalida . . ."

"You'll have to sedate me to make me *willing*," she muttered derisively, unsettled by the sense of his throbbing manhood like a bar of iron beneath her, his surety and monumentally strong arms around her.

"Will I?" he countered lazily, and she felt his hand gently stroke the side of her right breast, running his fingers vertically across its contour, stopping just screamingly short of caressing the nipple. She felt her whole body, independent of her will, arch up to demand that he feel that taut, rigid peak. His fingers responded by just lightly moving in a sensuously circular motion, close and closer still, but not *there*, and her body writhed in a mute plea. "Will I?" he whispered, mocking her words as her own body made the demand her mouth would not. He moved his magical hand away from her breast to explore the soft curve of her hip and thigh. His mouth touched hers lightly, just the barest breath of a touch. "Willing now?" His words fanned her lips.

"No," she whispered, her fingers digging into the hot skin of his muscular shoulders.

"Liar." He licked her lips, savoring their softness. "Listen to your body, Kalida. Your body doesn't lie."

"My body tells the worst lies," she whispered, turning her head to avoid his seductive mouth. His tongue touched her ear and she shivered at the sensation.

"I *will* have you." He pulled her closer, his hand sliding from the lush curve of her hip to cup her buttocks. "Willingly." His fingers contracted involuntarily against their undulating softness.

65

"Never," she swore.

"Forever," he corrected, his lips hovering above her mouth, his eyes smouldering as he concentrated on the movement of her lips that were now parted and waiting, belying all her denials. "You want me now," he added huskily.

"I do not want you," she bit out, pushing at him vainly with her free hand.

That faint sour smile played across his lips again. "Stubborn, stubborn Kalida," he muttered, and his mouth slanted over hers and took it ruthlessly this time, as if he meant to show her that her only choice was to comply with *his* will and that she had none of her own.

The hand that held her buttocks moved and ripped away the towel that covered the juncture of her thighs, and he began to caress the soft skin there, brazenly stroking, demanding admittance, commanding her compliance.

The soft sensual movements of his fingers compelled her legs to part, and she moved them without thinking to admit his questing hand. He stroked her gently, learning her, feeling her reactions and responses, in no hurry, either with his fingers or his mouth, and she moved against him voluptuously as he found her pleasure point and began his sensual massage.

The sensations he evoked were indescribable to her. She felt as though she could not get enough of his hand within her. Her whole body swelled toward him, demanding and giving at the same time.

He pulled his mouth away from hers to watch her face, loving the little animal sounds she made, whispering in her ear, "You want me now," and hearing her still deny him.

"No, no, I want . . . this. . . . I want—"

"Me," he rasped as her response heightened, and her body arched and moved frantically beneath his hand.

"I want . . . that," she sighed, feeling for one frenzied moment she had to escape his inexorable fingers and the unknown they impelled her toward.

"From *me*," he whispered savagely, his mouth claiming hers, knowing she was on the edge of hurtling away from him; his lips ravaged her tongue, her lips, her neck. "Only from me," he repeated harshly, and then his mouth closed over her tempting taut, straining left nipple, covering it, licking at it, sucking it in rhythm with her groans until her senses spun shatteringly out of control into a glittering convulsion of pure primordial pleasure.

Her body felt as if it had dissolved as his mouth and hands ceased their commanding pressure, and she moved closer to his heat, feeling melded to it and enveloped by it. His whole body was taut with a fine tension that came from both his response to her and from his own need. She felt that too and she did not know what to do or say to alleviate it.

"Kalida." His abrasive whisper penetrated her thick contentment. "Look at me, Kalida." The raw emotion in his voice flayed her, and her eyes flew open. "I want you, Kalida." Her head moved in a faint denial. She didn't want him to want her. She didn't. "Kalida!" His voice commanded now and she could not ignore it. His seductive hand rested lightly on her feminine mound but its very tautness communicated his suppressed desire. "Hold me, Kalida."

Her head reared up and her lashes lowered to shield her eyes. Her left hand, which had been clutching at his forearm, tentatively moved upward. Her other arm wound itself around his waist, and she felt as though some other self were moving her limbs. The flaring light in his eyes held hers hypnotically, and he was aware of every hesitant move of her hands. "Feel me, Kalida," he whispered as her fingers slid lightly over the corded muscle of his upper arm.

"Kalida!" There was a warning note in his tone. Her fingers tightened against his skin. "Yes," he murmured, "just like that."

"No," she demurred, arresting the movement of her hand.

"Yes," he said insistently, "from you, Kalida." He took her hand forcefully and placed it around his neck. "Like that. Hold me, Kalida." Her arm tightened and she became intensely aware of the shape of his body against hers, the sense of his burning need. His mouth touched hers, his tongue tracing the shape of her lips, tasting them, feeling them on his own.

"Deuce," she groaned, "I can't take any more. You don't want me, you can't. You just want any woman. Nothing is any different now than it ever has been."

"Everything is different," he growled, pulling the arm that encircled his neck downward across his chest and his taut male nipples that were so like and unlike her own. And downward still, to rest on the pulsating manhood that strained against his trousers. His hand covered hers, and then briskly unfastened the waistband beneath her fingers, releasing his hot, hard elongated maleness to nudge her hand.

She shuddered, and the moment stretched into a heavy war of wills between them, quivering in the air until he commanded huskily, "Touch me, Kalida."

"I can't," she protested. "I never—"

"I know. I know. Touch me, Kalida. I want your hand *there*—now." He watched intently as her tongue licked her lips; her hand made an unsure jerking motion and stopped abruptly. His hand grasped it uncompromisingly and settled her reluctant fingers around the proof of his desire.

She couldn't move. How incredible. And impossible. She felt desperate to get away from him, but he still held her in that inexorable grasp and her fingers were still wrapped around the heat of his rock hard masculinity.

"Kalida." His harsh voice came from far away, but she could not ignore it. "Tell me now what you're *not* going to do, Kalida."

She caught her breath, her eyes widening in shock at his rough words. He had shattered the mad moment between them, and she found it easy after that to remove her hand from his slowly contracting manhood, easy to withdraw from him, to summon up her resentment, which was always near the surface anyway. "I'll tell you," she bit out, using every ounce of strength to jack herself away from him. "I'm never going to be caught by you like this again. Never. And that's a promise."

"Don't count on keeping it," he said acidly, running his free hand insolently over her nakedness.

She froze under his touch just as an ominous pounding began on the door.

Deuce released her instantly, and she fell back against the pillows. He lifted himself off the bed as he smoothly fastened his trousers and threw her blanket at her. He did not look at her as he went to the door and admitted Ellie Dean.

"What on earth is going on in here?" she demanded, her eyes sliding to Kalida, who had muffled herself in her thin cover up to her chin, which did not hide at all the tempting curves of her body.

Ellie swung her gaze back to Deuce, her eyes kindling at the sight of his broad bare chest and the line of his body as he leaned sideways to grab his shirt. His expression, as he slid his muscular arms into the sleeves, was mocking.

"None of your business, Ellie." He buttoned his shirt as he moved toward her, and she began backing away from him, overwhelmed by the power in him, and the disdain.

He slammed the door in Ellie Dean's face almost as though he didn't even see her. She did not like that all,

69

not one bit, and she didn't care what Hal Ryland had told her about the reasons for it.

But a moment later, Deuce flung open the door and stalked out. Kalida's face, behind him, held a curious expression of relief mingled with yearning.

Ellie closed the door on her, her own relief palpable and distressingly evident to her.

Five

An eerie semblance of normalcy pervaded the house that night due, Kalida thought wrathfully, to Ellie Dean's presence, her motherly and solicitous aid, and her father's subtle approbation. Ellie and her father were clearly allied, and the sense was that they were a family; Kalida was leery of it while she could see that Ellie liked the notion very well.

It also annoyed her that her father never questioned Deuce's presence in her room. Quite the contrary, he went out of his way to assure her that he trusted Deuce implicitly and that he knew he would never do anything to harm Kalida.

"Oh, Papa," she said disgustedly as she picked at her dinner and they discussed the events of the afternoon. "Tell me how it comes about that you just happened to be up at winter pasture this afternoon with Eakins and the boys when I heard you say very clearly you were expecting them down here by the end of the week?"

"Eakins had a little problem he wanted me to handle," her father answered readily. "It didn't take above two hours for me to ride and come down, now did it?"

He beamed at Kalida, who sat stiffly in her wheeled chair across the table from her father, glaring at him. "It would not have taken Deuce above two hours to—" she began angrily, but her father held up his hand. "Really, Kalida; I thought the matter was settled. I should not be privy to things that go on between you and Deuce in private." He raised his fine white brows and shook his head. "Everything is going forward with great dispatch. Deuce had the papers drawn up already. He is anxious, Kalida, even though he pretends he is doing me the favor. That should please you. You should be very pleased indeed." He bent his head back toward his plate and so did not see Kalida's murderous gaze skim over him and lance into Ellie, who was nodding her agreement of her father's assessment. Hadn't she seen it herself. But then suddenly Kalida's anger dissolved into something akin to resignation and she said wearily, "No, I am not pleased, Papa. But everything shall be as you wish."

"Well of course," said her father.

"Because I have no choice, do I?" Kalida finished.

Her father's pale blue eyes held her darker ones for a long moment and then he turned away. "No, you don't," he said with uncharacteristic firmness. "It just has to be this way." He let a long, silent moment go by for this irrevocable statement to sink in, and then he looked back up at Kalida and went on. "But I wholeheartedly welcome Deuce as a member of our family, Kalida. Above and beyond my considerations, I still think he is a good match for you."

Kalida's beautiful face twisted into a mask of irony. "Truly, Papa, I am delighted that you had my best interests at heart."

"So I did," he agreed calmly. He looked at Ellie. "She seems up to snuff, doesn't she? Nothing fazes my Kalida; I wonder that I even needed to call on you to help. Except that it does worry me to leave Kalida alone at night, especially now that her legs appear to be useless. I'm glad you're here, Ellie."

Ellie's face was a study as her father delivered this moderately grateful little speech. Kalida shook her head hopelessly. Her father had been periodically going out at night for as long as she could remember, sometimes to nighthawk the herd, sometimes to hunt for marauders, sometimes to stand guard, and most times, recently, to join in the search for rustlers who had seemingly become more bold of late. There wasn't a rancher for miles who hadn't lost a substantial head of cattle, either in large droves or piecemeal, throughout the previous year, and mutual frustration had driven her father and their neighbors, including Deuce, to form their mutual protection society, which they had organized under the guise of being a gambling hall.

Never had her father scrupled to leave her alone at the ranch, particularly since Eakins or one of his men was but a shout away. However, in these bad times, Eakins and Bill, the range cook, were the only occupants of the bunk house beyond the corral, the only hands her father could afford to pay full time; during round-up he was forced to hustle up a string of day workers, none of whom looked any too respectable to Kalida. All of them now were away at winter pasture, and she supposed she ought to have felt appreciative that her father had given her immobile state some consideration.

It was obvious Ellie did not. She had not ensconced herself at the Ryland ranch for the sole purpose of trying to ride herd on Kalida for a second time. Her black eyes glittered as she assessed Hal Ryland. He was acting just a little too naive, she thought. Probably to impress Kalida, who was as sharp as a tack to begin with. Kalida understood perfectly how it was. They both did. Tacitly, they both allowed Hal Ryland his little fiction, but neither really expected that he had planned to leave them alone together this very night.

"Oh, but yes," he concurred, easing himself out of his chair. "Tonight's my poker night, as always once a month, Ellie, as Kalida can tell you. But I can see how Kalida was not thinking about that in the excitement of all that's been happening around here. Excuse me now, will you?"

They watched him exit the room, each woman with mixed emotions, and then they turned to look at each other.

"Well," Ellie said after a moment, "I don't suppose you can help with the dishes," and she began stacking the dishes, ignoring Kalida entirely.

"I'm sorry," Kalida said for want of something to indicate that she had a momentary sympathy for Ellie's position, but Ellie looked at her with a startled air. "What for?" she asked, puzzled. "Things will work out; they always do."

Not last time, Kalida thought, watching Ellie clear the table and disappear down the narrow hallway that led to the large square kitchen. This was really an oblong room her father had appended to the house, which contained the large wood stove, some tables and cupboards for storage, and a rude open stone fireplace for roasting. It had not existed during Ellie's first tenure at the ranch, and she expressed surprise that Hal Ryland had seen fit to build at Kalida's express wishes rather than her own. However, she also knew when to leave the past in the past, and she efficiently cleared the table while Kalida sat in her chair like a statue and waited for her father to come down and say good night.

He was dressed in dark clothes as usual when he reappeared and came swiftly to Kalida's side to kiss her on the cheek.

"I did *not* know this would be one of your nights out," she said angrily in his ear as his lips touched her affectionately.

"No," he agreed gravely. "Something came up, actually. We're patrolling Sweetland's borders tonight. A dozen head of Santa Linaria have disappeared, and you know how Deuce guards those damned steers. Well, anyway, Ellie need not know, and I'm sure nothing will come of this night's work. If someone made off with that many of that herd, you can be damned sure he isn't going to stick around to be caught at it a second time. He's got enough to breed his own. But—we'll do what we have to. I expect you'll get a good night's rest, and don't worry about me, Kalida."

She nodded and he went down the hall to the kitchen. She could hear his voice and Ellie's, and then the sound of his boots and the back door slamming as he let himself out of the house.

So now it was just her and Ellie. And if she were to give nothing away, she had to depend on Ellie to wheel her around. The situation rankled, but she knew she had no one to blame but herself. She wished she could think of a way out of it gracefully. She could not see engaging in an evening's light conversation with Ellie. Nor could she see lying in bed thinking about Deuce. She actually couldn't see going to bed at all.

She wondered what she was going to do all night.

The pleasant scent of smoke permeated her dreams; the sense of the comradery of the campfire, the physically exhausting work of the round-up; the warmth of weary muscles collapsed and prone before a crackling fire, a strong cup of coffee in hand. The murmur of voices, the snap and pop of the burning fire, so warm and so close when one slept, roaring in one's ear, hot now, intense, comforting . . . When had she lain down her head? The heat felt so good, she was so tired . . . She slept, a smile of memory of her lips, while the kitchen at Ryland ranch burned.

It began as a faint glow on the horizon, practically unnoticeable, almost unearthly, like a dim halo limning the outline of the far distance.

By the time it heightened into a shimmering orange haze against the black sky, the Sweetland range patrollers were sweeping across the back reaches of the Ryland pasture. They knew what it was, they did not know where Hal Ryland was, and they were frantic to reach the house before the disaster roared out of control.

They were too late. The upper story and the rear of the house were a mass of flames. Lying crumpled outside in front of the porch, in the dirt, was Ellie Dean, her clothing scorched and her skin grazed with burns.

Deuce came charging around to the knot of men surrounding Ellie, all of whom looked helpless and frightened that he was going to demand they forage into the burning building. Ellie was unconscious, he saw at first glance, but he dismounted anyway in a running motion, grabbing up her limp body and ruthlessly slapping her face, shouting over the grisly roar of the flames, "Where's Kalida? Damn it, Ellie, where's Kalida?" until she came to, shaking her head numbly.

She was dazed by his brutishness as much as by her fear when her eyes lit on the house. "I don't know," she screamed. "I don't know. She was in her bedroom—"

Deuce dropped her, literally pushing her on her back as he jumped up and sprinted around to the back of the house, to the little ell of the bedroom that Kalida had been occupying. The flames had not reached here yet, but they were inching closer and closer; the entire kitchen wing was a mass of charred and burning timbers and the second story above the ell was ablaze.

He could not reach the window, and he cursed himself for not riding back here immediately; but when he turned to run for his horse, he found five of his men right behind him, motioning that they would lift him to the window. Eight arms hoisted him ten feet off the ground, and he used the butt of his gun to break the glass. He never felt the cutting shards as he tumbled into the heat-stifled room.

And panicked.

Kalida was not in the room.

He screamed her name and couldn't hear his voice over the roar of the flames as he dashed through the open bedroom door into the main living room.

The whole wall abutting the kitchen was ablaze; the smoke choked him and brought tears to his eyes. He just barely perceived Kalida on the floor by the front door. Already the timber framing was smoking, and the insatiable flames were licking the curtains on the windows.

Deuce assessed the situation in an instant before he started coughing and gagging again. He pulled out his bandanna and tied it around his nose and mouth, and then he lunged toward Kalida's inert body. There wasn't even time to think. He hoisted her over his shoulder and turned back to her bedroom, only to find the door frame flaming.

Damn, and he had no other choice; the whole living area was blazing now, incandescent and like a furnace behind him. The bedroom was the only clear way out—if he didn't wait too long. The door was smoking and flames now visibly crackled across the lintel.

He shifted Kalida's body into his arms and plunged across the blazing threshold and straight to the window, determined to jump out with her.

But there was shadowy forms visible through the cracked glass, men on horseback waiting; he could hear their muffled voices as he blindly lifted Kalida's body upwards and through the broken points of glass. He could feel the flames roaring behind him, choking him, Kalida's weight being lifted from him, hands pulling at him as he climbed by instinct onto the windowsill, hands pulling at him as he seemingly fell through thin air, choking and sightless, to land on something firm, not an animal — a wagon? He didn't know; his eyes were streaming and he couldn't stop coughing, and he was moving, being moved away from the oven-hot heat of the fire.

More hands pushing him forward, voices commanding him to breathe and drink, pushing a canteen in his hand, brushing his hair and face with a sopping cool cloth.

Where was Kalida?

Impossible to talk. The fire was still close, endless. He determined he was now in a wagon, and it was being driven around to the front of the house where the rest of the patrollers waited and watched helplessly. He saw them as dark silhouettes on horseback, no faces. It was eerie.

His eyes cleared a little, and he was able, finally, to breathe without coughing and take a deep, cleansing drink of water from the canteen.

Now he could see Hal Ryland holding the collapsing Ellie Dean, and the rest of the men on foot surrounding but standing well away from the house.

He looked into the darkness that was lit up by the blazing fire. Behind him, in the flat bed of the wagon, lay Kalida, being tended by two of his own men. Before him, an aching, soughing sound made him whip around just as the roof of the house collapsed into a wall of flames.

She could still smell smoke and hear the roaring blaze, but something was different. The high-pitched screeching of the horses jolted her senses. Something was very different. She could breathe without choking, and she was cold. Yes, she was very definitely cold, although now she was aware that something rough covered her. But the horrible snapping sound—and the almost hysterical whinnying of the horses . . . She reached out her hand; she thought she reached out her hand to prop up her body but she hadn't moved. She heard voices and she tried to move again, this time more successfully. She managed to lift her head, but she could see nothing except bodies in black silhouette against the raging blaze of what used to be her home.

My God, she moaned inwardly, hoisting her body up with difficulty; there was nothing, nothing there. The barn! She jerked her head in the direction of the barn and was grateful she could see its bulk still standing. Against the firelight she saw the movements of men beating back the flames that had started to swoop along the wooden fences that butted the house, pulling apart the staves of the fences, almost as an afterthought as the fire started spreading outward.

She lifted herself into a sitting position, gulping in great breaths of the night air that was only faintly smoky this far away because the wind was blowing in the opposite direction. Everything was gone. And she couldn't remember a thing.

No, she shook her head consideringly, no, she did remember. She had awakened when the smell of the smoke finally started choking her; and she had run toward the most sensible exit, only to find the kitchen and the hallway engulfed in flames. She had immediately turned in the opposite direction, and she did not remember being felled by the smoke or anything of being rescued from the burning building.

But there was Papa—and Ellie; so he had gotten back in time to save her! She felt a wave of filial love and gratitude that she had been considered his most precious possession.

Every one of their neighbors, she perceived after a

while, had come to Papa's aid from the patrolling of Sweetland.

And they had come too late, she understood. The house was gone. Their home, their possessions down to their clothes were gone. All she and Papa had left were the cattle and the horses, the rangeland and her tacit promise to marry Deuce Cavender.

She did not know if that were enough for Papa to survive on. She watched silently now with the others who were still unaware that she had regained consciousness while the Ryland ranch burned to smouldering embers as the gray dawn seeped into the sky.

And then her papa approached the wagon and spoke to the driver, Deuce. "What now?"

"You'll come back to Sweetland, of course," Deuce said tiredly. "Ellie too. You'll stay as long as you have to."

"I'd rather," Kalida said suddenly and loudly, "camp out in the barn."

"Hello Kalida; I was hoping you were still out so I wouldn't get any arguments about this," Deuce said calmly, picking up the reins of his team.

"Kalida, don't be ridiculous," her father snapped just over Deuce's words.

"I won't be beholden to him on top of everything else," Kalida retorted.

"Consider it part of the marriage portion," Deuce interjected. "You getting in or out, Ryland?" he added as her father hesitated as to whether to climb in the wagon or to mount his horse. "Ellie?"

"I'm coming," she said, allowing Ryland to hand her up into the seat beside Deuce. She slanted a look at him. Oh, he did look weary and not a little angry. Well, so was she. She was damned tired of being considered an afterthought. She turned and looked at Kalida. Kalida was . . . as ever Kalida, even with her face covered with soot and her hair in a disgraceful tangle. "Poor Kalida," she

80

murmured.

"Papa," Kalida said imploringly.

"I'll ride," he decided, and mounted his horse alongside the wagon.

"We'll get cleaned up, have some breakfast, and then decide what to do about your situation," Deuce said, clicking at the horses. The wagon jounced forward and Kalida fell backward. As they bounced down the long dirt road, she turned to look back at the ranch. But there was no ranch. All that remained was just a sad-looking bunch of charred and smoking timbers, and a determined group of men armed with horse blankets beating at the last flicker of destructive flame in the ruins.

Six

Sweetland!

To Kalida, it seemed almost mystical that as they approached the sun was rising and wreathed the T-shaped two-story house in a hazy, glowing nimbus of light.

She had not been there in years, but she loved it instantly, with its early two-story log cabin fronting a long two-story ell that almost looked like another house had been appended to the antique one. It stood rambling and serene on the crest of a hill, and the newer ell overlooked gardens, fruit trees, and grazing pasture that was liberally dotted with tall shade trees and slatted fencing.

Perpendicular to the house, facing the drive, was a huge barn and stables. Beyond this, as far as the eye could see, was more fencing and grazing land. The air was sweet with the scent of hay and ripening fruit.

Beneath this tranquility, there was a sense of subtle energy, as though all activity were going on smoothly behind the scenes even this early in the morning.

This is what Papa wants me to have, Kalida thought as the wagon bounced to a stop by the porch that defined the entrance of the ell. She wracked her brain to remember what Deuce's family situation was and could only recall that there were numerous servants, hired hands, a competent foreman, a sister that she thought did not live at Sweetland but had been married recently, and an aunt. The aunt, his deceased father's sister, had come to Sweetland to nurse her brother five years before and had stayed on after his death.

Kalida's memory pictured her as a formidably bulky woman with a sharp face and tongue to match, but the reality was that she was tall, handsome, and had a physical impediment that necessitated her using a cane, which hampered her movements as she limped out of the house and down the porch steps to greet her unexpected visitors.

"Deuce, what's this?" she demanded in an unexpectedly deep and clipped voice.

"The Rylands' place burned last night," Deuce said brusquely, sliding down from his perch. He did not need to say more. His aunt turned, hobblings back up the steps and into the house, and even as Deuce lifted Kalida out of the wagon box, the older woman's voice could be heard shouting instructions to this or that servant.

"Ardelle is efficient, I will say that for her," Hal Ryland commented with a hint of admiration in his tone. He looked Kalida over with a critical eye as Deuce turned to carry her into the house. She looked weary and defeated; her features were smudged with soot, her nightgown was almost in shreds. She was shivering, as much from the cool morning air as from being in Deuce's arms, and she seemed unrepentant about that. She was a tempting bundle, Ryland had to admit, and he did not know how Deuce could resist her. But the one thing he was sure of was that this startling turn of events could not be allowed to have an effect on his agreement with Deuce.

"Hal!" Ellie's sharp, resentful voice broke into his reverie. He turned toward her apologetically and held out his arms. She braced herself against them, swung gracefully down from the driver's perch, and looked around her with an emotion akin to awe.

"This is lovely," Ellie breathed as one of the two men who had accompanied Kalida vaulted out of the wagon box and approached her. "You okay, ma'am?" he asked her respectfully.

Which was more than either Hal or Deuce had done, she thought. "Thank you, yes," she said gratefully as a middle-aged black woman with the straightest back she had ever seen came out of the house. "The men is going to breakfast down back," she said, addressing Ryland. "You come, you too, Missus, to the dining room where Miss Ardelle has laid places for you."

They followed her into the sun-flooded entrance hallway, both of them wondering where Deuce had taken the very obviously reluctant Kalida.

Damn him, thought Kalida, it just wasn't possible to remain stiff and unyielding the way he was carrying her. He was like some uncivilized savage, with his uncompromising expression and the tension in his arms. Perhaps she was too heavy, she mused; the thought that she was an unpleasant burden to him pleased her momentarily, but it paled before the grim reality of the situation — her and her father's dependency on him.

He stopped before a pristine white door as he felt the disclaiming movement of her head. She looked up to meet his glittering gray gaze. It struck her that he looked as wretched as she did, and Kalida felt a moment's compassion for him before she felt him swing her body downward and release her to stand on her legs. Damn, she just had time to think before she fell to the floor, an almost involuntary reaction as she instanteously perceived he wanted to trap her. God, she had to be quick-witted with him. The stone hardness of his expression told her as well as words that he was going to catch her sometime. She couldn't even imagine what he might do when the truth came out.

She watched dispassionately as he pushed the door open with one grungy work-worn boot, and she moved instinctively before he could reach down and lift her up again.

She wriggled through his long legs and pulled herself into the room, and then turned to look at him with a gleam of triumph in her eyes.

"My house is your house," he said mockingly. "Or soon will be."

"I haven't agreed to that," she snapped, looking around suspiciously. She knew where she was. The room was too bold and masculine to be anyone else's but his. The furniture was massive and ornate, newly purchased with new wealth, all walnut and marble, the bed with its eight-foot headboard and rich applied moldings dominating the center of the room. There was a matching step-down dressing case and a marble-topped washstand with a splash back and soap shelves. Near the window was an upholstered rocking chair with padded arms.

Deuce stood watching her as she assessed the impact of the room from her position on the floor. When her accusing blue eyes lighted on his tall muscular body, he smiled—rather unpleasantly, she thought—and said mildly, "You don't have to agree to anything—now."

She stiffened slightly at the tone and the implication of his words, and then she began struggling to move forward, cursing herself and the day she had ever thought that this kind of pretense would get her anywhere away from him. She felt as trapped as though she were handicapped, and as she pulled herself into a sitting position, she grated, "God, if I had the means and the mobility, I'd be so far away from here a Pinkerton man couldn't even track me down."

He came down beside her like a shot, his hand reaching

out to grasp her chin, to lift her head so that her eyes focused on his stone-carved face. "I would find you," he stated unequivocally in a hard harsh voice, and she had no doubt he meant what he said. "Kalida!" The timbre of his voice changed, and the merciless grip of his fingers changed to a caress against her skin as he traced the line of her face. "Don't fight me."

"I have to fight you," she whispered, mesmerized by the feeling of his fingers so gently limning the contours of her face. But she wondered where her strength was when he touched her. Where was her resolve? It would be so easy the other way, so extravagantly easy.

"Why?" The word was a breath between them as he leaned forward and touched her lips with just the slightest pressure.

Her whole body flinched in reaction, and she hated herself for not being able to control her feelings. "You'd eat me alive," she hissed, frantically trying to gain some self-possession. She was drowning in the sense of him beside her, all heat and sweat and an intensity she hardly had the strength to withstand.

"Oh yes, I would . . ." he growled, and there was no room left to maneuver as his mouth crashed down on hers with the sole intention of conquering, dominating, driving, relentlessly delving into the soft recesses of her mouth, tasting her in a way she could never imagine another man doing—ever. He held her head between his hands just so, and her own hands beat ineffectually at his long hard body, and it was as if she were caressing him; he tore his mouth away from hers for the barest instant and murmured against her lips, "You want me."

"No!"

He brushed away her heated denial with the softest flick of his tongue against her swelling lips. "You've always wanted me," he murmured in some satisfaction.

"God," she moaned, but it was too late; he forced her

stubborn lips apart once again and all she could do was dig her protesting fingers into the hot skin of his shoulders, where he felt it not at all. She was drowning in the sense of him, his taste and his scent, when he pulled away from her seductive lips and trailed a line of heated kisses down her cheek and chin to her neck and shoulders, moving his hands at the same time caressingly downward to the sooty remnant of a nightgown she still wore. And then he paused and looked at her through questioning, passion-smoked eyes.

She was as still as she would ever be in her life, she thought with a kind of horrified wonder. His hand was poised just above her taut, thrusting breast, which was outlined so visibly against the thin material of her gown. Just one movement and he would touch it, and she remembered full well what he meant when he touched her there and how he had touched her there. And she wanted it. She never thought she would admit that she would want to feel his hand caressing her nipples, but in that moment, on the floor of his room, oblivious to everything but that moment, with her back pressing against the molded siderail of his bed, she wanted him to. . . . But she saw that his intent was slightly different, and she thought that if he did as he intended, she could be in thrall to him forever.

And he watched every step of her thoughts as they were reflected in her cobalt eyes; they went from blazing blue to molten as she understood what he was going to do whether she willed it or not. His glittering eyes never left hers as he pushed aside the flimsy bodice of her nightgown and exposed the firm globes with their taut, inviting tips.

Very gently, he planted tender little kisses all the way from her shoulder to her chest, and then down the curve of her left breast, coming closer and ever closer to her yearning nipple until finally, thank heaven, finally he closed his lips and tongue around the lush crest.

He heard the deep hiss of her breath as she felt his moist tongue surround the nipple and lick at it, and then the hoarse groan from back in her throat as he began pulling at and sucking the pebble-hard nipple with all the wild control he could manage. And he wanted both nipples, and he wanted her right then and there, and as he eased his mouth back and forth from one luscious nipple to the other, he felt her capitulation; he felt her hands in his hair, pulling, her fingers sliding to his shoulders, pushing, her words, "Don't, please, no more," in a hazy desire so intense he almost exploded with it. Her words goaded him on as though the intensity of the sensations he was evoking in her caused her to deny their strength and what they made her desire.

She was weak with the molten feelings that slid like thick honey through her veins. It seemed as though the hot moist sensation centered in the pit of her stomach, between her legs, and in the two pinpoints of pleasure that this man, whom she swore she detested, was evoking from her traitorous nipples. It was almost unbearable, what she was feeling; there was a spiralling sensation, an unfurling, a reaching in her but for what she did not know. She yearned to feel his weight on her, hot and naked, and to open up to him in some way she did not understand. But she did not want him to stop suckling her breasts either, or to cease his provocative exploration of her body.

Was she suddenly on the floor—and naked—with her body arching up to meet the powerful thrust of his hips? Was she sane? Did his caressing her breasts make her totally mindless? She hadn't another instant to consider this because his mouth covered hers demandingly in a way that drove all thought out of her mind. She was rendered a wanton animal, reaching solely for his rapacious tongue and for the sensation that he could make her feel.

"Stop me now," he whispered against her bruised lips. He felt rather than heard her gasp of wonder that reflected his own sense of having her naked and willing in his arms.

Even Kalida, deep in the recesses of her mind, knew she should resist him now when he had given her the chance; but she was aware only of the opulent feeling of her body and her need to have him do more—of anything, of everything, whatever he wished—and there was no question of her pretenses now. She was wide open to him, sleek and silken beneath him, fierce in her consuming desire to have the more that she barely understood she yearned for.

He knew he should stop himself, that nothing should go further because he was taking the very grim chance she might hate him forever. But her response was so heady, and he felt the power within himself gather to the point of a need that nothing could stop and nothing could quench but his thorough possession of this one body, this one implacable, alluring woman. He seduced her mouth once again as he ripped apart his pants and rubbed himself lightly against the juncture of her thighs. He caressed her hot soft skin, warming her, readying her, parting her legs, exploring then her satiny core that was moist and ready to receive him, that met his hand with an eagerness and willingness that utterly enslaved him.

"Kalida . . ." Her name was a rough growl against her lips, rasping through her consciousness, piercing the ravishing sensations of his hands on her and his . . . She felt him poised suddenly, and then a thrust between her legs at the same moment his lips captured hers once again; a sense of tearing and a faraway fiery pain that almost made her scream it was so sharp and compelling. And then over that the sensation that she was joined, filled; that some empty place in her was empty no more.

She pulled her mouth from his and looked into his

face. And she couldn't tell what was there—except a kind of sadness for her pain. The joy she had felt turned over and deadened.

"Kalida?" Her name was now a soft caressing sound in the air between them, but somehow, she didn't believe it.

"Is that it?" she asked innocently and insolently all at once.

A crooked rueful smile skimmed his lips.

"Oh no, Kalida; we have a long way to go. A long way to go."

"Not today," she said, wriggling now against him, feeling suddenly as though she were pinned down totally and irrevocably.

"Today, Kalida." His voice was tense, impatient.

"Do it then," she challenged, even though she hardly knew what she was commanding him to do. Somehow the barnyard was not the schoolroom for her own actual experience. She wondered if she hated him for taking advantage of her, or herself for succumbing.

He braced himself on his elbows and looked down at her. He had to consciously pull back on himself to stop from devouring her sulky lips right then and there. Anything. This was not the way to teach her a lesson. He had prepared her for the future; that was all. She had the capacity to be an untamed wanton in his arms, and he wanted that from her—but he wanted her willing and understanding the nature of her desire. There was something petulant and disappointed about her now, as though she were either angry or had expected something that did not happen.

Well, he thought dispiritedly, enough had happened. And more could happen if he forced her and proceeded. He had learned something more about her this afternoon; he wondered if she had learned something more about herself.

With a short thrusting movement, he levered himself

90

backward and removed himself from her body. He was rather amazed that she looked shocked. They stared at each other for a moment, each trying to divine the other's motives, neither willing to give an inch.

All he saw was a beautiful, naked animal with wild, tangled midnight hair that spread in disarray over the Turkey red carpet beneath her bare skin, her eyes half closed, gleaming with something he could not define behind the lids.

"Come." He held out his hand and she reached for it, allowing him to pull her to a sitting position, no further. "Kalida . . ." The warning note in his voice did not put her off. She felt curiously deflated and empty. She stared at him defiantly now as he buttoned himself up.

"I could use a bath," she said suddenly.

He didn't like the connotation of that one bit, but since she would be sharing his room, he did not have to explore it now. A thorough cleaning off seemed, in fact, like a good idea.

"I'll have Prestina prepare everything for you," he said, turning away from her. He left her sitting on the floor in the middle of his room.

Seven

There was a knock on the bedroom door, and then it was thrust open and Ardelle limped in to find Kalida sprawled across the top of Deuce's bed, covered with the rough cotton spread she had pulled up from the mattress.

"Oh my dear," Ardelle murmured, and motioned to the two men behind her to enter. They carried in a copper hip bath and set it next to the fireplace. Behind them came Prestina with towels, soap, and a bucket of steaming water, which she poured into the boiler and gave back to the two men, who disappeared for barely five minutes, then reappeared, each of them carrying two equally full buckets of heated water.

"Enough now," pronounced Prestina. "I will help you." She looked meaningfully at Ardelle who was leaning heavily on her thick, ornately carved cane.

"Yes. You poor thing, Kalida. I must rummage in my closet for some appropriate robes until we can get you to town for some clothes." She raised her hand at Kalida's negative shake of the head. "But you must. Deuce will take care of everything."

"He has already," Kalida retorted.

"Dear Kalida, that's hardly an expression of gratitude to the man who risked his life to save yours," Ardelle said chidingly, trying to picture this wild hoyden of a child in Deuce's bed for the rest of his life. She couldn't see it, but if that was what he wanted . . .

"Deuce did?" Kalida whispered. Not Papa! She couldn't believe the unbearable pain she felt. To owe him *this* on top of everything else! To know that everything to do with their lives from now on rested solely within his hands! Oh, God, *his* hands! His damnable, compelling hands. She felt on the verge of collapsing at that moment; she couldn't conceive of one place within herself from which to draw strength. Her self didn't exist anymore. He had taken it, along with her very life.

"He did indeed, my dear. Try to be a little kinder," Ardelle advised, her tone just faintly remonstrative. Deuce did not deserve all the aggravation this child was giving him; nor did he deserve having to deal with the father. But all of that was his lookout. She could only stand by and pick up the pieces when the child hurt him finally and irrevocably as she could see, from her mutinous mouth and rebellious air, that she was bound to do. "Have your bath, Kalida. I'll find something for you to wear and later, after you've rested, I'm sure things will seem much less distressing."

She watched with admiration as Kalida seemed to visibly pull herself together, find her manners, and answer in a reasonably positive tone, "You're right, of course. They probably will. Thank you, Ardelle."

Ardelle withdrew in her slow hobbling gait and Prestina closed the door behind her. "Now, Miss Kalida . . ."

"I can manage for myself," Kalida said briskly, wanting now only to be alone and free to be herself.

"How can you do that, Miss Kalida?"

"I—" She didn't know how to answer Prestina. When she thought about the time and effort it would cost her, were she really disabled, to crawl across the room and hoist herself into that tub, it seemed ungracious and impossible that she would refuse Prestina's help. But then. . . . "Do you think," she rasped out suddenly, "I want *anyone* to see me helpless and crawling on the floor to perform the simplest act of sanitary caretaking? Do you? Do you? How do you think it will make me feel?"

Prestina's face turned impassive at this onslaught. "I am not *anybody*," she said painstakingly. "I am here to help you, and you will take my help. I will not leave the room until I have helped you."

"I don't care!" Kalida shouted, hostage now to her total frustration and the sudden release of tension from the shouting. "I want to be alone." Yes, that was exactly what she wanted. "Leave me alone, Prestina. I'll manage. If I can't," she added, softening her harsh tone, "I'll ring for you, I promise."

"I don't know . . ." Prestina said doubtfully.

"Go!" Kalida gritted, and Prestina realized finally that she was at the end of her tether. Without a further word, she scurried out of the room and slammed the door behind her, leaving Kalida limp against the pillows.

Quickly she made her way downstairs and down the center hallway to the back of the house, where Deuce impatiently awaited her in his office. "Well?" he demanded.

"It is just as you say, Mr. Deuce. She chased me from the room." Prestina's liquid brown eyes sent him a speaking look. "She is one stubborn lady, Mr. Deuce."

Deuce patted her shoulder abstractedly. "And see where it will get her," he murmured, with just the faint tone of anticipation in his voice, as he headed for the stairs. He took them two at a time and headed down the upstairs hallway, which dissected the house, toward his room. The room that had been his parents' room, which now bore no traces of his father's final, futile occupation of it. The room he had cleaned and refurbished and intended to furnish with new memories, new love. The room next to which was the old birthing room that his own mother had occupied delivering him and his sister. It was now empty but for a small rope bed and a bureau, and as he thrust himself into it, he smelled mustiness and a history he couldn't even recall.

But the most important thing to him was that the door gave into his own room which, from Kalida's perspective within it, looked like either the washroom door or a closet. Here, from his positioning safely across the room from the fireplace, he could spy on Kalida—and he didn't delude himself he wasn't doing just that—and ferret out her duplicity.

Carefully, silently, he opened the door just a sliver and then a crack more so that he could see Kalida's wilted figure sprawled dispiritedly on his bed, wrapped in his bedcover. The sight of her aroused intriguing possibilities; his unruly manhood snapped to attention and he clamped down hard on his wayward thoughts. And he watched.

Slowly, very slowly, she roused herself to the realization that the bath water was growing cold and she had very little time now to perform even the sketchiest of ablutions. With firm decision, she thrust away the cover and, pulling her hands through her inky hair, slipped off the bed. On her two rock solid legs and stark naked she went to the copper bathtub, tested the water, and climbed appreciatively into its depths.

The nervy little bitch, Deuce thought in admiration. The vixen. The flat-out gorgeous naked liar; the brazen witch . . . What he would like to do to her for the depth of her deceit. He had to forcibly restrain himself from lunging into that room and lifting her wet, glistening body from the water and . . .

No, there was time to wreak his own revenge; perhaps, just perhaps, his punishment was to stand and watch her all-unknowing sensual ministrations to her deliciously naked body: the swoop of the soap down her lifted arm, the barest vision of the swell of her firm, conical breasts above the water, the barest hint of their twin taut tips; the flexing of her leg as she held it up to wash it down with the sponge. The knowledge in his soul of what more lay quiescent beneath the water, enveloped by it, caressed by it, surrendering to its liquid embrace, giving in to its warmth in a way she would never give in to him.

Yet.

The ominous word formed in his mind even as she disappeared beneath the water for a moment to wet the top of her head, and then began rubbing the soap briskly through her sopping inky hair.

In another moment she was standing, reaching for the bowl and pitcher Prestina had put by the boiler that was full of cool water for the rinsing off of her body and hair. Her back was to him, and she stood and bent gracefully from the hip so that her body was one curved line, broken only by the enticing swing of her breasts as she leaned over, then straightened up, bringing the glazed china pitcher with her, looking like a water nymph with her streaming midnight hair, satin soaked skin, and lush naked charms totally revealed.

She tilted the pitcher over her head and fresh water coursed down the profile of her body, washing over her shoulders and slender arms, dripping down the slope of her breasts, drops hanging tantalizingly on her taut tipped nipples, sluicing down the hollow of her hip, sliding down her thigh to the vee of her flagrant womanhood, catching in the thick black bush of hair that guarded all her secrets; and from there, down and down the long, lean curve of her endless legs and tight firm cushion of her buttocks. She reached again, this time for a towel, which she hurriedly wrapped around her enticing nakedness before she stepped from the copper tub.

He let out a breath; how much more of watching her he could stand he did not know. He was filled to bursting with the sense of her, as a liar and the most desirable woman he could ever want.

Deuce took a deep, shuddering breath as Kalida removed the towel and began patiently drying herself off, and he remembered full well the day he had toweled her down in her bed. But this was nothing to watching her, privately, alone, with her having no knowledge of his presence, viewing her solitary ministrations as she rubbed the towel all over her glowing naked body and finally began drying her ebony hair, lifting it over her head and letting it fall to flow down her shoulders and her straight tense back, to curl wetly down her breasts and just gently caress her two voluptuous nipples.

The towel now went around her hips as though she were some primitive island woman. Kalida sashayed around the room, looking at things, thinking . . . what? he wondered as he gazed his fill of her long strong legs and her pagan breasts. Just what was she seeking? And how far would she go?

He eased himself back into the room as she turned and walked toward the door, her hips swaying enticingly. Knowing he was there? The audacious spitfire. The air vibrated for an instant with his indecision. He almost— almost—opted for letting her discover him there, waiting and watching. For just one instant he savored the impact of that meeting on her. But it was not time yet to expose her. In this way, or any other way. She was in his house now, a partner to the bargain he had made and the new one he would make with her father. That was all he needed. The rest would come, as fully and completely as he could make it, and later. He could wait. He had waited—for her.

When she opened the door curiously several moments later, she found an empty room, empty save the bed and bureau and a curious sense of heaviness that permeated the air—and meant nothing to her.

"This is perfect," Ardelle said with satisfaction, surveying Kalida as she finished struggling into the robe the older woman had brought. "Lovely with your hair and eyes, my dear. My grandfather brought it back from China, did you know? In the trade. That's where my Papa got the nerve and the money to go west. Grandfather was totally nonplussed that my Papa did not want to go to sea. But luckily there were three other boys who did. My Papa loved the land, you see, and this was ideal for him. But he used to like to take the family back to New York whenever Grandfather put into port. He brought us back many things. This was one of them which, though I can't wear it anymore, I treasure and keep."

Ardelle smiled at Kalida and Kalida smiled back without guile or hurt or anger. Ardelle was almost beautiful as she talked about her memories. She *was* handsome, with her glowing brown-red hair that was piled into a loose chignon on top of her head. And while her features were strong, almost mannish, she had a lovely smile and her skin was creamy white and showed none of the years she had spent on the Montana plains. She was kind, too, Kalida thought, trying dearly to make her feel at home instantly, and she was grateful for that.

"Another thing Grandfather brought which I still have is a little Chinese slipper. Have you ever seen one?"

Kalida shook her head, and Ardelle went on. "It is perhaps four inches long and just a beautiful little object—all deep red silk and embroidered delicately with gold thread. Oriental women bind their feet, you know. I keep it," she added, "to remind myself that everyone has a different standard of beauty." There was a heavy silent pause and then her sherry eyes rested again on Kalida.

"Well, there is a late breakfast waiting for us; I believe your father and Ellie are already at table, if they aren't finished, so we'll join them as soon as Deuce — ah, there you are. . . ."

She turned as Deuce pushed his way into the room briskly, followed by Prestina, his gray eyes hard as slate and focused solely on Kalida. She looked like an extravagantly exotic flower sitting in the middle of his bed. She was enveloped by the fragile silk robe, which was the same shade as her eyes; the colors glowed, from the deep blue of the background to the finely sewn golden threads that outlined the burgundy, green, and gold Oriental hieroglyphics that were sinuously woven all over the fabric. The thin silk draped across her body like water, hiding everything and revealing everything at the same time. She sat ramrod straight against the towering headboard, with her long legs pointedly straight out in front of her. Her eyes glowed with an edgy resentment of what was to come, and as she became aware of the direction of his smoldering gaze, she shrugged the two edges of the robe closer together, as if that were an effective barrier to his imagination.

She was not a little dismayed to see that Prestina did not bear a tray. She had been counting on taking this breakfast in this room, having discounted what Ardelle had said about going downstairs. Now it looked as though Deuce was going to carry her downstairs, and her whole body resisted as he bent toward her. "Your pack mule, ma'am," he said sardonically, holding out his strong, muscular arms that were now encased in a fresh white shirt.

Kalida edged away from his hands — and the memory of how they felt on her. "This is ridiculous. I'll have a tray here."

"Yes, that would be simplest and most convenient for you, wouldn't it?" Deuce retorted in a tone of voice that verged on nasty. She drew back as he went on. "But we're not here to make things simple and easy for you, Kalida. So while you still have your beast of burden, I suggest you make the most of it. He may kick you off rather sooner than you expect."

"Bullheaded bastard," she muttered rebelliously, knowing she could hardly make a scene before Ardelle and Prestina. She reluctantly shifted her position so that she moved closer to the edge of the bed where he could slide his arms under her legs and around her waist.

"I'm not the only stubborn ass in this room," he grated warningly as he lifted her high into the air and hard against his steely chest.

His hot hands burned her skin through the delicate fabric; she felt as though she were naked in his arms, that nothing was hidden from him by the veil of silk that surrounded her body. The hard, unbending steel in his eyes seemed to say she was totally at his mercy, dependent on him, a supplicant should he choose to make her beg.

And didn't the notion please him in the one instant it came to him! She saw that in his face, too, and she felt like clawing him. Her body went rigid and she turned her head away as he swiftly and efficiently carried her down the long straight staircase to the dining room where her father and Ellie Dean awaited them.

And as he placed her none too gently in an upholstered chair by the overloaded table, she mentally curtsied to the arrogant king of Sweetland—and all whom he controlled.

Look at her sitting there like a queen, Ellie Dean thought resentfully as she picked at her plate full of beans, bacon, eggs, and biscuit. And everyone's eyes were focused on her. She was like a living painting, so still and colorful, her expression enigmatic, her gossamer robe draped around her artfully, as though someone had arranged it for the best effect. Ellie hated her passionately in that still silent moment as Deuce and Ardelle sat down on either side of Kalida, across from Ellie herself and Hal Ryland.

There was something portentous in the air, but neither Deuce nor Ryland made any comment until after Deuce had filled his plate and Kalida's and settled back with a cup of coffee in his hand. Then he said to Ryland, "Danton isn't back yet."

Ryland nodded. "All right. I know he won't be bringing good news."

"Not likely," Deuce agreed in a noncommittal tone of voice, and began attacking his plate. Ellie watched him avidly, noting too how Kalida's hooded gaze alternated between him and her father with an angry, speculative glint that did not bode well for either. And why should it, Ellie thought. They were both overbearingly proud, the center of their own universes, not accustomed to relinquishing an inch of power or to feminine interference in any of their high and mighty plans. Yes, and she could just see Kalida thinking that, too. Kalida was the pawn — and the reward. But Kalida would not surrender readily, and because of that, Ellie thought hopefully, she herself had the minutest chance to make a dent in this vainglorious, male-dominated world. And she fully intended to grasp and take all that she could.

The punctilious arrival of Jake Danton, who was Deuce's foreman, only confirmed what they all knew already. The house and everything in it had burned to ashes. They had saved the barn by dismantling the corral fences and digging a trench along that side of the house. He and the boys had brought Ryland's string of horses up to Sweetland, a decision that Deuce had made without even consulting Hal Ryland and for which Ryland did not look very grateful. Apart from that, the boys had stayed until they had beat out every last glowing ember so Mr. Ryland could be assured that the conflagration was truly out. But as he had said, Danton reiterated, everything but the barn had burned.

"Thanks, Jake," Deuce said abstractedly, now totally immersed, it seemed, in the coffee grounds on the bottom of his cup.

Danton swept a long look around the room, his eyes resting appreciatively for a telling moment on the butterfly bright figure of Kalida. She was something, he thought, sitting there like a stone-faced queen in her robes that concealed and revealed all at the same time. He wondered if she knew it. He wondered if she had chosen it that way, if she were aware of how the fabric draped over the sweet swell of her breasts and the two luscious points of her nipples, if she deliberately thrust herself out that way to invite the eye and, perhaps, were there not others present, the appreciative comment. "I wish we could've done more," he said suddenly, wanting to extend his dismissal so he could gaze at Kalida's provocative breasts. "I gave the boys the morning, by the way, and we'll come back on in shifts this afternoon."

"That's fine," Deuce said, again with that distant tone of dismissal, and this time Danton knew he could not linger. He cast a long glittering look at Kalida's silk-shrouded body, and then let himself out disappointedly. She was naked under that robe, he would swear. She had to have chosen to wear that; Ardelle Cavender would never have allowed such impropriety at her table, even if her guest *had* just been burned out of her home.

Kalida stared after his retreating figure, not even seeing him, as if all hope were drained out of her.

There was a deadly air of futility in the ensuing silence. Deuce's stone-hard eyes swept from Kalida to her father and back again.

102

Kalida pointedly refused to look at either him or her father. And Ellie began to feel distinctly uncomfortable.

It was obvious Deuce was not going to speak until she and Ardelle left the room, and finally Ardelle realized it too.

She swept to her feet with uncommon grace, her hand grasping her cane, which was always nearby, and she said lightly, "Come, Ellie. We will spend the afternoon exchanging gossip instead of over dry, dull business." She limped across the room, took Ellie's arm companionably, and led her out of the dining room just as if a storm were not about to burst behind them.

It hung in the air for a long, long time, as though Ryland did not know what to say, nor did he want to hear what Deuce would tell him. Kalida still refused to look at either of them, for she knew whatever the outcome of this "business," her fate remained that same: Deuce would not renege on the proposal no matter what reverses her father faced.

And he would take advantage; she could just see him working up to it. The king was out to fill his own coffers no matter what the cost to others. The violent desire to oppose this imperious power shuddered through her. But how? *How?*

She started as Deuce began to speak.

"The situation is this: You've lost everything except the herd, the land, and your string of quarter horses. You have no reserves — yes? You didn't think I would look into that, Hal?" he asked parenthetically at Ryland's startled look. "As I see it," he went on in that flat expressionless tone that Kalida so despised, "your first priority has to be to rebuild the ranch and the herd if you are to be of any use to your backers — or me," he added with an ominous undertone. "What you can't afford to do this year is buy into Sweetland. I can't let you do it because it isn't sound business for me."

103

Ryland's face went dead white, and Kalida almost jumped up to run to him. "You bastard," she hissed, banging her fist ineffectually on the table. "You contemptible—"

"Shut up," he ground out, his huge hand crashing down over hers. "Just shut up." His fingers tightened around hers and he held her in an inexorable grip, as though she were manacled to him. She couldn't bear the sight of her father's defeated face across the table from her.

"What's your deal?" her father said warily.

Deuce's grip relaxed on Kalida's hand. "I'll buy the herd. With enough to finance the ranch and set up a new trail drive if you're willing to buy in Texas. Or negotiate a lease; that's fine. But your profits would have to go back into the ranch no matter what you did, and a new herd. Besides, you'd have to find a buyer, and at your price. It's quicker this way, Hal, and it will get you where you want to go that much sooner."

Ryland nodded. "And Kalida?"

"Kalida stays with me," Deuce said with heavy finality.

Kalida's body jolted upright from her chair. "No!" she shrieked, and then she realized she had stood almost involuntarily and she slumped herself back down into her seat quickly, her heart pounding wildly, hoping madly that Deuce hadn't noticed.

But his hard gray gaze told her he had. One dark thick brown quirked tellingly, and it seemed to her that his expression became stonier. But all he said was an inexorable, "Yes."

"Why?" she demanded, thrusting aside her heaving emotions and the fact she had known that this would be the ultimate outcome, that he would not release her from the previous arrangement.

Deuce's firm lips thinned as he sent her a scornful look. "I'm buying the cattle," he said at last, "and I'm buying you."

"That's crazy," Hal Ryland interjected suddenly. "I won't do it. Kalida is not part of our business together."

"She was," Deuce said inflexibly. "And she is. Maybe you don't quite understand, Hal. There is no deal without Kalida."

The unyielding tone of his voice nonplussed both Kalida and her father. He looked across at her and she couldn't quite read his expression. He was going to leave it to her conscience. *Her* decision. She could ruin him forever. Or she could save him at a cost to herself.

He didn't assume she was so naive that she couldn't perceive these things. There was no pleading in his limpid blue gaze, only a kind of resignation: He would go whichever way she decided. Unspoken, unacknowledged as before was the tacit understanding that he knew she would do what was right.

"Kalida must decide," her father said suddenly with just a trace of weariness in his voice. Kalida shot him a resentful look at his having voiced the fact aloud. Why must she? she wondered. Why couldn't *he* just tell Deuce Cavender to go to hell? A moment later, her rational sense took over as she enumerated in her mind the steps her father must take to get back on his feet. Clearly, this was the cleanest, fastest way, to sell out to Deuce. But to include her in the bargaining when he gained nothing but space to breathe again at square one! No, it made no sense. But you would have sold yourself for the syndicate, a nasty little voice within her chided, so why not to save your father's reputation?

Because I hate him, she thought fiercely in response; because he has to put us in this position in both instances and he's enjoying every last moment of making my father crawl to him. And reducing me to a piece of property he either owns or doesn't own.

Her father was looking at her strangely now, as if all she were thinking was reflected in her face. But in fact, her expression had gone totally impassive as she made these wrathful conjectures; her father could no more tell what she was thinking than could Deuce. And all Deuce was doing was lounging back in his chair, just watching her with those cold, slaty gray eyes and grimly set mouth. Ryland had to press his daughter; he could see very plainly that her acquiescence was the only thing that would bail him out and resuscitate his failing business and his good name. Deuce would not have had a thing to do with him otherwise. He wanted Kalida, and the rest of it—the syndicate, the cattle, his rangeland—was irrelevant.

"Kalida!" he said imperatively, leaning forward a little, trying to get a fix on what she was thinking. There was nothing. She didn't know what to tell him. The degree of animosity she felt toward Deuce and how much, or if, she could temper it were her only guiding factors. He wished she did not hate him so much; he wished that Deuce were a little less of a overlord in these parts. Of course an independent nature like Kalida's would chafe against that kind of overbearing arrogance. He perfectly understood it. He just wanted her to agree to Deuce's terms anyway. She had to.

But Kalida knew all that. "I have to think about it, Papa." It was the best she could do.

Ryland nodded, but his hands clenched in order to contain his impatience. Kalida must not see how desperate he was—even if she intuited it. He must play the part well. She must come to the right decision without feeling that she was being blackmailed. She must, damn it, and he knew many women who would have married for less. By God, it *was* a good bargain, and he swore he would have her committed if she rejected it. So he forced himself to say calmly, "That's only fair. I'll excuse myself then and get cleaned up." And he had to force himself to slide back his chair, stand up calmly, and walk out of that room without looking back, leaving Kalida alone with Deuce.

Another long, heavy silence followed. Prestina came in and cleared away the dishes without a word, not even commenting on the amount of food left over, and withdrew only after thoroughly rubbing down the plain pine harvest table.

Kalida sat like a statue watching Prestina, while seated beside her, Deuce observed *her;* she felt as if she were cornered even though he hadn't said a word.

She slanted a covert glance at him. The hard lines of his face were harshly drawn now, and he waited with a patience she never would have dreamed he possessed. A wave of heat emanated from him, but his flinty speculative gaze was unswerving. He expected her to speak, and he would do nothing to help her.

But then, why should he? she wondered. What did she want him to do? He had done enough already, she thought acrimoniously, and he hadn't even acknowledged that! But if she said the word to her father about what had happened this morning, she was sure he would be delighted.

He would wonder what all her fussing had been about. And he would see no obstruction whatsoever to either Deuce's plans or his own.

She had to face the facts: Neither she nor her father had any leverage at all over Deuce Cavender. She herself was the only bargaining chip they had. And she couldn't comprehend why he was so adamant about that. She knew he didn't care whether her father went under or not. He was using their bad luck to get at her. And the only conclusion she could reach was that she must give her father his chance to recoup, whatever it took.

She gathered her resolve together almost as if she were girding her body to ward off a physical blow and twisted herself to face him. "Deuce," she began, but one look at

107

his mocking expression stopped her instantly. "Take me upstairs, please," she finished imperiously and somewhat warily. She did not like that look one bit. It said he had plotted out all her thoughts almost before she did, and he already knew her answer because she had been trapped from the very moment he and her father had made their first agreement.

"Yes, ma'am," he said meekly. But his eyes! Cold stone as he hoisted himself up, pushed her chair backward, and bent to slide his large hands under her arms.

Like plucking some exotic bouquet, he thought grimly, and with one mightly flex of his muscles, he heaved her body headfirst over his shoulder as she shrieked, "Damn you, you lousy varmint! What the hell do you think you're doing?" even as she felt his huge hands clasping her legs and one of them moving slowly up the silky folds of her gown to her buttocks.

"Just steadying you," Deuce said calmly, cupping her bottom with one hand and holding her ankles firmly with the other. He began to move, and she pounded his back. "Put me down, damn it; I will not be toted around like a sack of flour. Deuce, put me down!" God, she hated him; she *hated* him and his hot searing hands that made her feel totally naked and helpless. She just wanted down so that she wouldn't have to think about his hands, or not moving her legs, or the rock solid sense of him beneath her, or the way she must trust him to haul her around like that. No, no! She had to think. She could not go on like this either. Her voice was grittily ragged as she hissed again, "Put me down, Deuce."

His body shifted and she found herself sitting primly on the edge of the scrubbed table. "Don't you look good enough to eat," he said sourly. "I hope you don't intend to stay here all afternoon to offer some variety to the luncheon menu." His tone of voice said she had better not, and she took it so seriously that she felt like attacking him at that very moment.

"I could kill you," she spat viciously.

"Do it," he challenged, his voice burning hard. "Do it; use your legs; come after me, Kalida. End the game." He watched her eyes narrow and then disappear under her half-closed lids. "I dare you, Kalida."

"God," she breathed, "if I could use my legs I'd kick you in a place you'd feel it forever, Deuce Cavender."

"And what do you think you've been doing with your damned words, my girl?" He moved directly in front of her. "Now. Do it. I'm here. I know you're not helpless." He leaned into her, bracing his arms on either side of her legs. Her blazing navy eyes widened and dilated as he forced her backward, so that she had to brace her body with her elbows. "Run, Kalida, run; this is your last chance. Run, or I'll take you right here."

"You're crazy," she whispered wildly, wriggling her body further back onto the table.

One viselike hand clamped down on her leg and pulled her forward again. "I'm not the crazy one, Kalida. You're the one defying *me;* you're the one who is going to ruin yourself and your father. So you'd better run while you have the chance." Now he watched her through hooded eyes, his face impassive, his mouth in an inflexible line. "Did you think I would carry both you and your father forever?" he finally asked harshly.

"You don't care about him," she accused, utterly numbed by his raw intensity.

"Yes, and you know just what I do care about, Kalida."

"No!" One of her hands shot out to brace itself against his chest.

"Yes." He pushed against her hand and her arm gave, falling back to the table and the support of her weakening body. His heat seared her, his incomprehensible anger beating in waves against her consciousness.

"I don't understand," she whispered as his mouth came

inexorably closer to hers.

"You understand everything," he rasped against her lips, and he claimed them like a conqueror, ravaging her mouth, moving downward to her neck, the flat of her chest, and the swell of her breasts under the thin, thin protection of silk that could dissolve at a breath.

He paused at the sight of the profile of one taut tip outlined against the center of a blossom, against the white hot radiance of the morning sun pouring into the room. "No," she whimpered, but it was too late as she said it. His hand had cupped her breast under the material, pushing it gently upward to meet the heat of his marauding mouth, and it melted the flimsy silk; it melted her, the succulent pulling of his mouth against that straining nipple, and she only wanted him to continue on and on. She watched as he held her and almost unnoticeably began, with his other hand, to push aside the waterfall of translucent silk so that he could fully feel the silk of her body. And she was lost. She would never run, not from this—this incredibly voluptuous wet tingling that enveloped her.

Never from this tight point of pleasure that pulled at her senses unbearably and unendingly. His golden mouth moved, first to her right breast to caress its tempting crest, then to her belly, and then slowly slowly downward. She felt herself writhing against him, feeling like a pagan goddess being worshipped as he began with luscious intent to show her all that it meant to be his woman.

His woman; the words reverberated as her senses expanded and whirled. Like the petals of a spring flower, wet from the rain, her desire unfurled, unrolling in a giant spasm of pleasure that sent her spiralling almost to the edge of unconsciousness.

And his movement stopped as she lay panting and breathless, and he allowed himself the moment to inhale her perfume, to caress the long line of her silken thighs.

He gently lifted them downward and sat up, and she raised herself onto her elbows at the same moment. "Don't ever do that again," she hissed, heaving herself upright and hurriedly pulling the edges of the gown together. How could she make him see she wanted no part of him when her body just as graphically contradicted her words?

She saw in his eyes he wanted more of her, and more, and her only thought was to run. To get away from him whose hands and mouth could wreak such havoc on her. Hadn't he said very plainly he didn't care about her father? Why *should* she sacrifice herself to that? *Why?* Why should she become in thrall with a man she hated, a man whose sole occupation was to demonstrate forcibly just how much power he wielded and to devil with whom or what got in his way? Oh, no. Oh, no. She ignored her tingling body and his cold gray glare as he perceived that, in spite of her raw and perfect response to him, she wanted none of him still. She felt dizzy with humiliation; no glory in that lush swell of pleasure that overrode her commonsense, only the notion that her decision had been made. Her father would have to fend for himself.

"So," Deuce said harshly, waiting, his patience wearing thin and thinner still at her rigidity and the stiffness of her body. She would yield to nothing, he thought, and he could admire her for that. And hate her for it at the same time; she had no sense at all of what she was preparing to give up. "Run, Kalida," he advised in a hard, threatening voice, leaning into her once again. "Run, because I'm not hardly done with you, and I hope you know what you're playing with and what you're denying, because you're going to lose on all counts. All counts. To me, Kalida. Your father can go broke for all I care, but you, my girl, are not leaving Sweetland. You can spend the rest of your damned life in my bed waiting for me, but that's where you'll spend it, Kalida. That's just about as far as you'll get."

She seethed at his words, at his arrogance. At his certainty that she had no choices, none at all, even though she was exactly sure that she would never consent to him, never. And even now he must show her he had the power as his body slanted over hers and forced her backward again. This time she did not hesitate to think; this time she acted. She had to have her legs to defeat him, and defeat him she would. She pulled her legs upward and kneed him in the groin. As he stumbled backward she thrust her feet into his midriff, and he lurched into a nearby chair. There was only a moment's break before he recovered enough to follow her, but by that time she had dashed out of the dining room on a mad run toward the pasture.

She could not get far; she was hampered by the thin stuff of her robe and its glaring visible colors against the new jade grass and the crystal blue sky. And by her bare feet. By her wild hair that streamed out behind her. By the crowd of wranglers who had stopped working to watch her.

He mounted his stallion at a dead run and sent him galloping after her, ignoring the pain between his legs and in his ribs. The bitch, the utter brazen bitch; she couldn't brazen it out, he thought, and good for me: I've got her where I want her now, and she is not going to get far. Not an inch beyond the spring. I'll drown her first. She'll never get away. Never.

Eight

She was not so far beyond the house, she saw, as she turned and looked behind her. Damn, she would never elude him this way. Kalida cut across the burgeoning spring lawn toward the little orchard. Here, among the trees that were fed by the little spring that sparkled in the distance, she might, just might, be able to hide from him. How was she going to escape him? She pushed away the obvious answer—that she couldn't. That it was barely afternoon and she could not depend on staying hidden until nightfall. That she had nowhere to go, and no way to get there. That she had no clothes save the flimsy silk on her back, with its brilliant colors that probably could be seen a mile away.

She groaned. The traps were everywhere; she would be better off to discard the thing, but she couldn't quite make herself do it. She slid it off and tied the sleeves around her hips as she proceeded further into the grove where the dappled shadows were cool and concealing. He would be looking for glimmers of color, and here her skin was radiant sunlight, her taut tipped breasts as heavy as the ripening fruit.

She did not look behind her as she threaded her way through the neat rows of trees, but she knew as surely as she knew anything that Deuce was following her, that he was perhaps even then skirting the very edge of the orchard, stalking her patiently and impatiently by turns, exasperated beyond measure with her deceit and her duplicity, as she was with herself, and waiting. Her breath quickened at the thought of him waiting. Waiting for what? Her capitulation? Ha! Even if he won this bout, he would never have that. Never.

Her body tensed almost in opposition to her thoughts, and she denied its message. She knew her body was weak, and she admitted he could get to her that way. Yes, the body could give in all it wanted; but the mind would remain hers. He would never touch her mind.

She was approaching the edge of the grove now and her heartbeat accelerated. Far in the distance, beyond the spring water that twinkled like sunlit diamonds in the early afternoon light, there was nothing but open pasture dotted with little copses of bushes barely large enough to conceal a mewling lamb let along a grown woman. And a small stand of young trees that shaded one small end of the spring. Not a line shack or a fence broke the rest of the landscape, and Kalida shivered. The futility of her flight was chillingly apparent.

She sank to the ground under the last of the row of apple trees. Everything was reassuringly still, the sun blazing hot, the air fragrant and caressingly warm.

Where was he?

On her hands and knees she crawled horizontally along the line of trees until she came to the edge of the short side of the grove. To the east was the house, sitting like a stately matron on a slight rise above the fields. Deuce was nowhere in sight, although she could see figures, horses, movement. She knew he had followed her. She knew she had hardly disabled him. But *where* was he?

Her heart pounded violently. All she could think was that she was trapped, trapped, trapped. And then suddenly, two huge hands grabbed her from behind around her silk-shrouded hips and she screamed as she was dragged backward, on her knees and into the granite wall of Deuce's chest. He toppled her onto her side and then on her back, and straddled her wildly thrashing legs.

He leaned forward, supporting his body with his arms, his eyes devouring the lush curve of her naked breasts before they swept up to meet her icy blue gaze. "It's a miracle," he murmured ironically, "how you so unexpectedly regained the use of your legs." Her hips bucked under him and he bore down harder on her body. She could feel his thick iron-hard staff digging into her soft flesh, even through the work-rough denims he wore. His arms surrounded her now as he braced his upper torso on his elbows, and his face was close enough for her to claw, close enough for her to glare into the flinty stone of his unyielding eyes that had no softness for her. Close enough to see every harsh, obdurate line of his face that told her he was adamant and determined. Close enough so that her traitorous body was aroused already by the feel of him on her, by the memory of his arrogant lovemaking.

"No!" She groaned the word out loud almost as if she were denying the feelings to him as well as herself.

He watched her face intently at this reaction. The permutations were almost amusing; he felt a softness toward her now because he knew he truly had her boxed in. But she would not look at him. Her eyes were closed first, as though she were wrestling with some inner voice; and then they were opened and looking far away, never at him. And he did not move. He lay sprawled on her, his arms surrounding her shoulders and head, and he followed the temporizing movements of her head with his eyes until he could stand it no longer; then he spoke, his voice rough with the impatience of waiting. "All your little tricks are useless, Kalida; you've done nothing but delay things and sorely try my temper to boot."

"You know what my answer to that is," she retorted, consciously tensing her fingers so as not to slap him. "My

115

God, I never even considered the thought that having a shrew in your home would deter you more effectively than someone who is incapacitated. You're just like every other damned man: You want everything all your own way."

"Yes I do," he said ominously.

"You can't have it," she countered defiantly.

"But I will have you," he contradicted warningly. "And you will agree, not only because it's the only thing you can do, but because you will *want* to—"

"You have a nerve, telling me what I *want* to do," she broke in disparagingly, moving her hands just a tad to get them in a place where she could do something to him for his godalmighty abominable arrogance. "That's not nearly what I *want* to do."

"—and because your luscious body wants to," he finished, ignoring her, his lips that close to hers, his head tilting slightly and his eyes darkening in anticipation.

Her body heaved in denial. "No! Never!" she spat, her hands slithering under his torso to push against his chest. It was like a wall, immovable and immutable. Nothing she could say would make a dent in it. His lips touched hers, and she hissed, "You bastard. You—" And then her words were cut off by his mouth on hers. My body will betray me every time, she thought wildly, as the nectarlike taste of his kiss seeped and flowered through her veins like a thick, sweet sap.

She could call him anything she wanted, she thought, but she would always be subject to the whim of her treacherous sex. And when her desire became full-blown, her resolutions deflated; and when he pulled away for the barest second and his eyes reflected that chest-thumping male triumph, it came back in full force. And she knew she had to force him away somehow, or she would lose this round, this moment.

"Let me tell you what I wanted," she whispered in a suggestive way, and she was gratified to see his head angle

116

closer to hear her more distinctly. She wondered just for an instant what he might have expected her to say. "I wanted Sweetland for Papa," she went on, her voice taking on a faintly vindictive tone. He reared back as she continued. "I wanted Papa to have the shares he coveted for so long, and that's all I wanted. And it's obvious you just loved effectively taking that away from him. Just because of that damned stupid fire. Just because . . . you're . . . *you* . . ."

The last word strangled in her throat as his large hand came up and covered her mouth. "You bitch. You rotten stinking brazen bitch, to say that—that's all you wanted," he growled. "*All* you wanted. *All*. And I took it away—forget his debts and his ruined house, and the loss of every personal possession he and you owned. *I* took it away. . . ." The sheer bravado of this statement totally left him speechless. "Goddamn, I must be so powerful that mere words can invoke my bidding. I told the gods to torch the house, and by heaven, it was done; is that it? That's what you envision? Goddamn hell. It's awesome, Kalida. Soon you'll tell me I got you with child, and I won't even have had the pleasure of that either. Damn you. Damn you . . ."

His fury was fearsome. He levered himself upward suddenly and sat back on his haunches. "Unbelievable," he muttered, pulling her to sit upright. "That's all you wanted—goddamn Sweetland. Fine. Fine. The bastard can have his damned shares, Kalida—next year, provided he can buy them."

She stared at him. "Why?"

He glared at her. Trust her for omitting the gratitude, the common courtesy. In her mind, obviously, everything he did had an ulterior motive. Which it did, but that was no concern of hers. "I'm willing to bet he won't be able to afford them. And that doesn't let you off the hook either, Kalida."

"I'll survive," she said sourly. "I'll abide by your agreement with Papa. I'll marry you."

"How delightfully condescending of you," Deuce murmured, his fury still at a high edge, his desire to strike back at her smoldering in a dark place where she could not begin to comprehend it. "But you may have noticed, my lovely Kalida, that since the unfortunate disaster, I haven't asked."

She was utterly thunderstruck. That was the bargain, that was what she had agreed to. Her heart sank as she realized he was out to punish her well and truly now. He told her to dress herself, speaking in that flat, impersonal tone that made her want to strike out at him, and he motioned her to start walking to the edge of the grove on the far side where he had tethered his horse.

They proceeded back to the house in a rare silence. Her bare feet began to hurt from all the prickles of unseen scabrous plant life that lay hidden in the green velvet swath of the field they crossed.

Her embarrassment was acute at having to be retrieved like some runaway field hand. She couldn't even begin to assess her humiliation at Deuce's hands. She wanted only to run and hide rather than face anyone upon their return. She had nothing to say. Nothing. Everything was plain and clear. The new bargain was that now she would remain at Sweetland in exchange for what Deuce could do for her father. The terms to be set were his now; her father would get Sweetland shares. And she had nothing more to say.

Even when her father came running from the house, babbling about her wondrous recovery with such sincerity that it was almost comic, all she could do was nod and make little noises of agreement until he asked her, *sotto voce*, "Have you decided?"

She looked up at Deuce, who had overheard Ryland's bald question, and she said, "I will do what Deuce wants," in a toneless voice that squarely put the burden on Deuce to define what he did want. She was suddenly not so sure he wanted her along with his power over her father.

Ardelle bustled in just then, murmuring reassuringly, nodding at Deuce's directions to put Kalida to bed instantly, since she should not overtax herself until they knew whether she was fully recovered or not. Kalida found it strange that he was acting as though everything were for real and nothing untoward had happened.

She allowed Ardelle to push her upstairs once again but was dismayed when she was shown to Deuce's room. "Why?" she demanded, wheeling on Ardelle, whose face registered bewilderment.

"My dear Kalida, we've a houseful of guests, with the men going out on patrol all this week. I don't think you realize it, but Deuce has lost half a dozen head of Santa Linaria this *month;* that's disastrous, and the syndicate leaders are eager to help rout out the rustler. But with you, your Papa, Ellie, and the rest of them here, there's not an extra room in the house. Deuce will be out all night anyway, so it's perfectly acceptable to me for you to use his room"—her sherry eyes pinioned Kalida—"as you will be doing soon enough," she added gently. "You must rest, of course; your body may well feel shocked at having the use of its legs again. I will come to see you later. We must talk about the provision of a wardrobe for you. But"—she raised her hand as Kalida started to protest—"that's for later. Be a good girl now and take your rest."

Kalida did not have the heart to argue with this kindness, nor the assumption that her presence in Deuce's room—in his life—was to be permanent. No, her argument was with Deuce, and she would have it out with him eventually, oh yes, she would.

* * *

Still later, Ellie Dean bustled into Deuce's room armed with a measuring tape. "Come; we make a trip to town tomorrow so that your father and Deuce can execute the necessary papers. So I need your measurements, Kalida. And don't stand on ceremony with this; your father specifically asked me to tell you that. You are not allowed to object, protest, or refuse, you hear?"

"I hear," Kalida said, astounded at the Ellie Dean who was fluttering around her bed, commanding her to sit and lift her arms and turn her torso. This Ellie's face looked younger for some reason, perhaps because her hair was streaming down her back, the first time Kalida had ever seen it unconfined. Little curly tendrils danced around her unusually animated face, and she was dressed in a pinafore, a grown-up version of the kind little girls wore, which Prestina had remade from the remnants of her one remaining dress and scraps of material she had hoarded away.

"I'm to shop for the necessities for both of us," she said when she had finally finished measuring and sat perched at the foot of the bed still making notes. "And Deuce has agreed that I can hire a dressmaker—Rosalie Dupuis, do you think?—to come out for a week and attend solely to *us!*" Her voice, calm though it seemed, still held an undertone of repressed excitement. She was perfectly willing to have Deuce pay to outfit her in a style befitting what she considered her status. And the prospect of a day in town alone with both Deuce and Hal was not an unpleasant prospect either.

"Deuce is very generous," Kalida murmured noncommittally. Ellie need not know the details of any new arrangement. Ellie seemed very happy to be at Sweetland and have the run of Deuce's money. Well, fine with her. The less attention Deuce Cavender paid to her the better. Ellie

120

could monopolize every moment of his attention for all she cared.

"When do you leave?" she asked, trying to summon up some show of interest.

"First thing in the morning." Ellie jumped off the bed as she said that, tucking her mysteriously annotated paper into one of the skirt pockets. "Deuce said it would be too much to ask Prestina to sew for us, you know. I think it's lovely he's offered to provide us with the dressmaker and whatever we want."

"Lovely," Kalida echoed as Ellie wafted to the door.

"I'll see you tomorrow evening, Kalida dear. Trust me, will you, to do the best for you?"

"With my life," Kalida said ironically. She stared broodingly at the closed door. She was getting in deeper and deeper. She could be bought for the price of a dress. And so, she thought meanly, could Ellie.

Ellie, who jounced along willingly and cheerfully in the uncomfortable buckboard seated next to Deuce at sunrise the next morning. Ellie, who chattered endlessly with a bright gaiety that did nothing to improve Deuce's humor as the miles wore on and on across the flat, rolling plains.

He himself was tired from the night's patrol and the loss of yet another bull from the Santa Linaria herd. And he was exasperated to the point of active dislike with Hal Ryland. Overriding all of these feelings was his intense desire to get his hands around Kalida's lovely throat, to shake her within an inch of her life, to make her admit everything she denied.

The sun burned down with an unconscionable morning heat that seemed to make steam rise from the very earth. Ellie's voice buzzed around him like a fly he wanted desperately to swat. Ryland continually wiped his forehead and complained of the temperature.

And Deuce resigned himself to the fact that it was going to be an excruciatingly long day.

Which was what Kalida was thinking when Ardelle and Prestina entered her room later on that morning with a breakfast tray. Prestina set it down at the foot of the bed, waving away her protestations and silently disappearing and closing the door behind her.

Ardelle laboriously pulled forward a chair and settled herself into it. "They've gone," she said, an unnecessary statement since the noise of the departure had awakened Kalida earlier than she would have liked.

"Yes." Kalida could find nothing to say to that. "How did it go with them last night?"

"We lost another bull, my dear, but really, that shouldn't concern *you*. That's Deuce's business."

"Of course, you're right." Kalida reached across the counterpane for the coffee cup, inhaling its aroma like it was a lifeline. She had no idea what to say to Ardelle, no idea what Ardelle knew or did not know about any arrangement between Deuce and herself. She sipped her coffee thoughtfully as she regarded Ardelle's handsome face over the rim of the cup. "I don't suppose," she said suddenly, "you could ferret out a shirt and a small pair of pants for me? I'd love to—" She stopped short at Ardelle's horrified expression.

"Kalida, really, you are *not* some calicoed eastern settler who has no other choices. You are going to be Deuce's wife. . . ."

"That's up for debate," Kalida muttered, reaching for a hot muffin from the tray.

"My dear, I don't care what kind of verbal scuffling you and Deuce are having between you. The point in fact is he will marry, and insofar as I know, he wants to marry you."

"Well, I don't know that," Kalida retorted, biting viciously into the muffin. "I don't know what stupid arrangement he and Papa have come to now."

Ardelle pulled in an impatient breath. "My dear, none of this matters. Whatever your status is to be here, you must become the kind of woman he wishes to come home to."

"Indeed?" Kalida paused, utterly beguiled at what that statement implied. "I'm not sure I understand what you mean, Ardelle." There, that put the burden of plain speaking on her.

Ardelle punctuated the air with her endlessly moving hands. "You cannot be a—a cowgirl, Kalida, if you live on Sweetland. You're a beautiful young woman, and Deuce is one of the wealthiest men in Montana. You can't go gallivanting into the barnyard whenever you want. Or on roundup, or into the branding pen. Or jump fences, or hunting game, or whatever it was you did when you were living with your father. Deuce wouldn't expect it anyway. You'll—you'll take over the running of Sweetland from me; I'll teach you everything. And I—I finally will be able to go home again," she finished wistfully.

"That's crazy," Kalida objected. "Deuce would never ask anyone to make that radical a change."

"Yes, well," Ardelle said disparagingly, "what Deuce says he wants and what he really does want are two different things. I promised myself that I would welcome whomever he chose with opened arms, and I would guide her with all the wisdom I've acquired over the years I've lived here. So you see, I know."

"Yes," Kalida admitted reluctantly, "you must know." She put down her cup and the remains of her muffin, and shook her head almost as though she were denying without words the vision of the future that Ardelle was conjuring up for her. Ardelle did not know that Deuce was on the verge of retracting all offers of marriage. And Ardelle would never countenance being replaced by a—a mistress. Yes, that was what Deuce was implying: Kalida

123

was to stay at Sweetland, all right, but the only capacity he possibly could have meant was as his bed companion, bought and paid for.

"Oh really, Kalida," Ardelle's kindly voice interrupted her musing with just the faintest touch of irritation in it. "You know married women have certain responsibilities, certain duties beyond those of running the housheold, and God knows, there's enough attendant to that! I'm sure you could even enumerate them for me. But then there are those . . . undefined obligations—you know what I'm talking about, Kalida. You bear his children, you behave like a lady, you *dress* like a lady, and you perform your marital duties with some degree of willingness, if not affection."

"Lovely," Kalida muttered sardonically. She was going to have no part of *that,* but Ardelle did not need to know it—yet.

"And in return, you'll have whatever luxury Deuce can provide: He'll pamper and care for you, you will live in this beautiful house—unusually beautiful house, yes, for the wilds of Montana?—and he will provide the servants when you need them and money for anything you could possibly want. And, you will have Deuce."

Kalida's stormy blue eyes meet Ardelle's. "Yes," she whispered. "And Deuce."

"And that is what he will want," Ardelle concluded, lifting herself out of her chair with the help of her cane, which as always was nearby. "Trust me, that is what he will expect."

Kalida watched her limp out. God, everything Ardelle had told her fit the picture perfectly. Deuce was king, and it *was* inconceivable that he would want anything other than cool royalty to grace Sweetland.

And the king was lavish with his gifts now that he had

gotten what he wanted. Kalida watched the wagon arrive back from town after sunset, laden with supplies, boxes, bags, suitcases, and an imperious-looking middle-aged woman whom she did not recognize but assumed was Rosalie Dupuis, the dressmaker.

Her father, she perceived, looked relieved, and Ellie looked excited as she gazed adoringly down at Deuce who had lifted his arms to assist her from the wagon. Her still unbound hair fell forward, almost into his face, and as he set her down she made especially certain not to drag the crisp cotton hem of her new ready-made dress in the dirt of the drive. Oh, didn't Ellie look just wonderful, Kalida thought, turning away in disgust. She must have had a fine old time spending Deuce's money. She had the very sensibility that knew exactly what to do with it.

She wrapped her gossamer robe more tightly around her at that thought. Her body stiffened with a kind of fine excitement that sent a riotous tremor along her veins. Ellie was exactly the kind of woman Deuce needed. Ellie. Ellie was ambitious, and she would bet that Ellie was tired of being the poor widow who ran the rooming house in town. And Ellie was still young, though Kalida had never realized it until she had seen her with her hair undone and that galvanizing impetus of money shearing years from her face, her body. Yes, Ellie. Ellie was smart enough to know how to distract someone like Deuce. If she could be persuaded to do it.

But why shouldn't she want it? Hadn't she counted on captivating Kalida's father once again? Wasn't Deuce Cavender a better alternative to being the stepmother of someone who was almost her own age?

Oh, glory, it was perfect. Perfect! Kalida hugged herself. Deuce didn't need *her*; he needed a woman to manage his home and give him children. And Ellie would revel in every last detail, she was sure of it. Ellie would love it. With no competition, not even from Ardelle.

And she herself could be gone the moment she had a skirt and blouse and a horse to carry her away from Sweetland. She couldn't wait. *She couldn't wait.*

But after the first euphoria of this perfect idea, Kalida felt a letdown that had her pacing the room agitatedly. Deuce was coming. She didn't think it, she didn't sense it; it was just the thought pulsating through her consciousness. Deuce would come, and he wouldn't be turned away by any discussion of the desirability of focusing his attention on Ellie Dean.

She didn't want to see him. She wanted nothing to do with him.

She froze at the knock on the door, and then her body tensed. Deuce would never knock. "Come," she called, and her father flung himself into the room and she ran into his outstretched arms.

"It's done," he murmured into her ear. "We're solvent again." His voice was buoyant with hope and just the faintest tinge of satisfaction. "We'll be back on our feet in months," he promised, holding her away from him so she could see his jubilant face. "I'm going to hire a crew to clear away the charred timber and get a builder to work on plans for the new house. As soon as that's in place, I'm heading south, Kalida, and I'm going to lease the pasture and bring up a new herd, and we're going to start again."

No, we're not, she thought, and wrenched away from him. "Not 'we,' Papa," she reminded him gently.

His face clouded with remorse. "It's almost the same," he said. "I'm doing it for you and for the memory of your mama. The ranch is your inheritance, Kalida; Deuce can't take that away from you."

"No," she said longingly, "just everything else."

Ryland paced slowly to the window and looked out.

126

"Kalida, if you were anywhere near realistic about this, you would admit there wasn't anywhere near 'everything else.' You keep acting like you're losing something, but you're not. You're gaining, you're winning. You have a place, a position, an inheritance now. You're going to win it all. . . ."

"Including a man I despise," she interrupted roughly.

"I don't believe that," her father said placatingly. "There's nothing wrong with Deuce. *Nothing*," he emphasized.

"He's a damned despot," Kalida retorted.

"He wouldn't even try to rule you," her father countered. "He knows you too well."

"Tell me that when you hear he may rescind his proposal. Now he's got you where he wants you. The thought has occurred to me that *he* engineered that fire somehow."

"Nonsense!" her father snapped. "You're letting your emotions override your good sense, Kalida. Deuce is not capable of that kind of meanness."

"That always assuming that you don't know what it is you have that he wants," Kalida rejoined stonily. "And I don't mean me."

"You don't know what you mean," Ryland countered angrily, his temper rising, not at her accusations but at her emotional state. He did not want to know the things she was thinking. He wanted everything in place and nothing to hamper his ability to spend the money that Deuce had paid him. He wanted none of Kalida's fanciful notions. Besides, he was absolutely sure that her head was being ruled by her last-minute jitters. Nothing else could account for the wild ideas she was throwing around. Deuce, an arsonist! "Deuce will tame you," he threw out, stalking to the door. "It's the one thing he can do with impunity that *I* can't."

* * *

Her father was being dense, Kalida thought abstractedly not for the hundredth time as she watched the twilight descend over the hills. But she had prepared him now, even if he thought her charges were fantastic. Oh, he would find out there was more to Deuce Cavender's openhanded willingness to finance him, she was sure of it.

She paced the room furiously, pulling at a strand of her inky hair without even being aware of it. She had done all she could with her father, she decided. She had prepared him for the fact that Deuce probably had an ulterior motive for offering his unstinting aid, and she had hinted that her own status with Deuce might change. If he refused to believe it, that was his lookout. Now all she needed was a skirt, a shirtwaist, and some boots. Damn, where *was* Ellie? She was getting a little tired of the thin silk robe that was wrinkled now, and crackled and clung to her body with her every movement. She had assumed Ellie would be up to see her the moment she entered the house.

She darted to the door, opened it and stepped into the narrow hallway. Voices wafted up the stairs, chiefly Ellie's and Ardelle's, and she moved closer to the head of the stairs to hear them more distinctly.

Yes . . . Ellie was clearly showing off the results of Deuce's largesse. Kalida slid her body down against the stair wall until she was on her haunches, and she listened with resentment to Ardelle's admiring voice as Ellie unwrapped packages. There was a murmur of appreciation and then Ardelle's voice said, "Yes, this will do nicely for Kalida. Where is she, anyway?"

An indistinguishable comment from Ellie preceded a silence, and then the appearance of Deuce at the head of the stairs, his arms full of materials, and behind him, Ellie holding a kerosene lamp high.

They saw Kalida crouched on the landing, her silken

robe a pool of riotous color around her bared legs, her hair in disarray, her eyes blazing molten blue, looking like some wild, untamed animal preparing to leap.

"Well, well," said Deuce mildly, "the stuff of my dreams: Kalida anxiously awaiting me at the top of the steps."

Her head jolted backward as if she had been struck, and she slowly slid herself upright, propping her body against the wall with her hands, bracing herself against some kind of onslaught.

"You must have continual nightmares," she said suddenly, her voice as bland as Deuce's.

"You silly girl," Ardelle interrupted impatiently. "You must dress for dinner. Now, Deuce . . ."

He turned to her. "*You* take this stuff to my room, you and Ellie. I'll see to Kalida." He lifted his arms and a waterfall of material drifted into Ardelle's outstretched arms. She made her way up the steps with surprising alacrity and an ungracious look in her eye. "Only because you say so, Deuce; this is just highly improper. . . ."

"Of course it is," he agreed, winking at Ellie who following, carrying bundles of underclothes. "But Kalida doesn't look in the mood to agree to anything, and I think I may have to persuade her."

"A neat end to your singularly successful day of buying everything and everyone in sight," Kalida muttered, squeezing herself against the wall as Deuce approached her.

"I haven't counted the cost yet," he murmured, settling himself directly in front of her and bracing his arms against the wall on either side of her shoulders.

"You may find it beyond your means," Kalida retorted.

"And you may find your vindictiveness will cost you more than you dreamed," he ground out.

"How could it? I'm a beggar now, am I not? I've saved my father, and I am here as you wish. You are about to supply me with the clothes on my back and the very food I eat. You need not be honorable, and all I need to do is provide the body, since my father has traded away everything else." She was trembling with a fine anger now, wrought up at having been left alone, at feeling imprisoned, at the duplicity of her father and *him*. Mistress, yes, and she hadn't even said the word, but she would. She would. And she'd make a fine one for him because even now, in the depth of this holocaust of anger she felt against him, she quivered at his nearness, responsive to the scent of him inches away from her and the memory of what his mouth could do to her, to any part of her. . . . She didn't know if she had the strength to resist that hot knowledge when every fiber of her being yearned to have him touch her again.

"Yes, give me the body," Deuce agreed harshly," and the rest I can take—willingly or unwillingly, Kalida. But the secret is—and you and I both know it—that it is more willing than unwilling."

"Then I'm a better actress than I thought," Kalida said sweetly, striking out with the first notion at hand as his mouth came closer and closer to hers, and his purpose became crystal clear that in spite of the presence of Ellie or his sister, he would possess her where and when he would.

Out of the corner of her eye she saw Ellie and Ardelle emerge from Deuce's bedroom and come back down the hallway, their eyes curious, more than curious because Deuce did not move and neither did she.

Deuce did not even look at them as he spoke to Ardelle. "When is dinner?"

"Half hour," she answered tersely, and limped down the steps without a backward look, followed by Ellie who turned one covetous glance to him before she disappeared downstairs.

"Thought they would save you?" Deuce asked in an

almost conversational tone of voice.

"They?" Her own tone mirrored disbelief. "Your grateful vassals? They wouldn't dare oppose you. They're as impoverished as I; you merely demand a different fealty from them.

"Oh God, you are a piece of work, Kalida. That unruly tongue of yours is going to get you into more trouble . . . so the only thing for me to do obviously"—he bent his head toward her again—"is keep you very . . . very busy," and his mouth settled emphatically on hers.

She held the wall; she would not touch him, even though her legs felt like buckling, even though his body covered hers as completely as if they were lying together. She could do nothing, not even prevent her disobedient body from responding to his outrageous seduction, and then she wanted to do nothing except answer the violent urgency of his will.

The darkness surrounded them. His hands moved from the wall to thread through her dark-as-the-night tumbling hair, to pull her still closer, more fully to his mouth and against his body. His long legs tangled with hers, his knee parting her legs. His right hand skimmed to her neck, her shoulder, and then the silk-shrouded curve of her breast and rested there, hot and all encompassing.

His mouth eased off of hers, and there was a long, taut moment of tension as she licked her bruised lips and felt, with every inch of her being, his one hand holding and feeling her breast; a breathless tense moment as she waited for him to find, in the forgiving darkness, the taut hard tip, waited for him to caress the straining nipple; waited, arching toward him, inviting his hand to move and his fingers to surround that quivering pleasure point. Waited in the tumultuous silence as though it were the only thing in the world she wanted. It *was* the only thing she wanted. She would die if he did not feel, in the next minute, the lush rigidity of her nipple. Her tense hand, unable to stand it, reached up and pushed aside the thin material of the robe; her whisper of a voice commanded, "Touch me, Deuce, now."

His hand and mouth moved simultaneously; his tongue found hers and instant his fingers touched her naked nipple, and she swooned at the rippling eddies of feeling that cascaded through her veins.

"Hang on to me, Kalida." His voice was the merest hoarse breath against her mouth as he eased away. He felt her hands grip his forearms, and her left hand urging his to her right breast, demanding that he strip away the flimsy covering and discover the naked treasure there. He cupped it, feeling its contour while he still held, between his thumb and forefinger, her turgid left nipple, just touching it, just enough to let her know his fingers were there. Her gasping moans told him she knew his fingers were there, and she begged now for him to caress her bared left nipple in exactly the same way. He held off, merely stroking the side of her breast while she writhed in anticipation, waiting again, waiting as his fingers came closer, and closer still, barely brushing the areola now, so slow, evoking feelings so thick and lush it was like she was swimming in sweet honey. She felt every movement of his hand now, in the silence that had grown molten with heat and sensual tension, every flex of his fingers as they slid with unerring precision exactly to the sensitized nipple that awaited them so eagerly, settling as gently as a breath around the taut tip.

She groaned ecstatically just at the sense of knowing his fingers surrounded each naked nipple, and the knowledge of what those fingers could do to her if they made just the barest movement. They didn't move. Her imagination supplied from memory the feelings that were as real as if he were caressing her, and the dark and the heat steamed up between them—because she knew, she knew at any moment he would caress her nipples and she would explode.

She felt her body arching toward him, luring him, inviting him, teasing him, enticing him to squeeze and fondle her. She wanted him to both hold her that way forever and to finish what he had started. The anticipation was electric and almost unbearable. He breathed her name into the stark silence and she jerked backward, contracting her stomach and hunching her shoulders. His fingers constricted, squeezing just the pebble-hard nub— just right.

She almost screamed at the dazzling sensation that shot through her whole body like a steam of glittering lights, a waterfall of them raining through every pore of her body. His mouth devoured her ecstasy and consumed it as his hands now devoured her breasts every way he could think of.

He growled unintelligible urgent words against her swollen lips, making her aware of her nakedness and feminity all at once, making her yearn for him—him?

He contained her ecstatic moans with his insatiable mouth. She was utterly soft now, pliant; he felt as if he held the world in his hands, and it still was not enough. He could never get enough. Her avid hips grinding against his thighs was not enough. Just feeling her ripe, straining nipples was not enough. He wanted more, and more, and his mouth ripped away from hers and followed a burning course to her jawline, her ear, her neck, the sensitive hollow of her collarbone, to the enticing cleft between her breasts.

Yes, she breathed, or thought it, or remembered it with such an intensity that he knew she needed the heat of his mouth against her right breast, trailing moist kisses directly to the heart of the matter. Yes, his lips pulled with a gentle tugging at the hard tip of her breast, and somehow her hands entangled themselves in his shadow-dark hair and pushed him closer and tighter, urging him

133

to taste and suck.

Her body heaved against his as his hot moist tongue touched her succulent nipple and began its lush exploration. His free hand grasped the curve of her hip, feeling her heated skin through the thin robe, crushing it mercilessly as he moved his hand still further downward, and then paused — and then, in sudden carnal decision, slid to his own belt, his tumultuous desire impelling him to seek the ultimate release.

She wasn't aware of when he removed his muscular thigh and replaced it with his hard, probing manhood, or when his hand slipped under her buttocks to lift her slightly to ease his shocking, gorgeous way within her feminine source that was so luxuriously ready to sheathe him.

Her velvet heat enfolded him, moist and tight, and he filled her so completely, so complexly, that there was no room for protestations or false denials. Even she, in the throes of her surrender and her demand, recognized that this was what she had wanted. This, the soft velvet words from deep in her throat murmured as he thrust upwards, moving his other hand now to hold her around her hips so that he was almost supporting her whole weight in his arms. He gently eased his mouth off her breast and crushed her body against his, holding her this way, with his hard, throbbing manhood deep within her, for a long, ravishing moment so that she could feel him deep within her, answering her need. And then his mouth sought hers without a word, and he began a slow, rhythmic movement that made no demand of her except that she give him everything.

The sensuous slide between her legs, the play of his lovely delicious tongue against hers, the sense of her nakedness against his clothed body, driving relentlessly into hers — these dissociated coherent sensations aroused her beyond anything he had done to her before; her hands clutched at his shoulders as his arms flexed with the burden of bearing the weight of her body. She was aware only of him and his raw male power that dominated her, that found exactly the right place to stroke, to heat, to drive against with all the virile force he possessed.

And still she felt fragile, feminine, liquid with enveloping passion, crystalline with the knowledge of his desire, and her own power and response to it. It was perfect; it was building, somewhere there were words—he murmured or she breathed, mouth to mouth—shrouded by the darkness where everything was possible. She was filled with the desire to attain the impossible, reaching again, in the same familiar way that was so different, expanding, climbing, yearning . . . And then it shattered—into a thousand sumptuous, wondrous fragments.

And then they were both still, the echoing storm of their shared ecstasy still reverberating between them. He was still rigid within her, still held her tightly against him. She felt like she might collapse if he let her go.

And suddenly the dark magic evaporated. She became a woman in the hallway being held in an incredibly intimate embrace by a man whom, when she was in her right mind, she could barely tolerate. And she had allowed him to get to her once again; she had allowed her reason to fly in the face of his captivating sorcerer's hands.

She struggled against him in her growing discomfiture; her senses were in total disarray, conflicted by the dazzling pleasure she had just experienced, and the method and the man with whom she had experienced it. "Let me go," she whispered fiercely.

"Really?" he murmured, his mouth seeking hers again.

She averted her head. "Yes." The word was as harsh and patently negative as she could make it. She felt frantic, overwhelmed and possessed at the same time. And he must have felt it, for he lifted her body slightly

135

and eased himself out of her without another word.

She had a distinct sense of becoming herself again as her feet found the floor, Without another word, as he was occupied with putting himself to rights, she stalked down the hallway toward his bedroom, where soft light emitting from the kerosene lamp Ellie had left showed through a crack in the door.

She pushed it open impatiently, dizzy with the ignominy of her shameless response to Deuce. And in a hallway, where Ellie or Ardelle could have sought them out at any moment and found them—the possibility did not bear thinking of. The transient ecstasy was utterly gone. She wanted only to dress and stay dressed forever whenever Deuce was around. And the fragile materials that Ardelle had heaped on the bed didn't look at all as if they would serve the purpose.

Deuce found her clawing through them a moment later as he entered the room. "What *are* you doing?" he demanded roughly as he pulled her away from the bed and into his arms.

"I am going to get dressed, thank you, and not in any of that thin, unusual garbage that Ellie saw fit to choose for me. I want—" God, she was perilously closer to tears. Kalida bit her lip. "I want a shirt of some kind, and a skirt."

"Don't be a child, Kalida. There are several dresses you can choose from here."

"I don't want a fashionable dress. I want the thickest cotton shirt you can find me and maybe that pinafore that Ellie wore, which covers the whole body, and I just don't ever want to be undressed around you ever again, never, do you hear me?" Oh God, she was dissolving now, and he was seeing her helpless rather than strong; she had to show him rather than evoke his pity and his protectiveness. She wanted nothing more of him, from now on. Nothing. Not after he had made her submit to him in a

136

hallway, for God's sake.

"*That* remains to be seen," Deuce said harshly, thrusting her onto the bed, onto the rainbow of silks and muslins. "Fine, if you think for one moment you can hide your gorgeous body from me, Kalida. You have yet to learn a little tantalization piques the imagination more than all the revealing silks in the world. You may be sure I'll be thinking about the tempting treasures beneath whatever rough clothes you choose to wear. I'll remember, Kalida, even if you pretend not to." He strode to the door and slammed it behind him.

She stared at it, and then hoisted herself upright to the edge of the bed. She would not believe there was no dissuading him. Once he saw her parading around in canvas and twill, he would get very discouraged.

She allowed her head to droop into her hands. She was so tired of fighting him—and tired of surrendering as though she had no will of her own. She just did not know how to fight him with her father's livelihood at stake. At that moment, she felt as if she did not know anything, and she was startled therefore when the door burst open and Deuce appeared, his arms full of clothing. "Take off your robe." His food pushed the door closed and he came by measured steps farther into the room.

"I can dress myself," Kalida said defensively, wrapping her arms around herself tightly.

"We do waste a lot of time in these futile arguments, don't we? Just do what I tell you."

She didn't move. He dumped the clothes on the bed and came toward her. "Don't forget that robe is one of Ardelle's treasures," he reminded her softly as he reached for the belt.

"All right," Kalida said abruptly, stepping back and away from his reaching hand. Anything not to be touched by him. To be touched by him meant enslavement to those hands. She slowly untied the belt and let the robe slip off

137

her shoulders onto the bed to pool in riotous color that contrasted oddly with the pale silks and muslins beneath it.

His face seemed impassive, impervious to her nakedness, but his eyes . . . His glittering charcoal-deepened eyes kissed her breasts, and she shivered. "Give me a shirt," she commanded curtly, stretching out her arm, ignoring the eyes, ignoring the sudden torrid heat that arose from his awareness of her naked body, and her own tacit acknowledgement of it. And the futile feeling that went guttering to her toes.

His all-pervasive perception of her was in his eyes; she knew in that instant that even his smoky eyes could arouse her when they grazed her with that all-knowing look of complete awareness. Her whole body stiffened under that sensual scrutiny, and her arm fell to her side, useless. She was not the one to make demands here; he was, solely with his hot gray gaze, proving to her finally, she thought, just how little power she had over her own responses.

But he was not finished yet. He saw the still barely suppressed defiance of her stance, and he wanted her all over again. But he stamped down heavily on that urge and picked up one of the thick cotton shirts he had brought back, unfolded it, and held it up for her to slide her arms into the sleeves.

They stared at each other for a moment. Kalida knew that if she came to him, she would be giving in, but he made no move to hand her the shirt. He stood a few feet away from her, holding it, waiting for her patiently — as patiently as he could under the circumstances — and finally after long, tense moments, she turned her back to him and extended one arm to slide it into the sleeve, holding herself as far from him as possible.

But it wasn't possible. His body was a wave of pure heat coming at her from behind, and as she slipped her left arm into the sleeve of the shirt, his arms folded around her body so that she had to brace herself against him, and his now-brusque fingers began buttoning the shirt, oblivious to her hands pushing his away.

And she could see—even she could see—how the fabric draped and outlined her breasts in a way that hid nothing, and how, as his muscular arms inched downward and pressed against the sides of her breasts, they thrust forward and how she reacted when his palms just accidentally brushed against her distended nipples.

She wrenched away. He pulled her back by the tails of the shirt and twisted her around to face him. His hands reached for her shoulders, and before she comprehend what he meant to do, he pulled her to him, wrapped his arm around her, bent her body backward so that arm was supporting her, and fastened his mouth to her left breast.

It took mere seconds for the heat and wetness of his tongue to seep through the coarse cotton. Her breath caught in her throat. The material was no barrier to his succulent exploration; it enhanced the sensation rather than hindered it. His tongue worked harder against the encroaching thickness, and she felt the two layers of stimulation curlicue thickly down between her legs.

"All right!" Her voice was hoarse as she capitulated. "Please . . . Deuce . . ."

He lifted his head briefly. "No." His mouth settled on her breast again.

She pulled his hair violently, and his head came up again. "What?"

"You win," she whispered.

The tension eased. "I knew I would," he murmured with a grown of satisfaction.

"Then please let me get dressed." Was she begging? Or was her urgent desire solely to escape him and his sultry knowledge of her? No matter; he had made his point. She could not escape his desire, or her own. Her defiant navy-darkened eyes told him as much as he slowly straightened his body, clamping down on the rising passion that would have made still further demands on her quickening senses.

He watched her look down at the shirt as he moved reluctantly away. There was a dark wet patch over her breast and she looked up at him accusingly. He pivoted to the bed and picked up the dark heavy cotton skirt he had tossed there. His expression was mocking as he turned and handed it to her. She took it without a word, and he watched appreciatively as she stepped into it, pulled it up over her long bare legs, and fastened it around her waist.

When she looked at him again, she could read in his blazing charcoal eyes exactly what he was thinking, and it was precisely as he had said: Cotton and twill were no barrier to his imagination. The concealment only enhanced his desire. She whirled away from him and reached herself for the serviceable pair of boots that were the last item he had brought and dumped on the bed. She pulled them on silently as he watched. They were tight.

She stood up and curtsied tauntingly. His eyes kindled a dark warning, and her body quirked at the remainder. The rough cotton felt raw against her skin, damp in that one place she did not want to think about, against her sensitized nipple.

"I'm hungry," she said flatly, moving toward the door, determined to ignore the dark patch of shirt and even more determined to get away from him.

"So am I," Deuce murmured, steps behind her and already reaching ahead of her to grasp the doorknob and block her way.

She felt the force of his body behind her. He pulsated with some emotion that reached out to her, and she shook her head. "Yes," he hissed in her ear. "Isn't it clear yet?"

"Nothing is clear," she gritted, "except that you own me and I'm starving." She reached out her hand to grasp his and pull it from the door.

She could not give in to the mind-shattering pleasure her body was beginning to crave; she couldn't. It would just mean she would be his chattel, and she knew she was nothing more than that to him—a piece of property in a deal. She had more pride than that, no matter how her body reacted to his closeness and to his touch. She would never allow herself to come to the point where her intelligence gave in. She would never take anything from him without a fight, and she knew many women who would not scruple to do just that, because that would be the easiest thing to do.

There was no torrid heat between them now, only a cool calculation on both parts, a battle of wills, as their eyes clashed.

"You can't go downstairs like that," he said finally, moving his hand from the door.

"Can't I?" she flashed back, grabbing her opportunity as he relinquished the doorknob. The telltale patch was drying. In the dim kerosene light it would probably look like a dark shadow. She grasped the knob, turned it, and flew out the door before he could stop her.

He let her go, his mind still on the taste of her cloth-covered breasts in his mouth. She would have to face them, not he. He wondered how she would explain it.

Nine

She slept alone that night, and thankfully. She did not have to keep on her clothes, and she did not have to fight her own overwhelming desires.

"Of course Deuce and the men will be going out tonight," Ardelle had said at dinner as if it were expressly understood by everyone. She was totally put out with Kalida, anyway, with her unsuitable dinner dress and that suspicious spot on her shirt. And Deuce being late. Only Ellie won her approval this night, with her tasteful new ready-made dress and her tacit and tactful taking over the duties of the hostess of the table. And that Hal Ryland, rather sitting there and looking smug and excited and hardly paying attention to any of the conversation or Deuce's instructions.

Ardelle herself spent at least twenty minutes detailing her plans for Kalida and Ellie the following day. Kalida squirmed in her seat at all the talk of being measured for new clothes and being treated to an in-depth tour of Sweetland. Part of it was that her father looked so delighted.

As well he should, she thought wrathfully, digging a rebellious fork into a slab of meat on her plate that she had barely tasted. Hadn't she bargained away the rest of

142

her life for his share of it?

And then there was Deuce, with his steamy gray gaze all over her, making her aware, too aware of herself and him. No wonder she had no appetite, for all her protestations of hunger! She felt suffocated between the three of them—Ardelle, her father, and Deuce!

Her eyes focused on Ellie, sitting so cool and serene at the head of the table, only the barest glimmer of a smile on her lips betraying the fact that she was enjoying her new status enormously.

Ellie. Ellie had pinned up her hair this evening, the better to show off the fancy lace collar of a second new dress, this one a trifle large but becoming nonetheless, with its glowing golden color enhanced in the subtle light. Ellie, looking so elegant and perfect and the lady of the house. Lady. Yes. The veriest lady, the picture of what Ardelle envisioned as the mistress of Sweetland.

Kalida's eyes narrowed thoughtfully. Imagine if Ardelle could be persuaded to become Ellie's champion instead of her own! If she could so disgust Ardelle with her antics and her contrariness that Deuce's aunt would want Kalida nowhere around. If, indeed, Ardelle could be made to perceive that she suffered in comparison to Ellie Dean's perfection.

And wasn't that just the logical extension of her initial thought as she had waited in the bedroom for Ellie's return from town? Hadn't she had that feeling as she had watched Deuce handing Ellie down from the wagon? Her plan formulated itself in its entirety even as she sat at the table and listened to the desultory conversation and watched Ellie directing the service. It was perfect, absolutely perfect. Deuce only had to be convinced she would not make a perfect mistress in any sense of the word. The contemplation of the means to that end gave her some degree of satisfaction as the dinner progressed, coffee was finally passed around, and her father and Deuce made ready for the evening's patrol.

Ardelle stood and signalled the end of the meal. "Madame Dupuis will be ready for us at nine o'clock," she said briskly, reaching for her cane, her words directed at Ellie as well as Kalida.

And it was Ellie who answered, "That will be lovely," as she pushed in her chair and followed Ardelle into the parlor.

Kalida hung back, seeing the first opportunity to put her plan into action. "I'm going upstairs," she announced upgraciously.

"Well you should," Ardelle snapped, turning back to her. "How could you come to the table dressed for the barnyard?"

"It was easy," Kalida muttered, lowering her lids over her gleaming eyes. How much more in character this was for her! And wasn't Ellie looking intensely interested?

"Be prepared for the dressmaker tomorrow," Ardelle continued, still in that chastising voice. "I'm really disappointed in you, Kalida. Good night."

Kalida nodded her head and turned on her heel. She couldn't imagine anything more delightful than an evening by herself. It seemed to her that she had not been alone for weeks. And then there was the relief of taking off the rough cotton shirt and the too-tight boots, and slipping on the crushed silk robe that she had so disdained. Now it seemed like the most comfortable garment in the world, and she reveled in its lightness against her skin.

Now, too, that Deuce was nowhere about, she could allow herself to go through the heap of material on the bed and separate out the bolts of silk, cotton, and gingham from the underclothing and the two ready-made dresses that Ellie had chosen for her.

The dresses were wildly inappropriate for her. One was a green checked gingham with a lace collar and ruffled hem, which had no defined waistline. The other was a plain gray silk that buttoned up the front to a plain white collar and fastened at the sleeves with mannish cuffs.

She tossed them aside happily and slid into the cool sheets. Lovely not to have to fence with Deuce or fend off his seductive hands. Delightful to think there might be a way out of this situation for her if she were clever enough to manipulate Ardelle and Ellie. Funny she had never thought of Ellie in just that light before. But then Ellie had always affected a certain staid, prim attitude that made people view her as the straitlaced widow that kept the boarding house. Interesting that she had other qualities, that she was still interested in Hal Ryland. That was obvious. But Deuce's arrogant masculinity seemed to appeal to her too.

Well, Ellie was welcome to deal with it. Kalida Ryland wanted no part of it, deal or no deal. And she was going to do her best to pull it off. Starting tomorrow. Starting with the dressmaker. She would kick up a rumpus with the dressmaker. That would be perfect. . . .

Kalida slept, alone, unaware that in the early hours of the morning Deuce wearily returned and, throwing himself tiredly into the upholstered rocker, sat and contemplated her alluringly curved slumbering body for the rest of the night.

Kalida awakened early, threw the abominable green-checked calico over her naked body, washed, and headed downstairs.

Even this early there was a sense of suppressed energy in the air, as if beneath the serene surface a hive of activity was commencing.

As she came down the stairs she could see Ardelle's white-garbed figure on the porch, blocking the open door, and could hear her voice talking to someone, low.

145

". . . obvious Deuce hasn't got the men or the time for this kind of intensive patrol." A mumble of agreement from—it sounded like—Jake Danton, whose body was blocked by Ardelle's standing directly in front of him. ". . . choice? I don't know. He's talking about hiring a professional now; I don't like it. He's fed up with spending all the time and energy and getting nowhere. Especially because of the Ryland herd having to be got down next week. I don't know where he's going to put them—maybe Morgan field, so as not to mix them with the syndicate herd until branding. I don't know. You'll have to figure it out next week. Meantime, there's this problem first. . . ." Her voice lowered here so that Kalida, who was listening avidly to this conversation, could not hear the rest.

Obviously Deuce had already gone, and if she didn't want Ardelle to catch her eavesdropping, she thought, she had better scoot. But she did. Ardelle almost collided with her as she unexpectedly came in the door, caught Kalida's arm with unerring accuracy, and whirled her around so she could look at her.

"Good God, that looks awful on you," she commented deprecatingly.

"I expect it was the best Ellie could do—on such short notice," Kalida said mildly, her cobalt eyes guileless.

"It had better not be the best that Dupuis woman can do on short notice," Ardelle muttered, releasing her arm and motioning her into the dining room.

Prestina was there already, laying plates and arranging baskets of biscuits and platters of eggs and freshly fried thin slices of meat. She looked up as they came in and tamped down on a smile. Miss Kalida looked about thirteen years old in that dress, she thought. And Mr. Deuce would not like it one bit.

Ardelle was wondering whether she had deliberately pulled her inky hair back and braided it in just that

146

childish way to emphasize the fact that her costume made her look younger. Just like Kalida, she thought, watching as Kalida seated herself and looked up at her, her face wickedly serene, her eyes bright and glowing with a lambent blue light.

Ardelle shook her head. *"Ellie* chose this?" she questioned disbelievingly.

"I?" Ellie's voice just behind her feigned innocence. "I never would have chosen green for Kalida. Madame Dupuis must have misunderstood my instructions."

Kalida's eyebrows zoomed upwards at this audacity as Ellie entered, dressed in still a third new gown, this one a wool and silk morning gown whose rose color set off her black hair and eyes. She seated herself next to Kalida with a stately grace, not meeting Kalida's quizzically mocking cobalt gaze.

Kalida lowered her eyes so that Ardelle, who was staring at her fixedly, could not see the triumph there. It was as good as if she had given Ellie the words to say — like a play where she was directing the action. Ellie obviously wanted what Kalida wanted and, she thought, she would be perfectly happy to direct Ellie into Deuce's arms.

A tiny smile wafted its way around the corners of her mouth, a contended, mischievous smile that Ardelle did not miss as she pointedly began directing the service of the meal.

There was a palpable release of the small frieze of tension as Prestina began pouring coffee.

Even Ardelle's displeasure seemed to have eased as she said to Ellie, "Yes, Madame *must* have not heard you correctly. We'll remedy *that* today," which statement did not reassure Kalida.

Ardelle turned to her next and announced, "Did you know your father is leaving today?"

"Yes, I am," Ryland said, striding into the dining room

147

just then, "but I wanted to tell Kalida myself."

"Papa . . ." she began, as if to argue with him right there, and he held up his hand.

"Come, my dear. Excuse us, will you?"

Kalida resentfully followed him out onto the porch, sat down on a rush-bottomed slatted-back rocker, and looked up at her father. "What now, Papa? Are you going to abandon me to Deuce?"

"Abandon you? The very idea! Kalida, you have some very strange notions in your head."

"Don't I though?" she murmured. "All right, what is it then this time, Papa?"

"Well, there is now working capital, as you well know, and I need to be in town to oversee things."

"But that's perfect! I'll come with you. I'd rather be in town than here," Kalida said cheerfully, knowing full well this pretense would not fool her father nor get her one step away from Sweetland.

"Kalida, my dear, you do know that's not possible. Not only would Deuce not allow it, neither would I. I intend to put up at the roughest lodgings—merely a place to sleep at night while I superintend the rebuilding of the ranch and begin negotiating for a new herd. I must be close to the mail and have access to the railroad and hire workmen, and none of that is possible here. And you are well aware of it. So what are you up to?" His tone was reasonable, his arguments were persuasive.

Kalida stared out at the vista for a moment. She could just see the diamond-drop sparkles of the spring away in the distance. What was she up to, indeed? "How important is the syndicate to you now?" she asked abruptly.

His harsh answer came instantly. "I want it."

She looked at him. The smooth joviality of his expression had turned hard, almost uncompromising. She would get no sympathy for her plans from him. He was determined to do what he was going to do, and he did not need the excess baggage of a meddling daughter to slow him down.

"Why?" His question was a guncrack in the silence.

She hesitated a moment and then plunged. "It seems to me that Deuce has bought and paid for, by contract, a certain amount of your property. I'm pretty sure that contract doesn't specify your daughter as part of that property. Or does it?" She tilted her head questioningly, not reassured that her father had the grace to turn away. "He isn't honor-bound to marry me," she went on dryly. "The terms of that agreement pretty well went out the window when the ranch burned down. And only my honor will keep me here, because otherwise there would have been no refinancing for you. But that's done now. And he doesn't need me here."

"But Sweetland . . ." her father prompted, turning back to her.

"He said next year, if you can afford it."

"Then you must stay," he said—calmly, he thought, but a certain urgency in his tone communicated itself to her. "You *do* understand that, Kalida. No matter what, you're bound to stay with him if he promised you that."

Her eyes darkened to navy as she regarded him. "And you just go off and leave me."

"It has to be." He was adamant; he needed her compliance on this. "No matter what, I still need Sweetland, Kalida."

"And I'm the price," she said, almost to herself. "Well, that's that then. I won't renege, Papa, but I still am going to try to get out of it."

"Remember where your first attempt got you," her father reminded her pointedly. "Don't jeopardize what I'm trying to do, Kalida. I won't have it."

"And isn't that the problem—what everyone will and won't have," Kalida said scornfully. "Except me. My sole contribution is to do what I'm told. Well, *I* won't have

149

that, Papa."

He looked at her closely; she was bluffing, he thought. There wasn't much else she could do. Deuce was determined, and she would not get away from *him*. It was the one thing he had counted on, besides the generous infusion of cash to his bank account. If he could pull off his own plan, he would be sitting pretty himself. And he wanted that. In a way, he felt Kalida owed him the chance to try to recoup. But he couldn't put it to her that way. All she saw was that she was being bartered like a piece of property. And she was. He hadn't thought she would prove to be nearly so valuable to him.

"You'll do what you have to," he said finally. "I *think* you'll give me my chance to get back on my feet before you do anything rash." He watched her face now, knowing how hard it was for her mobile mouth to keep from expressing her feelings. Her cobalt eyes clouded over and her firm lips worked to deny that she would do anything except what was good for herself. But she couldn't. He saw it and knew it. Her mouth twisted in resignation.

"You won't, will you?" he pressed.

"I have my own plans," she said enigmatically.

"You could love Deuce if you would let yourself," he threw out in desperation.

The thought amused her. "Why should I? All he needs is a decoration for his house and heirs. Anyone would do." Her eyes were bright again, as if she expected him to leap on this cryptic statement.

He didn't. "I'll be gone a month or so, Kalida. Please try to behave."

She stood up and held out her arms. "I'll be laying groundwork, Papa. Nothing more. Yet."

Her father put his arms around her lightly, noncommittally. "I do not like the sound of *that,*" he said sternly, warningly. "Don't complicate our only chance to recover what we've lost."

She kissed his cheek. "What if—what if Deuce turns out to have other plans?"

"What other plans? I know his plans; he has no other plans," her father said sharply, setting her away from him. Damn, but she looked so young and vulnerable in that ridiculous dress and that infantile arrangement of her hair. Just for an instant he felt a pang at the thought of leaving her.

"He *could* change his mind about me," Kalida murmured. "He might find he wants someone else."

Ryland shook his head despairingly. "Hold on to that thought if it comforts you," he advised her, "but don't be surprised to find it's just a daydream."

She smiled at him without rancor. It was obvious his mind was set: Deuce's money had bought the cattle and Kalida. Thank goodness he was going to town for the month. Otherwise he very definitely would have interfered with her plans. "Good-bye, Papa. Let me know how you're getting on."

"I'm *not* going forever, my girl," he said gruffly, sensing her capitulation to his wishes. "I'll be in touch. Let me know when Deuce brings down the herd, will you?"

"He said something about next week," Kalida told him.

"That soon? Well, he'll have his hands full if he pastures them on the Balsam Range, but that's his problem," her father said, hugging her again.

"He apparently plans on keeping them separate at Morgan field, Papa; they won't get mixed in with the syndicate. I expect he'll brand them there and then turn them out." She returned the hug, this time with reasonable emotion. She was sad at his going and desolated that Deuce would run their cattle, and she fully felt that her father was experiencing the same emotion.

He patted her shoulders as he released her. "It's all right, Kalida. I had already made up my mind that when it was done, I would put it behind me, no regrets. Deuce paid a very fair price, all things considered; I could not have expected more under the circumstances, and if I had had to market them myself, I could well have gotten less. I promise you, he means well with you, and you must give him a chance."

She didn't answer him, and he moved away from her, down the porch steps before she answered. "Don't make me promise, Papa."

He smiled at that, satisfied, and turned toward the barn with a wave of his hand, leaving Kalida, a rather forlorn-looking figure, standing on the porch staring after him. But he didn't see that. He saw his future ahead of him, bright with a certain kind of promise. He saw straight ahead of him, one step after the other. Kalida was out of sight now, and for Hal Ryland, she was out of mind.

"Stand still now, Kalida, and take off that awful dress," Ardelle commanded, hobbling around the small stool on which Kalida had been forced to stand in the parlor at Madame Dupuis's behest.

"I feel like a rag doll," Kalida said unappreciatively.

Ardelle and Ellie were both looking up at her, and Madame Dupuis, a rather tall, gray-haired, black-garbed haughty older woman, with snappy compelling dark eyes, was rummaging around in a huge black bag that she seemingly habitually carried with her, oblivious to the torrential tirade of abuse that Ardelle heaped on her because of Kalida's ill-chosen dress. She merely shrugged, sent a black look at Ellie, and went for her bag where she claimed she kept her measuring tape and patterns. Her search allowed her to hide her face and her mouth, which was issuing imprecations against the idle wealthy who thought they could get away with anything, even maligning her taste. Meanwhile, Ardelle Cavender was beginning to, in the midst of her dressing down, have doubts as to whether they should allow Madame Dupuis to even measure them if Kalida's dress were an example of how she could outfit them.

And Ellie's opaque black eyes glittered and just dared her to reveal that Kalida's dresses were Ellie's choice.

"Mademoiselle was in a hurry," she muttered as she tossed things out of her bag. "Haste was paramount; it mattered not what she wore so much as she had *something* to wear, *non?* One does not have dresses ready made on rack for every size and coloration every day, Madame; surely it is obvious no one would have *chosen* to outfit Mademoiselle so unless it were absolutely necessary to do so, and I was given to understand . . . ah! Now!" She looked at Ardelle, who was somewhat mollified by this semblance of an explanation, and she handed over her pattern books and fabric samples. Ardelle took them with more willingness than she had thus far exhibited to see Madame's work, scanning through them quickly and with an exacting eye.

"All right; these will do," she said at last, and Madame Dupuis let out a covertly held breath.

"I will have several skirts and shirtwaists if you please, and nothing fancier," Kalida put in, watching Ellie move gracefully to a chair by the window and sink into it with just the faintest air of boredom.

"Just take off the dress," Ardelle ordered, "and I'll have Prestina burn it. *Now,* Kalida."

Kalida shrugged, raised her arms to unfasten the hooks at the neck of the dress, and then shrugged her arms out of the sleeves and let it slide fluidly down the curves of her naked body into a gingham puddle at her feet.

"Kalida!"

This unladylike roar issued through the thin, firm lips of the most ladylike Ardelle.

Kalida shrugged again and bent forward to pick up the dress, a move that threw her breasts in sharp relief against

153

the bright light of the window.

"I suppose you hadn't a chemise to spare," Ardelle commented sarcastically.

"Not a one," Kalida agreed calmly, wrapping her upper torso in the dress. She turned to Ellie, whose glittery black eyes seemed fastened to her long bare legs. "Ellie? Didn't you say you had gotten some underthings for me?"

Her dulcet tone snapped Ellie's attention back to her. She rose from her chair. "I believe I did. Can I have forgotten to give them to you?" She sent an insincere smile in Kalida's direction.

Kalida stepped down off the little footstool. "I believe you did."

Ardelle said, "Please, Ellie. I want to get on with the measuring. At this rate, Madame Dupuis won't even begin to get started this week."

"Don't let me hold her up," Kalida interpolated, and Ardelle sent her a scorching look and motioned Ellie out of the room. Kalida sank onto a small velvet-covered sofa, musing on the fantasy of Deuce still being around the house somewhere and what might have happened if Ellie had encountered him. Would he be polite? Probably. Ellie did look particularly fetching this morning, but since Ardelle had not yet formulated her objections to Kalida, he would only see her in the guise of a particularly charming guest in his house.

But surely, Kalida decided, he would remember the drift of ladylike rose-colored dress in his upstairs hallway and the calm, deliberate way that Ellie seemed to go about doing things. And surely, when he was made to see how unsuitable she, Kalida, was, the early morning vision of Ellie in fresh morning rose would recur to him and, perhaps, send his desire in a totally new direction.

The thought was so pleasant that a small contented smile played on her lips. She was absolutely on the right track; she had only to think of the next thing to do when

Ellie returned with the chemise.

And, in fact, it seemed like only moments before Ardelle nudged her and handed her the flimsy length of cotton knit undergarment. She took it resentfully and slipped into it as Ardelle and Ellie watched, and somehow she felt more embarrassed by this act than having appeared before both of them stark naked.

"All right," Ardelle said briskly, "back up on the footstool please, thank you."

Kalida obliged meekly, her mind teeming. Madame Dupuis flurried around her with measuring tape, pencil, and paper, on which she took copious notes. *"Bon,"* she muttered at last, and motioned Kalida to step down. "Now, Mademoiselle—" She beckoned to Ellie, who looked around at Kalida and Ardelle, and then said timorously, "Could we do this in private?"

Ardelle thought a moment and nodded, directing Kalida to put on her dress in that same no-nonsense voice she had been using with her since last night. Kalida hid a smile as she slid the dress over her head, and then followed Ardelle into the hallway.

"Ellie's modesty is becoming," Ardelle commented, with a meaningful look at Kalida.

"I think it's stupid," Kalida said flatly, and was gratified by Ardelle's disgusted reaction. They did not speak for the ten minutes that it took for Madame Dupuis to take measurements and notes, and for Ellie to dress.

When they were invited back into the parlor, Madame Dupuis was all business. She had laid out her patterns and fabric samples on the floor, and sat in a chair beside them. Ellie was back in the chair by the window, looking like a flushed rose, and Ardelle and Kalida seated themselves on the sofa.

"Now," Ardelle said abruptly, "we have the underthings and shoes. Therefore, four dresses, one suitable for evening—I leave to you the styles and colors; two shirtwaists, two skirts, wool and cotton weave is suitable for working around the ranch when required I believe. You will start on the house dresses first, and perhaps a skirt and shirtwaist apiece so that we're not totally confined indoors."

"Colors?" murmured Madame. "A suggestion — ? The green would go better for Mademoiselle Ellie. Red and gray she can wear very well with her coloring. The gold taffeta also becomes her; I have only to take it in a little."

Ardelle nodded and looked at Ellie questioningly. "I put myself in your hands," Ellie said softly.

"*Bien*. Now, Mademoiselle Kalida . . . the blue, of course; and the rose is suitable, white, blue-gray, black, lavender-blue, perhaps. Always the blue for the eyes, quite lovely is Mademoiselle," Madame finished suddenly at Ardelle's quelling look. She bent forward and gathered up her samples. "It is time to begin."

"Yes," Ardelle agreed, "now we begin."

Kalida made a fuss. If they were to tour the ranch, she had to change; she just couldn't go gallivanting around in that light, horrifically unsuitable dress, she couldn't. Ardelle's expression became hectic as she excused her and led Ellie out onto the porch.

Kalida dashed upstairs quickly, pulled off the offending dress, dived into the cotton shirt and skirt, and peered out the window. From Deuce's room, she could just hear the drone of voices, but whether they came from the barn or the porch she couldn't tell.

She fully intended to keep Ardelle and Ellie waiting as long as possible, but her impatient nature did not allow her to sit still. She knew Deuce was cutting cattle on the Balsam Range; she had a deep yearning to be out on the range, unfettered and *helping*. Dangerous, that kind of yearning. It was just part and parcel of the things she had done at home, things she would never be allowed to do again.

She wondered what Ardelle was saying about her. She wondered whether she oughn't ease up on this first day of her campaign to earn Ardelle's dislike. But she couldn't control the situations, and they seemed to be coming thick and fast, with opportunities to be seized and used at the moment.

She contained herself for twenty long minutes before she appeared on the porch, ready for instruction.

Ardelle said, "Humph," reached for her cane, and led them around to the front of the house. Kalida was gratified to watch Ellie pick her way through the dust and dew-moist grass with disdainful little movements as she lifted her skirt and wrinkled her nose, as if to say, *is* this necessary?

"The original house," Ardelle was saying, pointing with her cane. "When my brother arrived here twenty or more years ago, he built a sod hut. Deuce was just entering his teens then, Camilla was just a little girl. They hardly had anything; and, in fact, when Asa first went to Texas, father cut him off without an allowance, since he wasn't about to follow in the shipping business. No, Asa caught western fever, and he had come up north with the original drives in the sixties and married after that, and then it took ten years and more for him to convince his wife that they were coming to Montana before it was too late.

"She died several years after they came; the life was too hard for her, I suspect. Nothing was like it is now. The original house was two rooms, with a stove for cooking and heating in the one room, and a stone fireplace in what was the bedroom. The kitchen had a dirt floor and she never could keep it clean, even with laying down canvas, even after Asa laid the plank floor. And no windows but the two original ones you see in front here, and muslin material for a wall covering with newspapers over that for decoration. Well, my sister-in-law came from a right well-to-do family herself, and it almost killed her to do the kind of work she had to do while Asa was out herding cows.

"She hated the gardening and she hated the chores, even after the children were old enough to help, and she finally took sick and got out of the whole mess." Ardelle paused, looking at Ellie's rapt expression and Kalida's cool disdain, which hid the fact she was listening avidly. Ardelle sensed it. She went on.

"Much as I came to care for Asa later on, Prestina came to take care of Lydia. By then, because the children were growing, Asa had raised the roof and added the two upstairs rooms. But privacy and patient care did not help Lydia. Prestina stayed for the children, and Asa calmly went about building his cattle empire. When he accumulated enough money, he built the new house, but Deuce wouldn't let him tear down the original house, and he uses the downstairs rooms—still the original sod that Asa boarded over as he enhanced the house—Deuce uses those rooms as offices for the syndicate.

"Five years ago Asa took ill—lived long enough to see Camilla married off to an English investor who had come to buy into one of the larger spreads. Anyway, that's the first house, and Asa built it and enlarged it with his own two hands. The barn"—she pointed now to the larger log-hewn structure that was set at a perpendicular angle a hundred feet or so from the house—"he built it too; you remember they used to site them like that because of the Indian attacks. This is the beginning of Sweetland, just what you see here, and the Musselshell River in the distance, and why Asa chose to settle here, along with its proximity to Bozeman. He didn't want any truck with Miles City—Milestown it was then—lawless place.

"It was better here. Most of those pick-up-and-go ranchers hunkered in along the Powder River anyway. It was getting too crowded, Deuce said, and they had gone on a survey trip to confirm that. No, Asa was happier here where there weren't too many neighbors to horn in on things. He had the whole shebang to himself, along with his connections in Texas."

Ardelle started walking, stabbing the ground with her cane to emphasize her words—or perhaps her anger at circumstances beyond her brother's control. "My father would have been proud of Asa, if he had lived to see this. But he didn't." She shook her head. "Then, of course, Deuce took over and made it bigger and better, got more money, *bought* the land, which, young lady"—she pointed at Kalida—"was perhaps one of the smartest things your own father did."

"His backers insisted," Kalida murmured, fascinated by Sweetland's history and where Ardelle was leading them—past the old corrals and the old barn, to the long side of the newer house, and beyond that to the bunkhouse and cookhouse, pointing out the laundry, the dairy, the garden, of course, the canning cellar, the sanitary facilities that were discreetly hidden by bushes and stood close to the house. More outbuildings behind the bunkhouse stored their hired hands' gear, housed the horses that were not on the range, stored the buckboard and flatbed wagons, the hay baler and other implements.

It was ten times larger than her father's spread, Kalida thought in dismay, and didn't account for the thousands of acres of grazing land and streams and valleys that were like gold to a cattle rancher.

"There are still chores to be done by the mistress of Sweetland," Ardelle went on as they walked. "We have two Cheyenne women who come twice a week for laundry, of course, because of the men, and Prestina supervises the house. We do the sewing, plan the meals, tend the garden, put up the fruits and vegetables. I help Deuce with his account books during summer and winter roundup, as well as I keep the books for the household expenses and make sure we never want for anything."

She looked at Kalida. "One is never idle at Sweetland."

"Does one never get away from Sweetland?" Kalida asked sardonically.

"Why would one want to?" Ellie asked softly.

Perfect! Kalida thought balefully. Ellie had all the right responses, especially the ones she could never bring herself to make.

"I never have wanted to," Ardelle said with a serious finality that put a period to that discussion.

"I should like to watch the cutting and branding," Kalida announced, daring Ardelle to dissuade her.

"I don't doubt you would," Ardelle agreed, giving the notion some consideration. "I suppose it does come under the heading of entertaining the guests, since you are still to be counted as our guests. Guests never tire of watching *real* ranch work going on."

"I never tire of doing it," Kalida snapped, put out by Ardelle's insinuations.

"I would not advertise the fact if I were you," Ardelle tossed back pointedly, her speculative eyes wondering whether Kalida would jump out of the carriage and take over the branding pen if indeed she did consent to take them.

She wheeled in the opposite direction, still undecided, when a figure on horseback barreled into the barnyard, hailing them with a shout.

"Danton," Ardelle murmured. "What the devil is he doing back?"

She moved backward slightly as he pulled in his heaving mount and dismounted in a supple movement, with an instant smile that included all of them. "Howdy, ma'am," he said respectfully to Ardelle and removed his hat, and Kalida had the impression that he wasn't being respectful at all. His bright hazel eyes skimmed over Ellie and herself, settling for the briefest moment on her breasts, and then he transferred his quicksilver look and attention to Ardelle.

"You were taking Hal Ryland to Bozeman," she was saying.

"Well, I'm on the way back to Balsam; Mr. High and Mighty Ryland—excuse me, Miss Kalida—didn't want to be taken nowhere. He wanted to be let off at the ranch to get his own buggy and proceed from there. I was just as happy to let him, ma'am. I didn't figure on losing a day to nursemaid nobody to town."

"Quite right," Ardelle said brusquely. "Meantime, Kalida had the itch to go to Balsam herself." She shook her head. "An hour of that should suffice for any woman with any sensibilities."

"You all figuring to go?" Danton asked, his eyes back on Kalida, who nodded, sensing an ally; and then to Ellie, who shuddered delicately thinking of all the sweat and noise, and then thought about all the men, including the not-too-unpleasant-to-look-at Jake Danton, with his dark curly hair, leather-tanned face, and knowledgeable eyes. She nodded also, and Ardelle gave her a disgusted look.

" 'Pears to me you and Miss Ellie should take the buggy, what with your being dressed so nice and all; Miss Kalida and I will ride." He winked at Kalida and bent a straight, serious look at Ardelle, who indignantly found herself committed to this jaunt, and with Kalida on horseback, too. Nothing was going right, and Ardelle was becoming furious with Jake Danton's high-handed familiarity with both Kalida and herself. Jake had a place, damn it, and he had better remember it.

She watched helplessly as he pulled the buggy from the carriage barn, and then went off with Kalida to the stable to saddle Malca and bridle a horse for the buggy.

Kalida felt a delicious moment of freedom in Jake's

161

company as they strode away. It was almost as if they were defying an enraged parent and getting away with it. Jake's manner was conspiratorial and just faintly overbearingly male, as though he were telling her he appreciated the fact she was a woman but he knew the boundaries. And Kalida rather liked his attitude; it allowed her a flirtatious freedom that wasn't fraught with sensual peril.

Jake was, in fact, very likable, and he made it plain he found Kalida very attractive too. "We're two of a kind," he said to her as he slung her saddle blanket over Malca's impatient back. "We're mavericks, and we live by our wits, and we grab for everything we can get. Don't we, Miss Kalida?" He cinched the saddle under Malca's belly with a brisk yank, and then paced around to his other side, where Kalida was stroking his sleek flanks and admiring Jake's efficiency. "Don't we?"

The urgency of his words pulled her up short.

"I never really thought about it quite that way," she said brusquely.

But she saw that abrupt reply had no effect. He was as close to her now as he could be without having intimate contact, and it was obvious from the expression on his face that he wanted that too. "You're a beautiful lady, Miss Kalida," he said softly. "I've been watching you."

"How could you have?" she said sharply. "I've been in my room."

"I saw you running from Cavender," he amplified, but did not elaborate. The vision of her streaking blue-gowned figure vanishing into the fields and the humiliated look in her vibrant blue eyes when she returned . . . and that robe clinging to her skin, which made her look almost naked. No, he wouldn't forget that, or the glimpse he had had of her nakedness through the window this very morning. The vision of those long legs and lush breasts would have turned a stone man alive, let alone a celibate cowboy who once a month had leave to relieve his turmoil at the nearest brothel in town.

She had flaunted her nakedness before two women. He wondered, as he was on his way to join her father, whether it was because she had no opportunity to flaunt herself before a man as she must be dying to do. A violent dream possessed him as he disappointedly had watched her pull up her dress and enfold her naked charms in it. And the dream had carried him through the morning and back to Sweetland again, earlier than he had expected, vibrating with a lust to just see Kalida again. And fortune had thrust her right into his hands, alone and willing, in the dank isolation of the stables for these very few minutes.

He had to convince her of his desire without scaring her away.

"Did you?" she murmured in answer to his statement. "So what?"

"You're scared of him," he said, moving closer, backing her against the stall wall.

"I'm getting scared of you," she snapped, looking wildly around, wondering how she could have thought that Jake Danton was a harmless cowboy who could possibly be a friend.

"Don't be scared, Miss Kalida." His voice had dropped. "I'd like to help you." But that wasn't true. What he wanted was for her to start stripping off her clothes of her own volition because she had been yearning to be alone with a man where she could reveal her nakedness the same way she had this morning, when he was watching and she was not aware of it.

But she made no move to unbutton her shirt or slip off her skirt; she stood looking at him oddly, and he had the wild idea that she knew exactly what he was thinking and she was sneering at him. But all she said was, "You can't help me."

Damn bitch, he thought, struggling to hold onto his control and his reason. She had no way of knowing what he wanted or that he had seen her. She couldn't feel the raging inside him. One day, he vowed, one day she would. But until then he had to play her along a little.

"Listen, Miss Kalida," he said urgently—urgent but not what she would be thinking; oh, no—but the sincerity in his tone was unmistakable, and he thought it was a rather nice touch himself, since he couldn't touch her—yet. "I know you're not in a good situation here. I do know that. And if you ever find a way out of it and you need someone to help you, you must promise to call on me. Say you will."

"I might have to," she said dryly, edging away from him and taking Malca's reins. He didn't stop her.

"You'll want a hat," he said gruffly, mesmerized by the line of her body outlined against the stall doorway where the light filtered through. "And probably a bandanna."

"I know," she said gently, caught off balance by the sudden change in him. It was as if two different men were with her. She was not wary of the one giving her all this kindly advice. She pulled a bandanna from her skirt pocket and tied it around her neck. He handed her a deep-crowned hat and caught up two others for Ardelle and Ellie, and then followed her out of the stable, bringing with him one of the dray horses and a bridle, admiring all the way the sway of Kalida's hips, and remembering the lush curve of the buttocks hidden beneath her skirt.

Kalida mounted Malca, who was as restive as she felt, and watched with mixed feelings as Jake skillfully bridled the horse and hitched it to the buggy. Here, in bright daylight, there was nothing menacing about Jake Danton. There was, in fact, something very attractive about his long, rangy body and his brown face and capable hands. He was foreman of the ranch, a man given responsibility, a man used to taking charge, a leader, a knowledgeable man, a man who knew his business. He was muscular in a thick kind of way, slightly fleshier than Deuce, a half head or so shorter. He wore his pinch-crowned hat at a jaunty angle, with the braided chin strap almost defiantly visible. There was nothing not to like about Jake Danton, she decided, as he looked up at her before he mounted his own horse in a kindly way that made her ashamed she had felt afraid of him in the stable.

Then he swung up onto his saddle.

"How far away is it?" Ellie questioned as he grabbed the lead strings of the buggy.

"Far enough so you don't hear the noise or smell the sweat," he said baldly, rapping the leather strap against their horse's nose to get him walking. His hazel eyes shot to Kalida. Yes, she had a faint smile on her lips at the humor. Very faint. Just enough to give him hope.

Ardelle, however, looked disapproving, and he was beginning to think it was her natural expression. She said nothing as he led the buggy to the dirt track behind the outbuildings that fed out into the pasture and the rangeland beyond. She took over briskly and Ellie shuddered delicately as the carriage jounced onto the well-rutted track. Noise! she thought disgustedly; sweat, heat, dirt! The words pounded through her head during the grueling half-hour trip. The only sustenance she could find was the thought of all the men, the lovely hired hands and the better-heeled ranch reps who always seemed to have lots of money in their pockets. All those work-hardened men in one lovely place with no other women around but herself and Kalida. The thought, in fact, was nourishing enough. Kalida just could not attract every last man of them.

Kalida was not thinking of the men; she was thinking of the pleasure of working and the freedom of the range—not typical feminine thoughts, she acknowledged to herself with a smile. Jake cantered easily beside her, companionable now, hardly talking except to occasionally point out some feature of the landscape she might have missed. His eyes, however, were focused on her breasts and his thoughts on his own elaborate plans, so that he was not aware of the noise that suddenly became obvious as they drew closer to the Balsam range. They heard that first, the ceaseless bawling of the cattle below the dust swirling above the rise that they were just topping. And then they saw the whole stunning picture.

A river of cattle streamed down from the foothills opposite and pooled into the lush grass of the Balsam range. The numbers were awesome, uncountable; the men were numberless. They seemed everywhere, whooping and prodding, galloping and changing direction on a moment's decision, a rope lashing out here to fell a calf like lightning, fastening it, tying and holding it; instantly two other men to help control its flailing body; and the third with the branding iron nearby to scald the flesh, the glint of a knife in the sunlight, cutting the ear, and then gone—a whoop and slap to send the calf in the direction of the holding crew. And then it began again.

Ardelle watched it all with a certain avidity, since she knew the dollar figure each head translated into. But it bored her after a few minutes, when it was obvious the work was well in hand—as it would be when Deuce was present.

Ellie sat beside her, aloof and disdainful, her eyes greedily sizing up the men on horseback, choosing, imagining, lost in a sensual daydream compounded of dust and desire.

Kalida and Jake, however, moved farther over the hill and down its slight incline to a place where they were silhouetted against the sky. Kalida's excitement communicated itself to Jake, as she seemed to watch everything, overpowered by the sheer numbers and the pageantry of

166

the movements. Her hat was tilted back, and she leaned forward in her characteristic way. Jake admired the long straight line of her back and the fact she did not ride sidesaddle. He imagined her strong, firm thighs gripping Malca's flanks, and he envied the horse.

A brisk wind whirled the dust up and around them, obscuring his reverie, and when next he looked, Kalida had dismounted and he was disgusted that he had lost the chance to catch a glimpse of her legs.

She stood on the rise, arms akimbo, looking this way and that, looking—although she didn't admit it—for Deuce, and when her eyes spotted him, she thought, Thank goodness; now I can keep out of his way.

She felt Ardelle's impatience behind her, and Ellie's hazy swoon, and a kind of thick resentment emanating from Jake; but that was a momentary sensation. Her whole attention was fixed on Deuce as he cut through the herd, chasing this calf and that, finally cornering one and laying it low. He was masterful at it, and she was happy to be able to pinpoint exactly where he was and what he was doing.

And she was happy that Ardelle was so annoyed. If there was one thing she had wanted to accomplish with this trip, it was to make Ardelle unsure of the kind of mistress she would make for Sweetland. And Ardelle was champing at the bit; her sensibilities were being assaulted every minute more she sat in that buggy and had to witness the grim work of the branding pen.

Kalida's satisfaction ran deep. Ellie must have fainted, so quiet was she. Exactly the proper response, she thought.

She was aware suddenly of Jake standing next to her. He had to shout over the noise. "Hard to talk."

She nodded agreement and moved closer to him. Their bodies touched and his fevered imagination had her turning just slightly more so that her breasts nudged him—

167

just so he could feel the softness of them. Just . . . But with her standing just so, he could look down at the sweet swell of them, and his memory would supply the rest. He bent his head so that his lips were just touching her ear and inky black tendrils of her hair blew back into his mouth.

"I don't see Deuce."

His words were very clear. And so had been her sight of Deuce's distinctive ramrod posture on horseback. She looked around frantically and still could not see him.

Damn, she thought, moving still closer to Jake to say something to him. Suddenly she was swooped up in the air, close against the sweating flanks of horse and angry man. "Deuce!" But her protest was lost under the sound of the herd and the thud of his stallion's hooves down the incline. They veered left to pound furiously hundreds of yards away from the branding pen, past the chuck wagon and bed wagons, out into the lush brush of the range where, finally, he pulled up, dropped her, and reached down his hand.

"Come up." It was a harsh, autocratic command.

She dusted herself off disgustedly, thoroughly shaken by his piratical abduction and by her fear he might have dropped her at any moment. His anger was palpable. "Why should I?" she snapped crossly.

"Because I'll come get you."

She stared up at him defiantly, her blazing navy eyes shooting sparks, her face flushed with fury. An avenging angel of the range, her hat flopping on her back, her midnight hair wild from the wind, the dust tight in her face, and she found somewhere the nerve to oppose the godalmighty Deuce Cavender! She wondered at herself as she watched him girding for a fight, controlling his temper with an unbending will that, if she had assessed it, might have frightened her still more than his anger.

"Come up, " he repeated inflexibly, and held out his

168

hand again. Kalida slapped it away. She knew that hand. If she braced herself against it and allowed him to draw her up in front of him, that same hand would slide around her and hold her tightly, and soon enough that hand would slide upwards to feel the underside of her breast and, more, to cup the whole. And then those fingers would entice the nipple, and if he did that, she would be captivated by that hand once again.

She never wanted him to touch her breasts again. Her eyes dilated wonderously at his dark expression as she rejected his implacable body and coaxing hand. She never wanted him near her again to give him the chance to touch her in the way that made her totally at his mercy, dissolving with pleasure, willing to acquiesce to his demands. She turned away from him and began defiantly walking away.

He followed slowly, still on horseback. "Heading back to Jake Danton, are you? Do you really think he can protect you from *me?*"

The goading words were too much for her. She turned to face him indignantly. "Do you think I *need* Jake Danton to protect me from you?" she retorted, knowing, just knowing, that response would kindle his simmering rage.

He swung his right leg over the pommel and slid off the saddle in one efficient movement. "Vicious cat," he hissed, taking a step toward her. "Sharp little claws you have"—another step, and she moved backward—"and a soft, strokable body." Still another step, and she moved again. "One only has to caress the cat in just the right spot to tame it." Now he paced toward her inexorably, his face hard and purposeful, his eyes coal-gray, burning with deep fires of intent.

Kalida turned then, even knowing it would be impossible to elude him. She started to run—a futile effort because he reached for her instantly and jerked her back, which threw her off balance. She fell forward, taking him full force with her, landing, face in the grass, with him on top of her.

She writhed beneath him violently and immediately knew it was a mistake. He responded instantly, his hips thrusting tightly against her buttocks so she could feel the hard length of his arousal. "Deuce—"

"No," he growled in her ear, and she thought the worst thing was not being able to see his face, to look into his smoking eyes and read his intentions. She knew what hers were—to get as far from him as she could as fast as possible. She moved her arms slowly downward toward his thighs as her heart began pounding with the fear of not knowing what he was going to do. He was silent above her, heavy, and the wind swirled around them like a cocoon. Her hands inched downward, and she hoped—in vain—that he had not noticed.

But he had. He grasped them almost instantly as they reached to pinch his thighs, and he lifted his body and thrust them beneath, against her bottom, against his iron-rod length where the flat of her palms now rested.

She moved against him and her hands caressed him involuntarily. "Deuce . . . no."

Her plaintive cry did not move him. "Yes," he breathed against her ear, his breath as hot as his growing desire.

"What?" she demanded, trying hard, and unsuccessfully, to hold her body stiff against his.

"I will tame the cat," he murmured, moving his left hand downward, sliding it lightly against what he could feel of her left breast. "I merely rub her here. . . ." His fingers stroked the outward curve softly, patiently, seeking a little further each time, retreating, and seeking again, until she was in a fever to either beg him to stop or demand that he continue. He did neither; she did neither. He merely continued the soft seeking strokes and her body did the rest: Her body demanded the enticements, her body moved alluringly against him, her body wriggled tightly against his hips to feel the length and hardness of his masculinity; and her body somehow of its own volition managed to turn slightly so she could free her breast to his questing fingers, which instantly slid across the sensual swell to the hard, swollen aching nipple thrusting against her crumpled shirt. His fingers surrounded the taut tip and she moaned. He squeezed it and she arched herself against his fingers, and his harsh hoarse voice permeated the swoon of honey that she floated in. "And she rubs herself against my hand, docile as you please, because she knows, my cat, that no one else will handle her in quite the same way. And she knows that my hands know exactly the right spots to feel"—his fingers moved and her whole body spasmed with shooting stars of pleasure "—and just the right spot to fondle. . . ." His fingers moved this time, pulling at her shirt, stripping it and the chemise away from her straining breast, sliding his hand over the naked swell of its creaminess to the taut, yearning tip, surrounding it once again and just gently . . .

"I can't take it," she moaned as her body stretched against him, demanding more.

"Oh, you'll take it, you'll take it and more," he promised harshly, "from me. Only from me, Kalida." He shifted himself slightly, still holding her nipple firmly in his fingers, and moved his right hand, this time urgently, to skim down her body to her skirt, to pull at the rough material, to pull at it until her leg was exposed. And then she felt his hand on the chemise, and then no chemise, and his hand hot on her buttocks, sliding downward to touch and stroke her womanly core, with her own urgent grasp giving him permission, begging him.

And then his questing hand slipped away, and she moaned with need, "Deuce—" But he was already pulling his throbbing shaft from its confinement; he lifted her

171

slightly so that she was braced on her knees, and he covered her, slipping into her with one primal thrust that produced within her a waterfall of sensation, unlike anything she knew. His naked heat within her branded her his. He had no need to say it: she knew it. No one—no one . . . He did not move for moments after he entered her. The iron strength and length of his manhood permeated her whole being. The delicate touch of his fingers on her taut nipple filled her with softness and an unfurling appreciation of his sensitivity.

But after a moment, she found she wanted even more from him and she began to move against him, inviting him to follow her, tantalizing him with the alluring rocking motion of her hips and buttocks. She heard his voice again, a thick growl that surrounded her, entered her. "You're mine, Kalida, mine."

She heard him; he moved in tandem with his words now, and she would never forget, never. Thrust for thrust, her body answered him, writhing against him, tempting him, demanding him to fill her again and again. The creamy feeling thickened inside her and became richer, deeper, eddying inward and outward in soft, thick circles, thicker still, and her body rocked with it, feeling each thrust to its fullest until the final shattering explosion that dispersed fragments of pleasure like pebbles rippling water.

He was deep within her at that moment, and somehow he sensed she did not want him to move. She surrounded and encompassed him; she felt every rock hard inch of him and she felt, just for that instant, like she owned him.

He moved and that sensation dissolved. His urgency for completion was overwhelming, but he did not make the mistake of moving too soon. He held the softness of her billowy breast in his hand, feeling its shape, wondering at its magic, at her magic; he felt her soft buttocks against the hard angle of his hips; he enjoyed the expression of satiation on her face, and he moved then, once he thrust, and twice, hard and harder still, again and again, wishing he could arouse her once more to glorious culmination, feeling her rocking against him and with him even though she was finished. One more thick thrust, and he shuddered with volcanic force deep within her.

And then there was quiet, and the sound of the wind above them, and the heat of the sun beating on them.

He still lay on her, and his hand still held her breast. The grass was cool under her cheek, and she felt expansively warm throughout her whole body.

Sounds permeated her consciousness: the faraway bleating of cattle, Deuce's even breathing as he lay on her, the thrum of his heartbeat slowing down. She became aware of the swirling wind and the hot sun, and a sense of vastness with herself in the middle of it, alone now. The feeling of completeness and satisfaction dissipated. She felt crushed, used. The sensual heat was totally gone, and even Deuce sensed it.

He lifted himself off her, and when she turned, he was dressed and holding out his hand to her. This time she took it, and he pulled her to a sitting position. She looked at him with icy blue eyes and saw he was looking at her still-exposed perfidious breast. She tucked it into the torn chemise mutinously, hating him, despising the power he could wield over her with a mere caress.

Oh no, she thought, she vowed, never again; she could not lose herself like that to him again. She couldn't. She would never let it happen again. She would thwart him, and as she gazed up into his shadowed face and shielded her dust-smarting eyes from the sun, she swore she would make him desire Ellie. Let Ellie be dominated by the brute, be absorbed into him, into Sweetland. She wanted no part of him.

Her fingers sought the buttons of her shirt, but there

were no buttons; he had torn them away. Her sweetly curved lips set grimly as she projected Ardelle's reaction. Ardelle would notice. Ellie would notice. Who else would notice?

She turned to look for the buttons, but in the deep tufts of grass they were hard to find. She stood up resignedly, taking a sweeping blue glance around. She saw limitless sky with scudding clouds, and a long swath of rangeland before her and gently undulating foothills behind. The wind lifted her tangled inky hair and she bent to pick up her hat, and jammed it on her head.

They were utterly alone, she thought, as she tucked her ruined shirt tightly into her skirt. But anyone could have come; anyone could have seen them lying in the cool grass; anyone would have known what she was allowing Deuce to do—what his hands had seduced her into allowing him to do. She felt impotent against his will and his unfettered knowledge of her. He had that weapon in his arsenal all right, and she was helpless to combat it, especially when she was part of the price of a new beginning for her father.

Nonetheless, she resolved, if she could somehow convince him to direct his unwanted attentions elsewhere and if she could alienate Ardelle, she had a chance of saving herself without negating her father's chance.

Her resentful cobalt eyes slanted a look up at Deuce. He was looking at her quizzically as though she were a puzzle he was trying to figure out. "What next?" she asked insolently, and his expression hardened, his eyes turning steely.

Damn her, damn her, damn her, he raged inside. The elemental sense of what they had just shared had not affected her for one moment, while he still felt shaken to the core. "You keep away from Jake Danton," he rapped out at her, and reached for his hat. He whistled sharply to summon his stallion, which pranced restlessly beside them

174

as he grasped her arm and pushed her ahead of him.

She dreaded facing the others. She strode beside him in a fury that she should have been put in such a position. She did not look at him; she never wanted to see him again, a gross impossibility that almost made her smile at the absurdity of it.

The walk back was unbelievably quick, accomplished with not another word said between them. Almost before she realized it, they had crested the slight incline of the hill and the panorama of cattle and men came into view. On the hill, where they seemed not to have moved in that half hour, Ardelle and Ellie still sat like statues in the shadow of the hood of the buggy. Jake Danton, now mounted, stood guard beside them. All three faces turned toward them as they approached.

Ardelle perceived Kalida's stormy face and her mouth tightened. Ellie immediately noticed her disheveled clothing and felt a spurt of envy and resentment, and she could not have told which was the strongest. And Jake's hazel eyes were instantly veiled behind his heavy lids, so as not to reveal the convetousness that possessed him as the details of Kalida's wrinkled skirt and buttonless shirt hit him all at once. His imagination ran riot, even as he calmly dismounted, untied Kalida's horse, and handed it over to her.

Up close, he could see her face was flushed, and the clever tucking of her shirt hardly disguised the fact that it had been torn. He totally ignored Deuce's thunderous expression and watched Kalida mount up with just the right amount of detachment to disguise the intensity of his interest.

And Deuce watched him. If he could have killed him then and there, he thought he would have. Danton's avid scrutiny, covert though it was, was not lost on him.

"I trust you're ready to return home," he barked at Ardelle.

Ardelle threw him a baleful glance, lifted the reins disdainfully, looked at Kalida meaningfully, and set the buggy in motion.

Deuce watched them leave, Danton a few feet beside him, still unmounted. He didn't need to be told to stay. And he knew Deuce would say nothing further to him. After a moment, he swung into his saddle and urged his horse down into the milling herd, leaving Deuce on the rise of the hill staring after the swirling dust.

Ten

It almost seemed as if Ardelle were creating an atmosphere conducive to her rebellion, Kalida thought later. Her disapproval was patent all the way back to Sweetland, and she did not speak to Kalida at all, addressing the very few remarks she made solely to Ellie and sending Kalida very telling glances from time to time that said, as plainly as if she had spoken: This is not the proper behavior for the mistress of Sweetland.

She went reluctantly back to Deuce's room to assess the damage; standing in front of the mirror that Prestina had brought for her, she was appalled by the extent of the visible ravaging.

"We find something for you to change for dinner," Prestina said placidly. "I fix the shirt for you."

Kalida ignored her as she turned this way and that, her cobalt gaze speculative, craftily considering the consequences of *not* changing for dinner. It was another perfect situation. Ardelle would be furious, and Ellie would look even more desirable by comparison.

She pulled the shirt apart a little further so the crumpled chemise was visible. Yes, that would ruffle Ardelle's feathers nicely, she thought with some satisfaction. She ran a hand through her tousled midnight curls. She wouldn't even do her hair. She would leave it as knotted and tangled as the wind had combed it. She would wash, certainly. Her face still felt heated and her hands grubby. The rest . . . There was a grass stain on the front of her skirt, she perceived, not easily discernible or removable, for that matter. The creases were evident, and though no one else could see her torn undergarment, she was very well—too well—aware of it.

In the end, the nature of Ardelle's expression of disapproval more than made up for any discomfiture. "You look," she said slowly as Kalida entered the dining room, "like a pig."

Even Kalida did not expect such a venomous attack and a hot wave of momentary chagrin washed over her. Her back straightened perceptibly as her sparking navy eyes swept over to Ellie, perfection in the muted gold gown of the previous day, bandbox faultless and serene, and perhaps covertly smug at the comparison between their appearances.

Kalida mentally nodded to herself; this had been just what she had hoped for. Her resentment faded, and she said frostily, "I'll take my dinner in the barnyard then," and turned on her heel and exited the room, almost colliding with Prestina, who had been listening.

"What did you do that for?" Prestina demanded.

Kalida stared at her. "Ardelle is a—"

"Don't you go saying nothing you gonna regret, Miss Kalida. I bring you tray, you go on upstairs," Prestina forestalled her. "You do that. Don't you let Mr. Deuce hear you been sassing his aunt and kicking up a rumpus here. Go." She gave Kalida a gentle shove toward the stairs.

Kalida moved, feeling as chastised as a child by its nanny. It didn't matter; she had created the effect she wanted. Ardelle had asked for it, anyway. So had Deuce.

She couldn't understand why she felt so desolated instead of triumphant.

In the morning, there was no evidence that Deuce h
returned the previous night.

In the morning, her rumpled clothing was completely gone, and in its place, spread neatly across the foot of the bed, was a garment she had never seen before—a high-necked plain blue cotton dress, with a narrow draped skirt and several rows of tucking down the bodice for decoration.

Such a ladylike dress, she thought sardonically, touching the material and examining the seams. Madame was a fast worker, undoubtedly urged on to finish the first item in Kalida's new Ardelle-ordained wardrobe. She had probably worked the whole night to stitch up this one dress so that Kalida might have something "proper" to wear. Something demure and constrained. Something that would utterly restrain her vital nature.

She fingered the row of round black buttons that marched up the bodice. The only good thing, she thought, a barrier to keep Deuce's hands away from her traitorous body. He would have a devil of a time undoing *those* in the throes of desire. Surely the time it would take to undo them would quench anyone's passion aborning. The notion made her smile. She had to wear it; there was nothing else. But that didn't mean she had to bind herself up in the fine lawn underthings that lay beneath it. Or wear the petticoats that Prestina had dredged up from somewhere, for it was a physical impossibility for Madame to have made those too.

She examined her hair. She had combed out most of the tangles last night after her bath. Prestina had insisted she take one to cool off her body and her "soul." Yes, well her soul was hot and sorely tried at this point. Her father was somewhere in Bozeman making all kinds of arrangements she knew nothing of, and in fact had no right to know anything of, and she was stuck at Sweetland, to all intents and purposes a "thing" to be used at will by its master.

She ran the brush through her black curls with more

force than necessary. Her hair was behaving willfully, flying every which way, as crackly as her temper. Her face, in the mirror, appeared drawn to her, and her eyes unnaturally large and glittering with blazing blue fire. She already knew she was after someone today. She was going to make trouble. She started talking to herself, but it did no good. She did not like feeling helpless and impotent, unsure and dependent. She wanted her father and their ranch back; she wanted things the way they had been before the fire.

Perhaps, she thought, I should see the damage for myself. And the idea calmed her. She should have done it days ago. Perhaps viewing the finality of it would reconcile her to the situation now.

She braided her hair briskly, thrust her feet into the too-tight work boots she had been wearing rather than the footwear that had been provided with the dress, and slipped the dress over her naked body. Without the undergarments and the petticoats, it hung on her. It flattened her breasts. It dragged on the floor.

She cursed. It was deliberate; it had to be that Madame had designed it in just this way, and that Ardelle would not accede to her requirement of shirtwaists and skirts rather than formal morning and afternoon dresses, which she *never* wore before coming to Sweetland. She had had one "good" dress before then, one dress that she utilized for all occasions that had required more than a skirt and shirt—weddings, parties, trips to Bozeman for visiting, or entertaining prospective buyers for her father.

But never for everyday wear; it just wasn't practical on the ranch, where everything had to be dun-colored to hide the dust and washable when the dirt caked too thickly on the hem or the collar.

This was impossible. She tugged off the dress, fumbling at the interminable buttons, and resentfully threw on the underwear and petticoats, and finally the dress.

Miraculously, it hung precisely right, the buttons now fitting gently across the swell of her breasts and curving sweetly in at the waist, to flow over her hips and swag up into the merest suggestion of a bustle.

Too suggestive, she thought angrily, grabbing up the narrow black waistband that tied around her waist to trail its ends over the slightly exaggerated back of the dress.

Oh, Madame was talented indeed, she fumed, as she made her way downstairs. She knew exactly how to subdue the body, and Ardelle was working mightily on the soul. Between the two of them — and Deuce — what chance did she have?

Ardelle was dressed all in white today, which emphasized the pallor of the face she turned to Kalida as she walked into the dining room once again. Something flared in the depths of her sherry eyes as they swept over Kalida, and then she nodded approvingly. "Just so, Kalida; do sit down and have breakfast with us now."

Kalida bridled, and then she noticed Ellie at the head of the table and sank into the nearest chair. Dear Ellie; she did not need her help. Ellie was going after Sweetland all on her own, Kalida perceived, or else why would Madame have altered her dove-gray dress so drastically? And subtly. Rows and rows of lace cascaded across the bodice now, directing the eye toward her bosom and the discreet vee of the redesigned neckline. And Ellie's hair, once again flowing down her back and drawn away from her face, emphasized her deep dark opaque eyes and her excellent cheekbones.

Oh yes, Ellie was firming herself up for something, Kalida thought, and she would be happy to help her. She nodded to Prestina, who had brought the coffee and a platter with biscuits and bacon, and nibbled at these while she considered Ellie and Ardelle's paper-white appearance.

181

"I am sure," Ardelle said after a while, "that you are much more comfortable in that neatly fitted dress than you have been in that ill-fitting shirt and skirt you were wearing."

"Well, actually I'm not," Kalida said firmly, calmly, not the slightest bit rudely, bud Ardelle reacted just as if she had responded snidely.

Her eyes flashed red fire, and she turned back to Ellie and murmured, "I don't know why Deuce persists," as if to herself; but of course she was speaking to Ellie. She and Ellie were seemingly very cozy.

Kalida hid a smile. "Neither do I," she said loudly, not pretending she hadn't heard Ardelle's comment.

Ardelle's pale face swiveled back to her. "I hope we can convince him then," she said plainly. "All you need do is keep up this reprehensible behavior."

"Thank you; I'll keep that suggestion in mind," Kalida said seriously. So Ardelle was beginning to understand. Except, she believed that this was Kalida's true nature. All to the good then. Better and better, in fact. Ellie was looking like a veritable queen of taste, tact, and propriety next to her. Surely Ardelle would bring Deuce to see that. And with her new stylish look in her hair and clothing, she seemed younger, more vibrant. More attractive.

More sensual.

Where did that thought come from? Kalida wondered, not liking it at all. She took a quick sip of her coffee and scalded her tongue. Sensual. Really. Ellie Dean.

But that's what Deuce would want, her implacable inner self pointed out pragmatically. Wouldn't he? Deuce would never tolerate a statue as the mistress of Sweetland. How many times has he told you he wants a willing, loving woman in his arms? Which hasn't been you. And could be someone else.

I don't like that thought, her mind shouted back.

Unnecessary to shout, the inner voice chided.

Damn it, Kalida clamped down on her unruly ruminations, I will not think about that.

She hid her harassed expression behind the coffee cup again and listened halfheartedly to Ardelle and Ellie discussing the gardening chores they were scheduled to accomplish that morning.

Ellie's dark head bent forward respectfully as she nodded and responded to Ardelle's words, but her eyes, her lambent glowing black eyes, were fixed pointedly on Kalida, as if she were saying, Here is how to get on with Ardelle, and why you are ruining your chance here, I'll never understand. But I'm willing to take up the slack. Very willing.

Kalida met the mesmerizing black stare defiantly. She was perfect at the head of the table, perfect with her ease and grace at directing the table and pouring the coffee. Perfect gracing the parlor waiting Deuce after his hard day on the range, pushing aside his hard-muscled body in its grimy, sweaty clothes as being too cowboyish for her parlor, so he must go bathe and change. Yes, she would do that, and she would be so particular and dainty about herself that anything else between them had to be impossible.

Or did it?

Ellie's hot eyes glittered knowingly as Kalida pursued her scenario. Ellie would have a separate bedroom and a closet full of clothes, and she would perform her chores without perspiring or wrinkling a cuff or dragging a hem in the dirt. And she would bring that cool capability to her bed, where once a month, she might allow Deuce to . . .

To what? Touch her? Undress her? Caress her marble skin, play with her, reach for her in the same way he had commanded her, Kalida?

No! The picture would not form; it just wasn't possible. Kalida smiled, a mysterious cryptic smile that wafted across her firm lips for just a second, and it squelched Ellie's confidence for one brief triumphal moment. Then Ellie squared her shoulders and stood up, throwing a challenge across the long table at her rival.

Kalida was jolted by the sight of her standing there, her body slender and curvaceously suggestive in the refurbished dress. God, Madame had been a regular machine during the night, Kalida thought ruefully. Or perhaps Ellie had done it herself. Ellie was, after all, a widow; she would have had to devise many economizing ways to make ends meet. How fortuitous she happened to be at the Rylands' when the fire broke out!

These linked but unsequential thoughts were broken into by Ardelle's impatient voice. "Kalida!" Again her face took on that obstinate disapproving look, for it was obvious she had startled Kalida. "You'll take gloves and basket and join us in the garden." An order, brooking no protest.

"I think not," Kalida said, wiping her mouth carefully and standing also. "I think I will go for a walk." She turned her back on Ardelle then and proceeded out of the room to the hallway and the front door.

She was shaking. She had fully expected Ardelle's long, omnipresent cane to snake out and hook her around her legs, tripping her to detain her. But nothing so melodramatic happened. There was silence behind her, and silence before her. And as always, the ever-present sense of latent energy. But none of it was apparent in the placid fields surrounding the house, none of the commotion of the range, or even the smooth machinery in Prestina's capable hands that made sure the house functioned smoothly.

Kalida stepped out onto the porch. So different from her own home, she thought with a pang. There she had done so much of the work. She had only to look at her hands to measure the depth and worth of her capabilities. Her father had relied on her so much, on her love of the

184

land and the joy she had taken in the mundane chores of the ranch.

Papa should have had a son, she thought. But he hadn't; he had had one all-fired stubborn daughter who loved to ride and hustle cattle, whom he had sold to finance his future. She had had great worth all around, she concluded as she turned right toward the barn rather than have to pass the garden where she was sure Ardelle and Ellie were working assiduously in the most ladylike way possible.

And, after all, Papa had to rebuild now. He couldn't possible *like* having to start again, with both house and herd, with having to renegotiate his life all over again. As she meandered past the barn and stables, she felt a huge wave of sympathy for what fate had dealt her father, and she paused a moment to whistle for Malca, who was prancing around the corral. Kalida climbed up on the bars of the fence to scratch Malca's ears and whisper assurances that she herself did not feel.

The change had not affected Malca. Malca did not have to build a new life, Kalida reflected as she continued on through the narrow pathways of the corral. But I will. I will have to. After all, there was nothing wrong with Deuce—except he was arrogant, high-handed, a bully, stubborn, dominating, and his damned hands kept getting in the way.

"No," she murmured, not even aware she had said it out loud; it was a negation of what she knew was not possible—making a new life at Sweetland.

But a strong, sure voice contradicted her insolently, "Yes," and her preoccupied gaze swung up and glanced off of Deuce's amused gray eyes. He was bare to the waist, with a towel slung around his muscular shoulders, and he was leaning lazily against the bunkhouse door. Beside him was a barrel of water which, from the puddles on the ground around it, looked as if he had been almost bathing in it. "I keep telling you," he added, still with that suggestive lilt in his tone, "yes, but you just don't listen, Kalida."

She flared up immediately. "You just don't hear, Deuce Cavender, any damned thing your highness doesn't want to."

He made a regretful sound. "I sure thought a contented sun-warmed kitty was strolling into my front yard this morning, pert and pretty with a nice new dress and maybe a slightly better humor; but I always seem to be out of luck, don't I, Kalida? You're always going to present the face of a lady tomcat, just spitting for a fight."

"Definitely *not* a candidate for mistress of Sweetland," Kalida agreed sweetly, changing her tack entirely as he moved forward aggressively. "I entirely agree. So since you have the cows and my father's life in your hands, you can rest easy that power is yours; and, if you really need it, a more willing woman is available for you right in your very home, one who urgently wants what you can provide for her."

He stopped dead at that one. His face closed up, except that his eyes became steely and reflective. "Yes, I have power and I have you," he said finally, "and I'm not giving either up. I don't care who the hell else is dreaming in my house."

"No, you don't hear," Kalida said sadly, and made one move forward, which incited him instantly to grasp her arms and prevent her from advancing.

"It's *you* who doesn't hear *me*," he gritted, his fingers digging deeply into her flesh. "And you can't see me for the fog in front of your eyes, either. You're a fool, Kalida. A stupid fool. And a provoking vixen. You think your defiant tongue will protect you from me, as well as you think you can entice every man jack on this place. But I tell you, you'll get nowhere any which way you try to outwit me, Kalida, and you'll do it at your own expense."

his mouth twisting on hers, seeking to overpower the words and the woman. He pulled her against him, and her other hand slid into the curly crisp hair on his chest, tugging it as his tongue invaded her mouth and sought hers. He did not play with her now; he wanted only to dominate her, to incite her passion, to make her wild with wanting.

The thick, round little buttons on her dress pressed into his bare skin, and he hated them. His hands began the torturous task of finding their way to her bare skin. There was none. His heated caresses felt the silky smoothness of fabric, draped and fitted beguilingly, a total impediment to his feeling her nakedness. He groaned in frustration. "Say yes now, Kalida," he commanded, removing his burning mouth from hers.

"No," she answered, her lips quirking slightly at his vain attempts to undress her. Perfect! Fifty more dresses like it, she thought as his mouth crushed against hers again, reaching for her, delving deep, nipping at the tip of her tongue as she kept withdrawing and then seeking his. Games, all games, and yet the yearning unfurling inside her was real.

No! Now her consciousness denied it, even as she savored his kiss and demanded his caresses. Damn, he aroused her so quickly just by his sensual, erotic kisses. She had to beware of his ravishing tongue as well as his enchanter's hands. And she was the one standing in the barnyard, allowing him to devour her in the most enticingly arousing way. She was almost at the brink of something. Her hands moved, she knew they moved; they were feeling his chest and his shoulders and the texture of the muscles corded beneath them. And she felt him pressing against her, ready to possess her.

This was impossible, she wanted to cry—impossible place, impossible dress. She couldn't reach for him, he couldn't feel her, not an inch of naked skin except her neck and face; she could lift her skirts, and he could ease the ache in her there, that way. But . . . no!

She felt herself reacting by pulling away. She didn't want that, she didn't want it that way. She was panting with the force of her yearning. His lips were an inch away from hers, touching her in quick little motions on her cheeks and lips, her chin, her neck, delving into her mouth again, kissing her tongue, biting her lips. "Kalida . . ." Her name was a hoarse rasp on his lips as he waited for her to say what next would be done. But he did not ease the iron grip of his arms holding her, and his kisses did not burn her the less. He wanted her there and then, but he did not demand it. He would not force her.

She wrenched away, her whole body heaving with the torture of unfulfilled desire. "No!" she ground out, hanging onto one shred of her heretofore firm resolve. "No." Her voice became steadier as anger overtook her emotion. "Not again. Not again, Deuce. Don't touch me again."

His eyes burned charcoal at her words. "That's a joke, you wanton bitch." Hell, his anger was every bit as steep and grinding as hers; she was denying every last thing between them once again, and he couldn't take that. He was going to force her to her knees one way or another, and he knew just how he wanted to do it and what he would do once he got her there. "Don't touch you. That's why you didn't walk away, right, that's why you stayed here, just demanding to have me put my hands on you. Don't touch you. That's *all* you want, you selfish fool, and I wouldn't touch you now if you were the last woman in Montana." He swung away from her in a towering fury and disappeared into the bunkhouse.

She watched him go, calm in some center that she did not know she possessed, undisturbed by the words; they were the very words she had wanted to hear, and now she had them and she felt a shimmer of contentment.

Perhaps now he would realize she was serious and he

would leave her alone. It was just what she wanted. Just exactly what she wanted.

She felt like a weight had been lifted from her, tension dropping like a huge yoke from her shoulders. She leaned against the bunkhouse wall, breathing deeply.

"Miss Kalida." A tentative voice broke into her reflections. She looked up, startled, and met the speaking hazel gaze of Jake Danton. "You're all right?" he asked with concern, hiding a certain excitement in himself at what he had just witnessed and what he had felt as he watched. And Deuce's words that confirmed everything he had felt about her — everything.

"Yes, of course," Kalida said firmly. "Why do you ask?" she added, a slightly sinking feeling inside her wondering whether he had seen Deuce mauling her in that appalling way.

"You looked out of sorts there for a minute; maybe it's the heat?" Jake suggested, wanting now to allay the fear he read in her cobalt gaze. He couldn't let on he understood, not yet, even though he had heard Deuce's words very clearly and had seen her responding to Deuce very, very clearly. Though why she had trussed herself up in that costume on a day like today, especially if she had intended to entice a man like Deuce, was beyond him. But now Deuce had disappeared in a rage, and he was alone with her. Jake was willing to give her time to get used to him, to be assured she could trust him. Nothing threatening. He hoped he could hold his desire in check. Just the thought of that ungirdled luscious body bared solely for his delectation was enough to send his male senses spiraling to new heights. He hardly heard her answer; he inferred it from her expression.

"Yes, the heat," she agreed. "The dress is too confining."

Oh, it is indeed, he thought gleefully, bending his head to catch her next words and to get a better look at the swell of her breasts under the tight bodice and march of glittering buttons. "You should have worn a hat," he chided gently, all concern for her predicament.

"I should have," she confirmed lightly, drawing tightly on her good manners to keep her talking rather than returning abruptly to the house. One more comment, and then she could leave. "But tell me, I thought you and Deuce were staying on at the branding corral."

"We slept there, sure, but Deuce is recording the first tallies this morning; then we go back. Tomorrow we bring down the mommas and their calves. Maybe you might want to watch that." I hope to God you want to watch that, he thought, remembering the look of her astride her horse, thighs gripping its flanks, breasts jouncing with every movement.

"I might," she said noncommittally. "I appreciate you telling me about it. And now I think I had better get back to the house."

He nodded wordlessly and watched the sway of her hips beneath the provocative draping of the dress. Suddenly she turned back to him as if she had had an unexpected thought. And in fact it did abruptly occur to her that he had been with her father when he had gone back to the ranch, and she felt an inexplicable urge to ask him what it was like there—now. "You've been to my home since—"

"You wouldn't want to go there," he broke in roughly, "honest you wouldn't." Hell, what am I doing? he wondered. He took off his hat and wiped his forehead with his shirt sleeve. She had flinched at his words, but her expression firmed up again. She looked at him with those glimmery navy eyes and said, "Yes I would."

"Miss Kalida . . ."

"Truly, Jake. I should see it, I should."

"Maybe." And maybe she was looking for an excuse to be alone with someone now that Deuce had tossed her aside. "Maybe you should," he agreed, his voice becoming hoarse with that consideration.

"Maybe you could come with me," she went on recklessly, and she knew why: She wanted to strike back at Deuce. But she didn't care. Deuce would never let her get three feet off the property; didn't he as much as say so? And hadn't Jake offered his help?

"It isn't pretty there any more," he said, warning her, warning himself that he should at least make a slight attempt to discourage her to ease his conscience. The same conscience that would replay his dreams tonight once again, dreams of her, framed in a window, but this time beckoning to him, and when he was within, slowly revealing her nakedness only to him.

"I need to go back," she said firmly.

"Well sure, I can see that," he agreed finally. "In a couple of days, Miss Kalida; I'm sure I can work a couple of hours free. We'll go."

"Thank you, Jake." She turned away, trembling. She knew, really she knew, exactly what she was doing. She went over it in her mind as she strode back to the house. She was playing on Jake's sympathy for her and Deuce's ridiculous anger about it, that was what she was doing. And she wasn't in the least afraid of touching off an explosion.

Deuce had preceded her into the parlor by only a minute or two, she deduced by the tail end of Ardelle's comment, ". . . didn't expect to see you so soon."

"I'm running an initial tally this morning," he said brusquely.

Ardelle's voice again: "Any trouble last night?" Her words held just the right note of disinterest, as though she were aware he would recoil from any further mention of the elusive thieves that had decimated the Santa Linaria stock. It was a sore point with him, although Kalida was not aware of it, but she made the connection instantly as he answered, "No, curiously; we didn't run a patrol last night either, and everything was fine. Too fine. We moved out the Linaria, and I'm not telling anyone where. That's the last of that, and I'm wiring up the boundary after we get this load to market."

"Good idea," Ardelle said briefly. "Do you need help on the tally?"

"Ellie can help me," Deuce said, turning then and looking straight at Kalida, who was standing in the frame of the parlor door. He had finished dressing in a thin chambray shirt and silver tooled belt that emphasized his hips. His hair was freshly brushed back, and his face was as hard as stone. His eyes, however, burned with that dangerous charcoal light as he motioned to Ellie, who glided after him demurely, throwing Kalida a snide sideways back glance as she followed him down the center hallway to the old house and his office.

Kalida stood still as a statue watching them, happy at the successful conclusion of her first-stage plan—that Deuce was turning to Ellie. She was happy. It made her supremely happy to see him choose Ellie to help him.

She couldn't let her expression reveal even a nuance of her agony. She turned back to Ardelle, who was already halfway across the room on her way out. She brushed past Kalida without a word, leaving the young woman alone with the stiff furniture and the stiffer silence.

She sank onto the little velvet sofa. What were they doing in that room? Her imagination began percolating with speculation, and she did not like the direction her thoughts were taking at all. She got up restlessly and began pacing. They were merely conducting business. They were closeted alone in that room counting cows. Counting calves. He was counting and she was writing, listing the numbers and the brands. The syndicate members. Of course. He was not bending over her to check her neat flawless handwriting nor staring down the vee of her neckline at the swell of her breasts. He was detailing numbers and she was copying them down and that was all.

She stared out the window that overlooked the front porch and the extended green fields in front. A timber fence enclosed the pasture, to separate it from the dirt and gravel drive in front of the house. She saw it, and she didn't see it, as her imagination ran riot.

And what if he put his big hand on her fragile shoulder in a complimentary gesture and he leaned over her all at once, to check again what he had said. Perhaps he had made a mistake; he was probably reading from roughly annotated crumpled pieces of paper that he had detailed right in the branding corral. And what if his hand gently slid downward and ever so discreetly brushed the tip of her breast — what then?

What then was didn't bear thinking about. She put her hands over her ears almost as though she were shutting out voices rather than obstreperous thoughts.

And there went Ardelle, limping quickly across the drive, in a hurry to get somewhere — unusual for her, she noted abstractedly, deterred for a moment and interested in what Ardelle might be doing outside. She was acting very strangely for a woman whose actions and opinions were usually so precise. She had made her way to a point midway between the house and the back field, which was still visible from the parlor window, and then she paused. And she waited, her cane tucked up under her arm. She just stood and waited.

And Kalida watched her, intrigued now, her thoughts deflected from what could be going on in Deuce's office. Why would Ardelle be standing in the middle of the drive and waiting?

A small mantel clock ticked away the minutes as Ardelle waited patiently and Kalida watched. After a while, Ardelle moved forward a few steps, and then back, almost as if she were wrestling with a decision to leave.

And then her face lifted and she moved forward again, quickly this time, and moments later hailed a rider who was coming from the stables. As he came closer, Kalida identified Jake Danton by the way he sat the horse.

Well, Jake . . . Of course Ardelle would need to speak to him occasionally about something.

He bent over courteously so Ardelle should not have to shout, and she said what seemed to be very few words to him before he straightened up, wheeling his mount back in the direction he had come, and Ardelle turned back to the house.

So much for intrigue, Kalida thought sardonically. The only intrigue that was going on was in that office in the old house, and now Ardelle was on her way back. Kalida's mind immediately jumped back to the possible reasons for their taking such a long time writing up a tally.

Prestina poked her head in briefly. "What you doing here by yourself?" she asked kindly.

"Thinking," Kalida said. The short, sharp answer had its effect: Prestina withdrew abruptly, and Kalida felt instantly ashamed of herself. She ran after her and apologized. "I am at wit's end anyway; look at me. I look like some porcelain doll that Miss Ardelle wants to keep on the mantel. I can't ride; I can't do chores. All I can do is stand still and let that obnoxious Madame measure me for more dresses like this one."

Prestina chuckled sympathetically, and Kalida looked at her consideringly for a moment. "Would you help me?" she demanded.

Prestina's open cheerful face became suspicious instantly. "You are trying to turn this house upside down, Miss Kalida. What you want me to do?"

"I need a skirt and a shirtwaist. I will absolutely

collapse if I have to wear this dress another minute."

"You will have to," Prestina said darkly. She ran her eye over the neatly fitting blue dress. "This is a good dress for you; I am helping Madame make the rest, you know. We'll see, we'll see." She turned away without committing herself further, and Kalida threw herself back into the parlor in a fury of frustration.

No one wanted to help her—no one except Jake Danton. Damn, what a situation. Deuce was busy doing who knew what to Ellie in the office, Ardelle was busy giving instructions to Jake and the dressmaker, and Prestina was sewing underwear or something. And she had to twiddle her thumbs, awaiting everyone's pleasure and everyone's decision about her life!

It was so unfair that she felt like beating down the door to that stupid little office and killing Deuce. He had no right to buy her and then go off and make love to Ellie Dean.

Later, she did not know how she contained herself. It seemed she sat in that parlor for hours before anyone else joined her, and it made her intensely determined to change what was happening and take some charge of herself.

But while she waited, she could not control her feelings or her imagination. She was tortured with visions of Deuce's hands all over Ellie Dean's willing body as they set aside the puny pieces of paper that were a mere excuse for them to closet themselves alone together, an excuse for Deuce to pay her back for denying she wanted him and to prove to her how easy it was—even if it was *her* suggestion—for him to find someone who did.

But she *didn't* want him; she just didn't want Ellie to have him either. But since he was so arrogantly, bullheadedly *male,* he would, of course, have to prove her wrong. And since Ellie was so blatantly hungry and desperate, she would grab any chance. Forget that she, Kalida, had concocted such a scenario for them so she could be left alone. It was becoming obvious, in point of fact, that nothing would change. Deuce would just keep her *and* Ellie.

That conclusion made her shriek with rage. She would kill Ellie Dean first before she would stay in the same house with Deuce making love to *her*. Doing the same things — my God — to Ellie that he had done with her . . .

Ellie was no temptress, one rational part of her mind pointed out with some sanity as a molten blue haze threatened to envelop her brain.

Neither am I, Kalida thought, and look at how he stormed my body with his caresses and his male dominance. Look at how hard I fought. What if Ellie succumbed so easily, in the same way; what if he were sliding her dress off her right at this very moment? . . .

"Kalida, dear —"

That oily voice . . . Kalida looked up, her eyes hot navy pools, and there was Ellie, smiling conspiratorially at her, her black eyes glittering knowingly, as if she saw every moment of Kalida's torment and was glad of it.

"We have lunch and fittings this afternoon," Ellie said, straightening up, and Kalida searched every detail of her appearance for some sign of disarray. Oh, but Ellie was clever; she would never do anything blatant. It would be some small sign, something only Kalida might notice.

An unfastened button on her bodice. Two. Kalida counted them; had Ellie been in such a hurry then? Or was it a lie? She stood up abruptly. It didn't matter now. It was war once again between her and Ellie, and this time Deuce — not her father — was the prize.

Eleven

There were no surprises for them in the array of dresses awaiting their inspection after lunch. Madame bustled around them, holding up each one to measure against size, coloration, suitability. Of necessity, the garments were simple — as simple as Kalida's blue dress — and her limited wardrobe was the one Madame had worked on first, since she had the least suitable apparel. Madame had altered the ready-made gray dress originally chosen by Ellie and had stitched up two more besides, a simple blue and white checked gingham pinafore, with white sleeves, and a blue plaid cotton that was trimmed with a white eyelet collar and undercuffs.

These suited her much better, Kalida thought as she tried on the gingham. They were not as fitted and they allowed her a freedom of movement — the freedom to breathe, she amended ruefully, taking that one off and sliding the mournful gray over her head. Even that, with the addition of a little trim and a little letting out, fit her better, and she felt a small jolt of gratitude, which she did not expect to feel, for the kindness and prosperity of the family that could afford to rescue its neighbors and never count the cost.

But then, she was also sure that her father would repay this benevolence as one of his first obligations, so that accepting Deuce's bounty did not trouble her at all. She lifted her arms and allowed Madame to wrap around her

199

waist a length of material that was the color of mud and the texture of wool. This was to be basted into the first of her skirts. Madame pinned, Ardelle and Ellie watched, and Prestina assisted quietly and capably.

After, Kalida had no choice but to button herself back into the wretched fitted blue, and then, with a nod of satisfaction at its fit, Madame turned her attention to Ellie. "For whom we must create but the one extra dress, since Madamoiselle already has the gold, the gray, and the rose that seem already made for her."

At this juncture, Madame chased Kalida out of the room, as Ellie required, her black eyes gleaming maliciously, and Kalida thankfully retreated.

No one was watching her now, she thought as she made her way downstairs from the bedrooms. She could just jump on Malca and escape.

Escape; yes, it did feel like a prison. The situation with her father and Deuce, the house, the dress, Ardelle's disapproval—all strands of a tightening web that circumstance was weaving around her, constricting her, controlling her, making her feel like the only course was for her to run for her life.

As she wandered through the open porch door she chastised herself for being fanciful. The heat hit her like a wall. The drive lay ahead of her. She had only to set her feet on it and start walking.

Yes, with nowhere to go and no money to support myself, she thought; and any alternative situation would probably lead to more unpleasant consequences than she could ever suffer at Deuce's hands. She had to make the best of this situation. That was the conclusion she had been avoiding these past weeks.

She saw Jake walking up the path, leading his mount, looking as though he were heading for the house. He seemed preoccupied, and when he lifted his head he was startled to see her. After a moment's hesitation, he hailed her, and when he drew up beside her, he took off his hat respectfully. "On my way to the bedding ground," he told her. "The boys will be spending the night there, now the cutting's done, Deuce too; I came to see if he was ready."

"I haven't seen him," Kalida said pleasantly, forbearing to say if she had, she would have done something awful.

"You be sure to come out to the Morgan field tomorrow, Miss Kalida, and watch them mommas and calves come home."

"I want to."

"Deuce is set to start off the drive tomorrow, so maybe after that, I'll have a couple of hours and we can take a quick trip over to your old home."

"I would like that too," Kalida said, warming up to his clear hazel eyes that regarded her so admiringly and courteously. He smiled, and she noticed for the first time, in the bright clear light, the lines that crinkled around his eyes and the dimple in his cheek. He really was very likeable, and she liked him very much at that moment.

He put on his hat and it shaded his suddenly sharpened eyes. "You wouldn't have happened to have seen Miss Ardelle, would you?" he asked offhandedly.

"She's up with Ellie, why?"

"No moment, Miss Kalida. Tell Deuce, if you see him, I've gone on ahead with the provisions. I'll see you tomorrow." He touched the brim of his hat in farewell; he had no time to linger with Kalida Ryland, much as he would have liked to. Business first, he thought swinging gracefully up onto his saddle. Get the calves in and the money herd out, and then I can pursue my fancies. Then, I'll have all the time in the world.

Kalida stared after his retreating figure, perplexed. She did not have the time, however, to follow an elusive thought that had occurred to her, as Ardelle's sharp voice intruded. "Was that Jake Danton?" She sounded cross, and Kalida wondered why.

"It was, and he said it wasn't important." She turned to look at Ardelle, who was standing over her right shoulder.

"And Deuce?" Ardelle barked in her ear.

"Hasn't left yet," Deuce interpolated behind them in his dry, flat voice that Kalida hated.

She spun away as he came down the porch steps, his bedroll slung over his shoulder.

"I'm on my way now," he said unnecessarily.

"Who's moving them out?" Ardelle asked.

"Hayes and Jenkins are taking them, and their boys. We're going to head up to Stoneface Ridge, probably at the end of this week, and bring back the Ryland herd."

"And the calves?"

"About a dozen Linaria babies, strong and looking good. Jake's crew will nurse them for the week."

"And you've put the Linaria bulls in hiding," Ardelle finished caustically, not even looking at him. Her sherry eyes were fixed on a point above his head, somewhere far away in a place he couldn't see, and Kalida could not understand. Not yet, at any rate.

"Necessary precaution," Deuce said briefly. "Just for the week; I can't take any more losses there, you know that."

"I know it," she said grimly.

"Where's Ellie?" he asked, effectively changing that subject. His steel-gray eyes raked over Kalida, who still stood uncomfortably by the porch steps looking as if she would rather be anywhere else but in his vicinity.

Damn her to hell, he cursed exasperatedly; she needed a damned week and more to ruminate on her sins. If they all came up and slapped her in the face, then she might be able to admit feelings she was hiding and desires she would not let herself feel. But oh no, the proud, almighty Miss Kalida Ryland was too fine for all that. She would let him go any which way, but she would never let him

202

touch her within, in the place where the fire burned. He felt as though he would never get in there, and he wondered whether he wanted to.

His frosty gray gaze discomfitted her, and he knew it from the way she was fidgeting. No memories of any kisses in the barnyard here; she effectively put away the reality of her dizzying response. Only he would remember, alone at night on the range with just the lowing of the cattle and the crooning of the nighthawkers to keep him company.

Goddamn hell, I waste too much energy wanting, he thought angrily, slapping his hat against his denim-clad muscular thigh.

"Cheer up, Kalida," he said abruptly. "I won't be sleeping with you tonight."

Her startled cobalt gaze rammed into him with its anger and resentment of his audacious comment. And to say it out loud in front of Ardelle! She clenched her fists to keep from swinging at him. "So happily *I* can get some sleep," she snapped back before she thought. The words sounded brazen, inviting by their very denial of what he implied. His firm mouth quirked consideringly as her lips tightened in dismay.

Ellie made her entrance just then, smiling and purring, Kalida might have described it as she turned away and stalked to the far end of the porch. She peeked over her shoulder. Deuce was saying something to Ellie, and Ellie was smiling. She grasped his muscular forearms and stood on her toes to kiss him, right on the mouth. A lingering kiss, one he answered deliberately, willfully, Kalida thought angrily, because he knew she was watching.

Fine. Ellie was perfect for him; hadn't she been saying that since they had come to Sweetland. Let him trample her. Let him swallow her up alive. Let him try.

She leaned against the porch railing as telling heat washed through her body. She couldn't reconcile the fact that she didn't want that — and she wanted it, all at the same time.

For the first time since they had arrived, Sweetland seemed bereft of life. It was just the three women, Prestina, and several aging ranch hands to oversee things and protect them if anything untoward happened.

It was eerie sitting in the parlor by lamplight, with Ellie doing some inconsequential embroidery, Ardelle sewing something else with detached intensity, Prestina sitting by the fire with mending, and Kalida herself pacing restlessly.

Ardelle was ready to slap her. Her restiveness was like a thunderbolt crackling through the peaceful atmosphere. "Sit down, Kalida, for heaven's sake. I am out of patience with you. You would think you never spent an evening at home at the Ryland ranch. However did you keep yourself occupied then? Your poor father!" she clucked, and bent her head back to her work.

At the ranch, Kalida thought, sinking into her favorite little sofa. It seemed a lifetime ago. What *did* she used to do? She used to do sewing — mending, as Prestina was doing now; she used to read. She used to keep a diary, but that had been burned to ashes. She used to play cards with Papa. She used to practice her guitar, but there was nothing at Sweetland that made music. Nothing. She couldn't remember what else, but she was absolutely sure every evening had been eventfully filled when she had been back at her father's ranch. But Ardelle would never believe it.

And she herself could hardly credit it. It seemed the wealthier one was, the less one had available to occupy oneself. It was another vision of her possible future that she did not like one bit.

She got up abruptly. "I'm riding out to Morgan field tomorrow," she announced defiantly, daring Ardelle to

204

forbid her to do it.

Ardelle looked up at her placidly. Only the faintest spark of red fire in her eyes betrayed her annoyance. But she only nodded and said, "If you must. How fortunate Madame is working on your skirt. And how nicely it will suit the occasion."

And how lovely, Kalida found when she flounced up to Deuce's room in a rage, that it was stitched and ready for her to wear, lying neatly across the foot of the bed with a fresh shirtwaist, and Prestina anxiously hovering, waiting for her to try it on.

"Yes," she said with satisfaction as Kalida modeled it for her, "that will do you nicely for riding. Mr. Deuce say you intend to ride, and how can you with that tight blue dress you cannot move in."

"*Deuce* said?" Kalida echoed, astonished.

"Mr. Deuce said," Prestina confirmed, taking the skirt and draping it over the back of the upholstered rocking chair. She turned back to Kalida. "Mr. Deuce, he want you to be happy."

Kalida shook her head and began unfastening the pins that held her inky black hair in its tight braid. "He wants me to be a possession," she contradicted, "someone else he has in his power and under his control. Something to use, to tell what to do and when to do it."

Prestina's smooth brown face came up behind her in the mirror. Her liquid eyes spoke volumes; they emanated pity, and Kalida's back stiffened.

"You misunderstand," Prestina murmured. "I have known him since he was a boy."

"Yes," Kalida snapped, "and I have known him since I was a girl. I don't misunderstand. I know exactly what he's like. I always have. He hasn't changed."

"No," Prestina said low.

"And he never will." Her sparking navy eyes challenged Prestina. Prestina's expression did not change; she shook her head and turned away, leaving Kalida to stare at her own rebellious face in the mirror and whisper, "He never will," to the reflection that was perfectly sure the words were true.

Her inner awareness that there was work to be done awakened her at dawn, and she arose with a sense of purpose that had been sorely lacking since she had come to Sweetland.

She thought about the calving all morning as she washed, dressed, ate breakfast alone, and prepared to ride out to Morgan range with Old Bruno, one of the three hands who looked after the house and pastures when Deuce and his crew were on roundup. And it seemed to her that, barring the calf herd was large, nurturing the calves was something she could do, something she had done at home, although their calf count was not nearly as high as Deuce's herd.

Old Bruno, who was a crusty, rusty-voiced older man of about fifty, cheerfully brought Malca to the porch for her, along with his own sway-backed mount. He smiled at her eagerness as she clamped her hat on over her rebellious black curls and made sure her bandanna was turned to just the right angle.

"No hurry," he told her as they walked the horses into the back pasture onto the dirt track behind the barns. "No hurry; they'll have started them moving about now, and it'll take about an hour to bring them down. And they'll spend the day watching over them, and after that Barney and I'll take over."

Kalida smiled at his kindly garrulousness. He was rather taller than she had expected, with sandy receding hair and a freckled open face. Everything about him was large and droopy, like a comfortable old shoe. He had worked for Deuce's father, he told her, from the beginning, and Deuce relied on him heavily for home chores and tending the horses and the newborn calves. He helped with the haying and the weeding and with some experiments Deuce was trying out of growing their own feed, since Deuce didn't think free grass would last forever and was worried about what might happen if the country went through another bad winter or two, like back in the seventies.

Kalida listened to this restful monologue as they maneuvered their horses through uncultivated pasture that she had not traveled before, enjoying the enthusiasm of Old Bruno for his work and his misplaced admiration for Deuce's foresight.

Old Bruno used to like to go on roundup and sometimes still did. His favorite chore always was rounding up the strays; it was one of his winter tasks, too, along with keeping tabs on the calves, and he enjoyed it so much because he liked having the time in the field alone.

"I used to like it too," Kalida said without thinking. Her cobalt eyes took on a reminiscent blue glow as she smiled at him.

"Did you now, Miss Kalida? Well, well."

"Yes, and I helped with the newborn calves too. We never had many, but any number always had to be looked after the first weeks, same as here. Before"—she swallowed for a moment because all of what Old Bruno had said brought back the days at home, the times she missed, and the tasks she was not supposed to do any more, and she felt a lump rising in her throat "—before I came here, I did a lot of work around my father's ranch. He couldn't rightly afford the kind of help Deuce has, so everyone pitched in, even me. I—I never told anybody but I even had hopes of breeding cutting ponies, except I never told Papa because I thought he would laugh at the idea."

Bruno's pale eyes surveyed her straight-backed figure and her capable hands guiding Malca, and he nodded sympathetically. "That'd take time and money, always assuming you could find the right combination of horse to breed."

"Exactly," Kalida agreed wryly, looking around curiously as they proceeded cautiously through unclaimed brush and towering trees. "Now, where are we?"

"Shortcut," Bruno cackled, and moved ahead of her. "Be there in a minute, you'll see."

She followed him cautiously, and within moments, they came through a break in the bushes into sun-washed open pasture that stretched verdant and rich into the horizon.

"Now we wait," Bruno said, a note of satisfaction in his voice. He reached behind into his saddlebag for his canteen and offered it to Kalida. She took it, sipped the cool water gratefully, and handed it back to him. He took a long swallow, capped it, and put it away. "Won't be long," he said, wiping his mouth with his shirtsleeve.

"We don't have to talk," Kalida told him, and he nodded approvingly.

"You've got the right spirit," he commended her. "Come, let's meander in a little ways."

They moved forward slowly, in companionable silence, and Kalida allowed the heat of the sun to suffuse her body and spirit. There was so much to love here, so much about Sweetland she could care about. So much she could do. If she would be allowed to to it.

Her sense of frustration intensified as she imagined announcing to Ardelle that she fully intended to work the calf pen. Ardelle would have a fit, refusing to let anyone in the house that had had her hands in cow chips all day long. Ellie, of course, would have had her hands busy doing genteel things all day long, so naturally *her* presence would be welcome.

She just didn't know why Ellie didn't pick up and return to Bozeman at this point. What was Ellie doing staying on at Sweetland, anyway? Kalida shaded her eyes over the brim of her hat and looked to the distance. Not a sign of trail dust yet. Just a quiet calm surrounding her, and a peaceful soul by her side who respected the silence and the need to be alone.

What *was* Ellie doing at Sweetland? The question kicked back in her consciousness again. Ellie had supposedly come to the ranch to take care of her, Kalida, in her hour of need, as a favor to her father. But she remembered it had seemed strange that after all that time, Ellie had come instantly the moment her father asked. She would have supposed there to be a residual resentment on Ellie's part. She had as much as chased Ellie away all those years ago, when they had challenged each other for her father's love. She had thought Ellie had given up and that pride would keep her from falling into a trap again. But no, Ellie had come. And then the fire and Deuce's offer of hospitality . . .

What else could *they* have done? But Ellie . . . She could have requested to return to Bozeman. After all, she had a life there, running a discreet little boarding house to support herself. Of course, it was not Sweetland. Kalida supposed that Ellie would not have been human if she didn't leap on the prospect of living at Sweetland for a while and have the bonus of allowing Deuce to replenish her wardrobe.

Yes, that was feasible. But it had been several weeks now. And if she herself hadn't been so blinded by her need to escape Deuce's control, she might have perceived sooner that it was possible Ellie had overstayed her welcome.

But it was also possible that Ardelle had invited her to stay on. And that Ellie had now set her sights on Deuce Cavender, since it was so patently obvious that Kalida Ryland didn't want him, and Kalida Ryland's father didn't want *her*.

And Kalida Ryland herself was doing an excellent job of pushing Ellie right into Deuce's arms, she reminded herself wryly. Was that what *she* wanted?

She didn't know what she wanted where Deuce was concerned. She did not like the power he had over her with his wanton hands, which knew exactly how to render her mindless and hot with reckless desire so that her will was suborned to her passion. She only knew she wanted things to be as they had been before the fire; she wanted to be young and carefree, her own mistress who answered to no one but herself.

But as she looked over to the horizon and finally saw the telltale cloud of dust that heralded the approach of the herd, she knew those days were gone forever.

Sweetland was her home from now on, and Ardelle the arbiter of her function there, until such time as she felt confident to relinquish *her* control. It was beginning to look like a losing battle for her on all sides, but that thought was lost in Bruno's excited shout over the bawling of the cows and confused calves. "Here they come, Miss Kalida! Ain't they pretty!"

"Look at the difference," Jake said loudly, close to her ear, as they walked the perimeter of the herd, which consisted perhaps of fifty head of heifers and about half as many calves. "The Linaria are very distinctive; look at the horns, the way they curve in, they're shorter and the legs are shorter, so they forage easier."

Kalida nodded to show she heard him. They were watching his crew settle down the herd, for this was to be their bedding ground for several days before they were moved into pasture on the ranch. Bruno was already in the thick of things himself, checking out the calves' hooves, mouths, and if the branding had taken clearly enough.

There wasn't much more for Jake to do here now, nor for Kalida to see, he told her, unless she was going to take active part in the work.

"Wouldn't I like to!" she said longingly, and he looked at her, startled. But her eyes were fixed on Bruno's work-worn old frame, and he didn't think she was even aware he had heard her.

"No reason not to get on to your old homestead then," he suggested. She turned to him so eagerly that he was transfixed by the blazing blue of her eyes and the keenness of her expression.

"Now?"

"A stop at the bunkhouse to get washed first," he temporized, "but yes, now." Her fervor made him almost willing to scrap that plan. It was almost like an overt invitation, and the thought of his dusty, sweaty body on her soft flesh aroused him further. But he clamped down on it. If she were willing today and not upset by the desolation of her old home, he wanted to be clean and fresh smelling for her. He hoped to God she wouldn't be upset by what she saw.

He made sure she was close behind him as they crosscut back through the shortcut that Bruno had taken and came out behind the barns again. He jumped off by the bunkhouse, adjured her to remain mounted while he changed, raced inside to get a towel and fresh shirt, washed himself sketchily from head to waist, and then donned the clean shirt.

Malca was prancing with impatience when he rejoined Kalida and mounted up again. This time, they directed the horses down the dirt and gravel drive in front of the house.

There wasn't a sign anyone was around as they came up to it, so that when Ardelle suddenly appeared by the old house, Kalida was so startled she almost caused Malca to rear back. She fully expected the older woman to prohibit their expedition, but Ardelle surprisingly said, "That might be a good idea."

"Why would you think so?" Kalida asked curiously.

"Perhaps when you see the futility of resurrecting that place, you'll mend your behavior and begin to live up to your father's part of the bargain," Ardelle said coolly. She stared at Jake then, leaning heavily on her cane, and she looked back at Kalida with frost in her eyes. Then she turned away and limped back behind the old house and out of their sight.

"She's a one," Jake said, shaking his head. "I never will fathom her. All right, let's get going; we've got a long ride, and we'll do it at a fast pace."

Kalida pushed her hat tightly on her head and urged Malca into a gallop. Malca hardly needed prompting; he was more than ready for a fast run after being cooped up in the corral for so many days. Kalida could hardly control him; she held on tightly and let Malca have his head as they raced through the pasture, off of Sweetland, and onto free range.

Jake kept behind her, his gleaming hazel eyes feasting on her hips and shoulders pumping with every movement of the horse. She was a pretty rider, at one with Malca's movements, always gauging the horse's motion, shifting with it, guiding it, aware of its temperament with an almost sensual sensitivity.

Malca knew the way. It was almost uncanny how he knew exactly where to go and when to turn. As they approached the stone markers of the Ryland boundary, Malca led the way across the familiar track and paths and pastures where Kalida had roamed so freely as a young girl.

Finally Jake skewed in front of her and motioned her to stop. Just beyond the field where they had halted was the remains of the house, and he wanted to prepare her.

"How can you do that?" she demanded, angry and anxious all at once. Her eyes betrayed her, now dark navy with a burning light that was not shadowed by the brim of her hat. Her mouth was as inflexible as her words. She would see it, without the preparation, even if the shock of it destroyed everything for her.

He let her go, and she pulled back on Malca's reins so the horse slowly picked his way through the field and finally came within sight of what remained of the house.

There was nothing. It was a huge square blank spot with footings marking where the frame had been. All the rubble was gone, all the charred timber had been removed. The only sign of the fire was the still-scorched grass around the perimeter near the footings and the missing pieces of fence on the barn side of what had been the house.

The barn still stood, gaping and empty, and the fencing was intact around the corrals and the herding pens. But nothing else remained of the house — not a shingle, not a clapboard, not a piece of glass from the precious windows, not a piece of the timber framing. It was as desolate as a ghost town, what remained of that one little inconsequential ranch that had been Kalida's world.

She dismounted with a heavy heart and walked into the blank space of the nonexistent house, wondering that something so substantial had been wiped so completely away. For it was not only the physical bulk of the house that was gone, it was also the substance of the lives that had been lived within.

She turned to Jake and shrugged. "Well, I guess that's that."

"I told you you wouldn't want to see your old home like it is now," he reminded her.

"Let's look at the barn."

They crunched across the drive and into the dark, open doorway space of the barn. It was cool in there, despite the sun beating down on it. Everything here was the same. There was still one carriage and one flatbed wagon in the stalls, and the scent of hay permeating the air. Intermittent light filtered in through the small windows

213

set high on either side of the loft.

Kalida looked up at the loft. "I used to play up there years ago."

You could play up there now, Jake thought, not moving, not daring to make one suggestion of anything he was thinking. He could almost feel her shaking herself out of her disappointment that the devastation of her home had been so complete.

"And hide from Papa sometimes when he had a chore I didn't particularly want to do," she added, with just the faintest sparkle of laughter in her tone. Yes, the memories were good ones. She went to the loft ladder and shook it. Still as steady as ever. In an instant she had mounted it and was climbing, while Jake stood below admiring the view.

"Come on up," she called when she had reached top. "Ugh. The hay isn't fresh, but the view is terrific."

Oh it is, Jake thought, and mounted the ladder. In a moment he was beside her, and the two of them were scanning out the opened doors that framed the fields beyond the house almost like a painting.

"If you hadn't known the house was there," Kalida said, sitting down by the railing with her feet over the side, "you would love the view."

Jake joined her, dangling his long legs over the side and discarding his hat behind him. "So," he said, because in actuality, he did not know what to say. Her mood had changed abruptly; she seemed carefree now, having girded herself against further hurt. She had gotten what she had come for—the final period put on her youth. Now she would have to deal with the reality of her situation and perhaps the revelation of her true nature.

Perhaps she knew it already, Jake mused as they sat in silence, and she merely liked to play games. In any event, he knew he must not make the first move. She must be allowed to feel the thickness in the air between them and the sensual implication of their sitting in the darkness in the barn. In an isolated place where no one could happen upon them. It surely could not have been chance that she had decided to climb up here and invite him with her.

He couldn't read her face in the dusky light from the windows. It played beguilingly over her cheekbones, emphasizing the movement of her lips when she spoke. It shadowed her eyes so he couldn't see their expression, and it limned the firm tilt of her chin as she looked at him curiously, as though she sensed he wanted something and was going to ask him what it was.

But she said nothing, and he sat very still, thinking of this shadowed darkness and how it would both hide and reveal her body if she chose now to stand up and slide out of her clothing.

"It is very restful to be here with you," she said finally, meaning it as a compliment. She was grateful he hadn't tried to talk or ease away her pain. She had needed to do that by herself; no one could come to grips with this kind of loss any other way. She reached out and touched the thick brawny arm that he had wrapped around his right knee.

He almost jumped at the feeling of her cool fingers on the hairy skin of his forearm, where he had rolled up his shirtsleeve. Now, he thought, if she would just slide her hand upwards and squeeze just a little, it would be like a signal for what would come. He knew the kind of smile she would send him—hot and knowledgeable, because she would be able to see clearly in his expression what he expected since she had to be very familiar with it. She knew just how to touch a man to arouse his interest and inflame his senses.

"Thank you, Jake." Her voice was husky, and the smile flashed at him, along with a dazzling slanting glance of invitation.

He didn't move a muscle. Come on and thank me, he

thought. Come on, and don't string me out any longer than you have to. God, but she was an expert. He could tell she knew what the darkness and her closeness were doing to him. And she was probably enjoying every minute of it. His anticipation of it filled him to bursting, and he thought it would be very easy just to grab her and strip away her clothes. But that wasn't the way he wanted it. He wanted her enticing him with the kind of uninhibited undressing she had performed in the parlor. The kind of impudent, audacious flaunting of her delectable nakedness that he had viewed through the window. The same abandon with which she had allowed Deuce to handle her in front of the bunkhouse. All that he wanted for himself, without coercion or force.

If she meant to taunt him, he would bear it; it would be part of the game, and he would have her eventually just as he had dreamed. It could be now. He watched avidly as the tip of her tongue played across her lips, wetting them deliberately to provoke him into doing something so she could deny him—this time. No, he wouldn't move. She was a tease, and she needed to play her games, and he would enjoy them, until she became aroused by his studied disinterest and would try anything to engage his attention. And he knew just how she would do it.

"Jake—" Her voice was throbbing with excitement; he could feel it. She could hardly contain herself. "I—"

And then the roar that shook the rafters of the barn: "DANTON!" And the huge shadow in the doorway, blocking the view, pistol drawn now, immense in shadow, threatening, blood-lusting. Deuce!

"You son of a bitch, wherever the hell you have Kalida, you move away from her because I am going to kill you and string up your ass. Danton!"

"Hell, Deuce—" Jake began. The words didn't scare him, but the emotion behind them did.

A shot rang out, just close enough to get him moving. "Shit, Deuce—"

"Get your ass down *here*." Another shot splintered above them. Jake moved, almost diving down the ladder. Deuce meant what he said; plainly he thought he had rights. Jake didn't know what rights he had, or whether he wanted to stay around long enough to find out. Deuce clearly didn't know about Miss Kalida's tendencies, and he, Jake, wasn't about to explain. But he was equally sure that the next time he saw Kalida she would be so sorry for what happened that she would want to apologize—somehow.

"All right," he muttered as he reached bottom. "My ass is here. And I'll tell you, just once, that nothing is going on here except Miss Kalida's sitting in the barn loft thinking about old times, and I didn't think she should come around here alone, because you never know what's skulking around an abandoned property."

"Hell and damn you, this property isn't abandoned, you shit, and you get the hell off of it, and be aware the only thing that's saving your ass and your gut is the fact you're a decent foreman. Get out of here."

Jake shot him a skeptical look and bowed sardonically. Deuce lifted his gun again, and Jake scurried out.

Kalida had not moved. She hated Deuce at that moment more than she ever had in her whole life. And she hated Jake for abandoning her. Both of them stared out the door after Jake, even though neither could see him. After a moment or two they heard the sound of hoof-beats, close and then disappearing into the distance.

And then there was silence, an impenetrable, dense, portentous silence that stretched until the atmosphere was as taut as Kalida's nerves. She stayed where she was, afraid to move, afraid of his explosive temper, which had not diffused with Jake's departure. Wary because he hadn't said a word, and he still held the pistol in his hand.

Suddenly there was a clicking sound and the creak of leather as he slicked the gun into its holster. "You can come down now, Kalida. I'm not going to kill you."

"You don't think that reassures me, do you?" she called down. "Come and get me." Damn, now, why did I do that? she thought as he started toward the ladder. Only fools issued challenges to the like of Deuce Cavender. Or had she some other reason, something deep inside her that she did not want to take out and examine? She admired the bend of his supple body as he agilely climbed the ladder. He had thrown aside his hat, and his straight black hair fell right into his eyes as he ascended swiftly and competently to the top of the ladder.

And when he stepped onto the loft floor, Kalida knew she was in trouble. Even though the light was too dim for her to really see his expression, she felt his anger. She couldn't even gauge the depth of it; it came from something she had no knowledge of. "So this is where the she-tom comes to rut," he said, almost casually as he looked around at the dark hay-scented loft.

"Always," she jeered rashly.

"You are as indiscriminate as a cat, you vixen," he growled, taking a step toward her, his rage becoming palpable. "What did that bastard do to you?"

"Nothing more than any man who had a spare hour to kill—with a vixen," she retorted, her resentment rising to match his fury.

"Any man," he echoed, and the flat, dry tone of his voice told her to move—and in that moment. She darted to her left and he dove for her, catching her legs and tumbling her on her back, into a pile of hay deep in the shadows of the loft.

"Perfect," she muttered hoarsely, cursing his temper and her desire to goad him beyond reason. Why, and why had she said it? She felt his body shift upwards and she pushed against him.

"Any man," he reminded her harshly, positioning his weight over her and onto her body with no consideration. "Any . . . man." His voice grated against her ear. "How many men, Kalida-cat? How many boys in the hayloft, you bitch? What did you let them do?" His breath was hot against her ear, as hot as his words. "Where did he touch you?" His words sizzled; he meant to kill her with his heat. She writhed against him in anguish. His own words inflamed him almost beyond reason. "Where did he put his hands, Kalida?"

"He . . . didn't —" She pushed against the rock wall of his chest with all her strength.

"You went off alone with this man, Kalida. Any man. And I find you alone with him in a dark barn and you tell me he didn't lay a hand on you? Hell, you must think I'm gullible; you forget I know Jake Danton doesn't do anything for a woman unless he knows he can get something for it."

She screamed with rage then and pushed against him again, his hard hissing words echoing in her brain. He was an animal, damn him, a goddamned stinking, stupid male animal, and all he knew was *that*, and damn him, he could go to hell thinking she would even allow Jake Danton to lay a finger on her. The thought of Jake and her together was burning him up, she saw. Well, she wanted him to suffer, and the idea of Jake touching her was making him suffer. She stopped struggling abruptly as she perceived the power she had because of this.

"And if he did?" she whispered impulsively.

"I'll kill him. I'll kill you," he said flatly, as if the darkness were witness to the promise. "Did he?"

She didn't answer; answering would alleviate his pain, and she didn't nearly want to do that. She felt a kind of contempt for him that it mattered so much. She forgot, in this heady moment, her feelings about Ellie.

"Did he?" He had allowed enough time for her to answer before he rapped out the question again. He felt frustration building on anger and desire at the way she was taunting him.

"What do you think?" she murmured.

"I think you're an alleycat with all the makings of a first-class tease of a whore. Did he?" His tone dared her to dissemble again.

"Deuce—"

"Kalida—" The frustration in him snapped suddenly. He moved off her, raised himself to his knees, and pulled her with him. Slowly, he drew her upright and close, and his slow, tense, languid movements scared her more than his words.

"What are you going to do?" she demanded in a whisper.

He didn't answer. His hands moved, surrounding her waist, pulling her against him. She felt his fingers unbutton her skirt, and it fell, with a little frisson of sound, to her feet. She heard a faint growl of satisfaction as he felt the underlaying garments, and he began with deliberate motions to unbutton the shirtwaist.

"Deuce—" she begged hoarsely, but he was intent now, almost finished with the buttons, parting the shirt, his hands molding her still-covered breasts against the fabric of her underwear.

"Everything comes off," he said harshly as he began sliding the chemise from her shoulders. "I want you naked in the barn with me; I want only that memory in your mind today." The chemise fell onto the heap of clothing at her feet. Then he knelt and removed her boots and socks one at a time, tossing them to one side. He stayed at her feet, looking up at her nakedness now revealed in the shimmering light as enticing shadows and hollows. He reached out for her, bringing her closer to him so that he could kiss the smooth flesh of her abdomen. His arms slid around her thighs and the sweet cushiony curve of her buttocks.

Her hands twisted themselves in his hair involuntarily as his lips teased their way lower. She moaned with uninhibited pleasure at the sensations only he could arouse in her treacherous body.

Just when she thought she could bear no more, he stood up very slowly, his hands sliding up her body as he raised himself, feeling her hips and the indentation of her waist, slowly sliding up her midriff and grazing the heavy curve of her breasts, up to her shoulders and neck to hold her immobile as his mouth buried itself now against her lips.

It was a long, languid caress; he sought her avidly over and over, kissing her voraciously until she had to hold onto him because her knees buckled. He held her tightly against his clothed body, to emphasize the power of his masculinity against her nakedness and the power her nakedness had over him. He was pulsating with need of her. His hands moved, following the line of her body to her buttocks, pausing there to cup them and crush them against his hips and thighs, to feel the movement of her body as he awakened her desire.

She felt out of control and she didn't care. Her heedless words were coming back to haunt her: He had only had to touch her, to remove one piece of clothing, and she was yearning for him, loving the sensation of her nakedness against his rough sweat-drenched clothing and hard, implacable body. When he pulled his mouth away and turned her body around so that her buttocks were pillowed against his throbbing manhood, she raised her arms around his neck and pulled his mouth back to hers avidly and awkwardly.

His hands now worshipped the front of her body. Her uplifted arms thrust out her taut tipped breasts in a way that demanded his caresses. His hands cupped them and

221

held them as his tongue ravished hers and his hips thrust against her writhing buttocks.

"Now." She heard the word as a guttural whisper against her mouth. "No." Her answer was moan and an invitation.

His tongue licked her lips. "Don't move." The merest breath. "Look."

"Don't stop," she groaned. Her eyes, now liquid blue with passion, slanted downward to see his hands, brown and long-fingered, holding her breasts, his thumb and forefinger just surrounding her taut protruding nipples.

"Now I'm going to make the Kalida-cat purr," he whispered roughly, and his fingers took each lush turgid nipple and held it just at the tip, knowing what the feeling of that would do to her. Her body reacted with a sinuous spasm and he could only imagine the cascade of sensation coursing through her as her moan of pleasure resonated through his. "Did that rutting bastard feel you there?" he demanded harshly as he played with the inflaming nakedness of her nipple. "Did he see you like this, hot and melting in his arms? Damn it, Kalida, damn you. . . ."

She hardly heard his words; the rough inciting syllables were like an aphrodisiac to her. Her head rested against his hard muscle-taut shoulder, thrown back as the ecstasy as his sorcerer's hands sent the lustrous thick sensations of pleasure shimmering through her veins. Her hands clutched his thighs, squeezing them, pulling them closer to her body so she could feel his hardness against her buttocks.

"Kalida . . ." He sighed her name hoarsely into her ear. Her luscious movements against him provoked him to an almost unbelievable arousal. No one, he thought in a haze of insane possessive feeling, could have made her feel this tumultuous upheaval of sensation except him. No one could make her grind her body so wantonly in pleasure

222

except him. "No one . . . no one . . ." he growled, unaware that he had even uttered the words out loud. He wanted her alluring body close, and closer still.

His iron bar of a left arm surrounded her suddenly, clamping her around the full curves of her waist, molding her even more tightly against him as his right hand slithered down the curves of her hips and thighs, slowly and sensuously.

She was totally his now, enslaved by his enthralling caressing hands, enraptured by the separate senses of his holding her as tightly as a bolt, his intimate exploration of her, and his impudent fondling of her deliciously taut nipple.

"This is mine, Kalida," he rasped, as his whole body responded to his sensual invasion. "This is mine," as his fingers felt the temptingly turgid nipple peak over and over, squeezing it and sliding his huge palm against its pebble hardness. "*Did* the bastard touch you?" he hissed, sliding his searching fingers still deeper.

His words whipped by her, through her; she was never conscious of anything but his voluptuous exploration of her nakedness. She felt him intensely all over her, within her. No one else could do this to her. No one else knew just where to feel her, just which way to caress her, just how to fondle her surging white-hot body. Her whole being glimmered at his touch, a recognition of what was to come; her body reached for his knowledgeable, driving fingers.

He wanted to throw her down on the sweet grass hay right there and take her savagely undulating body under his. He wanted to plunge deep into her sultry mystery and lose himself, to drive into her again and again and be sheathed in her sweet heat. But the urgency of her pulsating body compelled his hands, the moans that greeted every stroke and flex of his hard fingers drove him to mindless urgency.

He held all of her nakedness in his hands, and he knew she was rapturously aware of it and that only he could elicit this sumptuously primitive response from her. She was all liquid heat in his hands now.

Her fingers dug into his thighs as the crystalline feeling began building, slowly at first, liquid crystal upon liquid crystal, shimmering now, spreading through her veins, joining with the thick honey cloud of sensation from her nipples, white hot and glistening now, glowing, dazzling. . . . She felt her body expanding, the heat streaming and throbbing through every muscle, every pore of her skin, sheening it with all the liquid in her body. The satin heat in her rose higher and higher, and she drove against the luscious hardness that propelled the feeling until it exploded into a white-hot radiance behind her eyes and slowly drifted down to encompass her whole body.

Long moments later, she became aware of many small separate impressions: his iron arm around her waist, holding her so tight she almost couldn't breathe; the musky, earthy odor that melded with the scent of her sex; the dusky filtered light that concealed and revealed everything; the firm hand still resting between her thighs; the hard uncompromising body that still supported hers.

Her skin dimpled with cold and a wave of after-reaction. She struggled against his confining muscular arm, and it immediately loosened but still kept her restrained.

She sensed the simmering desire in him still, and she ceased her movements and let him hold her. He slid his right arm around her waist and turned her to face him. "Did he touch you?" he asked again, his voice strained and low, but without the intensity and the frightening hard ragged edge.

He couldn't see her lustrous cobalt eyes. He could barely now see the shadow of her face. The murky light seemed to illuminate only the line of her cheekbone and the sensual firm curve of her lips.

She hesitated a moment, unable to believe he was still after her answer, and then she shook her head. It was all she would give him, especially because she sensed it did not satisfy him one bit. If he could have commanded it, he would have had her detail every moment she had spent with Jake. But her resistance must have been apparent to him, for he let go of her suddenly and began searching for her clothes.

She made a move to help him, but he waved her away; when he had them all, he began dressing her, his hands strangely tender now as they buttoned the shirt, bracing her body so he could slip on her boots and slide the skirt over her head so she could fasten it.

And outside the barn, in a place where some straggly bushes effectively concealed an observer, close by the door at an angle that illuminated with startling clarity what went on in the loft, Jake Danton watched Kalida, his whole body suffused with hot resentment that she had allowed Deuce to do all the things he had been dreaming of — and without a protest, without a qualm, just as it was in her nature to do. Just as she would soon do for him too. He swore it, as he scuttled away before they became aware of his presence. He had learned a hard lesson about how to deal with Kalida, but he knew what to do now. He had only to take what he wanted, and she would fall into his arms.

Twelve

Kalida-cat.

Kalida could still hear the harsh hissing words reverberating in her brain as she stared at her drawn face in the bedroom mirror. Dress for dinner, Ardelle had said; Deuce was staying the night; Jake would nighthawk; he was gone already. And Deuce would not be keeping his promise about not sleeping with her, she thought.

Her glittering cobalt eyes darkened dangerously as she considered this. Why not? His men were gone. The rooms were empty now, and there must be any number of places she could settle herself in comfortably and he retire contentedly, knowing his honor was intact.

Sure. Kalida-cat. She moved her hands to her eyes and pushed up the corners. Nothing was different. He was still king and oppressor. Lord and owner of all he surveyed. Using any method to get what he wanted.

Her firm chin lifted and her hands pulled at her glossy black hair. Impossible hair. Everything was impossible.

Something had changed.

She had almost put a name to her discontent.

Kalida-cat.

Not a sweet, innocent face anymore. The face of a woman. A woman who could arouse a man's desire. His envy. A raging jealousy. A woman who was coming to know there was only one man she wanted touching her.

The man she hated. The man she could not bear thinking would touch another woman the way he touched her.

The mere thought of it sent crackles down her spine. She felt as though she were in a maze of confusion. How could she despise his arrogance and want his hands? How could he make her feel such a staggering capitulation by just putting his hands on her? And how could she feel such a fierce desire to become part of him when she was still consumed by this fiery resentment of the circumstances that had brought her here?

Something had definitely changed. She definitely did not want to hand him over to some other woman. Most especially she did not want him to become interested in Ellie, but she knew right well that Ellie was now intensely interested in him.

He could not possibly want Ellie after this afternoon!

She picked up a brush to pull it through her midnight curls, which were waved and tangled from the tight braid she had just unknotted.

Dress for dinner, Ardelle had said, most pleased there was a reason. A stern-faced, overbearing *male* reason who would sit there and allow three women to fawn all over him.

She hadn't changed *that* much; she was not going to fall all over his imperious, domineering, masculine high-handedness. She would sit and lick her paws in a corner before she would pay court to *him*.

She wheeled at the knock at the door. Prestina poked her head in. "What dress you wearing tonight, Miss

Kalida?"

"What do you think?" Kalida asked, thinking all the choices were positively atrocious.

"How about this pretty?" Prestina smiled, sliding herself into the room and thrusting something in front of Kalida's face. "Madame finished it minutes ago, so she can join you for dinner."

"It's lovely," Kalida murmured, touching the bodice. How clever of Madame! She had remade the hated fitted blue dress pattern, in black this time, of a heavier material more suitable for evening. The neckline was slightly more daring than even Kalida had ever worn, and the lightly poufed shoulders exaggerated still more the hourglass shape of the garment. The skirt was belled and drawn back and up in the hint of a bustle that Madame seemed to favor, and this time the buttons marched down the back of the dress. Its sole decoration was the velvet band that tied around the waist and trailed down the back of the dress.

For some reason, Kalida liked it a lot better than the blue, and still more and more as Prestina helped her slip into it, painstakingly buttoning it for her and tying the velvet band just so, laying its ends coquettishly over the little bustle.

Kalida stared at herself in the mirror. The black color of the dress gave her an elegance and imperious fragility. Her skin appeared translucent, pearly. Her unruly dark hair and the low-cut neckline seemed almost a frame for her face. Her eyes blazed cobalt approval at the gorgeous creature with the swelling breasts and exquisite posture that stared back from her mirror.

Prestina's hands lifted her heavy black curls off her neck and began pinning them, with expert little twists and twirls. Kalida made a negative motion, but Prestina was adamant. "You want the hair in such a way as to tantalize. You are showing your neck and your bosom, and soon enough, the man wants you alone in his room to take down the hair pin by pin, Miss Kalida, and we will make him work."

"I was thinking you might be able to find some other room for me to occupy," Kalida said testily as she nervously watched Prestina's hands arranging her hair. "Everyone's gone, isn't that so? Deuce has lifted the patrol and done something to protect the Santa Linaria; no one is expected back now or will need their room for another night."

Prestina nodded calmly. "This is true, what you say, but what you want is not possible. Mr. Deuce would not permit."

Kalida wrenched her head away from Prestina's gentle fingers. "And why not?" she demanded, whirling around.

"Mr. Deuce say," Prestina answered firmly, turning Kalida around again to face the mirror, her expression uncompromising. "We only do what Mr. Deuce say."

"Do we?" murmured Kalida. Everyone seemed so damned sure about that. Deuce must be spoiled, not having anyone oppose him at all in any way. So there it was, as simply put as possible. She would be coming back to this room, night after night, after boring days of doing what she could not imagine at this point, since Ardelle was not happy with her "cowgirl" proclivities; and here Deuce would be, and here she would be at the mercy of his desires.

And her own.

Oh no, she thought; she had some pride on that point even if it could easily be overcome. She still did not like the situation, and she still was sure the contract between her father and Deuce did not include his bedding her. Nor had she heard another word, since the fire, about his marrying her. What was he expecting? she wondered. That she would live out her days as his concubine? That she would be happy with such an arrangement that gave her no rights or a title, that would put her up to ridicule?

And on top of that, she was not to be allowed any privacy! Well, she thought, patting the intricate twists of hair that Prestina had woven into a delicate style to complement her dress, we'll see about that. Deuce couldn't be allowed to have it all his own way, especially when he had gotten everything he wanted already anyway.

Madame was speaking as Kalida entered the parlor, detailing, it seemed, just what Deuce was getting for his money. She looked like a gangling ostrich, dressed as she habitually was in black taffeta, with a piece of lace draped like a veil over the top of her iron-gray hair. She turned as Kalida entered and paused in the door frame. "Ah, here is Madamoiselle Kalida; does she not look resplendent in black?"

Deuce, who towered over them all, sent her a dark, inscrutable charcoal look, and said abruptly, "Quite." He couldn't trust himself to say more. She was quite beyond anything he had words to express. She looked almost ethereal in black. What saved the dress and the sense of her as some kind of illusion was the earthy neckline, exposing just enough of her breasts in such a way that anyone looking at her knew there was an exciting woman beneath the swath of black. His eyes rested on the swell of creamy skin. He felt instantly like he wanted to carry her off out of the sight of Ellie and his aunt and this babbling foreign woman whose words he barely heard.

But instead he had Ellie—Ellie with her hot black eyes and questing fingers, which darted here and there on his arm, pressing, feeling, inviting. Ellie stood too close and pouted just a bit too much, and next to Kalida's stark elegance, she looked almost gaudy. But for some reason, Kalida was playing some kind of teasing game designed to thrust him into Ellie's arms, perhaps, he thought, so she

230

could play at being righteously indignant. Whatever it was, he didn't understand it. Even now, a small smug smile played over her luscious lips as she watched them talking together. Even after this afternoon's thunderbolt experience in the loft. He didn't understand for a moment how she could think he would choose pallid Ellie over her, and he was rather amused, for one minute, to imagine how she would try.

He wasn't nearly done with Kalida Ryland today, he thought grittily, lifting his whiskey glass to her in a grim little salute. She understood what he meant. The smug smile widened and she turned her back on him.

Ellie said, "That was rather rude. But then, she still is a child." As if to say, I'm here, and I'm not.

Deuce gave her a thoughtful steely-gray once-over, as he considered Kalida's frame of mind, his own, and what Kalida meant to happen with Ellie. It wouldn't hurt, he thought, to give her a taste of her own medicine. It would not hurt at all for her to see him paying some attention to Ellie, who, by most men's standards, was a very desirable woman, particularly since she was no longer a virgin and, according to gossip he had heard, had had several fruitful liaisons as well as a successful business.

He smiled down at Ellie. "Yes, she is rather headstrong. Willful. Refreshing now and again." He shrugged, and Ellie stepped closer. No one could miss the gesture or her hand on his hard-muscled forearm, stroking the crisp cotton of his fresh shirt. It was almost as if she were inhaling him, and his scent stoked her ardor still more. If she could have sucked him inside her by aspiration, he would have been gone ten minutes ago, he thought ruefully. She was a predator and she had staked him out.

He let her ease closer because he felt Kalida's attention on them, although she did not seem to be looking at them directly. But she was aware of every nuance of Ellie's seemingly expert, covert movements. God, Ellie did it

231

well, she thought. There was an angle, an attitude, a stance ... and suddenly her body was leaning into Deuce, her breasts in the silky rose gown, now altered also drastically at the bodice, pressing lightly but firmly against his arm. Her fingers touched, skimmed, patted.

And her eyes! Those glowing black eyes, burning and innocent all at once. Kalida envied her. How *did* she do it? And how could Deuce be so stupid as to be taken in by her?

Of course he was. Ellie had a certain mature beauty. And, of course, her skin was flawless because she did not work out of doors, never had even when her husband was alive. And the eyes. They were wide, tilting, fascinating. Her mouth was also a fleshy pout of invitation. The new dresses certainly enhanced her body. Madame was so clever with a needle she even made it appear that Ellie had a bosom. And that bosom was pressed tellingly against Deuce's body.

Kalida was so incensed by the thought that she flounced into the dining room, where Ardelle was directing Prestina to lay the covers. Mindlessly, Kalida began to help, oblivious to Ardelle's scathing look until the older woman said tonelessly, "You may summon the others," and Prestina scurried out, very aware herself of Ardelle's anger.

Deuce appropriated the seat next to him for Ellie. Ardelle sat across from her. Kalida was next to Ardelle and Madame seated herself across the table beside Ellie.

Prestina tiptoed into the dead-silent room, and just as silently began to serve.

Kalida was not hungry. She had what amounted to a front-row seat to Ellie's antics, and she was fuming at how much Deuce seemed to enjoy her conversation and her little stroking touches as plates and serving pieces were passed.

A ripple of Ellie's laughter at something Deuce had

said to her in an undertone stiffened Kalida's spine. And then she completely missed something Ellie said to her across the table.

Ellie slanted an amused glance at Deuce, and then repeated her question. "I'm told you were at the ranch today. How did you find it?"

Kalida shot a bolt-blue glance at Deuce. "Devastating," she said coldly.

"You never should have gone back until your father had arranged to lay the foundation again. Really, to see it like that . . ."

"There was nothing to see. Papa had had all the burnt timber removed and the debris cleaned away. There's nothing there, Ellie. Nothing to see. Nothing"—again that explosive flash of blue ricocheted off Deuce's amused gray gaze—"to be upset about."

"If only you had known that, you could have saved yourself a trip," Ellie said complacently, smiling into her soup and then up at Kalida.

"And my foreman a lost afternoon," Deuce added without a shade of expression in his tone.

The bastard, Kalida thought furiously as a hot wave of anger suffused her whole body; not only was he reminding her about how he felt about Jake Danton, he was prompting the memory of what had happened between them. What could have happened between her and Jake, perhaps, if he had not come. Oh, she felt unreasoningly grateful to him. She could kiss his boots for interfering. At that moment, the thought of Jake Danton was infinitely more attractive than him. And she might, if this mood continued, set about to prove it!

If he caressed Ellie's hand one more time! Blast him and damn him to hell! She might well throw a knife at him if he did one more untoward thing.

And then Ardelle was speaking. "Personally, I don't blame Kalida for wanting to see the ranch. It was time.

She had to lay her hopes in that direction to rest. It's time for her to bear up to her responsibilities. And you've made a very nice start tonight, my dear. The dress is ravishing on you. You look quite elegant."

I don't want your compliments, Kalida wanted to scream. But she sat very still, her hands primly folded in her lap while Prestina cleared away the first course and returned to set out platters of meat, biscuits, beans, and corn.

"And compliments to Madame," Ardelle continued, "both for her speed and the excellence of her designs, and her willingness to come and attend us in this emergency."

I'd sooner have walked around stark naked, Kalida thought willfully, digging into the meat with a vengeance.

"Thank you," said Madame, nodding her head graciously. "It is a pleasure to dress two such lovely ladies."

"Now," Ardelle went on, and her tone turned brisk, "your plans, Deuce . . ."

Deuce's warming gray gaze swept down at Ellie. ". . . have changed," he interpolated smoothly.

"Really, Deuce . . ."

"Really, Ardelle, do I have to dot every *i* and put a period on every sentence so you may know to the minute what my plans are?"

"Yes, actually," she answered calmly, shooting him a sparking sherry-red look. "How else can I plan? Look, Deuce, we've had this argument for years, and we'll have it forever if you keep refusing to be pinned down as to your comings and goings. I can't even begin to account for how much food we waste just because you won't tell me *your* plans."

"I've told you as much as I know. The market herd moves out tomorrow. The rest stay at Balsam for summer grazing. The calves come here. Me and Jake are taking some of the crew to Stoneface Ridge for the Ryland herd. We'll cut and brand back at Morgan field, I think, and see what kind of shipment we can get out of them. That should take a day and a half, since Ryland hired his own day men and they're still with the herd as far as I know. We'll move out the day after tomorrow, be back by the weekend. Is that detailed enough?"

"And the Linaria?"

"Are being well taken care of."

"I'm worried about them. And our losses."

"We have the babies. And the remainder of the stud herd is safe. And being taken care of."

"I wish you would tell me where," Ardelle said fretfully.

Deuce looked around at the three avid faces listening. "No, you're all better off not knowing. You notice nothing's happened since I sequestered them. I still think someone on Sweetland is selling information."

"Don't get cocky," Ardelle cautioned. "They don't only steal the Linaria. Haskins was hit for a couple hundred head a few weeks back."

"I know," Deuce said, and a grim line appeared around his mouth. "That's why we're going to wire up after I disperse the Ryland herd. I'm damned tired of it, and damned tired of throwing money away. If the vigilante association can't do something about it, *I* will."

"I don't want to talk about it any more at the dinner table," Ardelle said suddenly, not liking Deuce's hard expression at all. And if some thieving rustlers found the Linaria—what then? Would he shoot to kill by his own deputization? Deuce was a formidable foe, as even she had reason to know. She was frightened for him. He was trying new methods, new mind games to deal with the thieves—games that could get him killed.

She looked around the table. Her words had sobered everyone, as if they had all thought the same thing. Ellie's pale hand gripped Deuce's wrist, and her round black eyes were riveted on his tense face.

Kalida looked at Ardelle. The older woman had a

strange look on her face, and Kalida could not tell whether she approved of Ellie's possessiveness or whether her mind was totally somewhere else. However Ardelle felt about it, Kalida was ready to throw things. She wanted Ellie to get her thin white grasping hand off Deuce, and she wanted Ellie to remove herself back to Bozeman as soon as was expediently possible, so that Kalida could deal with Deuce and his agreement with her father with some equanimity. As of this moment, she was consumed with rage at Ellie's forwardness and Deuce's blatant encouragement.

And she didn't care about cows or ranches or the Santa Linaria or her father's herd. Or anything. She slapped her napkin down on her table. And then stopped. Her first impulse was to leave the room. Ellie could have him, damn his hide, but she did not have to sit and watch them.

But her second feeling was stronger. She couldn't bear to think about what might be happening, and on that account, she was stuck in the dining room until dinner was over.

There was pie, dried fruit, cheese, and coffee afterwards, but she ate little of it. It seemed to her that there was a deeper tension surrounding them now, and perhaps it had come on because of Ardelle's intent questioning about Deuce's plans. He didn't like schedules or being kept in one place at someone else's behest. Something about what Ardelle had said had gotten him riled up, but only Kalida saw it.

Everyone else perceived him to have reverted back to his usual self. His reckless flinty gaze darted back and forth between Kalida and Ellie, with whom he began a desultory conversation when they adjourned to the parlor after dinner. And Kalida didn't like that either. She didn't like anything tonight, and finally she decided she would excuse herself.

236

"Well, really, Kalida." Again that chiding tone in Ardelle's voice.

"I'm tired," she said testily. "I've had a long day."

"Yes, I expect you have," Ardelle agreed, thinking she could not very well disapprove of Kalida's antics this afternoon when she herself had given her the go-ahead to ride with Jake to the Ryland homestead. A mistake, certainly, but Kalida sensed her displeasure anyway. And didn't care, of course. And that was just like her.

"Kalida will go and hide in her room," Ellie said, just loudly enough so Kalida could hear, "like a disappointed child. But come, Deuce, we have delicious things to talk about."

Kalida pounded the wall as she climbed the stairs. Oh, he could have the brazen old witch, what did she care? She was old, anyway. Old and desperate. Maybe she thought Deuce was desperate, since he got to town so rarely. That had to be it. Any old woman would look good to a man who hadn't seen one in months.

Ha! The idea was laughable. She shoved in the door of Deuce's room, scanned it briefly, grabbed up her silk robe, skirt, shirtwaist, and underthings, freshly washed and pressed by Prestina, as well as her boots, a hanger, and her brush, and slammed down the hallway looking for an empty room.

There were several, all dimly lit by guttering kerosene lamps, always ready, and she blazed up again in anger at Deuce's presumption that she would even choose to share a room with him if another were available. She wanted to be as far away from him as possible, but there weren't that many rooms from which to choose. One was obviously Ellie's, since the dove-gray dress was hanging outside the wardrobe door almost as if Prestina had just pressed it and hung it there so as not to wrinkle it.

She certainly did not want to be anywhere near Ellie, whose room was right at the head of the stairs and down the hall from Deuce's. She proceeded to look in the line of doors on the opposite side of the hallway. Here was Madame. There was Prestina. The next was empty but, she thought, her father might have used it. There was a book on the table and her father was an avid reader, and she knew that no one else at Sweetland was. The next room was empty also, and so was the one beyond it, which was directly opposite Deuce's room.

She chose the former room, which put her far enough away from everyone, she thought. By the dim light of the ever-present kerosene lamp, she could see it was a pleasant, nondescript room that was obviously reserved for unexpected company.

She closed the door and spread out her few belongings. What a pleasure to occupy a totally featureless room, alone and private. She turned down the lamp and lay down on the bed fully dressed. Bliss and peace, alone at last.

But what were they doing downstairs? She could hear nothing through the thick door. No, it was none of her business. Her mind jumped from that notion to the idea of busyness. And the forthcoming roundup of her father's herd. God, if she could only go! A day and a half on the trail, scrounging out straggling calves, keeping them moving, always mindful of the money on the hoof; sharing the cooking chores because she could do that well, and the men liked her coffee and her biscuits; earning the respect of the men for doing the work as well as any male. And she had done it; she could do it. It had been necessary to do it when her father had not had the money to hire the extra day hand.

She would do it, she thought suddenly. It would be insurance. It was something Ellie would never think to do. Whether Deuce liked her coming or not, it was something Ellie couldn't or wouldn't do.

Nostalgia cemented her resolve; one way or another she

was going on roundup. The thought that Ardelle would disapprove did not deter her either. And Deuce?

She was the collateral for her father's deal. She wondered if, once the cattle were dispersed to market, her worth to him would diminish. If once he got his money, she would be of no use to him.

Well, that wasn't strictly true, she thought wryly; she was of some use to him. Except if it weren't her, it would be someone else. It would be . . . Ellie.

Oh God, I can't keep my mind off of what they might be doing . . . She sat up abruptly. What if they had all gone to bed? What if, at this very moment, Ellie were expecting Deuce in her room, steps down the hallway?

She wondered if she would hear them.

She didn't want to hear them. She just didn't want them to be together. Ellie had pushed a little bit too hard at the dinner table. Damn her pale hands and obsidian eyes. Damn Deuce's supercilious feudal overlord attitude, sitting at his very own dinner table and insinuating that Ellie Dean pleased him to the point where she might find him in her bed!

What you wanted, the small undaunted voice in the back of her mind announced with smug satisfaction.

She had heard it before; she tamped down on it and replaced it with the vision of Ellie's bedroom, which she had just entered not a half hour ago. She could see it clearly, with its painted pine furniture, relics from another era but comfortable and homey enough for the guest room, softly lit, inviting, with Ellie's essence permeating the room. She would be seated in the center of the bed, only the sheets wrapped around her, loosely, her dark hair flowing straight and glossy down her shoulders, her black eyes glittering with dark fires that would beg to be quenched.

That was the thing about Ellie, that faint air of mystery that no other woman could penetrate: It demanded a man's logic, a man's mastery. The pure male insolence of someone like Deuce Cavender.

No!

Yes! And if someone like Deuce wanted a woman like Ellie . . . The thought was torture. Ellie, of course, would have discarded her rose gown and underthings, and her bare body would be just barely covered by the thin revealing sheet. She would hold her arm under her breasts to push them forward slightly (she would have to, Kalida assured herself with some satisfaction), and after a moment, that would not matter. Deuce would have stripped away the sheet, and it would not matter.

And then . . . And then Ellie would have the pleasure of those large, hot knowledgeable hands exploring and discovering. Only Ellie would be receptive, not abrasive and disparaging. She would allow . . . She would not . . .

Of course she would—anything Kalida would not. And what had Kalida not? . . . she asked herself in consternation.

Her body quivered; she could not spend a night like this, wondering enthralled by the vision of what might be happening, probably *was* happening.

Her imagination was too vivid; the picture she envisioned of Ellie entwined in Deuce's arms, his mouth ravishing her saucy breasts, scorched her consciousness and nearly drove her wild with longing that it was she experiencing the unbridled pleasure of his virile tongue.

She had to stop it and face the fact Deuce was not going to come looking for her this evening. Whether he was with Ellie or not was irrelevant. She had wanted privacy and now she had it. She could now curl up with her ultimate desire and derive the fullest pleasure from her solitude.

The brazen little bitch, he thought, as he stood in the door of the room where Kalida all unknowingly slept. It was very late. He had left everyone and gone off by himself, first outside to the porch and subsequently to his office, where he knew no one would seek him out. He had had enough of Ellie—and Ardelle, come to that, after a half-hour—and he had felt that Kalida ought to have time to stew over the outrageous little plot she had created and to assess the consequences.

Certainly she had looked upset, as he had paid obsequious attention to Ellie, and it was obvious she was very close to stamping pettishly out of the room at one point.

He had not expected her to abscond entirely. Her claws were out again, ready to rake him over. Well, she didn't know it yet, but she had met her match. He was the man who would tame the cat.

"Kalida!"

His voice roared all up and down the hallway an hour later, waking Ardelle and Madame and Prestina, who grumblingly shut their collective doors in his face. Only Ellie hung in her doorway, pulsating and seductive in her thin lawn nightgown, which she had not bothered to cover with a robe. "Deuce?" her low, throaty voice inquired with a touch of curiosity.

"Kalida in your room?" he demanded roughly.

"Why no, and why would you be looking for her, when *I'm* there?" she wanted to know in her roundest, huskiest tone. Just the faintest hint of poutiness permeated her words, but she instantly saw the mistake of doing that. He was after Kalida, for whatever reason, and there was no doubt about it.

"She took something of mine," he growled enignmatically, thrusting open the door across the hallway.

Ellie shrugged. "I'd like to take something of yours,"

she whispered invitingly.

He shot her a baleful look and she retreated; there was no way to warm him up in this kind of mood. She turned on her heel and allowed her gown to slide alluringly off her shoulder to expose part of her back.

He never noticed. He was rapping on the next door, his voice commanding over the din, "Kalida!" Ellie slammed her door behind her, his voice a concert of harsh syllables behind her.

"Kalida!"

She heard him well enough. His first bellow had awakened her along with the others, but she had been damned if she were going to be pulled to his highness's side like some puppet at his mere demand.

And then again, but this time Ellie's voice intermixed with his in a way that sent a shiver down her spine. He was coming from Ellie's room to her! His gall was staggering.

She hoisted herself up into a sitting position on the bed and waited. He started banging on the door. Dimly she heard the slam of another door—Ellie rebuffed.

Good!

His first rammed into her door. She wasn't even trying to evade him. "Take me if you can," she called out recklessly, and she did not know what precipitated such volatile rashness—Ellie's voice, perhaps, or her own nightmares, opaque but there, festering. Things she was not admitting to herself. The desire to incite his desire, to control *him* in the only way she could. All those things fused in a moment of heady power over him that provoked her brash command, and he answered it resoundingly by crashing through the door.

She was sitting in the middle of the plain pine four-poster bed, her back against the undecorated headboard, her knees drawn up to her chest. Her midnight hair curled in wild abandon all around her, half pinned up, half falling to her shoulders, its disarray a testimony to her troubled sleep. It shone stark black against the white-washed wall above her head, merging with the shadows cast by the guttering wick of the kerosene lamp.

"Good evening, Deuce," she said coolly.

"Aren't you the clever minx?" he murmured consideringly as he shut the door and paced around to the opposite side of the room. "The spitting cat turns tail and runs."

"Takes on protective coloration, perhaps?" Kalida suggested, cringing a little as he drew closer, dangerously closer.

"My darling Kalida-cat, you could not hide that coloration in the desert, let alone anywhere on Sweetland. What the hell do you think you're doing?"

His tone was reasonable—too reasonable; she had the grim feeling any excuse she tendered would be brushed aside like a whirlwind. Nonetheless, she girded herself, without moving a muscle, and prepared to do battle. "Well, I was sure that, since the patrol was disbanded—for this week at least—that you meant for me to have a separate room and some privacy."

"You were sure, were you?" he asked silkily, pacing back and forth in front of her bed, his shadow moving edgily back and forth over the blanket rail. "So sure?" He wheeled on her, his eyes flinty charcoal, glittery at her audaciousness. How far did she think she could push him? he wondered. How far would she try? The glint in his eye turned speculative. What was she expecting him to do? The obvious, most probably, as though he were some savage with no feeling but that in his loins. Yes, she surely was expecting some fierce response, and God, one part of him wanted dearly to give into the ferocious desire he felt.

But the thought of luring her by doing something unexpected appealed to him even more. To make her beg

243

. . . His eyes smoked up and the force of his hunger assaulted his very vitals. To compel Kalida to beg . . . He drew in a deep, heavy breath.

And Kalida watched him, her eyes sharpened to every subtle movement as his initial anger evaporated before her intent blue gaze. She immediately became more wary. In this mood, she fully expected him to hoist her up over his shoulder and carry her back to his room just to prove the point that her defiance was no match for his invincible male strength. Damn it all, she thought; it would never get that far. In her heart, she knew it; if he touched her, she would not struggle *very* hard.

But he didn't intend to drag her back to his room, kicking and screaming. "You were wrong," he said suddenly.

For a moment, she thought he was reading her mind and her heartbeat accelerated. "Wrong?" she queried innocuously, as she realized he was not referring at all to her fantasy, or to her secret knowledge of what she would or would not do if he were to approach her.

"You were meant to share my room, Kalida, no matter who is or is not staying in the house. I don't take it kindly that you took it on yourself to renege on my arrangements."

Of course not, your highness, she thought contemptuously; your word is law, your household members are your vassals. So what if he calmed down from his initial rage; his intention was the same. He would punish her now by ignoring her, and she would wind up back in his room, and that would be that. He had probably had some evening with Ellie; no wonder there was no vigor left to deal with her. It was just as she had thought: He would keep them both and damn anyone's opinion.

"All right, I give up," she said, swinging her black-sheathed legs off the bed.

He held up his hand. "I wouldn't dream of discommoding you." The hand moved to his shirt, and he began unbuttoning it.

"What are you doing?" she demanded.

"I can sleep here just as well as anywhere else," he said, removing his shirt with a deliberate politeness that did not fool her one bit. "Come. I promise I won't lay a hand on you."

"Two hands," she prompted sarcastically, watching him distrustfully.

His skin seemed darker in the lowering lamplight, his matted chest broader. Every muscle constricted as he bared his upper torso and sat down heavily on the opposite side of the bed, looking at her over his shoulder.

"No hands," he said with a crooked smile.

"You *must* be tired," she muttered. "All that dinner and then all the rest . . ." And she would have to face Ellie's gloating black gaze in the morning.

"All what rest?" He bent forward to tug at his boots, amused at her reaction to his blatant undressing. She hadn't expected that. She still sat on the edge of the bed, holding her black-clad spine as stiffly as possible, trying to minimize the impact of her dress against her ivory skin, trying desperately to figure out what he meant to do.

He pulled off his boots and tossed them across the room, where they landed with a resounding *thunk*. Then he pulled the pillow out from under the bedspread, punched it down to make it more comfortable, and set it up against the headboard. He lifted his long muscular legs onto the bed, settled his head and shoulders against the pillow, and folded his arms across his chest.

"All what rest?" he repeated conversationally, contemplating the rigid back still facing him, the perfect posture and the tumbling black hair that blended with the heavy tactile material of the dress.

"All the energy you must have expended on Ellie," she

said reluctantly, her voice somewhat muffled. "No wonder you're tired. This afternoon with me, this evening with Ellie . . ." Her voice trailed off. She knew she was on very dangerous ground here. She wondered whether she wanted to deliberately goad him; it seemed like the words spilled out of her almost of their own volition. Perhaps she wanted him to deny it, or to be pushed hard enough *to* touch her. "It's been a busy day," she finished lightly.

"Scratch, scratch," he murmured appreciatively. He was really beginning to regret he had said he wouldn't touch her. That comment at the very least deserved a hard shake, perhaps more. Definitely more. If only she were facing him, she would see it in his smoky gray eyes. But her face remained adamantly averted.

"Kalida." His tone was still pleasant, but a vein of iron underlay his commanding statement of her name. She refused to turn.

"Good night, Deuce." There, that should put an end to his little game. She stood up, fully intending to turn down the light, and his steely voice stopped her. "Sit down, Kalida."

She sat. He could have reached out and whipped her back as easily as he tossed a rope, but compliance was easier.

"Facing me," he added, in that chippy tone, and she twisted her head toward him, sending him a disdainful blue look over her shoulder.

"Facing *me,* Kalida," he said dryly. And he waited. It was so hard for her to have someone else order her. There was reluctance in every line of her body, and in the length of time it finally took her to shift herself so that her whole torso was turned to him and he could clearly see her face—and her unwillingness.

"You're playing cat and mouse with me," she accused angrily.

"Ah, but who is really the cat and who is really the

mouse?" he murmured. At this point even he did not know. He shifted his body forward and slithered closer to her. "Shall we find out?" He was six inches away from her now, and the heaving of her breasts was obvious against the confining line of the dress.

"You weren't going to touch me," she muttered under her breath, girding herself against the assault on her senses by his overpowering maleness.

He moved even closer. "Not with my hands," he agreed huskily, and his mouth slanted across hers, holding, waiting. "Nothing has changed," he whispered. "Nothing." His lips brushed hers, a mere breathless movement against them, so intense it sent a glissade of sensation spiralling through her.

He knew it; the faintest tremor shook her body. He had to lace his fingers together to prevent himself from touching her, but he swore he wouldn't, and he meant not to. She would have to demand it. Voice it. Want it.

The light surrounding them flickered as the wick burned still lower. He could still see her features now that he was so close. Her eyes flashed navy under the half-closed lids, covered lest they give something away. But her lips were slightly parted and he couldn't tell if it was an invitation or she meant to say something. Probably the latter, he thought ruefully. He waited, assessing her reaction.

She remained motionless; if she moved, she would dissolve against him. She had no defense against anything he could do to her except to prolong her ultimate capitulation.

She felt a suppressed excitement course through her, as if the power had suddenly shifted to her, compounded by the initial arousing touch of his lips and the knowledge of what would come and how he would pursue her.

"Kalida . . ."

He meant for her to acquiesce; he did not know who

247

held the control here. Her expression turned haughty, her navy-darkened eyes glittering with insolent challenges. She sat as still as a statue, daring him to tear away the trappings.

His fingers tensed with the overwhelming desire to strip away the elegant dress and reveal the sleek voluptuous nakedness beneath. He knew every inch of that delectable body, and he meant to taste its succulence tonight. But not yet. Not quite yet. Not until *she* was pulsating with the yearning to have him explore and taste her perfume. Not until she was white hot with wanting him, begging him . . . It was time she understood the nature of her own fierce primitive desire.

And he waited, feeling her excitement expand as the knowledge of the tempestuous passion between them sizzled in the air, in their minds, in their slowly, tantalizingly aroused bodies, lured by the incandescent thought of what could happen.

If only he would just . . . she thought, licking her dry lips nervelessly. She wanted him to seize her and hold her; she wanted him to crush his mouth down on hers just so, to feel the softness, the pliancy of her lips, tasting them, yes, pulling away from them too soon, hovering so close. She leaned forward an inch in invitation, and he captured her lips again, gentle, soft, feeling their texture. Releasing them with just the slightest pressure.

She was ready to scream; this was not nearly enough, and he sensed her urgency. He loved her urgency, but he wasn't about to give in to it, in spite of his own unruly craving for her. His mouth came down on hers again in that same slow, exploratory tasting way, pressing harder this time, feeling the shape of her lips with the firm tip of his tongue. And pulling away again and looking at her in that *knowing* male way.

She met his smoky gaze with a baleful blue look and folded her shaking hands primly on her lap. That provoking action earned her another innocent, devastating caress of her lips, which left them tingling with yearning long before she was ready. The realization made her furious and bold all at once, and resentful that he should know it.

"Say it," he murmured, watching her revealing eyes.

"You want everything your own way," she hissed, pulling back.

"Everything," he agreed huskily; he had said it before. He waited for a long, long moment, and then teased her lips again, bedeviling them with little smacking kisses. His refusal to taste her, to kiss her fully, inflamed her still more. She would never importune him but she sought to tempt him, thrusting her tongue between his lips each time he touched hers. He nipped at her for her impudence, sucking her lower lip violently as punishment, refusing the invitation of her tongue, ignoring the wanton wet enticement.

"Say it." His voice was harsh with unleased tension, and she responded by impertinently sticking out her tongue at him.

"You brazen bitch," he growled, "who the hell gave you the right to do that to me—to both of us? Say it now, or I'll leave the room."

The air vibrated with his thick hot urgency. Who was in control now? she wondered grimly. Her body was in control. Her body wanted what was hers to have for the price of a mere few words. Her body demanded the ecstasy of his ravishing tongue against hers. Her body spoke for her, whispering the words, "I need to taste you."

"Yes . . ." he groaned, and covered her mouth instantly, seeking her tongue, surrounding it with his lips, tugging at it, sucking it until her yearning body writhed in exultation. Her arms, of their own volition, sought his body to pull him closer to her. The lush thrusts of his tongue drove her to unbridled excitement that shimmered through her veins; his heat and voluptuous wetness swirled through her senses erotically, compelling her hands to feel him and stroke him in concert with what his delectable tongue was doing to hers.

His whole body was taut and erect with massive sensual tension. And yet, he still had not touched her. He braced his body against his arms on either side of her thighs, and he did not once, as his provocative tongue enslaved hers, touch her. She wanted him to touch her.

But he must know that, she thought dimly, he wanted her. His need was palpable; his succulent tongue had aroused her to an almost unbearable excitement. She felt liquid with her own honey, ready for anything he wanted. And still only his hot tongue possessed her.

"Deuce—" she pleaded fretfully, her hands sliding all over his hard muscular arms and chest, raking his skin lightly.

He growled deep in his throat, delving into her mouth again for the luscious taste of her.

She wrenched away. "Deuce—" Her voice was shaky, her need all-consuming. *Why* was he not stripping away her dress and caressing her fevered skin?

"Ummm." He licked her lips, nibbling at them, rimming them with the firm tip of his tongue. "What is it, Kalida?"

"What are you doing?"

"I'm devouring you." His tongue skimmed against the lush curve of her lower lip.

"Is that all?" she managed to whisper. Did she have to *tell* him? Had she ever had to tell him?

"Is that all?" he echoed in wonderment, pausing in his pursuit of her delicious tongue, pulling back and regarding her swollen lips and passion-glazed eyes. "Is there more?"

"Deuce—"

"Well, is there?" His soft voice caressed the air as his

soft lips gently wafted across hers, pressed against them, wet them, seduced them. "You tell me, Kalida," he whispered, his mouth still against hers. "Is there? Do you want there to be?"

"Yes," she breathed, and tilted her head to give him her willing tongue once again. "Yes." He filled her mouth and she could not get enough of his taste. "Now," she pleaded, gripping his tense hard-muscled arms.

"Tell me," he commanded huskily. "Tell me." He crushed her lips again with his own, seeking her once again with wet gossamer strokes that aroused her senses, mastering her satin tongue, dominating it, loving it. "Now . . ." he ordered in a voice barely above a breath.

"I want you." Her own voice was shaky with her own wild need, not even a whisper.

"Show me."

"Oh God, Deuce . . ."

"Show me." His voice became stronger, less a prisoner to his rigid rampaging masculinity as he determined to finish what he had started. He bit at her lips, demanding entry to the silken recesses of her mouth, thrusting his bold way within as deeply and firmly as he would her body. Yes, it would have been far easier to tear away her clothes and take her willing nakedness and possess it. It would have drowned the raging fever of desire that he had never experienced before. But it never would have satisfied his need to hear, from her own lips, of her wanton need for him. To hear her demand the delights of his ravishing tongue; to have her beg for the ecstasy of his sex.

She quivered under the expert manipulation of his wild kisses. She gave herself to him, wholly, wantonly, willing him to undress her, take her beneath him, and fill her as hard and deep as he could. And still he did not touch her. She felt like tearing off her own clothes, but the damned dress had hooks and buttons, and even as she thought it, her hands flew shakily behind her neck to work the fastenings as best she could. While his tongue coaxed her and inflamed her with its wet erotic movements, her tense fingers ripped at the buttons, finally feeling them come apart—an ecstatic feeling—as she lowered her arms and began shrugging the sleeves off her shoulders.

First one sleeve and then the other, and the wretched undergarment, as she played with his insistent tongue and dueled with it. Then suddenly her breasts were bare, and she reacted to the cool night air against her hot skin. Her nipples hardened, and she arched her back artlessly as she wriggled out of the dress and underwear and tossed them across the room. She wore little else—just garters, stockings, and shoes, and she kicked the shoes across the room impatiently.

He stayed her hands as she reached for the garters, pulling his ardent mouth away from hers to gaze at her with his coal-dark implacable eyes.

"Deuce—" Her swollen lips formed his name in the air; her whole body yearned toward him.

"Tell me now, Kalida," he murmured, riveted by the sight of her taut-nippled breasts and the erotic dark stockings encasing her long strong legs. He envisioned those legs wrapped around him and her body beneath him, convulsing in blinding ecstasy. His hands lifted themselves from hers, and she whispered, "Touch me, Deuce. I need to feel your hands on me, all over me. . . ." Her words became an urgent command, compelling him, inviting him to enfold her in his arms, to take her avid lips and tongue once more, to feel her nakedness against him for all time.

He lay her back against his arm to support her, freely moving his left hand up and down her body, seeking out the tempting curves and the enticing heat of the root of her feminity, discovering anew the sleek lines of her hip and thigh, the luscious curve of her breasts and buttocks.

He felt her everywhere, with lingering, lavish caresses wherever she demanded by the delicious little sounds in the back of her throat. She quivered at his touch, writhing against his hands tantalizingly, lifting one sleek black-clad leg to angle it outward so that nothing would be denied his rapacious fingers.

Her sultry heated words goaded them both on. "Yes, do that; yes, more, yes again." Breathless sounds in the encroaching darkness that would soon swallow them up, surround them like a blanket. Her insistent hands pulled at his remaining clothing, feeling the tight hard ridge of his elongated manhood prodding at its confinement, pulsating with its rock solid tumescence against her hand.

Their mouths crashed, open to each other, ravenous with tempestuous, uncontrollable feelings, sumptuous and consuming. And when his hand, gliding upward from its intimate caress of her velvet cleft, deliberately and incisively grazed her lush, rigid right nipple she groaned and swooned at the rush of pure molten feeling that flooded through her.

"Hold me there," she breathed through the haze of thick honey that enveloped her. And he held the tight hard nipple just so between his fingers, devouring with his smoky gray eyes that the picture that she made, lying naked in his arms, her long black-stockinged legs open to him, his fingers gently fondling her taut nipple while her hand pulled brazenly at his swollen manhood, yanking at the buttons that kept it bound tightly against his body.

And then the lamp dimmed and flickered out altogether. The darkness enfolded them, enhancing his wanton caresses, emboldening her to pull away the last barrier to his lusty manhood. Her hand audaciously grasped its hard strength and everything in him felt her strong, euphoric fingers. She held him tightly, and he held her just so she could feel the brief, exquisite glissade of his fingers on her nipple peak. His ferocious tongue settled against hers, demanding her, tasting her again and again, dizzyingly, until he released her and moved to her lips, her neck, and down still further to the swell of her breasts, where his sultry tongue replaced his sensitive fingers.

Her powerful response to his ravenous sucking drove everything from his mind but the need to possess her. Her body heaved against his, beckoning, beguiling him with her movements. His wet hot tongue surrounded the dazzling point of pleasure at the tip of her nipple, and thick gold poured through her veins, spreading outward and downward, melting into her feminine fount, becoming liquefied, shimmering.

She reached for him then, and with a sinuous movement, entwined herself around him, opening herself to him and luring him with her powerfully undulating hips.

He poised himself above her, regretfully removing his mouth from her luscious breast, and with one ferocious virile thrust, he plunged deep into her exquisitively moist, tight sheath.

Her femininity enfolded him, and the sense he felt of his possession of her took his breath away. He had waited for this moment the entire evening and he reveled in it. God, how he wanted her, how he had always wanted her. And in this moment of her quivering submission and voracious demand, he gave himself to her with total abandon.

She felt the turbulence in him as he rested deep and throbbing within her honeyed warmth. He filled her so tightly and completely that the whole elemental maleness of him encompassed her entire body. She held him tightly, her hose-clad legs wrapped around him, her hands gripping him, her mouth seeking the hot nectar of his. She wanted him to stay and she wanted him to move so she could feel every inch of the hard driving slide of his maleness stroking her; she loved his heated nakedness and the knowledge of what it could do to her. Her body tensed, enjoying the thick elongated feel of him nestling within her, anticipating the lusty thrust of his firm hips.

He possessed her mouth as fully as he possessed her body. His insatiable tongue caressed every inch of it as he lay quiescent on her, savoring her moist readiness. And then he became aware of just the faintest impatient wriggle against his hips. Just the tiniest pressing undulation of her body. And then her urgent sigh, "Deuce . . ."

"Kalida . . ." He breathed against her mouth, every inch of his primitive maleness aching to plunge into her provocative femininity. And he waited, lavishing hot little licks all over her lips and tongue, her eyes and face; he thrust his tongue against hers again and again in the same torrid movement with which he would have propelled himself into her velvet core. He heard her moans of rampant need, and he slipped his right hand downward, to slide under her buttocks, to cushion her and lift her alluring femininity even more snugly against him. He felt as if he had, with that one sultry motion, pushed his massive rigidity even deeper into her wanton heat.

Her buttocks constricted in response, and her body surged with a telling demand. "Deuce . . ." She was begging now, ripe for his delectation, the thick nectar of her sex surrounding him, potent and tantalizing. Her shameless provocative movements tempted him, enchanted him. The unbridled longing in her voice enslaved him.

"Yes," he murmured, lifting her lower torso still harder against his male hips. The message was powerful and clear: He possessed her fully with his virile maleness, his caressing hands, his rapacious mouth.

She rocked against him fiercely, commanding him to move, to caress her satin core with long, sliding, opulent strokes. To find her secret center and arouse her ravenous desire.

He took her then, driving into her white hot passion

255

with tempestuous lunges. There were no words for the blinding ecstasy of sensation that consumed them. Her legs slid down his sleek sweaty flanks to brace against the back of his knees so that she could open herself to him still more. Her sizzling gyrations matched the cadence of his thrusts, movement to movement, and each forceful drive sent shimmers of heat through her very core. She invited more, enticing him with her hunger, her ardor, her demand, tempting his lusty manhood with every torrid surge of her hips. She could not get enough of his bold, hard-driving masculinity.

And he was equally determined not to give in to her enticing blandishments. His vigorous thrusts gradually subsided into long, slow languorous strokes, which sent radiant tendrils of sensation rioting all over her body. She swiveled her hips against the molten lunge of his iron rod, seeking surcease and reaching for the incandescent glow of culmination.

His body tautened and tightened as her urgency compelled him. She twisted against him wildly as the glow heated up, and his hot thrusts stoked it and stroked it into a piercing, smouldering flame. Her voluptuous movements drew him with her, igniting his desire.

Her hands moved involuntarily all over him, feeling the planes of his back and shoulders, sliding and squeezing all over the curve of his buttocks, beguiled by the hard softness of his body and the contrast with hers. Her fevered body plunged in concert with his, pushing him to his limits. She knew it. She could feel the tenseness in him as her hands explored his nakedness. His heat seared her, arousing her still more. The lambent glow expanded slowly, luminously; her ripe femininity ground against his granite length violently as the glow deepened to red hot, blinding and brilliant.

Every sense in him answered her final need. He heaved his body upward for one final thick, hard potent thrust, and a cascade of fire shot in a raging torrent through her veins.

There was silence. Pure pulsating mindless silence. His weight pleasured her, as did the feel of naked skin against naked skin. The still stiff maleness of him deep inside her. The slick wetness of his seed moistening her most secret place. She felt full and sated, her body lightweight, floating. She did not know if he were awake or asleep. She lay quiescent in the torrid silence.

A tickling sensation and a sense of warmth woke her. She became gradually aware that now he was lying naked next to her, his granite length rock hard and prodding her hips and thighs gently. She heard the sibilant sound of her name being whispered over and over, and felt the soft press of his lips against her ear and neck, the weight of his hairy muscular leg entwined with her black-sheathed limbs.

She shuddered with a palpable excitement as he awakened her with his sensual stroking. The silky skimming touch of his right hand caressed her cheek, her neck, her shoulder, cupped her left breast, and slid with potent purpose to her womanly core.

"Kalida . . ."

"I'm here," she sighed, and turned to face him, offering him her lips and tongue. He took them with sultry possession, twisting his rock hard body against hers and pulling her snugly against his hot length.

Her body strained against the consuming arousal of his kiss. When he removed his mouth, she could have screamed with disappointment. But his lips trailed down to her breast to taste her burgeoning nipple and suck it to a stiff peak, downward still more to taste the nectar of her feminine fount.

His hands slid down her body concurrently with his

mouth, feeling every silken inch of her, settling finally on the edge of one stocking-clad leg. Now his avid mouth followed his stroking hands as they gently began removing the stocking from her right leg, rolling it down, following it with his mouth and tiny succulent flicks of his tongue along the tender inner flesh of her thigh, sliding the flimsy material down and kissing and sucking the luscious skin of her inner leg with moist flutters of his greedy tongue.

She held herself violently still as the hot wet trail of his tongue came to rest on her instep as he stripped off the stocking and tossed it aside. She felt the flat of his tongue hot against her foot, and she angled her leg outward to give him better access to her thighs as the wet heat began its exquisite lingering course back up her satiny inner flesh.

Slowly he licked and kissed his way back upward, sliding his tongue across her abdomen to the tender silky skin of the opposite thigh, pulling, caressing the soft material of the stocking downward, stroking her heated skin with his wet wanton tongue, sliding the wetness deliciously along her left inner thigh in a downward glissade that bared her long strong leg and ended with his lips sucking at her foot as he caressed the last inch of material from her toes.

His whole mouth cupped her leg as he slid his pliant tongue sensually back up her ankle, calf, and inner thigh. The hot wet of his tongue lapped at her skin, tasting every inch of it as he languorously sucked his way up her leg, pausing just at tenderest part of her thigh to nibble moistly at her soft, fragrant flesh.

Each hot little nip drove her wild with excitement. Her body quivered, tantalizing him with her responsive movement to the succulent motion of his sultry tongue. She felt his hands extending her legs, lifting them and angling the left one so that his smouldering tongue coursed deliciously downward in a long, luscious slide right to her moist, churning center, his avid mouth positioned against her welcoming warmth.

Her wildly constricting hands pulled at his hair, pushing him ever tighter against her clamoring body. Her hips heaved upwards, and he reached for her buttocks and held them in a tight hard grasp as she opened up to him totally, her body convulsing in succulent spasms that left her breathless and trembling.

He shifted himself away and upward, to lie next to her. "From me, Kalida. Only from me."

"Yes," she whispered, leaning over him, seeking his mouth, wanting to devour him in the same ferocious way.

"You are mine," he growled, opening his mouth to her, yielding to her own voracious need. He pulled away from her ravenous seeking suddenly. "You want me, Kalida."

"Do I?" she demanded in a breathless whisper. Her arms wound around his neck and pulled his mouth to hers. His tongue darted out at her lips, licking them and biting them, memorizing their soft succulent shape, and then delving between them to find her provocative tongue.

His hands cupped her buttocks, sliding over their pillowy softness, squeezing them, following their tempting line to caress her from behind.

Her alluring mouth, beneath his, shaped a startled "O" at the delicious sensation that soon aroused her to smouldering need once more. She ground her buttocks languidly against the firm thrust of his fingers and arched her body to shift her position so that her breasts grazed his poised tongue.

He lifted her body over his so that his lips and velvet tongue could feast on the taut rosy crest of her jutting left breast. Liquid heat cascaded in a torrent through her veins as he seduced her pebble-hard nipple. She pressed her body against his elongated granite length enticingly, tempting him, luring him, entwining her soft feminine legs with his hard muscular male thighs, arching her long sleek back to give him perfect access to her lush nipple and her churning buttocks against his avidly exploring fingers.

She moaned as he sought her right breast, as his hot tongue licked the tight taut nipple, curled around it, settled against its luscious enticement, and squeezed it finally with a firm compression of his lips.

"Deuce," she hissed through the thick glistening haze of undulating pleasure.

"You love it," he growled, sucking the luscious nipple with firm lavish strokes of his tongue.

"I can't bear it," she whispered, throwing her head back ecstatically as he pulled harder at the firm, tight nipple tip.

"You can bear it—from me," he breathed against her hot skin. He was aching for her; his turgid length elongated still harder and stiffer with each torrid movement of her ripe, alluring body. One hard, long thrust and he could be enfolded in her satin heat, making her writhe with unbridled ecstasy. He wanted her at this moment beyond anything he had ever felt for her. His rapacious fingers began their sinuous delving into her moistness, adoring the way her plunging hips responded to his sensual probing.

She undulated against the sumptuous sensations he was evoking, feeling all open and powerfully naked to him. She loved everything he was doing to her; every impassioned caress sent a ripple of sinuous feeling spiralling through the center of her body. She invited his hands and his mouth to take her. Her surging hips clamored for his rigid masculinity.

"Oh yes, Kalida," he breathed, "I'm taking you; be aware of it. *I* am taking you, hot and willing"—he shifted her now, poising himself below her "and no one else"—his hips heaved—"in my arms, Kalida, and in my bed"—and he thrust up into her pulsating feminine core—"now. . . ."

She felt new, intense separate sensations: his hot naked massive length filling her deeply; the tight succulent pull of his mouth now on each lush nipple; the sense of her free sensual nakedness above him; the movement of his hips below in snug little thrusts that urged her to move with him with a swinging rotation of her hips.

"You love it." She hardly heard his sibilant words, but they were there suddenly, stroking her consciousness as tightly and fully as his manhood coaxed her sex.

"What do I love?" she whispered, her hands kneading the muscles of his arms and chest as his hands blatantly caressed her buttocks.

"This." One hand moved to her breast and fingered the ripe tip of her nipple. "And this. And what else your luscious conscience only knows, Kalida. You're mine now." He braced his body so that his torso was upright. "Tell me what you need," he ordered huskily.

"Cover me," she moaned, the words a throaty breath in the air between them. But he heard her, and the sultry need in her. With one mighty tug, he rolled her over on her back and lay his weight on her body as she craved.

Her long, strong naked legs wrapped around him, and her hands boldly slid over his sleek, hard muscular shoulders. She was breathless with anticipation now, seeking his mouth again, writhing impatiently against the enticing hardness that still joined them, entreating him to move and fill her with his sumptuous passion.

"Kalida—" He kissed her swollen lips gently at first, murmuring her name like a litany. He feasted on her succulence as his undulating hips began giving her a taste of what was to come.

Her whirling hips quivered with her demand. "Take me if you can," she whispered.

"Oh, I will," he growled. His hips shifted, lifting in a

long smooth slide that left her feeling bereft as his thick length poised itself to possess her fully.

"Now?" she breathed, goading him just that little bit with the poutiness in her throaty question, taking the tip of his tongue between her teeth provocatively.

It worked. He thrust his tongue forcefully into her mouth at the same moment he drove his massive maleness into her straining feminine heat. And then out again, and then in, with a fierce thrusting cadence that thrilled her. She yielded her body to his virile stroking, meeting each lunge with shameless abandon, matching his movements with the savage surge of her own.

She was made for this—made for him, she thought recklessly in the throes of her silken surrender. He had only to seduce her with his virile masculinity; she wanted it, she needed it. His vigorous thrusting slowed suddenly, as he sensed her coming capitulation. He wanted her to feel all of him as he possessed her intimately, pleasuring her in a way that no other man could ever duplicate.

"You're mine," he growled raggedly, deep in his throat. "Your nakedness is mine, Kalida; your body is mine"— and his left hand swooped down to possess the curve of her hip—"your breasts are mine"—and up to caress the tight hard nub of her nipple—"your lips are mine"—and he covered her mouth violently.

Her body writhed at the words she knew were true. She could never deny her need to possess his maleness, to have him slowly invading her with the shimmering glissade of feeling that only he could evoke. To feel it building with each leisurely stroke, all glistening heat, surrounding her, cushioning her in a haze that tantalized her with luscious eddying cascades of sensation. Filling her, molten and gold, glowing and rich now, expanding within her, filling her and filling her again, rich and hot and dazzling as the feeling exploded into a ravishing white glow of pure radiant pleasure.

He gave her the enchanting moment, as she acknowledged with her sobbing moans that it was he who was connected to her, he whose lusty thrusts commanded her potent climax.

And then he plunged his rigid length into her fiery body blindly and mindlessly, releasing the torrent of his passion deep within her.

Thirteen

In the morning he was gone before she awakened, but she fully expected that. She stretched luxuriously, exulting in the euphoric memories of the night before, refusing to think of anything but the cataclysmic pleasure she had shared with him.

Shared with *him,* her mind echoed, and her willful body bolted upright. Nothing has changed, he had said. He had said he wanted her, threatened to have her any way he could, and now *was* having her, and she was falling for his inexorable, artful seduction.

But nothing had changed; she was still the collateral for a business deal. She was still immured like a piece of porcelain on a shelf at Sweetland. Her father had only done the barest minimum of his plans to restore and reorganize his ranch and his cattle herd. And her choices were just as limited this minute as they had been yesterday.

The only clear thing Kalida knew was that she wanted Deuce, and she did not want to precipitate him into Ellie Dean's arms.

She looked around the room that was still permeated with the powerful scent of their lovemaking. Her dress lay crumpled on the floor where she had flung it; her stockings were a pool of sensual black beside it, a reminder of his devastating seduction of her and her convulsive response. Even as she remembered it, her body reacted.

God, she desperately needed to get away from him, from her volcanic surrender to his touch. She jumped out of bed and ran to the little wardrobe where she had hung her skirt and shirtwaist. And stopped. The lush naked figure coming toward her was herself, with her jutting, proud rose-peaked breasts and all the firm, responsive curves that Deuce had wantonly explored hours ago. Her midnight wild hair was tangled and tousled with her sensuous head tossing, and her cobalt eyes reflected a deep lambent glow of satisfaction that was not manifested in her somewhat petulant expression.

She did not *want* to be in thrall of Deuce Cavender's body and hands and wayward tongue. He could never lay a hand on her again, for all she cared, she vowed, dragging out her clothing frantically as if it would ease the ache in her loins and the pulsating memory of the night before.

She picked up the wrinkled undergarments from the floor with trembling fingers, remembering it had been she who had removed them in such overwhelming haste. She threw them on the bed, hating them, and picked up the black stockings Deuce had so deliciously stripped from her long legs. The memory of him caressing and kissing her feet aroused her instantly. She held up the crumpled stockings and the thought came unbidden into her mind: I want him to do that again.

Her naked body recoiled. She did not; she did not want him to touch her again ever. Except . . . She sat down on the bed and began sliding on one stocking. She secured it with an elastic garter and began with the other one. Her hands began shaking. She knew what she was going to do, she couldn't pretend she didn't. But not because of Deuce, because *she* wanted to. *She* wanted to wear the hose, and she elected not to wear the undergarments. She ignored the excitement of her pulsing body and the stiff peaking of her nipples and what she hoped, in her secret heart, would happen.

She buttoned the shirtwaist over her jutting hard-nippled breasts, breathless with a feeling of anticipation. The skirt came next, lifted over her unruly black hair and sliding down over her upper torso to be buttoned by her nerveless fingers. She slid into her boots as she ran a brush through her tangled inky hair.

She felt her nakedness beneath the clothes intensely, as well as the slight constriction around her thighs that defined the length of the stockings on her long legs.

It was no matter, she told her reflection; Deuce would be gone the whole day, busy moving the summer herd out to market and settling in the others to summer pasture. Tomorrow, he would be on his way to Stoneface Ridge.

He wouldn't be thinking of her. All her little plots and plans would go to waste.

Except somehow she was going to get to Stoneface and help bring down her father's herd.

The thought calmed her wildly pumping heart. It was crazy. Her knowledge that Deuce would love to discover her nakedness made her heart accelerate unbelievably. Her navy eyes glittered with a sultry light. It just wasn't going to happen today, she told herself. No matter how much she might want it.

Kalida was still shaking with that fine sensual tension when she left the room. She hardly expected the first thing to be dealt with was Ellie, who came barging out of her room at exactly the same moment.

"Good morning," she said coolly, instantly in control as those feelings evaporated at the sight of Ellie.

"Kalida," Ellie acknowledged. "We seem to be keeping the same schedule today." Her opaque black eyes swept over Kalida as if she expected to see some visible evidence

266

of what had happened between her and Deuce. But Kalida was clever. The only telltale sign of the evening's passionate ending was the slight swelling of her soft lips, which she kept touching somewhat self-consciously.

Ellie did not like that. The ease with which the one time gangling, bluntly outspoken child had captivated Deuce Cavender was galling; somehow, in the short space of several years, she had assumed a relentless sensual power that overran anything in its path.

Including Ellie, who once again had the unpleasant feeling she was an afterthought. She was tired of being overlooked and left behind. Tired of petulant babies like Kalida robbing her of what was rightfully hers, taking away chances, and making her invisible. Someone would pay for Kalida's insolence, she vowed, preferably Kalida herself.

But she showed none of this condemnation to Kalida as, in inimical amiability, they proceeded downstairs where Prestina awaited them. Ardelle was nowhere around, and they elected to take breakfast on the porch. It was a curiously silent meal until Prestina removed the plates and platters and served the coffee. Then Ellie settled her sedate gray-dressed figure into one of the wicker rocking chairs, Kalida perched on the porch railing, and they sipped their coffee in a wary silence.

"You're over the shock of the ranch?" Ellie asked suddenly, her black eyes focused straight ahead.

"I have to be," Kalida said, wondering what Ellie was after with this conversational gambit. "I can't change it."

"No," said Ellie, "you can't." She sipped her coffee broodingly. "It was surprising that all the rubble had been cleared away."

"Papa said he was attending to it."

"But so expeditiously," Ellie said. "That kind of decisiveness is more Deuce's style, don't you think?"

"I don't think; Papa intended to take care of it, and he

did," Kalida said firmly. Oh, did she not like what Ellie was implying. What other nasty little remarks did Ellie have up her sleeve? she wondered.

"Have you heard from him?" Ellie asked after a moment. Even she was curious about that; it was almost as if Hal Ryland had disappeared off the face of the earth.

"No, but he hasn't been gone that long."

"Not yet," Ellie murmured into her coffee cup.

"He'll be in touch with us," Kalida reiterated. Ellie must hate her father, she thought, for her to be so vindictive. She did not have to stay and listen to Ellie's viperous comments. "*Do* you know where Ardelle is?" she asked abruptly.

"How could I?"

Kalida put down her cup decisively. "Good, I'm going riding."

"Kalida—" Ellie started to say, but Kalida had hopped off the porch railing and taken off in a brisk stride toward the stables. Malca was waiting, fresh and frisky.

She saddled him up and mounted, being careful to arrange her skirt to protect her nudity. With a liberating sense of freedom, both from her nakedness and her escaping the house, Kalida guided Malca from the corral and down to the shortcut leading to Morgan field.

When she was within minutes of it, she could already smell the earthy tang of the cattle. As she got beyond the trees, she could see the milling herd slowly moving under the careful prodding of Old Bruno and several of Jake Danton's crew. Jake was nowhere in sight, so she circled carefully around to the tail end of the drovers. No one noticed her; she had no idea how any of them would feel if she were to present herself among the hired hands.

Carefully, she picked her way to one side of the jostling cattle, on the shady side of the pasture.

From here, she could see the trail and the great green swath of pasture. She could see the line of cattle proceeding forward slowly and congestedly. She could see Old Bruno bringing up the rear.

She followed them slowly, certain that no one had seen her, keeping her distance, enjoying the morning and the luxuriant feeling of her covert nakedness.

Suddenly a calf broke from the herd and ran laterally at first, behind the herders, circling back then toward Old Bruno, and then bucking out toward the scrub brush. Bruno whipped around, saw Kalida, and hollered at her. She took off after the calf like a shot, barreling Malca at an angle to the calf's run, breaking ahead of it, and wheeling the horse around so that she was running head on into the calf. It veered toward the trees and she raced after it, whooping and zigzagging, angling across to reach the trees before it did so she could cut it off. In an instant, it wheeled and cut back across the pasture. Kalida chased it and ran it back into the herd.

"You'll do," Old Bruno shouted across the bellowing herd.

She pulled Malca to a walk and took up the opposite drag point from Old Bruno. Yes, he thought, she'd do. She knew that had been a lucky break. But she'd proved she would do, and Bruno welcomed her on the crew, and that was all that mattered.

Her shining cobalt eyes searched the landscape as the trail down to Sweetland's pastures advanced at its own leisurely pace.

Another calf broke, heading for the trees, and Kalida followed it carefully this time as it crashed into underbrush and skirted bushes. She urged Malca on cautiously but quickly to try to get ahead of the calf, who now was becoming confused and bewildered.

Kalida pushed Malca ahead so she could circle around in front of the disoriented animal, and then with her hand, she slowed Malca's walk so that the crackling of the underbrush would not scare the calf.

She jumped when she heard the low murmur of voices somewhere ahead of her. Deep in the wooded field. Surrounded by thick trees and leafed-out bushes. Who?

She edged Malca closer, her heart beating wildly because she did not like the conclusion she leapt to. Deuce. Alone in the woods with some other woman. No! She slid down from Malca's back.

She bent low, after tying Malca to an overhanging branch, and almost crawled to the point where the voices emanated. Whoever they were, they were on horseback, speaking very low and not laying in the bushes caressing each other.

She held her breath and ducked behind a nearby bush. And then she let out a breath and shook her head. Ardelle. And Jake Danton.

Ardelle must have come out for a ride and met Jake. They certainly weren't hiding; their chance meeting just happened to be secluded.

Thinking that, she still bent her body low as she made her way back to Malca. For some reason she did not want them to see *her;* there was no reason why not, she thought, except Ardelle would probably be very displeased that she was riding drag point with the calf herd. As good a reason as any. She untied Malca, swung onto his back, and picked her way back to where she had last seen the calf.

It was several hundred feet beyond that spot. Very slowly she approached it, got in front of it, and chased it back out of the woody thicket onto the trail. With very little effort after, she prodded back into the herd and was pleased again at Bruno's approbation.

She rearranged her skirts and prepared to enjoy the rest of the unhurried trip back to Sweetland.

There was a flurry of activity at Sweetland. The market

herd had been sent off, and the rest of Jake's crew was preparing to leave for Stoneface Ridge.

"Tonight?" Kalida demanded of one of the men.

"Yeah; old Deuce decided not to waste any time, ma'am. We're pulling out in an hour or so, and he reckons we can be back by tomorrow night."

Dismayed, Kalida uncinched her saddle from Malca's back. Damn and damn, he would not be with her tonight, and she would have no time to formulate some plan to get her up to Stoneface with him.

She nodded to Jake as he passed by on his way to the bunkhouse, and then as an afterthought she ran after him. "I heard right? Deuce is pulling out today for Stoneface?"

"Yep, Miss Kalida." He took off his hat in a mocking gesture of respect. "Figured we'd save a day. But don't let him see you talking with me."

"Oh Jake, I've forgotten all about that," she said airily. Well, she hadn't. And not because of Jake either. "Bye, Jake," she said abruptly, turning back to the corral.

He stared after her a moment, his hazel eyes narrowing. The stable was empty now, since all the horses were being gathered up for the remuda. She would be alone in there for several moments. Perhaps he could help her somehow.

Perhaps she was inviting him to help her. Perhaps, since she had mentioned yesterday's incident, she had obliquely implied she was ready to apologize to him. Perhaps she was waiting, brimming with excitement, for him to follow her. She would be naked under her clothes, and she would just be unbuttoning her shirt. Yes, she thought, now that his mind was really on it, that he had seen the bulge of her nipples beneath the shirt. He was absolutely sure he had seen those taut nubs jutting against the material.

He started walking forward purposefully, imagining her waiting for him, her luscious lips in a pouty expectant smile. I'm so sorry about yesterday, she would say huskily.

That bastard barged in before I could show my gratitude.

Yes, he thought, that was just how it would be. And then she would, finally, show her appreciation for his friendship.

In a riot of anticipation, he strode into the stable.

"Kalida!"

A hoarse whisper penetrated the darkness and Kalida stopped short—and Jake ducked into a nearby stall.

"Deuce?" she said uncertainly as she put up Malca's saddle and edged around the opening of his stall.

He was a tall, formidable shadow in the dusky light.

"You're leaving," Kalida said, and she knew her voice sounded accusing. He came closer and she backed against the stall wall breathlessly.

"I am," he concurred, his voice still husky. "In an hour or so; it makes sense. We're finished. I'm not too excited about hanging around here any longer than I have to. . . ."

She drew in her breath sharply. Not too excited indeed!

"Except," he added huskily, "for the fact I have to leave you for tonight."

Her mouth opened, and she said nothing. The air was thick and tangy with the musky scent of horse and masculine sweat, portentous with the scent of her knowledge of her nakedness and his memory of it.

"What—what are you doing here?" she finally managed to ask, licking her lips nervously. The movement arrested his dark gaze.

"You know what I want," he growled. "Come closer, Kalida."

His preemptory command set her hackles up, angry as she was that he was leaving today. "Why?" she asked petulantly, knowing what would goad him almost more than anything else she could do.

272

"You know why. After last night . . ." He was becoming all out of patience with her. He had almost thought she would send him off with a proper farewell, be anxious to leave the taste and scent of her with him to carry through the night. The thought was almost unbearable anyway, the way her brazen body had enslaved him last night. He could hardly bear to leave her. He could hardly wait to kiss her; it was all he was going to get to do with her tonight. His body was already taut with that thought and the memory.

He moved closer to her. "Come, Kalida; kiss me. I need the taste of you to get me through this night."

Her cobalt eyes glittered; he could just barely see them in the murkiness. He knew she would never acquiesce peacefully, and he was prepared for her resistance. He caught her in his arms and pulled her close to him. "Kiss me, Kalida." He bent his head to hers, and her lips parted and her body shuddered in anticipation.

He felt so hard to her questing hands. His body was rock tough, steamy with his sweat and his seductive male scent. His mouth came down firmly on hers for the briefest pressure of a kiss. "Open your mouth to me, Kalida," he murmured, nipping at her recalcitrant lower lip.

His voice was so alluring. His lips pressed hers gently over and over, without the heaving demand that he felt to just plunge his tongue into the hot recesses of her mouth. He coaxed her with his tempting lips and his provocative words, and his sinewy arms held her powerfully tight. She could not get away, but she could submit. Oh, but this was not submission, she thought, as his mouth dominated hers once again. She might feign unwillingness because it was her nature not to yield easily, but she knew she wanted his lush kisses if she could have nothing else of him tonight. And she knew how unbearably his kiss would arouse her, and she did not know how she would

273

be able to stand it.

Nonetheless, she wanted it, and she was aware that her resistance was exciting him unendurably, that his heated kisses were becoming more and more demanding. That her willing lips were starting to respond to the thrust and probe of his firm tongue. That his voluptuous sucking of her lips was driving her to the edge of her limits, and that where he was concerned she was beginning to have no limits.

"Ahhh, Kalida," he whispered roughly, "I need to taste you. Open your mouth to me. . . ."

His words thrilled her. "Take me," she breathed, and opened her mouth to his, almost fainting with pleasure as he filled her tender recesses with the full force of his hunger.

She pulled away from him for just an instant to whisper, "Don't go." It was all he would let her say before he claimed her pliant lips once again, taking them between his teeth, nipping and sucking them provocatively for even suggesting such a thing.

She loved the little punishment so much she brazenly tried to tempt him again. "Stay with me," she begged breathily, beguiling him by sliding her bold, brazen tongue all over his insatiable lips. She felt a purely female thrill of triumph when he groaned fiercely, "I can't," and she could feel his whole body yearning for him to say that he would. His massive manhood pulsated like an iron bar against her body as he held her. His arms tightened and tightened with each tempestuous caress of his hot tongue as if he would never let her go. And she felt as though she could never push herself tightly enough against him. That the only thing that would sate her craving for him was to take him inside her eager warmth. She had only to tell him to lift her skirt and she was ready for him.

His sultry mouth captured hers again fiercely. This time, he had no time to listen to her smouldering words.

274

This time, his intimate caresses told her that it was almost time for him to leave her.

She couldn't bear for him to leave her with just his luscious taste tonight. Her body writhed against him wantonly, seeking to tempt him; her lush tongue enthralled him with voluptuous promises.

He knew what she was doing. "Temptress," he growled against the silken glide of her tongue against his. "Vixen. The answer is no." He covered her mouth again with his pronouncement, giving her no time to try her provocative blandishments. He plunged into her tantalizing mouth again and again, unable to pull away, unable to walk away from her luscious provocation.

And then he wrenched away at the sound of someone calling his name.

Jake!

"Almost ready to move out," Jake said, walking firmly into the shadow of the stall where Kalida stood still in the circle of Deuce's arms.

"Really now?" Deuce said calmly.

"Bruno's got the chuck, and Barney's driving the bed wagon, and the wrangler's all set with the horses. It's just you and me and we can head out."

"All right, Jake." Deuce turned to Kalida. "Your enticements almost worked, Kalida-cat. I'll see you tomorrow."

He let go of her and strode away, leaving her and Jake looking after him.

"You okay?" Jake asked her.

Kalida looked at him, puzzled. "What do you mean?" Her full attention was on Deuce and the moving out of the roundup crew. How could she insinuate herself with them?

"You were mighty cosy there with Deuce just now," Jake said suggestively, his eyes resting on the hard peaks

275

of her nipples against the thin shirt. Yes, he was right; she was naked under the shirt. And she had been kissing Deuce ferociously, letting him . . .

"Was I?" she asked thoughtfully.

"Kalida . . . Miss Kalida, there's no call for him to treat you like that if you're a guest in his house. Even under the conditions he agreed with your daddy," Jake said.

Kalida now swung her gaze to Jake. "That may be, Jake, but it's none of your business."

"Your daddy didn't give him permission to kiss you like that, Miss Kalida," Jake said chidingly, with half-serious indignation that he thought disguised very well how much *he* wanted to do exactly that.

"Supposing *I* wanted him to," she shot back before she thought about the implication of her words.

"Did you now, Miss Kalida?" Jake murmured suggestively, moving a step closer. And wasn't it just as he had thought? She was as willing as he had ever dreamed. "I'm glad to hear that," he added. Glad to hear, he added mentally, of anything she wanted so that he would know, when his turn came, what she wanted him to do.

He toyed with the thought of commanding her to take off her clothes. She had a glazed look in her eyes, and her mouth was ripe from Deuce's thrusting kisses. Her passionate juices had probably aroused her to the point where she was desperate to have someone take control of her. Otherwise, he thought, she might turn her voracious appetite to just anyone.

How long did she expect him to wait?

"Did you say Bruno was tending the chuck?" Kalida said suddenly, as it occurred to her that if she were to thank him for his encouragement this afternoon, she would have a reason for hanging around the outgoing drovers.

It took a full minute for his mind to snap back to the moment so he could fully comprehend her question. And anyway, what did she want with Old Bruno when *he* was here? "Yes," he snapped abruptly, almost pettishly.

"You'll have to excuse me, Jake. I must get back to the house."

"What for?" Jake growled, grabbing for her arm as she turned away. His hand grazed the tight nub of her nipple as she slipped out of his grasp and he felt its hot hard sensuality clear down to his loins. She had done that deliberately, he swore. She was a tease, damn it, an out-and-out wanton tease. She gave him a taste here and a feel there, and all the while she willingly gave everything to Deuce Cavender.

She smiled at him in that pouty kind of way that told him she knew exactly what she did to him. "I'll see you tomorrow," she said in her most beguiling, he thought, tone of voice, the one that promised a thousand delights and would probably yield none.

"You will," he agreed roughly. The only thing holding him back from grabbing her was his determination not to force her. He would not compel her at all, even if the waiting were an agony. It was all part of the game he knew provoking teases like Kalida played. It just made her final capitulation that much more explosively sweeter.

And it would come soon, he thought, because he would make it come soon.

Jake was out of her mind before she even left the stable. He *was* acting strangely. And she wished he hadn't grabbed for her like that. She was sure it had been accidental but she didn't like the feeling of anyone touching her but Deuce.

She had no firm clear idea of what she was going to do. She only knew she wanted to go, and Deuce's reluctance to leave her merely fueled that desire. The fact Ardelle wouldn't like it any too well was no detriment either. Nor was the thought of not enduring Ellie's company for one minute longer than she had to.

The reasons for her to find a way to accompany the crew were mounting up, much to her satisfaction. As she approached the house, she could see the chuck wagon drawing around the corner of the house to the kitchen and storerooms. She followed it slowly. She could hardly pretend to be a sack of flour and hide away in the food box. But the thought was tempting. She wondered if there *were* anywhere she could stow away.

She waved to Bruno as she rounded the corner of the house. Prestina and Ardelle were already lining up kegs and boxes on the back porch.

"Good you are here," Ardelle called to her. "You can help."

Kalida's cobalt eyes flashed. Was it possible Ardelle actually approved of something for her to do? She picked up a bag of coffee beans and a package of dried fruit and lugged them over to Bruno, who was fitting each item lovingly into the wagon with the intensity of a man outfitting the woman he loves. Kalida was always surprised at the amount of gear and food that could be packed into the chuck, everything from bedrolls to tool boxes to a barrel full of water enough to last several days. And in its honeycomb of cabinets that were built into the opposite end from the driver's seat, a cook could store everything from flour to coffee to sickroom necessities, his pots and pans, plates and silverware, rope and ammunition, and a crock of starter for bread and biscuits.

Bruno took the coffee and fruit from Kalida and found a cranny to house both bags. "Glad you came along this morning," he said gruffly.

"Wish I could come along this afternoon," Kalida said lightly.

Bruno shook his head. "It won't take no time to get them cattle down to Morgan field. Then you come watch the cutting and branding, Miss Kalida; that'd be fine."

Kalida wrinkled her nose and hoisted a sack of sugar onto her shoulder. That wouldn't be fine at all. Not at all. It wouldn't be like *being* there. The tin box of matches next, and then a hefty container of molasses went into the chuck box.

Kalida gazed longingly at the wagon bed. Wouldn't it be easy and perfect if she could just hop up there and hide under a bedroll?

Prestina handed her various cooking utensils, which she passed to Bruno, who stored them on shelves underneath the chuck box. Wouldn't it be wonderful, she mused, if she could slide in there with tool box and the flour sack? And—an idea lit up in her mind—didn't Jake say something about the bed wagon travelling out too? What if . . .

No. Yes. She eyed Bruno, who was shifting boxes and implements, then picked up a package of salt and brought it to him.

"Oh, I got that already, Miss Kalida, and thank you," he said, his hands busy and his eyes referring to a list on a small crumpled piece of paper.

"Sorry," Kalida said, but she was not at all contrite. Her sparkling blue gaze lit on the piece of paper. "You have a check-off list?" she asked with a show of curiosity.

"Surely. I don't often get to go you know, but sometimes . . . Anyway, the trail drives vary, so we have a stock list of equipment and supplies for all kinds of lengths of trips. This here's for a short one. So's we don't waste food, you see."

"But a lot of men will be going," Kalida said audaciously, hating to use his kindly attention to her questions for her own means. But she didn't see any other way. She didn't. "Where is their gear?"

"Oh, there's another wagon coming up from the carriage barn. Barney's driving. I believe he's loading up now same as me. We'll shove off in about fifteen minutes."

Loading up. The words struck a chord in her. Besides Deuce and Jake, a half-dozen other men were going on this drive. Not to mention their gear. Six, maybe eight or more, bedrolls were being packed onto that small commodious wagon. Hiding places. And they were leaving in fifteen minutes.

Oh my God, Kalida thought in a frenzy; she couldn't have said when the actual plan of hiding aboard the wagon struck her in its entirety. She only remembered making the connection: gear—hiding place. She had to get to that barn before Barney drove out! She smiled at Bruno. "You'll be back tomorrow," she concluded conversationally, hoping that her frantic haste to get away now was not obvious to him.

"Barring unexpected trouble, yes." He poked around a moment more. "That's about it, Miss Kalida; whyn't you go tell Miss Ardelle and save Prestina the trouble of carting more supplies outside?"

Fifteen minutes. Kalida nodded and raced into the house to find Ardelle. She delivered Bruno's message tersely, along with a not very inventive excuse for herself so that she would not be looked for after the wagons had left.

Ardelle was busy with her own concerns and never questioned a word. Funny, Kalida thought, and dismissed it from her mind. The next trick was to manage to get herself down to the carriage barn without anyone seeing her.

She went back out the rear door. The wagon stood at the ready; Bruno was not there. Damn, what if he had gone to help Barney? . . .

Casually, she strolled in the direction of the barn, noting that everyone was busy and surely no one would come looking for her. She only hoped no one noticed the direction in which she was going. She wondered, just for an instant, what Deuce was doing. And then she slipped behind the first of the outbuildings and flattened herself against its back wall.

All was quiet.

She moved slowly, her heart pounding in a resonant drumming in her ears. The storehouse. The dairy house. Skirt the bunkhouse, where there was obviously the most activity. The barn. The carriage barn. The small rear door, which she opened stealthily. The sound of Barney's wizened voice echoing in the vast space.

The front doors were open, and she could see Barney and Bruno loading the rear of the wagon. She would have to wait. She slipped into the door, ducked onto her knees, and crawled as close as she could to the wagon.

Go back to your own duties, Bruno, she beseeched silently. It must be close to pulling-out time. How was she going to climb into that wagon with Bruno hanging all over it?

Suddenly the whole space was inundated with noise. "Time to move 'em out," an unfamiliar voice shouted, whooping its way down the dirt track.

Bruno brought the horses, which had been tethered right out front, and he and Barney hitched them to the wagon.

"Eh now, don't get lost," Bruno cautioned as he turned to leave. Barney cackled and tested the cinches.

Obviously a joke between them, Kalida thought, not amused herself. She inched forward until she was at the very edge of the wagon box. What if Barney came back to check the gate? Did she even know how to release the damned thing? She would have to climb over it and hope that her weight didn't sag down the rear axle. Was she crazy? She slithered up to the gate and reached up to grip the edge. And froze. Barney had turned and was looking in her direction.

A long moment passed, almost as if he were trying to

determine if he had seen or heard something and what it could possibly be. He stood motionless beside the step leading up to his driver's perch. Kalida held her breath.

He finally decided it was nothing. Kalida watched him step onto the little support and knew this was the moment to hoist herself onto the wagon gate, so he wouldn't feel her weight sinking the back end.

One, two—and she lifted herself just as he pulled himself into the driver's seat, tumbling over onto the bedrolls and, oh God, extra saddles, she crammed her arm and hip against the rocklike protuberance of a pommel and cursed the moment she had thought of doing this.

But extra saddles!— Meant extra horses. Meant she would ride—if Deuce didn't send her right back. She burrowed under the bedrolls as the wagon jolted forward. Deuce wouldn't send her back. She could convince him of her usefulness.

She smiled to herself as the wagon hit daylight and convened with the crew. She would convince him. She had ways.

The trip was almost unbearable, hidden as she was in the saddle-worn bedrolls, with the heat of the waning sun beating down on them and no protection. And no water, because she hadn't thought to bring a canteen. Only the thought of the quickness of the trip saved her from expiring from the heat and her thirst. Her father had gone there and back, and the trip had taken two hours.

But that had been one man alone, not a train of cowhands with two wagons. Damn and blast. And she couldn't move. The wagon was now surrounded by several cowhands, almost like an escort. The damned wagon didn't travel any too fast either. They would make it, the desultory discussion around the wagon was, by nightfall, a nice leisurely trip, and then fall into bed and out at first morning light.

The trip was interminable, the time passing with excruciating slowness. Kalida lay beneath the suffocating bedrolls and dared not move a finger. Her limbs were in agony, cramped beyond endurance. Her mouth was so dry she was sure one more breath would choke her. There was no air, no surcease from the endless jouncing over the rough track up to the ridge. She wished she had never thought of this idea. If she could have hopped out and walked back to Sweetland, she would have.

And if Deuce discovered her now, she was sure he would send her back. So she had no choice but to keep still and endure the agony. It could not be much longer.

And time passed. She stretched a tentative toe at one point. Her clothing was beginning to chafe her naked body, and there was no help for that. She sucked her finger to generate some moisture in her desert-dry mouth. It didn't work.

The rocking and jouncing of the wagon grew worse. It was ascending the trail; she could tell by the slant of her body and the slight shift in the wagon body.

Maybe, just maybe they were almost there.

It seemed to her that after a while the air grew cooler, the sun less intense. The relief she felt was tangible.

And supplanted by a new worry: What would Deuce do when he found her? A chill shot through her. Her little escapade might not sit so well with him after all, in spite of her initial feeling she could convince him of her serious intentions.

What if her presence thoroughly disrupted everything and distracted the men, what then? After all, she did not know Deuce's crew the way she had known the few regulars her father would hire on at roundup. And he knew Eakins and the cook would be there to protect her anyway. But Deuce headed a large-scale operation. His hands were tough, accustomed to months without a woman, and probably saw every female as fair game. She might have let herself in for something she had no way to control. Oh, Deuce would protect her, she thought, but he couldn't be with her every moment.

And from the conversation she had heard, these men seemed hardly gentlemen; there was a good deal of discussion about spending the fruits of their labors in Bozeman. They seemed very well acquainted with this and that lady of the evening—and in bawdy terms—and whiled away a good portion of the ride comparing notes. Just as easily they might be talking about *her*, Kalida thought, and she did not hide from herself just how interested she was at his peek into the male mind. She would not want them talking about her in just that same way.

The end conclusion, of course, was there was nothing she could do about it. Her impulsive action had landed her in this rash position, and sooner or later she would have to talk her way out of it with Deuce, and eventually Ardelle too, probably not succeeding with either. In sum, this was probably one of the stupidest things she had ever done, she decided.

The road seemed to level off at this point, and within minutes an animal scent permeated the cool air. Ten minutes later the wagon jolted to a halt, and Deuce was shouting something unintelligible. The answering voice sounded like Eakins. The wagon jerked forward again, slower this time, as if it were moving into a set area. The voices got closer, and Kalida could identify Eakins clearly now. And his words. Numbing words. "Mr. Ryland didn't tell me about no sale. How am I supposed to let you move in and take out this here herd then?"

"On faith," Deuce retorted. "He was supposed to send word."

"Well, he didn't send nothing, not even the pay; so's the

men left. It's just me and the cook now. . . ."

Kalida's heart sank. What on earth was her father up to, to leave Eakins in such straits? And she, who could confirm Deuce's ownership, didn't dare move.

"Well," Deuce said consideringly after a long, heavy silence, "we're going to set up camp here, and one of my men is going to return to Sweetland, and we'll get to the bottom of this."

Nice of you, Kalida thought, clenching her fists. He didn't even defend her father. He sounded rather like it wasn't unexpected. She didn't like that, she didn't like it at all.

All around her she could hear the sounds of the crew settling in. She knew what they would be doing—setting up the rope corral for the horses several hundred yards away from the camp, and each hand herding in his string to bed down for the night.

At this point, too, Old Bruno would have pulled into some kind of protected place, near rocks or trees, set up his stake poles, hung his canvas awning, and started his open fire. The rest of the men would be finishing up with their horses, taking some water, and finding their spot for the night. Already the smell of coffee hung in the air, the first likely food Bruno would have set on the camp fire. Dinner would be simple, since on a short haul like this a side of beef could be managed, wrapped in a tarpaulin to keep it fresh for the day or two the men would be out. A slap or two of that plopped in the Dutch oven with water, potatoes, a lick of dried fruit, and flour for thickening would take no time to boil up and would be served with quick-rising biscuits and the coffee.

Kalida's stomach growled as her brain assimilated the tantalizing smell of the coffee. A lot of noise now surrounded her, a lot of conversation. Eakin's adamant pronouncement that nothing was going to be moved in the morning. Deuce's stark silence. A demand from

Bruno: "Somebody fill that kettle so I can get the water boiling for cleanup," and the clarion call from Barney: "Unload your gear, men!"

Kalida cringed as lantern light was strung above the wagon bed. The reckoning was at hand. From all around her, hands grabbed for the bedrolls and spare saddle gear. In a moment, her dun-colored skirt was revealed.

"Well, I'll be good goddamned," a voice said wonderingly. "Hey Jake, get over here. Someone tell Deuce."

Jake's stark, frozen face appeared over the side of the wagon, dumbfounded by the sight of her where he was dreaming he might find her. The nature of her, he thought excitedly, that she would come after any men in any way she could. The nerve it took to hide away, to stay hidden all those hours. Not even he had been aware the wagon carried anything but the excess gear and bedrolls. And hadn't he spent the whole trip up thinking about her, wondering when he could and would take his chance with her? It was as if she had read his mind and had pursued him with the express intention of making those dreams real. Yes, she was looking and sounding disgruntled. But she was stiff from all those hours curled up alone and in the dark of the wagon. And the other men were so bedazzled by the sight of a woman that they hardly knew what to think. But then, they didn't know about Kalida, and he did.

He helped lift the remaining rolls of bedding away from her, and Kalida smelled fresh air for the first time in hours.

She shifted her stiff body upright, and then cast a flashing blue look at the crowd of men encircling the wagon. The look in their eyes! As if she were some exotic creature. And Jake, with that lambent light deep in his eyes; it made her correspondingly wary. The only thing to do was brazen it out. She wondered if she had the nerve. The thing to do was assume an indignant expression, and her eyes darkened as her mood became petulant. "It's about time," she shot out in a voice to match the mood.

Perfect—and she almost got away with it, except Deuce came marching up the instant the words left her mouth. In the lantern light, he looked bemused, amused, and just a whit annoyed—and all at once.

"Damn, you took your time getting here," she complained to him, forestalling whatever he had been going to say, hoping to deflect the anger she expected him to feel.

"It's for sure you didn't enjoy the scenery," he rejoined calmly, and her bolt blue eyes shot up in surprise. She hadn't expected this dispassionate acceptance of her appearance. She had envisioned rather more dire consequences, and she wondered whether she weren't disappointed.

Then she looked at Jake, his glittery eyes and a crook of his eyebrow saluting her, and the thought—which never should have been given an instant's life—flew from her consciousness. She waited with barely contained equanimity while the men unloaded the wagon and drifted off, their ears still tuned to the conversation they knew must follow.

Deuce watched them all, making sure they were aware of his scowl as his glowering charcoal gaze followed them.

Kalida wriggled, stretching her cramped arms and legs, avoiding that foreboding face.

"So now," he said finally as the last man meandered around the camp fire and took a plate from Bruno in preparation for being served dinner. He turned to her. She made a pretty picture sitting in the wagon bed, all disheveled from being covered for these long hours, looking slightly irritated, her cobalt eyes longingly following the exit of his men to the chuck. She must be hungry, he realized, and dead thirsty. "What *are* you doing here?" he asked finally. He sure as hell couldn't account for it unless the strength of the feelings he had aroused in her were enough to precipitate this rash action.

She turned a snide look on him, almost as though she could read his thoughts. She was furious that the tone of his voice assumed that anything *he* had done had compelled her to chase after him. The overweening male nerve of him! "I wanted to help bring down the herd, of course," she snapped at him, flexing her legs experimentally, ignoring the fierce burning flash in his charcoal gaze.

"That's some story, you vixen. And not half the truth."

"The hell with you." She stretched her arms and shifted so her legs were under her and she could lift her body up on her knees. Oh Lord, she hadn't quite expected them to be just that stiff.

"Go on, Kalida. You're tellimg me you're after cows and not . . . something else."

"You put it quite succinctly, but yes. I'm after cows. And maybe something to eat." Definitely something to eat, she thought, and something to drink. She felt like she could swallow a lake.

"Well, my scratching cat, be that all as it may, I'm rather happy you made your way up here. Eakins over there seems to think *he* owns the herd and not me. So I'd take it kindly if you would convince him otherwise." He almost softened as he perceived her struggling to stand up. "Come, Kalida; I'd forgive a lot for that." He held out his arms.

She slapped them away. "To get your hands on the herd?" she asked sweetly, pretending to misunderstand. Her shaky limbs just would not permit her to climb over the back of the wagon the same way she had climbed in.

"To save a few days and a lot of aggravation, cat. Come on, I'll carry you if it's necessary."

"Just lift me down; I'll manage the rest." She would have to; just being that close to him was wreaking havoc with her senses. She had the strange sensation, as his strong arms lifted her down and held her too tightly, too long, that the herd didn't matter. And her father didn't matter.

All to the good, she thought ruefully as her feet touched the ground; if she had been Deuce, she might have gone after her careless, feckless father with a gun. But he was not to know that. She leaned against him heavily. "My legs are stiff," she explained tightly.

"Of course," he agreed reasonably.

"If only you had provided proper accommodations for a stowaway," she went on musingly as she limped with his help to the camp fire.

"Perhaps," he said in an undertone as he sat her down by the fire, "the sleeping arrangements will be more to your liking."

"None of your arrangements have been to my liking," she snapped, out of patience with her recalcitrant body and angry with herself altogether for even attempting this reckless escapade and for confronting his all-fired masculine conviction. He would have it all his way, no matter what her motivations really were, and the fact that she had gone haring off without thinking of such mundane things as food or sleeping arrangements, in his eyes, only lent credence to *his* theory. So all her protestations must seem coy and just a little too arch in their denial.

Nevertheless, his humor improved over the roasted meat and gravy, and he was most solicitous to her, providing her with water and coffee almost the minute after she sat down. And all the while his coal-dark eyes burned with a different message — and it was one she could not refute.

"Of course you're sleeping with me! Where the hell else did you think you were going to sleep? With Jake?"

Kalida flounced away from him. Dinner had restored

the warmth to her body, and she was now fully ambulatory, enough at least to get away from him when she needed to.

He stalked after her, reaching for her arm and wrenching her around to face him. "Are you crazy, Kalida? You really think you're going to take a blanket and settle down under the trees and expect nothing is going to happen to you?"

"It never has," she said shortly, wresting her arm out of his grasp.

"When you were a young 'un, maybe," Deuce growled, yanking her back to face him. "You aren't hardly a youngster anymore, Kalida, and every last man of them can imagine what is under that dusty skirt and what they would do with it, since they all haven't had a woman since they can't remember when. Tell me how you're going to fight that kind of single-mindedness."

"I shouldn't have to," she interpolated.

"Uh huh, and you shouldn't be the only woman around to tempt them," he finished, "let alone me. But I promise you, Kalida-cat"—his grip loosened, almost like a punctuation to his words—"I won't touch you."

She drew in her breath at his words. Good. Perfect. He would keep his end of the bargain. She had corroborated his right to the cattle with the poor perplexed Eakins, and now he was going to take care of her. He was going to sleep with her and not lay a hand on her. And when she considered how ardently she tried to prevent him from coming here, she felt a huge wave of disappointment. Why was he so angry? Why was she?

"That will be just fine," she agreed, finishing the last dregs of her coffee. Already, the camp fire area was empty of the men. Bruno and Barney were doing the cleanup, dumping the dishes in the large kettle that had been heated to boiling earlier. Breakfast call would be at four-thirty, with the expectation that the herd would trail in the Morgan field by ten o'clock at the latest, allowing for an hour or two for them to corral the strays.

Kalida handed Bruno her cup and plate. His reaction to her sudden appearance had been simple, and perhaps the most honest. "You hadn't ought to have done this, Miss Kalida; this ain't no place for a lady."

And she said, "I'm no lady, Bruno; I'm a cowgirl, and I wanted to help."

Bruno shook his head. "You ain't gonna do much of that, Miss Kalida; Mr. Deuce wouldn't let you."

"Mr. Deuce has no say about 'letting' me," Kalida retorted huffily and was instantly sorry that she had vented her anger on him.

But Bruno hardly noticed. "You'll see, Miss Kalida. He wields a strong hand, Mr. Deuce."

And don't I know it, Kalida thought ruefully as she followed Deuce's long, strong figure into the twilight shadows of the surrounding rocks, holding a small lantern high so that he could pick his way through the rocks and find a suitable area to spread out the bedroll. Finally he nodded, and she set the light down on a flat rock nearby and watched him dismantle his bedding.

With the expertise born of years on the range, he deftly unrolled and laid out the first layer—a tarpaulin, on which he spread a quilt and over that a thin blanket. He had another quilt ready to lay over Kalida, and he stood patiently holding it while she resisted kneeling down on the bedding.

"Kalida." His tone of voice told her he would pick her up and haul her down like the most rambunctious calf if she did not get down on the blanket that minute. And that she understood. She got on her knees, settling herself in the approximate place he indicated with an insolent reluctance that made him snap the second quilt down on her curvaceous body with conspicuous impatience.

He kicked aside his meager bag of possessions that had

been rolled up with the bedding, snuffed out the light, and slipped down next to her. Meticulously, he leaned forward and pulled up the lower half of the tarp, which brought the quilts up over them snugly and still left the upper portion of the oblong of the tarp to cover them should it rain.

"Settle in, Kalida," he advised, wriggling down into the quilts, "it's going to be a long night."

She lay down resignedly and turned her back to him. It had been a damned long day, she thought. She wasn't up to anything much else but combatting her sensual awareness of Deuce lying next to her. That would use up anyone's strength. She took a long, deep breath. "I *am* going to work you know," she said challengingly into the dark.

"You've done your work for today," he responded in that flat, hateful voice that made her want to smack him.

It was obviously no use talking to him; he would think what he wanted to anyway. And she would not admit anything except her original intention. So she refused to be goaded by his statement. She lay tense and overwrought beside him, warmed by the heat pulsating from him, chilled by the thought of the situation she had put herself in.

She had no business coming on roundup. Her father had sold the herd; it was Deuce's business now, plain and simple. The impulse that had driven her spontaneous behavior seemed rash and ill thought out—the actions of a child. And she was sure that Deuce would not scruple to let her know it in no uncertain terms. When *he* was ready to. Damn, he held all the cards; it was galling to think he could—and would—call her bluff at any time.

Around them, the night had a life of its own, compounded by the whirr of the insects, the whickering of the horses, the subdued movements of Bruno as he finished cleaning up the chuck area. Beyond them, the first shift of the night guard was patrolling the herd, their low crooning mingling with the intermittent bawl of the cattle as they settled them in for the night. Above them, the rustle of leaves from the trees overhanging their bed made a counterpoint to the tense silence between them.

After a long, long time, she had to shift her cramping body and was dismayed when her buttocks jammed into his rock hard thighs. His arm immediately surrounded her waist, pulling her even tighter against him. She felt him behind her, lifting himself slightly onto his elbow, and then the breath of his voice in her ear. "Kalida."

"No," she whispered fiercely, her hands pulling at his arms.

"Contrary cat," he mocked, his voice still light, low, hardly discernible. She heard it so clearly. "Kalida, stop your nonsense now and turn to me."

"I won't." That was as resolute as she could make it as she felt his lips against her jawbone and his tongue tracing the line of it.

"Surely you will," he contradicted softly. "I'm desperate for the taste of you. Kalida . . ."

"Stop it," she groaned, turning her head and burying it against the blanket beneath her.

"Kalida . . ." He moved his hand to tangle in her night-black hair and tugged it sharply. Her head lifted and he grasped her chin, twisting it over her shoulder to meet his avid mouth. His tongue covered her mouth voraciously and delved between her lips hungrily. His hand moved slowly down her shoulder, sweeping to the curve of her breast to cup its fullness and touch the budding nipple. Her body reacted instantly with a resistant wriggle.

He knew why. He pulled away from her and pushed her gently onto her stomach, imprisoning her hands beneath her body. Her head faced away from him now and he had to force her to turn it toward him. She knew what he knew, and she did not want him to touch her.

293

He sensed it and made no move to kiss her again. His hand idly played up and down the sensual arch of her back. He had not shifted his own position at all, and he could just lean forward to touch his lips to her ear. "Admit you came here because you wanted to be with me," he commanded in that soft, low dangerous voice of his.

"A fairy tale," she jeered just as softly. She pulled in her breath as his hand began shaping the line of her lower back and buttocks. If he got much further, it wasn't likely she could pick up and run. He already knew she was wearing nothing underneath; how could he help drawing his own conclusion from that? Yet his coaxing hand was not demanding. It gently skimmed her curves, feeling the line of her body beneath her clothing, never probing. Just *there,* caressing and audacious all at the same time.

And he lay propped beside her in just the same way, moving his hand all over her body in the deep dark night, as though he were visualizing what she looked like and how her body was responding to the feel of his light, bold caresses.

She felt herself stiffening as his hand sought her curves lower and still lower. Then, finally, he shifted, easing himself down so that they lay side by side, face to face. His hand rested on her buttocks now, its warmth and shape penetrating even the thick material of her skirt. Her heart started pounding; she was panting with the tension of him next to her, his hand on her, and her fear of what he would uncover next.

The air between them vibrated with a kind of taut excitement. His hand constricted and she knew, in that extravagant dark moment, that he fully intended to expose her nakedness and her deceit.

He moved still closer to her and she caught her breath as she felt his probing tongue lick her unyielding lips. She shook him off, unwilling to submit to his lush kisses when she knew what he was going to do.

He nipped at her lower lip, pulling at it, nibbling it, sucking it, murmuring her name, commanding the caress of her tongue, whispering to her, coaxing her. "Kalida, kiss me, you want to kiss me," and he swirled his tongue against her lips. "Open your mouth to me, Kalida. I'm hungry for you." Here she shook her head violently, and he bit her lips with ravishing little nipping movements that again she tried to deny.

His hand moved then, sliding the coarse canvas of her skirt upward. She wriggled against his hand, a negating motion that made him all the more determined. His voice came at her in the dark, a seductive breath, not even a whisper, hardly a sound at all. "You're naked under this skirt, Kalida." His mouth covered hers in a violent movement as his fingers contacted her bare skin. "Kalida . . ." He reached for her again, seeking to part her lips, again unsuccessfully. "Let," he murmured against her mouth, "me feel your body."

Her body writhed tellingly at his words. If he kept it up, she would have no more secrets. Everything would be his. His hand lay just at the curve of her buttocks; she felt it there with an opulent awareness of both its heat and weight, and what it could do and where it could touch her next. And she would not be able to stop him; she didn't know if she wanted to stop him. She imagined his hand moving, large, hot, encompassing, and where it might move, what she would feel, and she wanted him to move it.

"Deuce . . ." She breathed his name.

"Kalida . . ." The barest murmur against her lips. "Tell me." His tongue glided over her lips, wetting them, tasting them, seeking entry. "Kiss me, Kalida." He covered her mouth again, willing her to open it to him. Her lips trembled under his as his hand pushed her skirt up over her hips and uncovered the lush curve of her buttocks.

She caught her breath as she felt his hand slide onto her naked skin and pause just at the small of her back. A deep chord sounded within her, like a mallet hitting a gong. It resonated deep inside, its reverberations eddying outward, downward, and nestling in that heated naked place just beneath his hand.

He felt her uninhibited response to his touch. His avid mouth collided with hers, seeking, nipping, delving against her lips again and again. "Kalida, luscious naked Kalida, I have you in my hands now." He formed the words almost soundlessly against her lips. "Open to me, Kalida."

Her body jolted sensually against his powerful thigh, and her lips parted for him.

His hand moved, at the same moment his sultry tongue invaded the lush recesses of her mouth, filling it and entwining with her tongue. Two separate sensations assaulted her senses—the wet heat of his devouring tongue and the heavy sensual motion of his hand exploring her soft curves. All her resistance caved in. She admitted it to herself, in the throes of her unbridled pleasure in the movements of his hands and tongue. She had wanted this, this close containment with him, his feeling her body in this slow sensual way, his sensuous words arousing her.

His questing hand audaciously stroked her luscious flesh, sliding closer and closer to her churning femininity. Her whole body remembered the feel of his fingers teasing her just this way. She shifted upward slightly to entice the exquisite caress.

"Kalida . . ." His vibrant whisper thrilled her. His tongue caressed hers voluptuously, hot and wet, endlessly demanding. "You're naked for me . . ." another ravishing kiss, "you want me . . ." his brazen fingers entered her velvet moistness, "you belong to me . . . Kalida . . ."

She was drowning in sumptuous billowing sensations.

She heard his erotic words, and her left hand worked itself out from under her surging body to grasp his taut shoulder, raking and wrenching it with the force of her galvanic response. Her mouth savored his now, kiss for kiss, touch for touch, her tongue as fervid to taste and caress as his.

Her body turned, of its own volition, toward him against his insatiable fingers. Her right hand reached for his chest, for the buttons of his shirt, pulling, unfastening them as fast as she could with her trembling fingers, sliding the flat of her palm against the crisp hair on his chest, feeling his bare skin beneath.

Her body convulsed as she touched him. It was almost as if *this* had been what she was waiting for, this intimate caress of his naked skin. The things he was doing to her receded beside her need to feel *him*.

When he sensed that, his own hand moved, slowly retreating from her lush welcoming warmth, sliding back across her buttocks and downward to push the front of her skirt out of the way, arresting its exquisite movement just at the tempting line of her thigh. His fingers flexed against her silky skin, and she wrenched her mouth away from his to murmur softly, "Don't leave me."

His lips hovered above hers consideringly for a moment. "What shall I do, Kalida?" He posed the question almost before he had realized it, softly, lovingly, feeling as he had the evening before at Sweetland, that he wanted all of the desire to come from her, all the words and the burden of yearning to possess. And yet, the question sounded harsh, a backlash against her continual retreat from her refusal to admit the reality of her feelings. It wasn't possible she didn't know them by now, only that she refused to accept them. Yet she was here, in his arms again, naked and willing, and he waited, flicking his tongue against her lips, licking them, covering them with biting little kisses intended to storm her senses, and he knew he did not have to do even that much.

"Deuce—" Her lips felt swollen under his sensual onslaught. Her body felt fraught with tension. His hand remained poised on her thigh; if she wriggled just once, she thought, she could coax it to slide right into her sultry warmth. Her body writhed in tiny tenuous thrusts that he must be feeling, and yet he made no move to assuage her hunger.

"Kalida." Her breath of a name on his lips crushed against hers once more. "Kalida . . . Kalida; you will drive me away from you with as much passion as you welcome me—when I force you to."

"No." Her breathy denial was gorgeously quick. "I want you."

"When you can't help yourself," he murmured dryly, and his hand moved then, feeling its provocative way to the juncture of her thighs, making her writhe with exquisite sensation. "A fine excuse, Kalida"—a ragged mutter as his fingers delved deeper into her pulsating warmth—"especially when you walk around naked under your clothes. God, Kalida, I wish I had that excuse. I wish I could deny it was for me. But it was, wasn't it? Admit it, you came for me; you dressed for me."

"Deuce—" She undulated her hips against his exploring fingers, her mouth seeking his now, desperate to say with her kisses what she would never admit in words.

"You're a luscious wanton animal," he growled, refusing her lips, "for *me,* Kalida; understand it, only for me."

She heard it, she understood it; in the core of her being she knew it. She couldn't help it because she loved her own fierce surrender to his hands and to his rock hard masculinity. She loved his mouth, his tongue, his body, his scent. She loved being in thrall to the sensuous things he did to her and to his response to the things she did to him. He had known forever what she was only comprehending now: She had always wanted him. She was coming to want him forever.

"You can't run any more, Kalida." Torrid words, uttered in that breath of a whisper against her ear. The truth, she thought, straining her smouldering body against him. Her left hand began a torturous trail of longing down his body; his right arm, which supported her shoulders, moved upward to her neck and pulled her mouth against his. "You ran *to* me, this time," he rasped against her lips before he devoured them again.

Had she? she thought wildly; she had without knowing it, or consciously — but she was consciously giving herself to him now. It was he — and only he — who was there, evoking such wondrous sensations from her body. Only the two of them in the primitive dark, driving each other to fierce, enthralling surrender.

Her frenzied fingers worked apart the buttons of his pants with shameless urgency, feeling his massiveness throbbing beneath her hand, his excitement building with hers as the material fell away and she took him in her wanton grasp. Her whole body convulsed as she wrapped her fingers around his taut, elongated length with ferocious ardor. Her fingers moved then, glorying in his massive strength. And as he audaciously thrust his fingers into her feminine heat, her own fingers brazenly explored the tempting granite length of him, learning its shape and texture and how her hand could evoke the same staggering response from him that her body did.

She tasted his powerful response to her wanton exploration. Her whole body surged against him voluptuously, ravenous for him and the volcanic pleasure that his virile length could arouse in her.

His lips and tongue released hers for the space of a breath as he murmured against them, "Oh no, Kalida. This time, I want you to touch the force of my desire. I want you to know exactly what you do to me."

"I know it," she protested in a breathless whisper.

"Good," he growled, and took her lips once more. She was liquid with the opulent sensation of his exquisite caresses, awash in a voluptuously euphoric haze of pleasure.

His knowledgeable fingers created the most delectable feeling deep within her. Her body quivered as a riotous heat began its radiant course up and down her body. Her fingers constricted against the ravishing length of him in response, the driving essence of his manhood heightening the wanton undulation of her hips against his hand. She frantically massaged him as the powerful eddies of feeling rippled over her, lanquid and shimmering at first, and then in a storm of sumptuous white-hot culmination that cascaded through every pore in her body.

He stopped only when he was sure he had wrung every potent drop of spiralling pleasure from her clamoring body, and he covered her mouth and face with luscious little kisses that, in their hot wet ardor, reflected his own bursting urgency.

"I have you now," she whispered, enthralled by the intensity of the climax that gripped him then. And afterward, the thrumming of his heart against her chest, as he rested in satiated peace, was sweet music; the languid touch of his lips against hers was a homage to the magnitude of his surrender.

The night enfolded them as he cradled her close, and she held him lovingly in her hand.

And outside the glimmering circle of their sensual exploration, a dark brooding figure listened to each low, vibrant word of submission and surrender. The bitch, he thought, the lousy teasing bitch. First she strips herself for two lousy goddamned women, then she lets that son of a bitch handle her any which way he wants to; she invites me for a ride to show her gratitude, she goddamn allows him to chase me away and then lets him feel her nakedness, and now . . . He drew in a deep, salacious breath. There certainly were benefits to volunteering to nighthawk, he thought, his own body aroused by the tantalizing sounds he had just listened to. And Deuce had accepted his offer without a comment, and he knew damned well why. Deuce had intended to seduce Kalida tonight; his mind was solely on her luscious naked body and what he was going to do to her, and he couldn't have given a good goddamn what Jake had said—or anyone else for that matter.

The high and mighty son of a bitch. Wait till he found the temptingly luscious Kalida in the bushes naked with someone else. Deuce would hand her over then; he would just chase her whorish body out of his life forever. And Jake planned to take it willingly into his.

Fourteen

"Rrroll out!" Bruno shouted, banging a spoon against his washing kettle. "Onnn up. Come and get your vittles. Rrroll 'em out, men."

It was just daybreak. The second shift of the night guard staggered into camp bleary-eyed. Everyone else rolled out of their bedding sluggishly. The fresh brewed aroma of coffee filled the air. Bacon sizzled in an iron frypan and Bruno was already whipping out a pan full of biscuits, still shouting at the top of his lungs, "Get 'em on up, boys; time to roll. Rise and holler, men, coffee's on the boil."

Kalida struggled awake with a start. Damn, she had fully intended to get up in time to help Bruno set up for breakfast. But after the extravagant sensuality of last night, it had been difficult to do anything but sleep soundly and fully, her sated body entwined with Deuce's, her hands nestling against him. Impossible to think of responsibilities and chores. Impossible not to think of his powerfully virile body that was all hers, every last granite inch of it.

But it was not beside her now. Some internal clock had prodded him awake even earlier than Bruno. She had not felt him leaving her. His warmth still encompassed her.

302

All of that dissipated as she wrestled with the bedding and pulled down her skirt, making sure everything was buttoned before she lifted herself from the rumpled bedding and set about folding and rolling it back into its compact shape.

Then she made her way cheerfully to the chuck tent, where the night guards were wolfing down their food in preparation to taking an hour's nap before the drive got underway. The rest of the men were at a nearby stream, washing and changing into the one fresh shirt they had brought with them.

"Someone had best go with you," Bruno commented doubtfully as she petitioned him for a spare pot in which she could put some water so she could wash herself privately.

"I'll do it." Jake's voice, gentle and helpful, behind her. She whirled and smiled at him. "Good morning, Jake. You don't happen to know where Deuce is, do you?"

"Probably washing up," he said noncommittally, his innards tightening up at her mention of Deuce. "Let me take you to the stream; I could use a good wash up myself after last night."

Kalida hesitated a moment. At least I know him, she told herself. The only one else is Eakins, or Deuce. Barney and Bruno are both busy. Oh damn. She nodded and he motioned for her to follow him into the bushes beyond the chuck.

"I hope you slept well," he said sardonically as she fell into step beside him, knowing just how well she had slept. Her sensuous whispers still reverberated in his mind. "Some folks don't take to sleeping outdoors, surrounded by all this wild life and nature. The thought of prowling animals keeps them uncomfortably awake. And sometimes the noise of the cattle, or that awful drone those cowboys make when they're singing to the herd." Prowling animals, he thought; that's me, on the prowl for a gorgeous wily heifer.

"No, I'm used to it," Kalida said, becoming comfortable with his homey conversation. When he was like this—considerate, chatty, friendly—she had no qualms about being with him. She reveled in the scent of the morning air that freshened considerably as they got further away from camp. The distance they seemed to be covering did not seem to be unduly far away.

She was surprised, therefore, when he stepped through a copse of bushes and beckoned her to follow, to find they were alone and far up the stream from the other men, hidden by an undulating bend from their sight but not their sound.

"Found this place yesterday," he said, stooping at the edge and scooping up the cool water to rub it over his hot face. "I thought you perhaps might like to take a bath rather than just wash."

"With you watching?" she jibed, kneeling several feet away from him with her iron pot and filling it.

"With me *guarding* you," he emphasized slowly, curbing his anger at her teasing taunt, which sounded as though she wanted him to and was deriding him for wanting to. What a potent combination she was, all knowing and seductive; a flirt and a chaste tormentor. She couldn't have driven him wilder with desire if she had tried. Everything she said seemed to him to have a second meaning. But because she was a woman, she could pretend there had been no suggestive meaning to her words, that he was reading something into them she couldn't possibly have intended.

He cursed women; he cursed this gorgeous midnight-black-haired witch who was driving him crazy with a wild need just to see her naked.

"Thanks for the offer, Jake, but this will do me fine."

He thought he heard the words, "Thanks Jake, that will be fine," and that she made a movement to turn and undress; that she trusted him not to look until she told him she was ready for him to consummate his desire. He thought she had divined that he knew what kind of woman she was, and he was willing to be her prey, as long as she was willing too.

But she made no move and she said nothing, her whole attention fixed on the minimal ablutions she was performing out of one little stinking pot of water when she had the whole wide stream to cleanse her naked body. At that ultimate mind-boggling tormenting gall, he blew up.

"Get your goddamned clothes off and get your ass into that water, Kalida," he exploded, wrenching her up with a jerk. "Do it! Now!"

Her cobalt eyes widened in real shock. "Are you crazy?"

"Are *you?*" he sneered, pulling her toward the water. "How long do you think you're going to play this whore's game with me, you bitch? You think I'm crazy, letting you flaunt yourself around everyone else and renege on your invitations to me? Or letting that goddamned Deuce fight your way out for you? Oh no, you tease; this time—this time you do it for me." He reached out and pulled at the front of her shirt.

She screamed and beat at his hand, yanking her body backward to try to counteract his superior strength pulling her forward. "You're out of your mind. I never—"

"Deuce doesn't have a clue what you're like," he grated. One button popped open, and then another. He stared at the vee between her breasts. "He never saw you flaunting your body; he doesn't know how you love to play and tease, does he? He doesn't know the goddamned half of what he's in for. But I do . . ." He pulled again and another button flew open, exposing more bare skin.

"God, what are you talking about?" she shouted, dragging herself backward as hard as she could, knowing her reverse tugging would give him better purchase to pull at

305

her shirt.

She didn't care; he was out of his mind with some fantasy about her that had no basis in anything real. She had had no idea he was this obsessed about her or anything she had ever said or done with him. What *had* she done with him to set him off like this?

Their grappling was like a tug of war. He pulled and she resisted, and every tug pulled apart another button to reveal more and more of her nakedness. The sight of it heightened his frenzy. He was almost at the point where mere words would never calm him down.

"Look at you," he growled. "You walk around naked under your clothes and you expect no one is going to notice? Or do you do it because you know everyone is going to notice? What do you suspect, you bitch tease? What do you expect to happen when you do things like that? Or when you strip off your clothes in front of an open window—you expect no one to be looking, do you? Or did you know someone *was* watching? You know what *I* think? I think you knew and you wanted it, Kalida. That's the kind of bitch you are. And then you protest your innocence—you never intended it to happen, did you? You just happened to be naked, you just happened to put your breast in the way of my hand, you just *happened* to ask *me* to take you back to your *deserted* home. Who the hell did you think you were gulling?"

She twisted wildly against his overwhelming strength, which was heightened by his frightening determination to bend her to his will. "You have misread everything," she panted desperately. "Nothing you said is true."

"I didn't expect you would say it was," he said archly, and she knew then she could not convince him of anything; he had the story set in his own mind and nothing would change him. And because she let up her guard for just an instant, her taut opposition to him wavered. He grabbed at her shirt one more time and, with a huge, forceful tearing jerk, pulled it right off her back.

"Now," he whispered, mesmerized by the sight of her gorgeous jutting breasts and her tumbling mane of midnight hair curling wildly down around her shoulders, just above the slope of those enticing mounds. "Oh, now I can look *my* fill."

His viselike fingers still held her arm, but the moment was stark still as his glittering hazel eyes devoured the sight of her taut tipped breasts.

He shook himself out of his fantastical reverie suddenly and commanded. "Take off your skirt now, Kalida. Slowly, so I can anticipate what is to come."

Her blazing navy eyes challenged him. "You'll have to let go."

"Of course." Obligingly he released her arm while with his other hand he produced a gun in a fluid motion that was almost imperceptible.

Her chin came up as she saw the sun glinting off the barrel. He nodded his head and waved the gun at her. "Oh yes, I mean for everything to be just as I imagined for all this time, Kalida. Take off your skirt."

Damn and damn; her nerveless fingers slid to the waistband and undid the buttons there. She looked at him appealingly, and he shook his head wonderingly. "It is incredible how you have that look, Kalida. I swear, I should have invited Deuce to see you like this. He'd know just what I mean. Take it off, bitch."

He cocked the gun, and she let the skirt slide to her feet to expose her naked torso and her black-clad legs. His eyes blazed up in a passion when her legs were revealed.

"Well, well," he muttered, walking up to her, and then around her, waving the gun and examining her from every angle. "And well, well, well again. Is this how a nicely reared young woman dresses? You look like the show-off tease of a whore you are, you bitch. And you play innocent virgin, with your airs and your righteous looks.

307

Your eyes smoulder with passion beneath that guileless look you do so well, Kalida. You're a teasing, tormenting bitch, and I finally have you to myself."

He moved away from her now and, still brandishing the gun, gazed at her statue-still nakedness first from the front and then from the back. He didn't touch her, not yet, but the agony was in knowing he would want to and not knowing when. Her fear was becoming palpable; she couldn't see how to escape him. She couldn't see anything except his passion-crazed eyes assaulting her.

He licked his lips thickly as he gazed at her. "I wonder," he said after a while, his voice as thick and muddy as the dirt below his boots, "whether you're sorry you didn't get a chance at the other men. I just wonder if you weren't planning to bathe in front of all those men in the stream in all your glorious nakedness. Whether you were planning to flaunt yourself and tease them the way you've taunted me." The image of her body and other eyes having the privilege of watching her seemed to torture him. He closed his own eyes for a moment, his facial expression hard, almost murderous.

Then he opened his eyes and smiled, a peculiarly cruel little smile. "But that's what you're like, isn't it, Kalida? That's what Deuce-almighty Cavender doesn't know about you." He walked behind her, and she felt the metal head of the gun slide down her spine, chilling her with his cold purpose and his insane intention. "You know," he rasped in her ear, "one part of me would love to see all those men coveting your nakedness. I just would love to see their eyes as they watch you take off your clothes and reveal all your naked charms, and those erotic stockings. I'd let them feast their eyes on you. I'd even let you walk around so they could see everything. And then, my tormenting bitch, I'd kill them all."

Oh my God, her mind screamed in a panic; he was really crazy. He was insane. Something about her tipped him off and he had become hog-wild insane; she had to do something, because she was certain he intended to kill her. It had to be; it was the only way he could keep her for himself. Her body started shaking and her fear-wracked brain would not operate. Her cobalt eyes glazed over and she almost collapsed right where she was standing.

"Ah Kalida, my closeness makes you tremble. You ache for my touch. You want me." The nose of the gun pressed into her back. "Don't you? Why not tell me then? I've been dying to hear you say it."

"Jake." Her voice croaked his name, so clogged with horror she could hardly speak. "Jake—"

"I'm here," he muttered, still standing behind her with the gun a hairsbreadth away from her body. If only she would show him her desire for him, he thought he could put the bloody thing down. Then he would know she meant to share her naked delights with him and only with him.

She took a deep breath. She did not know what to do to reach him through his obscene obsession. Her desperation was turning into sheer animal panic now, and her total nakedness made her feel so vulnerable that she almost gave up because it seemed too impossible to fight him stark naked. The shaking pervaded her entire body as if she had a fever, and she was not reassured that he pretended not to notice it. If anything, he perceived her to be in the grip of a growing, unchecked passion that any moment would explode into the stuff of his fantasies. And how could she combat that?

"Jake—"

"No excuses now, I'm waiting to hear."

Her heart fell to her feet. She just couldn't reach him that way. She didn't know how she could reach him. She swallowed hard, reaching for something in herself that would give her the strength to *do* something other than

309

just stand and be terrorized by him.

Any move she made, he could easily sight her with the gun. She was as good as dead if she even tried an escape. Nor did she think she could cajole him with sweet words. The set of his mind was such that he would see right through the false sincerity of her words. If she could even conjure up the right words. No, she couldn't play that game, and she couldn't run away, not straight away. She could not hope that anyone would come looking for her. The best she thought she could do was the water. If she could get to the water, she might have a slight chance to outwit him.

She let out her tightly held breath. "What do you want me to do?" she asked him huskily, turning her head just slightly so she could see his shadow behind her out of the corner of her eye.

He was nonplussed by her question. In effect, she had done what he had dreamt of her doing: She had taken off her clothes and her body was now solely his, for his eyes and anything else he might want. But no, he thought, something was missing—the life in her cobalt eyes; the glowing hot knowledge deep within that told him she knew what she was doing to him, and she wanted to do it. She wasn't teasing him the way he wanted her to, as it was in her nature to do. She was stone-still and terrified, and she wasn't supposed to be scared. She was supposed to *want* what had happened.

"You do it," he said finally.

She felt a flash of hope. He didn't know. "You tell me," she said carefully, trying to gauge how far to push him.

"You know."

"I don't know," she contradicted him. "I don't even know what this is all about. I came with you to get washed up, nothing more, Jake."

"No, you came because you've been aching to be alone with me so you can seduce me by flaunting your body."

Her heart sank. No hope this way. He could not be reasoned with, and he was becoming edgy with disappointment that she wasn't apparently eager to strut around, revelling in his fixation about her. "Let me wash myself, Jake," she begged him. "And then we'll go back to camp and forget this whole business." She knew the words were futile; she just had to say something.

"No, we're not going back to camp," he said with heavy finality.

She had to see his face now. She wondered whether she had it in her to be the tempting tease he seemed to think she was, whether her attitude would make the difference in whether she escaped or not. Her fear only made him irritable; he expected something of her she was not delivering, and her participation in this crazy fantastical idea he had of her had to be what it was. If that were true then, her cooperation would gain her time. Since he had not made a move to touch her, she had to assume his real purpose was only to look, and that her job was to entice him by displaying her charms.

He had taken care of that part, she conceded angrily, and now she had to decide whether it was worth risking herself with the other.

All of this went through her mind in the space of several seconds. She made her decision as quickly and whirled around to face him. "All right, Jake. You've got it right. It was all just a game to torment you." She smiled, and she knew it was a nasty little smile born of her growing contempt for him. It fed her attitude, her stance, the expression on her face—especially when he reacted to it, and positively. She was disgusted by the way his body tightened up attentively and his eyes burned with a strange little light.

He was waiting for her to prove her words to him. She sent him a scornful look, with her heart thumping wildly at the chance she was taking. But it was what he wanted.

She was astounded to read it in his face.

And he had known it: She had been putting on a performance for him — just like her, just what he expected. The tension in the hand that held the gun eased a little and he lowered it slightly, waiting for her to tell him more, his eyes feasting on her tempting curves now that she evinced her willingness to drop her pose of resistance.

Her eyes flashed as his arm lowered just that little bit. Yes, and if she could say the next right thing to get it down a mere inch or two more, she was going to run for it.

What did he want to hear? What would a woman, driven to taunt a man like that, say to hold his interest once everything else was revealed? Would she, perhaps, want to know if she pleased him?

Her cobalt gaze grazed his consideringly. His eyes were fixed on her quivering breasts. The moment could not have been more perfect. She only hoped she could get the right amount of archness in the tone of her voice.

She moved her hands slowly to cup her hips, murmuring, "Do you like what you see?" and hating herself for the sly playfulness that crept into her voice, which was exactly what he expected to hear.

His glazed eyes moved upward to meet her bright-eyed gaze. "Very much. I just don't know why you made me force you."

Her cool blue eyes narrowed. "Because," she said slowly, in a petulant voice that came from someplace she did not know, "you needed for me to do that." Kalida was saying words she could barely believe were meaningful, and yet they seemed to have meaning for him, even though they spewed from some part of her that understood what he understood without knowing she knew it.

The gun came down still further. "Yes," he murmured, "you have it exactly right. It's all a game, isn't it, you bitch temptress? When I get my hands on you . . ."

And those were the dangerous words that set her off. She whipped around and bolted straight for the water—the wobble of a stream that was just deep enough to cover her—cursing her dark stockings, her night-black hair, her smooth white body that would show under its clarity like a reflecting mirror.

Two shots rang out behind her as she leapt into its cold depths, in and under in one headlong dive that could have killed her if anything hard had gotten in her way. She heard him faintly behind her screaming, "You goddamn stinking bitch tease whore," and shots ringing out wildly overhead that sounded muffled beneath the two or three feet of water she was immersed in. She paddled forward very slowly. The mountain stream was frigid, and her hands and feet were already feeling numb. His voice and the gunshots began to recede altogether, and she made her way limply to the far side of the stream to take stock of where she was.

Her streaming black head popped out of the water. She was downstream a considerable number of yards away. Jake was a small ridiculous figure now, hopping up and down in frustration at both her defection and that of his weapon, which she saw him hurl into the water.

Ahead of her was the bend of the stream, around which the rest of the crew supposedly had been performing their morning ablutions. She wondered whether Deuce were seeking her now, if Bruno had told him where she had gone. If he were totally out of patience with her for causing this disastrous, unnecessary delay.

She had no sense of how much time had elapsed since she had walked off with Jake, nor any idea of what she should do next. Except get out of that water and dry off before she froze in the warm spring morning. How incongruous. She pulled herself over onto the opposite bank beside the stream and huddled there in the sun. Reaction set in and she began shaking in earnest, as much from the cold as from her narrow escape. There was nothing there to warm her, but she couldn't conceive of trying to get back to camp without some kind of clothing.

She couldn't have been gone longer than an hour, she reasoned. It was just possible the night crew was done resting and had come upstream for their wash up. It was even likely that one or two of them were bathing and their clothing might be lying someplace close by; she might even be able to "borrow" a shirt on the sly. Anything was possible, she thought.

Anyway, she ought to be walking rather than sitting hunched up, and if she could find some clothing in the bargain—well, all to the good. She hoisted herself up painfully and stretched her cramped arms and legs with the stupid stockings that shrouded them like a second skin. God, the ideas she had! She began walking slowly, berating herself for her obtuseness and the self-centeredness that had precipitated everything that had happened.

How was she ever going to explain to Deuce why she had returned stark naked and where her clothes were!

That not-so-very-amusing thought kept her company as she tentatively proceeded downstream along the muddy bank. As she rounded the bend, she heard voices and the splash of water. She drew in a tight, deep breath. It might still be okay, if she could just figure out how to filch a shirt without being seen.

She angled away from the stream now, ducking down low so that her presence would not be obvious. But she felt the same sensation as she had when she had dived into the stream—that her wild inky hair, damning black stockings, and white skin made her eminently conspicuous, and the only sensible thing to do was to get down as low as possible and *crawl*.

And she did, thanking Providence that the ground near the stream was spongy and rock and bush strewn, and that the bushes had leafed out enough to provide a modicum of protection for her if she should need to conceal herself.

Slowly, she inched her way toward the ribald noise of the men until straight ahead of her, spread out on some boulders, she could see their clothing: rinsed-out shirts, tough dirty denims, boots, socks, gunbelts, hats. A fresher-looking shirt hanging from a protruding branch . . . Her cobalt eyes lit on it and she began moving toward it, turning backward every few seconds to make sure someone wasn't coming.

The tree from which it hung was directly in line with the path from the stream, with no bushes or rocks in the way. It meant she had to somehow get around the far side of the tree before she could make a grab for the shirt. Her desperation gave her the patience and the strength to keep down on the ground rather than bolting for the tree, and very slowly she crept around the rocks and bushes nearby and over to the broad base of the tree.

Only then did she stand up, bracing herself against the rough bark, and her hand reached around the breadth of the tree trunk, outstretched, ready to snatch at the material.

And she heard the men. Her heart accelerated; she pulled frantically, and it came away with a sharp little tearing sound.

She tossed it over her shoulders to the shout of "Hey, lady" behind her, as one of the hands ran after her and caught an enticing glimpse of her bare back and buttocks and her long, flashing black-clad legs as she raced away.

Her mouth was dry, and she was totally out of breath before she felt she could stop. The silence behind her told her no one was following her, but still she couldn't quite be sure until she had gotten a long way from the stream. At that point, she collapsed onto the ground to catch her breath and button the damned shirt, which was miles too big on her.

She heard the reassuring lowing of the cattle behind her; she wasn't hopelessly lost at least, but she wasn't close to camp either.

It was the one moment in her life she wanted to see Deuce more than anything else in the world.

But the silence around her was eerie, complete, punctuated by the buzzing of insects and the faint cattle call. And her only course was to start back that way.

She took another deep breath and stood up. The shirt was ridiculously long; it fell almost to her knees, and it was so wide that it hung from her body as if she were skeletal. She could not have chosen a more effective cover-up if she had created it herself. Moreover, it was thick cotton chambray, wrinkled but protective. She resolutely rolled up the sleeves and turned in the opposite direction, toward the faint bawl of the cattle.

And she walked. She knew the soles of the stockings were rent and torn full of holes from the undergrowth; she could even feel little twigs poking her, but she didn't care. Damn that Jake; damn her ideas, damn everything! What had happened made her night with Deuce recede far into the background, almost like something *she* had dreamed. Maybe she had; maybe she had imagined that things were possible with him and that everything he had said was true, but when she would finally wake up, she would find it was all a daydream. . . .

Someone was following her. . . .

She pulled up tensely. Someone was behind her, quiet as an Indian . . . Jake! Terror seized her. How had he known her whereabouts? God, he was clever; he must have an innate scent to track his prey, she thought wildly. No water to dive into here. Very few trees and rocks, which told her the grazing pasture was not far away. Maybe she could dive under the cattle to protect herself.

She was getting crazy now; she had to think.

Slowly she moved backward, her bolt-blue gaze striking off any likely spot where he could be hiding.

Backward and backward again. In a moment she would veer right, toward a thicket of bushes that would afford her some protection.

She counted mentally to herself, shifting her body ever so slightly to make the turn and gear herself to run.

"Kalida!"

Whose voice?

She froze. Terror made her immobile, unable to think. Her heart pounded unbearably hard, as if it could beat its way right out of her chest. She had no coherent thoughts except that Jake might have his gun and use it on her now.

She saw him before she heard his voice again, and she instantly recognized the bend of his body, the particular ramrod posture, the set of his muscular shoulders, the walk.

He walked toward her across the field, and she waited, possessed by a different kind of terror: Oh God, what was Deuce thinking as he strode closer and closer, but still too far away for her to read his expression.

And then it didn't matter. She bolted into his arms and he held her so reassuringly close that it didn't matter.

"Are you all right?" His voice in her ear was expressionless except for a faint tremor beneath his words.

She nodded, and his fingers dug into her tangled night-black curls and lifted her face to his.

"Did he hurt you?" Again that flat concealing tone. Only his eyes were alive, burning charcoal, boring into hers.

"No."

But did her navy-darkened eyes flicker as she answered that question so emphatically? Was there something deep within them that spoke of her withholding something? He

317

couldn't tell for sure. He couldn't tell, and he could hardly bring himself to ask his next question.

"Deuce—" She was wary of the absence of emotion in his voice. His fingers tightened, tugging at her hair. The emotion was there, raging below the surface. She wanted to reassure him, and she hardly knew how to begin.

"Did he . . . touch you?" The words were out, with nothing in his voice to betray him. Nothing.

She denied it instantly. "I promise you, Deuce, he never touched me." She searched his coal-dark gaze and could not tell what he thought, what he believed.

"Kalida . . ." He pulled her tightly against him again, his hand still wrapped in her hair, flexing against the shape of her head, fraught with the things he had left unsaid.

Her body shook as she buried her head against his taut muscular shoulder. His arm around her was like iron. And she needed that secure feeling around her just at that moment. She needed him.

"I could have killed him," Deuce said suddenly. "I could have flat out murdered him." And this time, the chilling emotion was in his voice.

"I am *not* riding chuck," Kalida said adamantly as she surveyed the ruins of her shirt, impatiently balled it up, and threw it into the pile of Bruno's kitchen garbage.

"I don't see as how you have any choice," Deuce said practically, nodding at Bruno. "You are hardly dressed for a tough four-hour drive on the trail."

Kalida sipped from the hot, strong thick cup of coffee that Bruno had fixed up for her from the dregs of the morning coffee pot. God, it warmed her all the way down to her toes, which were now encased in her battered boots and tucked under her sorely wrinkled skirt.

Deuce was right, she thought, but that didn't mean they

couldn't devise some temporary solution. Look at how nice that shy towheaded Joe Slim had been about her keeping his shirt. Surely someone else had a spare pair of . . .

She voiced the thought before it was even completed in her mind.

It made him laugh. He didn't laugh easily, she had learned, but when he did, the most enchanting lines appeared around his eyes and down his cheeks. "Not likely," he said, still amused by the thought of Kalida's slender, strong legs encased in some hulking male's underdrawers. "Good thought, though. Inventive. See you later, though. You can help Bruno pack up." He flashed a funny grin at her. "Woman's work, Kalida."

"I know about it," she said dryly, watching him lope off. He grabbed a hat and a rope, disappeared into the remuda, and reappeared several minutes later mounted. He waved and was gone.

"Miss Kalida . . ." There was Bruno. "Now you miss it, but that's a lot of head of cows out there, and you can't go haring off after them like you used to. It ain't right. You shouldn't even be here. And Mr. Deuce wasting all that time checking out where you had got to. And now Jake gone." He shook his head. "It ain't right. Come help me. Things'll get better once we're on the trail."

Unwillingly she set her mind to the pack up. She washed the dishes and the pots from the morning meal and loaded them into their niches on the back of the chuck. She wrapped the leftover food into airtight packages and stored them in the wagon bed. She helped Bruno dismantle his tent, and they rolled that up and tossed it in the wagon.

And then there was nothing to do but wait until the strays had been rounded up and they were ready to roll.

But Kalida's mind wasn't on that. All the time since she had returned with Deuce, she had been envisioning the scene between him and Jake Danton. He could have killed him, he said. He felt that violent. But how had he confronted Jake? What had Jake told him? He hadn't forced her to go; he had only used a situation that had come to hand as expediently as possible. She certainly could be said to bear some of the blame. Deuce might well consider that he had cautioned her strongly enough about Jake the afternoon they had gone to her old homestead. And stupidly she disregarded it.

Oh God, *what* had happened between them? He must have trailed her from camp to the bathing place, but of course no one would have seen them.

And then he would have tracked them further upstream, which made sense; she would have done it herself had Bruno given her the information that she had left camp with Jake. And knowing Jake, as Deuce obviously did. But he must have found Jake long after she had gone.

She couldn't begin to imagine the scene—or the words that must have passed between them. Enough so that Jake was sufficiently defeated and had left. Left for where? With what? They had walked; his horse was still in camp.

Damn and damn. She had caused all this. She had no business being upset about it. But she was.

She walked to the edge of the pasture where two of the men were guarding the herd, riding around it in concentric circles, trying to contain the milling mass of flesh that sensed somehow it was going to be moving soon. Their sole job was to prevent a stampede, and they—and Kalida—knew from experience that the slightest sound or movement could set it off. It was one reason she kept well back into the trees; she had seen it happen. She was smart enough, she thought ruefully, about *that*.

If only she had some underclothing, she could be out there riding and not thinking about Jake Danton and his lascivious eyes. Or what the confrontation between him and Deuce had been like. Or her own blame for what had happened. If she had only dressed properly yesterday . . . But she hadn't the slightest notion she was going to wind up sharing Deuce's bedroll that night. And she *had* spent the morning on horseback, dressed as she was, and it had been no hardship. But that had been only an hour or so. Four hours plus was another matter altogether. She considered that thought carefully. She needed those underdrawers.

She turned slowly and carefully back to the camp, frustrated that everything had been packed up. Even a spare pair of trousers would have filled the purpose, she thought. She wondered if there were a pair someplace.

Bruno was the only one in camp, the only one who would know. He kept the laundry bag. It was, in fact, jammed into the wagon bed with the remains of the food and Bruno's bedroll. She didn't even think about whether she was going to ask him. He was busy, his back turned to her, doing some sewing or something.

He was a better homebody, she thought ruefully, than she was. She hoisted herself onto the spokes of the wagon wheel and began rummaging through the packages and bags. And finally, in a coarse flour bag near the gate, she found what she was looking for—a pair of dusty wrinkled denims that might have even been Deuce's. She whipped them out, closed the bag carefully, and ran for dear life to the little bit of privacy she might find behind the fully loaded bedwagon.

The pants were terrifying long. When she rolled them up, the cuffs were so thick she could not jam them into her boots. She had to cinch the waistband with a piece of rope she appropriated from around one of the bedrolls. The impromptu belt and bagginess of the pants bulked out her skirt to a conspicuous degree, but she didn't care.

She would be ready to ride when Deuce returned.

How could he have held out any longer? he wondered as he slowly trailed behind the herd on the left side, and Kalida matched his pace on the right. She was born to ride the range, he thought. Born for loving. Born for . . . me. Damned stubborn and determined. Bossy. Dangerous. He could think of a thousand adjectives to describe her, including goddamned unthinking. Check that to beef-witted. Hell. He wasn't going to think about that goddamned bastard and Kalida together. It was enough she had gotten away from him unscathed.

At least she said that. He slanted a coal-hard gaze at her mounted figure several hundred yards away. How devious was she? he wondered. Would she try to protect him? Or—another insidious notion occurred to him—herself?

The son of a bitch had had her at gunpoint; he had forced her to strip for him. It was inconceivable he wanted nothing else from her.

And when he imagined Jake Danton touching her . . .

He had no idea what he had said to Jake. He remembered tackling him and beating the hell out of him. He vaguely recalled all the filth that Jake had spewed at him, reviling Kalida, calling her names, telling him that she was nothing he thought she was, that he didn't know the kind of woman she was and Jake couldn't wait for him to discover the truth. He wanted to be there when Deuce finally understood everything about Kalida.

He didn't even try telling Jake he knew all about Kalida, more than Jake could ever perceive about her or dream about her. Everything. He had studied her for years, wanted her for years. Loved her for years.

Believed her. If she had said nothing more had happened, nothing had happened, despite Jake's insinuations to the contrary.

But Jake had threatened her with a gun. . . .

If he *had* put his hands on her . . .

If he *had* felt the softness of her skin . . .

If Kalida had wanted it, as Jake had intimated . . .

If Kalida were being evasive about what had really gone on between them . . .

If . . .

He studied her erect body from across the dusty trail. If he would ever know the truth . . . He felt right then like grabbing her and beating it out of her. No, not beating it out of her. He felt like branding her body as his all over again. Imprinting himself on her, in her, invading the deepest recesses of her mind and soul so that she would know she belonged only with him.

He couldn't let the likes of a piece of filth like Jake Danton destroy her. If he ever returned to Sweetland, he would kill him, pure and simple. And enjoy it. And then his memory of his hour with Kalida would be dust.

Only he would remember it.

And Kalida.

If it had happened as Jake had said.

And Kalida were lying.

He wondered if he would ever really know.

Fifteen

He had never seen her as determinedly exhilarated as she was on the long, interminable dusty trip back to Sweetland. The herd poured into Morgan field about five hours later, and Eakins, Joe Slim, and Bruno volunteered to turn them out so the others could pull in for the afternoon.

Deuce looked at Kalida for a moment, sitting rigidly on her mount, her face flushed, her hat dangling now by its strap down her back, her midnight hair in wet curly tendrils all around her face, her eyes blazing cobalt, and he felt a distinct ambivalence about her. Damn it, Jake's dirty work was having its effect, even with him gone, Deuce thought angrily, but he couldn't stifle the words he spoke: "I'll nighthawk."

"Aw, hell, Deuce, you don't need to do that," Joe Slim protested, running a sweaty hand through his straw-colored hair. "I'll take the shift."

"I will," Deuce said, daring his range hand to argue with him. He felt feisty, spoiling for a fight, desperate maybe to hit out at somebody because of Jake Danton's searingly suggestive innuendos.

"I'll relieve you later," Joe said resignedly. He knew that look. You didn't oppose Deuce when he had that look on his face. He motioned to Eakins and Bruno, and they turned back to the pasture. The others rode off, leaving Deuce alone with Kalida, and Barney to tend to the chuck. He followed behind them slowly as they made their way back to Sweetland.

It was mid-afternoon by then. Ardelle was seated on the porch almost as if she were waiting for them. She *was* waiting for them, and what appeared to be her calm repose turned into incendiary anger as Deuce and Kalida approached.

She tore out of her rocking chair like a bullet and met them at the porch steps. "You *fired* Jake Danton?" It wasn't really even a question; it was pure untenable outrage.

Deuce dismounted and tossed his hat up onto the porch before he answered. "I did. How do *you* know?"

Ardelle sputtered for a moment, and then calmed down enough to say, "He came back for his gear. He came by here to tell me. *Why,* for God's sake?"

"If you know he's gone, you must know why," Deuce said calmly as he tethered his horse with finely defined precise movements, which were the only thing that kept him from walking away from Ardelle at that moment.

"You caught him with that . . . with Kalida, in a situation *she* provoked."

Kalida's eyes jolted open in shock. Ardelle's animosity was tangible and real—what she had hoped to arouse, yes, but never thought to hear her voice. But worse than that was the story Jake had told her, *Jake's* version: They were together, and *she* had provoked it. Her eyes blazed navy, and she tipped her hat back onto her head and forward slightly to hide her expression from Ardelle. She knew she wasn't going to like the rest of what Ardelle would say, and she didn't even know if Deuce would defend her.

He braced himself against the front porch steps with

one dusty boot and leaned against his muscular thigh. Kalida could see how tautly he was holding himself and that Ardelle perhaps could not perceive his anger was about to be unleashed on her. Depending on what she said. On what he chose to believe.

Kalida sat very still as Deuce contradicted softly, "He deliberately got her away from camp to harass her, even to the point of drawing a gun on her. I don't care what he *told* you."

"And I don't care what you believe. You obviously have no notion of what a reprehensible slut this woman is, and you never have. I'd believe anyone over her, *anytime*," Ardelle shot back angrily, "and she's cost us a good foreman in the bargain." She stamped to the center of the porch where she could look up at Kalida. "Your father's no good, and you're no good, as you've taken great pains to show me this week. And now I believe it, and I hope to hell Deuce gets rid of you and comes to his senses about Jake. He can operate more successfully without you than he can without Jake Danton, I'll tell you." She whirled back to Deuce. "You'd better think about that, Deuce. You'd better rethink all your plans, for that matter."

She turned and hobbled away, and the thrust of her fury stayed behind. Deuce stared after her thoughtfully, and Kalida cringed. Her words seemed to have had an effect on him. She couldn't believe the nightmare this was becoming.

And then Deuce catapulted himself onto the porch and into the open doorway of the house, shouting for Prestina. She came at once, and Kalida watched as he spoke with her, his words seemingly quick and sharp, and Prestina's comprehension immediate and forthcoming because she glided down the steps with Deuce and they approached Kalida.

Deuce held out his arms for her, his stormy gray eyes kindling with something she couldn't read as she allowed him to lift her down from her mount. "Prestina will take care of you this evening—" he started to say and she interrupted.

"Why? Do I need taking care of?"

"I think you might," he said consideringly, still holding her, still searching her softening cobalt gaze for something he could not see beneath the brim of that almighty huge hat. "Go with Prestina, and don't get in Ardelle's way until I clear this up with her."

"You won't clear it up," Kalida said. "I made very sure to be on my very worst behavior this week. She'll believe what Jake told her." She gave him an unsure smile as he released her. "The question still remains, do you?"

He took her arm and walked her up the steps. "I believe you need a good hot bath, and I believe I'm a man short in the field is what I believe. And I believe nothing will be accomplished today by talking about it. Maybe tomorrow," he added sharply at her stricken expression.

"After you spend a long hard night thinking about it, you mean," Kalida hissed in disgust, pulling her arm away from him. "Fine. You do that. I'll sleep easy tonight because I *do* know the truth."

"Mr. Deuce say you take this same bedroom tonight," Prestina said as she stopped in front of Kalida's "privacy" bedroom. Kalida's spirits sank a little further. There was no undoing what had happened, and beyond that, Deuce had to take her word on faith. His relegating her back here told her that he didn't—at least today.

On the face of it, she knew it sounded impossible. And who knew Jake better than Deuce? Of course it didn't seem probable to him that Jake, armed with a gun, hadn't forced her to do all kinds of unspeakable things. And of course Jake would be vindictive—she had escaped him, hadn't she? All his plans and dreams had slid through his fingers. She had lied to him and he probably felt she had cheated him out of what he felt she had promised.

And she had; she had done what she needed to to get away from him.

She turned to Prestina. "You don't have to try to make things better. I think a bath sounds very nice. My skin is all burned and dusty and chafed from these horrid denim pants."

"Yes," Prestina said, lifting the hat off her head. "You have not had so good a time as you thought. You pay for someone else's malice."

"Yes," Kalida whispered, awed that Prestina understood, "I pay."

"I hear him say all those things to Miss Ardelle," Prestina said, helping her undress. "I don't believe him. You care for Mr. Deuce; you don't go doing those things when your heart is with someone."

Kalida stared at her. "*I* care for Deuce? Nonsense. You don't know what you're saying."

"I know," Prestina nodded. "I know." She patted Kalida's shoulder and helped her into bed. "You rest. I draw the water and heat for your bath. You be still."

But Kalida couldn't be still. After Prestina had gone, it seemed like her mind filled to bursting with a hundred different images, and all of them were Deuce. Her mind was full of him, and his seeming rejection of her was almost unbearable. The afternoon's events superimposed themselves over the picture of him, blotting it out, totally obliterating it in fact as well as in her reverie. Deuce would never want her again with the fury and passion that he had. Never touch her again if he thought Jake had put a hand on her. Never kiss her again. God, the thought was enough to drive her insane. Never arouse her body to exquisite culmination. Never look at her in that burning flinty gray way of his, or whisper her own innermost feelings to her. Oh yes, she cared for him. Too late to know it now. He had known it, even before he had put that outrageous proposal to her father. He must have, to have even suggested it.

And what she had put him through!

Her whole body flinched at the thought that it could have been different if only she had been just a little bit honest with herself. Just let herself admit the feelings that he aroused in her. Then there never would have been all this tussling; there never would have been this sensual war. Jake never would have weaved a fairy tale about her and acted on it; Ardelle would not be angry with her. There might not, she thought, even have been a fire; no Ellie, no complications.

Just her and Deuce and all those warm, delicious feelings he knew just how to evoke.

And now there was nothing.

Deuce was gone, and Jake's insinuations were going to ruin everything.

Everything.

The heat of the bath warmed her aching muscles, and nothing more. She lay in the bed wide awake, wrapped in the rumpled silk robe, letting Prestina take care of her, feed her, cosset her, reassure her.

But in the end, she was dead alone in the dark room, unable to sleep, listening for certain footsteps that she did not hear, that would not come.

She paced the room, looking out the window at the futile darkness that was unrelieved by even a hint of a moon. The night sounds did not comfort her. Nothing could comfort her but Deuce.

And hadn't *that* taken her long enough to figure out, she thought disgustedly. She wanted him. She felt frantic with wanting him, and she knew she had no right to want him. Not now. Not with Jake coming between them.

She threw herself back onto the bed. She couldn't even recreate yesterday's ecstasy. It seemed as though her life had begun anew when Jake had brandished the gun and commanded her to strip. And because of that, she could not have Deuce now that she finally admitted she desired him. She wasn't even free to love him — now that she knew she was coming to love him — because the possibility existed he believed Jake and not her.

If only she had acknowledged all of this just one day earlier. *One day.*

And the worst thing was she had done it to herself. Stupidly, unwittingly, not reading the warning signs in Jake's untoward behavior, not recognizing her growing feelings for Deuce.

She wasn't aware of the tears coming; they just seemed to *be* there suddenly, with nothing to cushion them but her own guilty conscience.

She buried her head in the pillow, her silent sobs shaking her whole body.

Ten minutes of self-pity was all she could stand. Tears were a weakness, and western women did not cry easily. Kalida Ryland did not ever cry at all. She couldn't remember ever having cried about anything — except when her mother had died.

It was insane to cry over circumstances she could not now change. Her tears diminished abruptly.

And then she heard his step in the hallway.

It was interesting to him, as he paused at his own bedroom door, that he would not have been surprised to see Kalida in his bed waiting for him.

And he did not know whether or not he was disappointed that she wasn't. He didn't even know why he had come back to the house when he could just as easily have bedded down in the bunkhouse.

He threw his gear bag down on the far side of the room and whipped out of his shirt and boots.

Kalida! Her name was a siren call; he knew why he was back. She was a fever in his blood, beating away: Kalida, Kalida. Kalida and Jake. Kalida and Jake. At the Ryland barn. At the stream. In the stable? In the fields? What did Jake know about Kalida that he didn't? The thought pounded away at him all night as he rode over Morgan field and the Balsam range. He couldn't concentrate for thinking about it; he was damned sorry he had elected to ride and damned ecstatic when Joe Slim turned up to relieve him.

Kalida. She hadn't even known Jake before she came to stay at Sweetland. She had been innocent. He couldn't imagine what had happened in the space of time since her arrival to drive Jake to that kind of excess.

What had Kalida done to him?

He had been over that one all night, and he just couldn't conceive that she could want anything from Jake.

He knew Kalida; her response to him was perfect and all-consuming. There was nothing Jake could give that he couldn't. Nothing.

Or did he just want to believe that?

Nothing. But she had driven Jake to pull a gun on her and she had taken off her clothes.

She had been alone with him and the gun and her nakedness, and she expected him to believe that *nothing* had happened between them.

God, he hadn't even asked *her* the details; he wasn't sure he would be able to listen with equanimity. She had dressed for *him* and undressed for Jake, and he couldn't see farther than that without blood-red anger coursing through his body. He couldn't even sit still thinking about it. He was up and pacing, staring out the window, unaware even of the flickering light of the ever-present kerosene lamp that limned his bare upper torso with intriguing planes and hollows.

If someone waved a gun at him and told him to strip, he would tackle him, he thought grimly. But of course Kalida could never have done that. She had truly been at the mercy of Jake's gun—and her wits. And she had gotten away from him.

But what had happened before that? Why had Jake taken her off alone like that, planning enough in advance so that he had a gun to threaten her with?

What did he *imagine* she had done to him?

It was the first time he had posed *that* question to himself, and for some reason the tight tense knot inside his gut unraveled slightly.

He leaned against the window frame, staring out into the black, black night, thinking of Kalida standing naked before Jake.

The picture tortured him. What else could she have done?

She could have screamed.

He would have shot her instantly.

She could have tried to talk him out of it.

Maybe she did.

Try.

And still, Jake would have wanted to and he must have reached out and touched that satiny skin. . . .

He ran an agitated hand over his face.

It wasn't possible that that hadn't happened. He had to conclude that Jake had had his hands on her, and he wasn't sure if he could live with the knowledge of that—and Kalida.

And then he looked up and she was there, half in and half out of the room, hanging onto the door as if it were her only support, looking impossibly exotic and desirable.

He hadn't thought what he would do if she showed up in his room. His first thought, as he paced toward her very slowly, was that if he had a gun on him right this very minute, he would draw it, then make her undress and show him every last goddamned thing that Jake had made her do with him. And his second thought . . . There was no second thought. He thrust his hands into her tumbling midnight curls roughly and pulled her to him, covering her mouth as though he could blot out Jake by force.

He sought her deeply from an endless wellspring of torment that could not be assuaged. Had Jake tasted her? Had he reached for her in just this way? Did he know her shape and texture, her passion to be kissed like this? Did he know the subtle wanton shape of her body against his, her eager hands, her passionate femininity? . . .

He pulled away from her mouth violently, sliding one hand down to surround her neck. His other hand tugged her hair, pulling her head back slightly so he could read her dew-wet eyes. She had been crying. For whom?

For her damned self, probably. He bent over her and took her upper lip between his own so softly, so gently, that she felt the tug straight through her whole body. His tongue delicately rimmed the silky inner skin, constricting his lips around it, pulling away ever so slightly and returning once again to hold it between his lips, savoring the taste of it in a way that was so totally opposite his ferocity of the moment before.

And then he played with her lower lip the same way. She felt shooting stars of pleasure all up and down her body, which should have reassured her and didn't. She met each light caress equally, pressing her body, a little bit closer to his each time, her hands on his taut muscular arms and moving with each rich little kiss.

She hadn't expected this; she had expected pure molten anger from him, violence, words. That could all still come. The way he was looking at her with those flinty gray eyes, the taut restraint of his body against hers, did not bode well.

"Deuce—" she murmured against his lips.

His whole body tightened. "What is it, Kalida? Isn't this what you've come for?" His mouth covered hers ruthlessly, and she could not pull away. He held her against his body with brutal strength, hot hard strength that made her struggle against it. He believed the worst; and he believed he could wipe away Jake from her consciousness by his very violence.

And then it let up. She could feel his arousal; his body lengthened, hardened, elongated against her. He didn't want that; she felt it in him. He did not want to be seduced by her tonight. He thrust her away from him angrily.

"You'd rather hate," she said acidly, even as she understood what he was feeling. She was aching for the gentleness again. Why couldn't he be that gorgeously gentle with her and let go of the rest? But he couldn't, and she felt bereft.

"It's hard not to." He was back by the window, his arms folded almost like a barrier against her. His body burned from the pressure of hers against it, and he felt as though the soft fullness of her breasts was imprinted on his chest. She could get to him; she could get to anyone. God knew she had gotten to Jake.

Hell. "Go back to your room, Kalida."

That flat, awful voice. She had to crack through it. "I need you tonight," she whispered.

"How the hell do you know what you need, Kalida? How the hell do I?" he said disgustedly.

"You know," she said plainly, coming farther into the room, closer to him, close by the bed.

"That was not the story last night," he countered.

"You were at great pains to tell me it was," she retorted, coming still closer. "I found out it was."

"Really, when?" he shot back, and she drew a sharp breath at the implication. He could easily think it was

334

after Jake had gotten done with her. Damn it, damn him, damn him. She wanted him so desperately at that moment that she thought she might do anything to entice him, to accomplish the same end that he had tried with his suppressed violence—to get the vision of her and Jake together out of his mind.

And he thought she looked ravishing, standing before him in that slide of a silk robe with its riotous flowers reflecting his vacillating feelings to a perfect degree. Her face was flushed from his insinuations, and it only made her cobalt eyes stand out even more blazingly against her skin and the color of her robe. Her tumbling midnight hair reflected the restlessness of her night alone in the other room. She is gorgeous, he thought dispassionately. The crumpled robe only enhanced the line of her body; it draped around her like a waterfall. Her breasts were fully visible through it, to the thrust of her nipples against two huge white silk blossoms on her chest, and it fell alluringly around the curves of her hips and buttocks.

If he just put out his hands to her, he could drown in the solace of her luscious body and never think of what might have happened.

He couldn't stop thinking about it. His smoky gray gaze rested tellingly on her breasts, and she saw exactly what he was looking at. Her breath quickened with anticipation, but she saw from the set of his face that he was not going to touch her. And that he wanted her terribly.

She had to do something. She could not leave the room with nothing resolved. Her eyes darkened to navy as she considered what she must do. She held his smoky gaze, challenging him to demand that she leave.

And she saw that he did not have the strength to do that. Her hands lifted almost involuntarily and touched her silk-shrouded breasts. His eyes fired up, and she moved her hands slowly downward on either side of her body, watching his burning eyes follow them, his expression never losing that set obstinate look.

She had to move him. She lifted one hand from her thigh, where it had come to rest, and pulled gently at one end of the sash around her waist. It fell away gently, trailing down her body to graze her bare feet.

The edges of the robe opened to reveal a line of enticing naked skin and a hint of her lush femininity.

His whole body tensed. She could not have done it better if she had planned it. Had she planned it? He didn't care. The shadow of the swell of her breasts invited his eyes, invited his hands. He had only to decide just when to take her. And he would take her. No one could refuse such a blatant invitation.

"You win," he said in that awful flat tone. "Sit on the bed." There was no reason not to, he thought; she wanted it.

She sat, easing herself backward so that she could brace her upper body on her elbows. More of the robe slithered away from her body, as she had intended, to reveal her breasts, her thighs, and the long length of her bare legs. She sent him an expectant look. His arms unfolded from his wall of a chest, and he stood surveying her with his hands on his hips.

"You *are* something," he said finally.

"You want me," she answered with deep grave surety. It was the one thing she did know; no matter what he still felt about Jake, his desire for her was unabated.

"I'd be crazy to reject your offer," he agreed, and only then did he moved forward, lean the hard line of his body over her, and touch her, drawing his hand from her cheek down her chest and straight down the line of her body. "I'd be crazy," he whispered as the sense of her sex and her silky skin jolted through him. His kissed her waiting lips, a firm, pressured, undemanding kiss, a frustrating kiss. She bit his lips as they moved over hers, demanding more, determined not to let him get away with giving her less.

The heat of his hand enveloped her sex, and her lips moved against it as her mouth moved to invade and conquer his. She was the aggressor now, avidly seeking his tongue, seducing him with the writhing of her hips, demanding his ardor.

He stradled her thighs then, his hand still resting on her straining femininity; bracing his body on his other hand, he leaned his weight into her, forcing her downward, off her elbows and onto the bed, where her wild inky hair made a tumultuous counterpoint to the blue cover.

Her one hand came up and rubbed his hard bare chest; the other slid down his muscular forearm to the hand that remained tightly against the juncture of her thighs. His mouth hovered over hers, dueling with her with an intensity that was not playful.

She flicked her tongue against his lips, impatient with his making her wait until he was ready to kiss her. Her desire flared like a living thing, touching him, enveloping him.

"You'd tempt the devil," he growled, grazing her lips with his and pulling away violently.

"You *are* the devil," she retorted huskily, running her hand up his chest now to his shoulders and urgently flexing her fingers against his taut skin to bring him closer to her.

He came down heavily on his elbow and, bracing himself, removed his hand from her to support his body just covering hers, over her but not touching her. His heat came at her in waves, and his mouth was touching hers and drawing back, feeling her lips between his and pulling away, tugging her lips, licking them, feeling their texture and shape as if he had never tasted them before.

He could have kept that up all night, but his own body betrayed him, moving with the rhythm of his exploration of her lips, acceding to the warmth and weight of her legs wrapping around him and sensually gripping his body. Her eager hands made a torturous glissade of motion up and down his torso, raking his chest, pulling him closer to her, closer, wanting him to feel her naked skin against his. Wanting him, against all reason, to take her with the explosiveness he felt.

His body still braced over her, Deuce took her incendiary mouth, invading it, filling it, and Kalida opened herself to him totally, willing him to possess her this way. His hands surrounded her wild lustrous hair, thrusting themselves into it, holding her head immobile. Her own hands pulled at him, felt him, held him unmoving against her, teased him, and slid down his body to caress his throbbing manhood that strained against the confining material of his pants. God, she wanted him; she pulled frantically at his belt and the impeding buttons, her fingers trembling against his bare skin as she slowly released them one by one.

He didn't move. His mouth still owned hers, his tongue still stroked hers with slow soft movements, and his whole body tightened and poised for the touch of her hand on his hot granite length. What if Jake had forced her to? . . .

He caught his breath sharply as her fingers grazed the taut area just below his stomach and slowly pressed downward to grasp and feel and free his masculinity.

She knew what to do; he had taught her himself, hadn't he? She pushed aside all the restraining material, and both her hands felt him, held him, stroked him until he was dizzy with wanting her. Her hands, somehow, had learned what more to do. Her touch was soft and firm, loose and tight, caressing and urgent all at the same time.

Did you do that with Jake?

That was the thought that was holding him back. And she knew it. Her torrid caresses told him she knew it because she fully intended to tempt him beyond his resolutions. Beyond rational thinking. And she was coming close to it. Closer. Her hands were magical in their enticing play and his desire was raging totally out of control. He felt himself sliding one of his hands under her buttocks and lifting her upwards and against his hard thrusting length, then with one tight lunge, he drove into her wet, welcoming warmth.

He eased her downward, drawing his mouth away from hers now so that he could see her face and look at her lush, sultry body that opened for him so shamelessly.

Her glowing cobalt eyes flashed him a tantalizing look, inviting him to settle his weight on her; her hips pushed upwards in taut little movements that betrayed her urgency. Her hands rubbed his taut shoulders and neck.

She didn't understand this long hesitating pause, or his reluctance to lay his body on hers. He nestled within her, unmoving, looking at her as if he were going to say something, and she knew exactly what.

But he didn't say it. Without warning, he levered his body so that it was being supported by his hands and arms both, and he could gaze at the whole of her body beneath him and the motion of his body within hers. He was not going to touch her; he was going to watch. Very slowly he began the languorous stroking movements that she yearned for.

Her hands grabbed his wrists as if they were anchors as his movements became more powerful, steady, stroking her velvet sheath rhythmically; his shrouded gray eyes told her nothing. Hers, she thought, melting into the molten thrusts of his lusty length, must have told him everything.

Her fingers constricted against his wrists with every surge of feeling. Her hips churned against him provocatively, enticing him to plunge deeper, harder, faster. Her head lashed back and forth with each compelling exquisite stroke of his potent masculinity. It was all so simple, she thought somewhere in her radiant euphoria, one man and all this pleasure.

He read it all in her face, in her hot blue gaze, in her urgent convulsive movements against him. She was so beautiful, with her body framed by the flimsy robe, all of it open to and possessed by him. Only he could cause this cataclysmic pleasure in her. No one would ever see this— her lusty fiery demands, her body writhing and twisting beneath his.

No one could compel this incandescent response from her except him. In that moment, he loved her for it, and for letting him see it in all her vulnerability.

He loved her.

Her body was all his now, hot, wiling, open, hungry for him, answering him, demanding him.

Everything in her reached for him then with fierce, unbridled desire as he plunged to the very depths of her sultry core and away again, over and over, filling her endlessly with piercing swelling sensations that billowed through her, expanding, filling her, spiralling slowly and rapturously from her honeyed center to burst in iridescent radiant shards all over her body.

He watched every movement, every nuance of her response and her culmination. He bent over her mouth to savor it again. His body plunged backward as his mouth claimed hers. He plunged into her luscious heat fiercely, possessively, driving his massive length home again and again and again until his lusty movements exploded his torrent of passion deep into her body.

Only then did he settle his hard weight onto her and allow her eager arms to hold him. He had no thoughts of anything but the cascade of feeling that still pulsated through his blood.

Her warmth enfolded him; her nakedness enthralled him. He was content just to lie in her arms for the rest of the night.

It was Joe Slim who pounded on his door the following morning, his voice hoarse with urgency. "Deuce, damn it, wake the hell up! Something's happened. . . . Deuce!. . ."

He awakened raggedly to that noise—the pounding and Joe's sharp imperative tone. And what the damn hell was Joe doing in the house? What the hell was going on with Ardelle? He reached for his pants groggily and pulled them on. "Hell, Joe, hang on. . . ." Shit, what the hell was Joe doing in the house? He groped for his boots, slanting a glance at Kalida to see whether she was awake. She was watching him, her expression quizzical, her body curved into a sinuously tempting line under the cover.

He stood up, shrugged, and strode to the door. He flung it open impatiently. "Yeah, Joe? What in God's name are you doing here at this godawful hour? Isn't Ardelle downstairs?"

"No, I didn't see no Miss Ardelle. Listen, Deuce, we got trouble. Something's happened . . . bad." He paused expectedly, nervously even. He didn't know how the hell he was going to break this damned news to Deuce, worse because that roundup lady was with him, right in the room. Damn!

"What is it?" Deuce asked brusquely. Joe's respectful diffidence was sometimes aggravating, the more so because Kalida was awake and waiting for him.

"The goddamn cows are goddamn gone," Joe burst out.

"*What* goddamn cows?" Deuce demanded, all his senses alert.

"Them goddamn cows," Joe whispered, pointing at Kalida. "Them ones we moved down yesterday to Morgan field. They're goddamn gone. Up and goddamned vanished, every last damn one of them!"

"And the men?"

"Left goddamned unconscious in the field. Damn it, Deuce, I don't see how—" Joe broke off as Deuce's face tightened into a blazing, menacing mask right before his very eyes.

"Yeah, well, I goddamned well see," Deuce said tautly, turning to look at Kalida who had bolted upright at Joe's news. Kalida's blatant seduction, he thought savagely, done with an express purpose; clever little bitch. Too bad she had no conception of her father's real character. Too bad he talked her into abetting his little schemes. "Oh yes," he said tautly, pinning Kalida with his stone-hard gray gaze, "I goddamned well see everything is beginning to make goddamned sense."

Sixteen

He stormed across the room and hauled Kalida out of bed. "Get dressed, you bitch. Get your lying traitorous body out of my bed and downstairs. Now!" he roared at her, wheeling around, grabbing his shirt, and flinging his way out the door with Joe Slim.

She reacted slowly, utterly bewildered by his treatment of her. She reached for her robe, which she had discarded in the aftermath of their sublime lovemaking, and slipped it on thoughtfully.

Her father's herd — Deuce's herd — some five hundred head of cattle were missing. Yes, she understood that. She could not comprehend what Deuce understood or what it had to do with her.

"Kalida!"

His bellow up the stairs sent her running to her bedroom, where Prestina waited for her with a pitcher and bowl for her morning wash up.

"This be serious, Miss Kalida," she said gently, sponging down Kalida's back. "All those cows disappeared. You say how."

"I can't," Kalida said, shimmying into her shirtwaist and staring into the mirror at her nimble fingers buttoning it up. She couldn't say anything at all this morning;

343

she felt like her whole world had rocked sideways and that everything she knew from the night before did not exist anymore. It was the only thing she cared about. Deuce's cattle could go to hell. But obviously he thought somehow she had something to do with their disappearance. How could she have?

She tried, as she brushed her wildly tangled inky hair, to figure out what he possibly could be thinking. Nothing made sense, she couldn't come up with a theory that remotely involved her with this catastrophe. It had to be a random happening, the gang of rustlers that had staked its claim on Sweetland and the Linaria. A mistake, possibly. How did a thief determine the breed in the dark?

She threw down the brush and let Prestina braid her hair into a long plait down her back. "You must hurry," she cautioned. "He is raving angry."

"All right, I'm done. I suppose I will find out what the judge and jury down there has decreed before too long," Kalida said grimly. Yes, and she would be tried and convicted before pressing her own case, too, or even hearing the charges. Just like with Jake.

She couldn't bear to pursue that thought, but it pursued her as she finally made her way donwstairs. Her cobalt eyes were dark with apprehension, and her hands were shaking just a little. The residual force of Deuce's anger was tangible. She found she was just a little frightened.

It was eerily quiet as she came down the steps. Everyone was on the porch. She could hear Deuce's hard voice rapping out brisk questions, and low hesitant voices answering them.

She looked up at Prestina, who was following right behind her. Prestina nodded at her and mouthed, "I bring you coffee. You go there," as she slipped behind Kalida toward the kitchen.

I go there, Kalida thought warily. I go to a hanging. She held onto the door frame as she stepped out onto the porch.

The first person she saw was Ardelle, and her vicious, accusing sherry-fired eyes. "Here she is," she said flatly, turning away.

Deuce looked up from a sheaf of papers he was examining. Eakins stood by him, his expression baffled. "Sit down someplace," Deuce said sharply, his eyes flinty. He turned back to Eakins. "All right; this is the pre-drive tally then. Mr. Ryland took the tote, am I right?"

"With me assisting," Eakins corroborated, looking utterly cowed. As anyone would have been, Kalida thought angrily, with Deuce's awesome glare dissecting him.

"Hell," Deuce spat. "God, I might have goddamned known it." He slapped the papers down on the flat of the porch railing and stalked away in a fury.

Kalida looked up as Prestina offered her a coffee cup, taking it gratefully and going to the far end of the porch to find an unoccupied seat. Ellie and Joe Slim sat closer to Ardelle, and two unfamiliar men leaned against the porch railing.

She took a deep hot, gratifying sip of the coffee, almost choking on it when Deuce whipped back to her and demanded, "Where is your father?"

"I haven't seen him since he left," she said resentfully. "Why?"

"He knew we were bringing down the herd," Deuce said unequivocally, staring into her face.

Kalida hesitated the merest second. It was true; *she* had told him. She remembered it distinctly. Her face whitened but she nodded her head. "Yes."

"From you," Deuce persisted, his frustration simmering under his question.

"Yes," she said low, and Ardelle leapt up.

"You see, you see? She has been a package of trouble

345

ever since . . . I can't tell you when. You see, Deuce, you couldn't even trust *her.* I could have told you that, but you wouldn't have listened. God, you have always been so goddamned stubborn where she is concerned."

She drew herself up then, as though she had said more than she had meant to, and sat down heavily in her chair.

"So when he planned his raid, he contacted you to create a little diversion," Deuce concluded, his voice dripping contempt. "And you did it very well, Kalida; very well indeed. Imagine my trusting you to the point of leaving only three men on guard, and Joe. Imagine my thinking you actually had some conception of your father's character, and you actually might be somewhat relieved to have him suitably occupied elsewhere. Imagine my stupidity and gullibility, you bitch."

"Stop it!" she shrieked. "What the devil are you talking about? What are you saying about my father? He didn't—"

"I would gamble Sweetland on the fact he did," Deuce interrupted harshly.

"But my father . . . you . . . I didn't . . . When could he have contacted me, for God's sake?"

"At your ranch; the barn with all its little crannies? A message in the haystack, perhaps? Some willing go-between. I mean, what the hell do you think your father has been doing all this while?"

"Planning the renovation and getting together his new herd," Kalida said staunchly. "The wreckage is cleared away already. Do you know that?"

"Yes I do," Deuce snapped. "Because if you think I would have left it to your father to get it done—"

"WHAT?" Kalida screamed.

"I'm telling you, I arranged it directly after we signed the papers, Kalida. Don't tell me you didn't know."

"I didn't know," she said dully, sending a searing blue glance at Ellie, who raised her eyebrows as if to say, I

346

warned you.

"You didn't know?" he repeated scornfully. "Now why don't I believe *that?* Your father is a scoundrel, Kalida, an out-and-out scoundrel who calls a good bluff and knows how to read a man's soul. And you, my lying bitch, are the perfect accomplice. You have just the right air of innocence and restraint. You conned me, Kalida. And I'm admitting it in front of everyone here. You and your father twisted me straight around by my tail and left me hanging."

"No!" Kalida protested. "No."

"But yes, the perfection of it is dazzling. Your father played perfectly on my feelings for you; he's known it forever, believe me, Kalida. He has a sense of those things very fine and innate. He made the arrangements, and then he burned down his house to get me to rescue everyone. And didn't I just fall into the plot, galloping up to Sweetland with the lot of you and offering to buy and help. Damn. You see how it works out, Kalida. He took the money and ran. And he saw a chance to get the herd back—double his money—if you'd just provide him with a little information and volunteer to occupy my attention as best you can, and the end result is several thousand dollars out of my pocket and one brazen bitch out of my life."

"Oh God," Kalida groaned. "Deuce, I know nothing of any of this."

"Forget it, Kalida. No other explanation makes any sense. There's the tally—" He pointed at the papers on the porch. "He didn't do it alone; he got my men and he got the cattle and he thought you'd got me so he'd have some control here, but he miscalculated on that one. He's got nothing here. You've got nothing, Kalida, except my cordial invitation to leave."

She couldn't believe it; she couldn't even assimilate all of what he had said. Disparate details intruded: the raging anger boiling under his words at her betrayal; the whiteness of his knuckles as he leaned against the porch railing confronting her; Ardelle's vicious little half smile; Ellie's contemptuous expression . . . She couldn't take it all in. Her father's perfidy, her indictment . . . Where on earth would she go?

She got up and stumbled blindly into the house, and into Prestina's arms. She could hear Ardelle spitting, "Your punishment was too good for her," and his slamming voice, "Shut up, Ardelle."

"Come, I help you," Prestina murmured.

"I'll be all right," Kalida sobbed. "I never cry."

"You cry for lost love," Prestina said, moving her up the stairs and carefully. "You cry for your father. And you cry for what cannot be . . . yet."

"I'm not crying," Kalida said through gritted teeth. She straightened her back and pushed away Prestina's comforting hands. "I wouldn't waste my tears on the likes of *him.*"

Ellie rocked back and forth contentedly, staring out at the broad fields of Sweetland. Ah, Sweetland . . . She loved it too much already. She would love to remain here forever. Kalida had conveniently botched her chance with Deuce. How good of her to leave the way clear. How deeply she had misconstrued Kalida's motives. Kalida was in love with Deuce, even if she didn't know it, and she would never get him back now. Imagine how stupid she herself had felt when she finally realized that Kalida's original little ruse, when Ellie had come to nurse her, was not a ploy designed to drive a wedge between her and Hal Ryland.

She marveled at her own misreading of the situation. She was sure Kalida had known that she and Hal had had an ongoing affair for years after the young girl precipitated Ellie's removal from the Ryland ranch. She had been sure Kalida had arranged her little accident in order to keep Hal home with her more, never expecting he would ask Ellie Dean to come to the ranch.

And then, when she saw how ardently Deuce was pursuing Kalida, her only thought was to speed up his courtship somehow so that she and Hal could make their own plans. Which he never would have done if Kalida were still living home. It had been so easy to leave the stove burning dangerously all night. It never occurred to her until later that Kalida might have died.

Or perhaps, deep in her soul, she *had* wanted that, but she couldn't examine that too closely. What happened was what she had hoped to accomplish: Deuce had invited them all to Sweetland, and she was sure proximity and propinquity would change Kalida's mind about him.

What it did, instead, was change Ellie's mind about him. How fortunate she had been that Kalida was intent on confirming Ardelle's bad opinion of her.

How fortunate that Hal had found some perfectly devious way to stealing back his cattle. She loved the symmetry of it. She hadn't half hoped to even have a chance to make Deuce really take notice of her. But tonight . . . Tonight she would take that chance, because Deuce never wanted to see Kalida again. Deuce felt betrayed. She could sympathize with that. Deuce needed a more mature woman to handle his hot male passions. He emphatically did not need a child like Kalida.

As for Hal, she had never been sure when or where he would turn up, even in the best of times between them. And now, of course, he was more or less an outlaw, and she might never see him again altogether.

She had to grab her chances when and where she could, she thought, and she'd infinitely rather have Deuce in her bed than Hal. It was just a matter of degree. Right now, Deuce had more to offer.

Ardelle was arguing with Madame. Madame had not nearly finished the garments Ardelle had ordered. Ardelle was sure Madame would accept the money in lieu of services and pack in preparation for returning to town later this morning, along with Miss Kalida and Miss Ellie.

Kalida's eyebrows shot up. Ellie too? The thought was the only diversion she had had for an hour at least. Her brain felt like a sea of mud, clotting up every coherent thought, sinking her deeper and deeper into its depths. Nothing made sense. Nothing. Her father's perfidy least of all. Her father was not like that. . . .

". . . that kind of decisiveness is more Deuce's style . . ." Ellie had said that.

Her head whirled. Her father had always been at the cutting edge of trouble one way or another every year since they had come west. But that didn't mean . . .

What did it mean? Had he been desperate enough to trade her to Deuce *and* expect she might have helped him in some little fraud he intended to perpetrate? He could not have done that, not to her, not to Deuce. But he had pushed for her marrying Deuce. Pushed hard. Would he laugh now if he were told it wasn't remotely within the realm of possibility? Would he rescue her if he knew that Deuce had abandoned her?

The questions whirled around. What had he planned? Supposing all his little plots hadn't worked? What if Deuce hadn't wanted her? What if the house hadn't caught fire? Did he have a contingency plan?

Oh God, I'm starting to believe Deuce, she thought wretchedly. The bastard against her own father. He believed her father had schemed and defrauded him. He believed the worst. Her capitulation to him had taught him nothing about her; her feelings for him were rendered meaningless, part of a hoax, a ruse.

350

How could she live without him? How could she forgive him for his suspicion and mistrust?

There was a hard rapping at her door. Kalida opened it warily to find Ellie standing outside in a seething rage. "Can I come in?"

"If you must," Kalida said ungraciously, surreptitiously wiping away her own tears. "What do you want?"

Ellie strode around the room for a moment as if she needed to release some of that voluminous anger inside her. Her black eyes utterly burned with an animosity that was not, for once, directed against Kalida.

"I have something to tell you," she said finally when she had calmed down.

"What could you possibly have to tell me?" Kalida asked coldly, wondering if Ellie knew that she would be leaving this morning as well.

"Something about Deuce. And your father."

Kalida's blue gaze flashed at Ellie and then turned away. She must not show too much interest; Ellie was just in a mood to play with her. "What about Deuce and my father?" she asked finally in as neutral a tone as she could manage.

"Didn't you wonder why Deuce was adamant about clearing away the rubble from the fire?"

Kalida shook her head. She hadn't given it a thought. "Why?"

"Your father mortgaged the property," Ellie announced vindictively, sending Kalida a hard look that commanded her to make the obvious connection. She did.

"To Deuce," Kalida said slowly, her heart beginning to pound unbearably hard. "He owns the property now."

"He can foreclose," Ellie contradicted, "but yes, he could well take title to it."

"Oh." A wealth of comprehension in that one small

351

word, Kalida thought, examining it like a piece of fruit she had taken out to eat. Her father had sold away her inheritance to get what he wanted. Yes, that explained a lot of things. A whole lot of things. The only thing it didn't explain was why she had been made to feel like she was the collateral for her father's whole life. She just didn't understand that. But everything else was clear. The money didn't even enter into it. Deuce had wanted the ranch, pure and simple, and by this convoluted way, including shunting blame for his losses onto her father, he had gotten it. Her father had done what he expected, and he didn't need her any more. All explanations simple and neat, the undercurrents torturous and mind-boggling.

She slanted a hard blue look at Ellie. "Why are you telling me this?"

Ellie swallowed and started to speak. And then changed her mind. "You should have known about it; I should have told you when I saw your father hadn't."

"Too good of you," Kalida murmured. Ellie had something else on her mind—she had to. She just was not one to offer confidences or help. If you had the money, she was willing to do anything, even put up with the antics of a fifteen-year-old motherless child. But she was not a friend.

"I understand we have to leave, all of us," Ellie said suddenly. "What are you going to do?"

"I don't know," Kalida said frankly.

Ellie considered her for a moment through her glittery black eyes. "I think you should come home with me. If your father tries to contact you, I would be the first person he would write to or come to see. I promise you that's true."

Kalida shook her head. "I can't do that." At the moment, however, she didn't know what she could do, and it was plain Ellie knew it. But why was Ellie offering her succor? She was the last person Ellie would ever want to help.

"But you have to," Ellie said practically. "Where else would you go? You'd only get into trouble anyway."

"Really?" Kalida snapped, at the end of her tether with Ellie's kindness. "And tell me what you get out of it, please."

Ellie's obsidian eyes narrowed appreciatively. Kalida knew there was no love lost between them. She couldn't confess the half of what she would be getting out of Kalida's agreement to her proposal. Ellie shrugged. "You know your father and I have been lovers for many years." And she saw by Kalida's jolted expression that she didn't. It was rather pleasing to her to be the one to finally tell Kalida that all her little ruses and games had had the impact of a fly on her father and Ellie's affair.

She went on. "He made a lot of promises." The tone of her voice darkened. "A lot of promises. Anyway, he's gone, as we know. I'm not sure he'd get in touch with me other than to learn your whereabouts. You might say I'm doing him a favor, and myself a favor."

Kalida sent her a scornful navy glance. "I don't believe that for a moment," she snapped. "What if my father never comes back for me?"

"Trust me, he'll hear about what happened at Sweetland soon enough. There is no way he can move out five hundred head of cattle in a day, let alone a week. He'll come looking for you."

Yes, Kalida thought, *that* made some sense. She couldn't bear the thought of being beholden to Ellie now. "You just want to use me," she said suddenly, as the thought occurred to her that everyone had wanted to use her, from her father right on over to Deuce. It made her feel as though she had had no control in any of the events of the past week, let alone now, in the whole of her life since they had come west. Her father had chosen Ellie over her; her father had always known Deuce had wanted her; her father had planned sometime to use it—to use Ellie even—to cheat his backers, to sell off the ranch and abscond with the money. Her father *was* a scoundrel.

"We'll use each other," Ellie said sardonically. "Neither of us can do anything without your father. So let's join forces and smoke him out, and that way you won't be reduced to begging from Deuce Cavender. You don't," she added bitterly, "want to take alms from Deuce."

No, Kalida thought violently, I don't. If I never see him again, it will be sooner than he deserves. The bastard, the full complete and absolute bastard, to even think she would abet her father in his stupid schemes. Damn him.

She didn't think to ask Ellie why she sounded so vehement, so wounded. And Ellie was extremely grateful for that; Kalida had had enough shocks for one day. Ellie certainly did not want to confess that she had been on her knees to Deuce herself, not an hour ago, after he had announced that she too would be leaving with Kalida; that her determined effort to make an ally of Ardelle had come to nothing; and that Deuce would not even consider her sensual offer to ease his troubles and his mind the best way she knew how. The offer had been pure desperation, a last shot at something she saw dwindling away by dint of Kalida's own stupidity and naivete. But Deuce wanted no part of it.

"It won't work, Ellie. Just cut your losses and go back to town with Kalida," Deuce had said harshly. Ellie Dean, of all people, he thought angrily, slamming his hand down on a nearby surface.

"Deuce," Ellie's voice had lowered, the timbre becoming huskier, suggestive, "haven't you felt anything from me in these past days? That day in your office—? Wasn't it obvious how I felt?"

"Yeah, you were running the dollar count through your brain, Ellie, and liking the sum total very well. I had a lot of fun watching your face as the numbers grew. . . . Did you say something?"

He obviously enjoyed tormenting her, Ellie thought, her anger at his sloughing her off so lightly consuming her. He would pay for that, she was going to make him pay rarely for this rejection of her. He could have at least invited her to stay the night. He could have sampled what she was offering, and then he could have refused her. But he hadn't even been that kind. He was bent on humiliating her in the worst possible way, and now her sole intent was to wreak revenge on him as well.

And the whole crux of her scheme was Kalida.

Prestina handed her the envelope. "Mr. Deuce say you will need some money."

Kalida did not look up from the case she was packing. The abominable nerve of the bastard, giving her money, she thought wrathfully. And as quickly, her anger died and she thought, why not?

She snatched the envelope out of Prestina's hand, hoisted her meager little bag onto her shoulder, and stamped out the room and downstairs. She tossed the bag out the front door onto the porch, where Joe Slim was waiting with the carriage for the luggage, and she proceeded down the center hallway to the ell of the old house.

Deuce was in his office, as she expected; hiding, she sneered to herself, as she burst in and waved the envelope in his stone-hard face. "You bastard, sending Prestina up with this to give to me. You couldn't face me, could you? You thought I'd throw it in your face, didn't you? But you know what, you son of a bitch? I earned it, and I'm keeping it; there is no goddamned reason I shouldn't get something out of this deal, since you and my father walked off with every other goddamned thing. You got what you wanted, you bastard, what you were aiming at all along, and your injured party act almost fooled me. You had this deal wrapped up so tightly you couldn't lose if you were robbed blind. God, I hate you for that. I *hate* you. And I'll take your money anytime, Deuce Cavender. It's worth as much to me as it is to my father."

She wheeled and flounced out of the room, her body shaking. Slowly, she walked down the connecting corridor, back into the main house, and out the front door, where Ellie and Madame Dupuis were waiting.

Madame looked indignant, even as she was tucking what looked like a wad of bills in her huge bag, and Ellie looked—it was hard to characterize how Ellie looked. She was staring up at the house, her black eyes glittering, her expression ominous.

"It's time to go," Kalida said abruptly, climbing into the carriage.

"Yes," Ellie said, "it is very definitely time to go."

Seventeen

What was it about Ellie's place? Kalida found herself wondering several days later, after she had been comfortably installed in an upstairs bedroom, had made her honorable offer to help Ellie in her housekeeping for her roomers, and was even now in the process of changing beds and sweeping bedrooms. She didn't know; something wasn't right. And yet nothing seemed out of place, including Ellie's restrained hospitality.

Ellie had made her feel welcome, had given her a nice bedroom, had explained that a friend had taken over running her house for the time she had been away. It was a simple situation: When her husband had died, she had had no choice if she were to stay solvent and independent. She had taken in boarders, mainly transient men who were mining the back hills of the Crazy Mountain or Big Snowy. They would come and file their claim, exchanging their dust for dollars, and they had spare change to spend for a decent room for the night, with a homey atmosphere and good home-cooked food.

The men had a need, Ellie said, and she had filled it.

And she was rather pleased with herself for defining it. The money was good: Those men were willing to spend for the right ambiance. And the fact they didn't stay meant she had more rooms to rent. She made out, Ellie said, very well, especially over the winter when those men needed a place to stay when the weather stopped their eager prospecting.

She had help too. There was Bonita the cook, an older woman with long glossy black hair that she wore coiled around her head like a crown. And there was Charlotte, a down-on-her-luck actress who had been abandoned in Bozeman on her way to Miles City, and who was hoping to open her own theater in town and make a success of it by choosing her clientele the way Ellie had in her successful boarding house. She had flaming red hair and an irrepressible good humor that was helped by the fact she was not very smart. Kalida doubted she would ever make a move to achieve her dream, and Charlotte didn't seem to care much; it was just something to hold onto.

And there was world-weary Lorena, of the flashing dark eyes and voluptuous body, who didn't talk much and saw everything. And she didn't like Kalida. Kalida had usurped her job for one thing, and Lorena was reduced to removing slop jars and dusting, polishing what little silver there was, and cleaning the parlor in the morning. Doing the beds was a hell of a lot easier and took up damned less time.

Lorena took great pains to let Kalida know it, too, and when Kalida offered to switch chores with her, Ellie intervened, saying she would not have Hal's daughter cleaning slops and that was the end of it. And, she added meaningfully, if Miss Rose of the South Lorena didn't like it, she was perfectly welcome to leave.

Lorena sizzled and stayed.

But even that little incident did not define for Kalida what seemed essentially wrong about her new home. Of course the time was passing with exaggerated slowness, and her impatience increased in direct contrast. That could have been part of it. Or was it the glowing little looks that Ellie kept slanting at her, almost as if her eyes were patting her and complimenting her thorough work? No . . . Ellie never said anything, she never praised. She just expected everyone to pull together and at the end of the day create the proper setting and surroundings for her paying guests.

Other than that, their time was their own after they finished chores. They were expected in the dining room at five-thirty, freshly washed and dressed up. They had to help with setting up the table for dinner and took turns helping with the service. Kalida volunteered for this one night when it was Lorena's turn, and she relinquished her post sullenly, without at all feeling that Kalida was making it up to her. It gave Kalida the chance to view the guests without having to gird herself for dinner table conversation with them.

She put on the voluminous white apron that Bonita provided and took the soup tureen. She discovered it was not easy balancing a tray of hot soup and opening doors, nor was it easy to rest the tray at a certain point on the table and dole out the steaming liquid into the shallow plates of men whose covetous eyes were constantly on her as she worked.

There was Mr. Humas, a rather older gentleman with soft brown eyes and a ruddy complexion; there was the dashing Mr. Brackett, who was a lot younger and had dangerously sparkling blue eyes and long black hair, a devastating combination that was topped by an elegant figure and a mischievous smile; and there was Mr. Wilder, with his wind-burned face and straw-colored hair, pale eyes and somewhat emaciated body. He looked like he couldn't get enough of the food Kalida was dishing out, and she made sure to inquire if he wanted additional helpings, in spite of Ellie's warning looks.

Kalida ate in the kitchen, interrupting her meal to provide service, trying hard not to notice the hot eyes of the men following her every move in her dowdy gray dress, one of the original dresses Ellie had chosen for her on that original trip to Bozeman. The fateful trip where her father had signed her away, and her legacy. The trip that was predicated Deuce's desire to help—no, not to help; to dominate, totally run right over, and possess everything in his path.

And now he had everything. He had paid everyone for services rendered. The loss of her father's herd was probably meaningless to him. Her father had probably given him a good price to begin with, better than he should have in order to advance the machinations of his plot.

So that was that.

And there had been no sign from him at all in the days since she had arrived at Ellie's. Nothing was right.

After dinner, Mr. Humas engaged her in light conversation, but she had nothing to say to him either. He was a sweet older man who wanted to talk about his perpetual hunt for the gold and his adventures, and she could listen to him with one ear. If he said anything untoward, she never heard it, and she went up to bed alone at about nine o'clock, well before the others.

"That girl is a strange one," Mr. Humas said to Ellie.

"I'm breaking her in," Ellie said sweetly. "She does try to escape the reality of the situation by just avoiding it altogether, but I'm going to put my foot down about that very soon. I can see you were very taken with her."

"She's a good listener," Mr. Humas agreed, "but she didn't seem to understand about the rest."

"Mark me," Ellie told him, "she'll understand about the rest and be making overtures to you before the week is over. Meantime, let me freshen your drink, and you can sit and tell me some of the things you have been doing while I was gone."

Mr. Humas left the next day, after patting Kalida on the cheek and murmuring so only she could hear, "Well, little gal, I expect next time you'll be ready for some honest masculine company," a remark that left Kalida's mouth agape and her cobalt gaze staring after him in perplexity. She whirled on Ellie, who had been listening avidly.

"What did he mean by that?" she demanded, but she was already afraid she knew.

And Ellie dissembled. "These men are lonely, Kalida. Isolated from women for months at a time. You really could have been nicer to him. It would hardly have required any effort at all. And so little would have satisfied him."

Kalida's gaze sharpened. "How nice?"

"Just as nice as it is within your conscience to be," Ellie said sweetly. "You'll have another chance tonight."

She allowed Kalida the rest of the day to assimilate what she had said. It was too much time, too much. Now that Kalida knew what was really expected, there was nothing to stop her from walking out the door—except the pull of contacting her father. She had no money—or had she? No friends—except Ellie. Nowhere to go, unless she had contact with her mother's family somehow in the east.

Usually such circumstances were the perfect lever to push a girl into working for her, Ellie thought, but Kalida wasn't any girl. She had pride a mile high and an independent spirit that just begged to be broken.

That thought led her to search Kalida's room thoroughly. And with some little difficulty, she found the envelope stuffed with banknotes and counted it. Unusually goddamned generous of Deuce, she thought grimly, tucking it away. And lucky she had found it. Damned lucky all around.

Later that evening she said to Kalida, as Kalida prepared to don the apron for the dinner service, "You know, I did tell Mr. Humas that you were only service help, but he was so attracted to your beauty. You are beautiful, you know, and men are going to want to be with you. And since I pride myself in making this rooming house a place where men feel at home, I can't have you or any of my help denying them the pleasure of your company. It's part of the . . . benefits of their choosing to stay here, and why they always come back."

I'll bet they do, Kalida thought; no wonder she had felt something was off. Ellie's generosity *had* been too good to be true, and now she saw why. Ellie wanted her body, and not her father's at all. Or both. She wasn't sure. She began untying the apron briskly, her cobalt eyes blazing with an odd comprehending light. "You know *I* don't have to choose to stay here anymore."

"No," said Ellie agreeably, "you don't have to." Her obsidian eyes positively glowered as Kalida threw off the apron and ran up the stairs. Ellie motioned to Charlotte to resume serving and she slowly followed Kalida to her room where, as she expected, the girl was ransacking her belongings searching for the money Deuce had given her.

She was so frantically involved in her search that she never heard the closing of the door or the telltale click of the tumblers.

She only knew she couldn't find the money. The envelope was gone, the money was gone, and she knew just who had taken it. There was no question.

She darted for the door and pulled it. Locked! Locked! She banged on it with all the force in her arms. "Ellie, damn you, let me out of here. Now. Who the hell do you think you are? Just give me back the money and let me out of here."

Ellie by that time was back at the table, but it soon became obvious that Kalida was not going to tire of shouting and rapping on the door, and it was beginning to interfere with a pleasant evening's meal with two more-than-passingly-attractive gentlemen. She pushed herself away from the table, murmuring, "Excuse me, gentlemen; my recalcitrant daughter. So hard to keep these youngsters in line. If I ever told you what she had been planning to do . . ."

She took her time going up the stairs, trying to plan exactly what to say to Kalida to insure her cooperation. She supposed, given all the options, she had no choice but to make her feel trapped and, subsequently, obligated. She hated to do things in quite that way, but she would. She would do what she had to in order to wreak her revenge on Kalida.

Kalida's rage had continued unabated, along with a spew of curses and threats. Impatiently, Ellie banged back on her side of the door. "For God's sake, Kalida, *what* do you want?"

"My money," Kalida growled. And my freedom, and never to see your blighted lying face again. And never to ever find my father.

"I know nothing about any money," Ellie said smoothly.

"Then let me out of here."

"I can't do that, Kalida; you haven't shown your willingness to be cooperative. It will be easier for me to have you entertain my guests in your room." And wouldn't it be delightful, she thought, to pay Kalida's percentage — little as it would be — from Deuce's money.

"I am not going to entertain anybody," Kalida shouted, feeling cornered and helpless. She ran violently around the room, looking for something to threaten Ellie with. "I'll jump out the window before I do that."

"Oh my dear, you can't. Unless you break the window altogether. It's bolted and screened from the outside," Ellie said helpfully. "You know this is the room I give all my skittish and reluctant girls. It really helps them come to realize that my way is best. You have nothing to lose by helping me and my poor woman-hungry guests, and everything to gain. They have a *lot* of money, Kalida. And they like a *lot* of discretion and a guarantee that things will remain relatively the same from one visit to the next. They like knowing I take care of my help. They pay *big* for that, Kalida, and when you begin to enjoy your work, *I* pay big. That's what I want you to think about tonight, Kalida. There isn't much else you can do. Jobs aren't that easy to come by for a girl who has been immured on a ranch for the last seven or eight years. You can't round up cattle down the main street here, and there aren't many who would hire you.

"Deuce won't save you; I don't even know at this point if your father will, but that's hardly to the point anymore."

"So you lied," Kalida interrupted.

"I lied, but on a slim hope that might come true. Yes, I lied."

"Why, Ellie? Why me? You could have left me to starve in the street."

"But you wouldn't have, apparently, would you? Even in his flaming anger, Deuce was generous with you. Much more, my dear, than he was with me. And that's why."

"You threw yourself at Deuce?" Kalida whispered, interpreting Ellie's last remark. "After everything that happened, you dared to think he would want you as a substitute?" Oh, she knew what kind of mushy ground she was treading on here. She knew, and she knew Ellie had the key and the power and she had to get her goat somehow if she were to have any means of fighting her. And Ellie was enraged by Kalida's words.

364

"Now you know, my dear. Two rejections all on account of one Kalida Ryland. It's a bit much even for me, and I'm rather hardened to that kind of thing. Deuce didn't even give it a moment's thought, Kalida, and I'm aching for him to finally see exactly where you've gotten to," Ellie sneered with just a hint of triumph in her voice. "I'm going to try very hard to see that it happens. But meantime, we'll await the return of Mr. Humas and he, gentleman that he is, will show you the ropes in just the proper fashion."

She turned to leave Kalida's door and, as an afterthought, turned back and added, "If you continue screaming and banging on the door, Kalida, I will come up here and kill you with my own bare hands."

Well, would she? Kalida wondered as she stared out the window the following morning. Charlotte had brought her a semblance of breakfast and no sympathy.

"Oh honey, everyone has nerves. It's perfectly easy once you get the right attitude. And you're so beautiful all the guests will want to spend the night with *you*." Her voice betrayed no envy; she didn't expect to be beautiful, and not even to be used, but she rather liked all the attention the men gave her, and not having to make a commitment to one and lead a drab and drudgery-filled life. She said as much to Kalida. "Honestly, once you get the hang of it, it's fun. And the guests all sweet-talk you and give you presents and money, and all they want is a few minutes of time with you. I kind of thought it was a fair exchange."

"Did you?" Kalida murmured, thinking of her few minutes' time with Deuce — each time. How could she accept anything less than that? How could she bear it?

"Well, sure. The men all are real nice, and Ellie treats you real good, and you've got a room and your meals and she even provides some clothes. And there's lots of free

365

time, and she gives us money too. And all for letting some nice guest spend some time with us. I really think you are not seeing this in the right way, Kalida. The guests would just *love* you," Charlotte concluded, putting away the untouched dishes. "You think about it. You could have so much fun and none of the work of being a wife. I think it's made to order."

"I will. I'll think about it," Kalida said dryly, watching her maneuver out of the room. She almost had the thought of trying to knock poor Charlotte over and make her escape, but then she saw the interesting bulge in Charlotte's apron pocket. So for all Charlotte's chattering ingenuousness, she had a side to her that was owned by Ellie. She would do whatever Ellie told her, including give Kalida a talk to rally her spirits and try to convince her of the saneness of acceding to Ellie's plans for her. And she would kill for Ellie, plain and simple.

Kalida realized she was shaking. She hadn't quite perceived the danger as being as real as it was. Ellie would kill me, she thought, Ellie is in a rage over my father and Deuce, and she blames me, that's the long and short of it. And she wants to make me dependent and a whore, and not necessarily in that order. She will pay back my father no matter what she has to do. But what she hopes to do to Deuce is anyone's guess when the bastard doesn't give a damn anymore.

A lead weight descended on her heart. That was true, and it shouldn't make a difference what she did now, she thought. She could perfectly well do what Ellie wanted. Charlotte's artless description of her duties was more or less to the point, insofar as she could envision it. And she was sure that, even though Charlotte was shy of giving graphic details, the essence was still the same as what she had experienced with Deuce. She would let some strange man touch her and kiss her, take her to bed. And for that, Ellie was willing to provide many benefits and some money, and allow her to receive all the attention she could handle.

She could, she supposed, do worse. She hadn't much choice as to getting a job; there weren't many to be had in town for a woman. She could teach school? Hardly. Sell at the mercantile store? Boring. Raise vegetables and sell her produce and preserves? Would not get her any kind of livelihood very fast. Raise pigs? In whose backyard? Throw herself on the mercy of a handful of long-ignored relatives who hardly remembered her anyway? She didn't even know where to reach them.

Well now, she thought practically, Ellie's proposal was beginning to sound more and more attractive.

Don't even think it, her inner voice reprimanded her harshly.

Well, I will, she retorted to herself. Why not? Why the damn hell not?

Ellie let her stew still another day, with the naive coercing chatter of Charlotte to keep her company in the morning. Charlotte made things sound like a bed of roses. Charlotte loved her work, anyway; she would never do anything else no matter what she said.

Ellie listened from behind the door that morning.

Kalida must have been asking questions because Charlotte sounded all animated, as if the Kalida were finally getting into the spirit of things. "Well," she was saying, "this is really about how it goes. The dinner and all you know. And after, sometimes—not always mind you, but most times—the gentleman indicates there is one of us he would like to talk to, see. And then we talk, kind of get to know each other a little bit. It makes it a little less . . . businesslike, because he has made his arrangements with Ellie, see, so we don't have to take care of any of that.

"So we talk, and after a little while with the talking, the

gentleman might indicate something like he finds me very comfortable to be with, and perhaps we could be alone someplace. And—well, you know, sometimes you say yes immediately, sometimes you play him along a little longer. But eventually, you suggest you can be alone in your room, which is conveniently discreet, and you meet him there. And by that time, of course, you have slipped out of your dress and you are ready to have him kiss you— and whatever."

"Charlotte!" Kalida gasped, feigning shock and knowing full well Charlotte would take her seriously.

"Don't you like to be kissed?" Charlotte asked sweetly.

"Oh God," Kalida muttered. She raised her voice, "Go on. What happens next?"

"Well, that depends on the gentleman, of course. But they all seem to like a little kissing and touching you. Maybe if you like them well enough, you might let them undress you still more. And then you get on the bed, and you don't have to really do much more unless you've got a mind to. You can touch them if you want—that's always good, except I don't care to do it—and you let them have their way with you, because that's always over quick. And that's it," Charlotte shrugged prettily. She smiled. "You meet a lot of men that way, and sometimes one or two come back steadily so it's like being married almost—for a while. But you don't have to do the rest of that stuff, and they feel like we're not cheap and they can enjoy themselves a lot more. Wasn't Ellie clever about that?"

"Oh yes, Ellie *was* . . . so very clever," Kalida whispered, seeing it all pass before her eyes, paling in comparison to what she had known with Deuce. This wouldn't even be a kind of substitute; this would be an absolute living hell. "I understand things better now," she said to Charlotte, and Ellie, listening avidly through the door, nodded with satisfaction.

She was sure Kalida did understand now. It only remained to drive the point tellingly home.

And it wasn't Mr. Humas whom she enlisted to help her. It was almost as if Providence were watching over her, and the gods smiling. Joe Slim came striding down the main street of Bozeman late that afternoon, in town doing errands for Deuce and seeking to assuage his own loneliness.

Ellie grabbed him right off the street, and he was more than passing glad to see her. "Have dinner with us," she invited. "You know, the boarding house? You could even stay the night if you wanted to."

He looked around Ellie's neatly ordered living room, felt the thick homey aura of the house, and nodded, "I'd be right happy to, ma'am."

And during dinner, as he was shooting direct fulsome brown looks at Charlotte, Ellie leaned over to him and asked whether he was so lonely he wanted to get acquainted with Charlotte—or perhaps another lady she had in mind who was upstairs.

And Joe, diffident Joe, who would rather die than confess to having carnal thoughts about Charlotte, who was the most beautiful woman he had ever seen, chose to go upstairs to meet Miss Ellie's more willing, experienced friend.

Ellie opened the door slyly, calling, "I have someone here to meet you, my dear; I hope you're presentable." And Joe blushed, while inside the room Kalida leapt to her feet and backed up against the window, fully expecting to see the salacious Mr. Humas walk in the door.

But . . . "Joe!"

His knees buckled. "Miss Kalida!" He whirled toward the door but it was closed now, and as he tried the knob, locked.

"Oh God, Miss Kalida . . . I can't—I couldn't . . ."

"No, of course not. Oh Joe, she's keeping me prisoner here."

"Surely not, Miss Kalida." Joe looked around him and regained his equilibrium somewhat. The room was luxurious, the bed looked comfortable and clean, the furniture was polished. "No, you're imagining things. I'm sure Miss Ellie brought me to the wrong place. It's good to see you're settled fine here with her. It relieves me to see you so comfortable. I think Miss Ellie made a mistake. She . . . invited me to dinner, you know. She made a mistake." He went back to the door just as Kalida cried.

"Joe, listen to me. I'm a prisoner here. She won't let me go."

"No, no, you went with her, I remember," Joe said, turning the knob and relieved this time to find it was open. "You're not a prisoner here; you could walk out anytime, just like me." He opened the door and turned to Kalida. "Have you been all right, Miss Kalida? Is there anything you need I could tell Mr. Deuce?"

"No," Kalida snapped, watching him walk out the door. She darted to it the minute it slammed shut, but it was too late. Ellie had locked it again. She heard the low murmur of voices beyond, receding. Ellie had made a mistake.

Ellie didn't make mistakes, she thought wildly. Ellie made plans. And now Deuce would know; how could Joe help but tell him? Tell him what? That he found her ensconced in a nice room raving about Ellie's maltreatment of her. God, she had never thought anyone's hate could run as deep as Ellie's. Ellie wanted to torment her. Ellie wanted to give and take away and show her exactly who had the power over whom. Ellie wanted to *reject* her.

Ellie returned shortly thereafter. "My apologies, my dear. He didn't believe you, and I told him you had been rather under a strain since the theft of the cattle and Deuce's turning you out. But he'll tell Deuce, don't you think? And Deuce *will* come, of course, if only out of curiosity. Deuce," she added lightly as she turned away again, "knows all about me." The door closed softly, the lock clicked into place, and Kalida allowed herself to feel this further betrayal.

Deuce knew about Ellie. He knew about her father, he knew all about Ellie, and he never did a thing, never said a word. Welcomed everyone and put Kalida in the middle so he could blame her when her father finally deceived them all. She was meant to be a pawn all along, she thought with a finely wrought new insight. She was meant—what was she meant for? she wondered despairingly. Not to be Ellie's dupe. Not to be the object of revenge. Not to lie down for the mighty King Deuce Cavender, about whom she had been outrageously right all along.

She had to get over that hurdle, her ungovernable feelings for Deuce. If she could make that—and what better way to do it, she thought suddenly, than to reduce the memory of the sex between them to a commodity she could bargain with. To use what he had taught her, to use the body he had for that brief time cherished, to turn their fierce joining into something any man could buy for any price. It might make her forget him; it might reduce the memory of the ecstasy to something manageable, maybe even a nightmare she once had. It might demean her so totally she could never rise back up again. But what did that matter? He would see—if he even cared to see—that the sensual delights she had found in his arms were obtainable elsewhere, and that to her, their union was nothing special, just a waystop on the road to other things.

Yes, she thought, falling into her bed, wouldn't that be perfect, hellishly perfect? And she couldn't even cry for the loss of that innocence.

Mr. Humas returned, chafing and eager to see Miss Kalida who, Ellie assured him was ripe and ready to see him. But didn't he want dinner first?

"Oh no," he assured her. "I've been dreaming long hard dreams about that little gal and I want to see her as fast as you can get me to her."

Lovely, Ellie thought, leading him upstairs to Kalida's room. Just lovely. "Yes," she said in a low voice, "you know, Kalida has been so sorry since you left that she wasn't a little nicer to you. I mean, she knows how hard you work and how little time you have to play and find companionship. She was beside herself that she might have hurt your feelings."

"No account, no account," said Mr. Humas, who was shaking with anticipation to see whether Kalida was as lusciously beautiful as he remembered her.

Ellie surreptitiously slid the key in the lock while she rapped briskly on Kalida's door. "Kalida! Mr. Humas is here to see you."

Kalida sat up in her bed, her resolve in place, and called back, "Fine," and Ellie repressed her elation. She could not have asked for anything better. She swung open the door and they both gazed at Kalida's seductive pose. She lay on the bed, in a nightgown and wrapper that Ellie had supplied her, her body curved temptingly, her cobalt eyes blazing feverishly, and her inky hair in disarray all over her pillow. "Come in," she said huskily, swallowing hard, feeling that now the moment had arrived she couldn't possibly go through with it, even though she had been preparing for it for at least a day and a half.

Ellie was going to test her now, and she had better perform. Ellie said it in her sweetest conversational tone, but Kalida knew she meant it. And since she herself had determined to do it, she didn't object at all. She gowned herself accordingly and waited.

And waited.

And now finally the moment was here, and it was the lecherous Mr. Humas whose eyes almost popped out of his head at the sight of her. He looked as if he would devour her without any preliminaries whatsoever, and Kalida shrank back, flinching at the sound of the lock turning as Ellie discreetly withdrew, throwing an airy little salute in Kalida's direction.

"Mr. Humas," Kalida began, her voice a throaty scratch.

She felt under the gun again, helpless, not in control at all. Yes, this would make a mockery of what she had felt with Deuce, and yes, it was fitting to let it end this way, but she couldn't do it, she just couldn't do it. She watched wide-eyed as he approached the bed. . . .

Ellie listened outside the door for a moment, then went away satisfied, her obsidian eyes gleaming. She had bent Kalida to her will, and it hadn't been all that hard to do. Deuce had crumpled her pride, her father's perfidy had smashed it, and Ellie's plans reconfirmed it. Nothing could be better.

She went out of her way to say a special word of thanks to Charlotte. "The things you told her must have hit a nerve. She received Mr. Humas without a protest. He's up there with her . . ." She broke off as Lorena poked her sultry head into the parlor.

"There's someone here asking for Kalida," she whispered, motioning behind her.

A jolt of fear shimmered along Ellie's nerves for an instant. It had to be Deuce. She hadn't expected him quite so soon; she had been sure he would simmer over Joe's information for at least a week.

"Tell him," she said sweetly, "that Kalida is occupied at the moment."

"Occupied—how?" Deuce demanded, shoving Lorena aside and stalking into the room. "What the hell is she doing here anyway?"

"What you would expect," Ellie said in that same sweet reasonable tone. "I made her an offer and she made a choice. A good one, too. I think she'll be quite popular." Her black eyes kindled as they swept over his long muscular body. God, she would have loved . . .

"Bitch," he spit at her. He reached into his pocket and threw a thick wad of bills at her. "Take me to her; I don't care what the hell she's doing. I just bought the rest of her time for tonight." His stone hard eyes stared her down, daring her to make another light suggestive comment, daring her to try his patience one step over the line.

But she was experienced enough with men to know when not to push. "As you wish," she said neutrally, thumbing through the money, the generous money for a man who had thrown the bitch out of his house. Damnation, he was getting to her again. He was willing to pay for Kalida, and he never would have stepped foot into her house if Kalida weren't here. "I'll take you to her," she said, concealing the rage that was starting to lick at her vitals. She would be very happy to take him to her. She wanted to revel in the pain on his face when he saw her servicing the voracious Mr. Humas.

She led the way upstairs slowly, and he followed behind her, a seething presence that could erupt any which way at any moment. A dangerous man—she liked that, she would have liked it better if it had been for her. But it was for that child-bitch Kalida, and he deserved what he was about to see.

Again, she surreptitiously inserted the key as she listened at the door for some clue as to what was happening within. All she heard was Mr. Humas grunting and groaning, "Oh honey, oh beautiful, did you miss me? Don't fight me, honey. Tell me you want . . ." And she knew Deuce was hearing every word too, because the look on his stony face told her he had heard enough. He shoved her aside violently and slammed down the door like some towering avenging angel.

The sight that met his eyes made him see blood red. *"Get off of her."* The words were not a command, they were a threat. The portly older man was lying directly on Kalida, trying to pull her gown off her shoulders, and while she looked flushed and breathless, she did not look in the least mortified to have Deuce break in on them. *"Get off of her."* The second command was an animal growl, which was followed by his grabbing the man by his neck and heaving him off Kalida's barely clothed body. "Get him out of here. Get him away. I'll pay his time, just get him the goddamned hell out of this room or I will kill him."

He issued this threat in a more normal voice as his flinty eyes raked Kalida's body ruthlessly, yet no one in the room was in doubt that he meant what he said.

The man scrambled to his feet, with Ellie taking his arm and murmuring to him as they left the room. Deuce backed up against the open door, still observing Kalida and not liking her blasé attitude at all. He slammed it shut with a savage backward kick of his foot and folded his arms across his chest in a rough movement that told Kalida he was just that short of folding his hands around her neck.

Too bad for him, she thought defiantly, shifting her body up against the headboard and giving him a light-ning-bolt blue glance that told him better than words she was not grateful for his interruption. She'd be damned before she let him see that.

His mouth tightened and he paced toward her like he was stalking her. She supposed he would rather have her cowering and mewling at his feet, she thought, but she would not back down to him. Not to him. She hated him;

she hated his coming here and seeing her like this. And she refused to back down an inch to him. He didn't scare her. His fury was just a lot of noise in her ears. He was the one who had abandoned her, after all.

He stopped just shy of the bed. "So, my feline Kalida, you landed on your feet, right at home in the cathouse."

The words shocked her into anger; he had gone one step too far now. She slid off the bed and reached for the bowl and pitcher on her washstand. With one unholy thrust, she heaved it at him, her blazing navy-darkened eyes triumphant as he ducked and the china smashed against the door.

He crawled to the side of the bed, swooped up, and vaulted across the bed to grab at her. She eluded his grasp, just barely, and darted across the room to the bureau, her hand groping across its top to find an object to throw. Her fingers picked up a china pin box, and she hurled it forward with all her strength. It crashed against the wall above his head.

He levered himself upward just in time to see her grab an oak-framed lithograph that was hanging above the bureau and fling it at him. Down on the floor again, in a crouch this time, with enough momentum to catapult himself at her and tackle her to the floor before she could reach for something else to throw at him.

His weight was so familiar. . . . She couldn't allow herself to relish it. She squirmed frantically, working her body upwards; his hands held her hips, tugging them toward him.

"You don't understand, Kalida-cat. I bought you for the night," he hissed in her ear, and she whipped her wildly tousled head back and forth in negation.

"You bought my removal from Sweetland," she retorted harshly, "nothing else."

"Don't say that, you vixen; Ellie would be up here like a shot, and you'd see the full depth of her depravity. You take what you get in this business, and tonight you have me."

Her eyes blazed molten blue as her face set in stubborn, unheeding lines. Oh yes, he could already tell she would fight him full bore. She wanted nothing to do with him, even on a paying basis; she would have preferred that pig, Humas.

He pulled himself off her, taking her limp right hand to draw her to a sitting position. "Come, my cat. We'll have the night, and perhaps, if you please me, I'll retain your services from now on."

She went for him with her nails, managing to scrape them across his cheek before he wrestled her hands behind her back. "Oh, you are the vixen, Kalida. One week on the town has turned you into a pouncing cat. It makes me wonder whether you didn't lure poor Joe in here with your lurid tales just as bait to get at me."

"Why would I do that?" she demanded sweetly as he pushed her toward the bed. "I never wanted to see you again."

"Surely that's why you stayed in Bozeman," he drawled, thrusting her face down onto the mattress.

"What was I supposed to do?" she snapped, wriggling against him as he straddled her legs.

"Get out of town while you could," he growled, coming down heavily on her writhing body. "And now it's too late, Kalida. Now that you've discovered your full potential, I'm sure there will be no stopping you. And I'll be the one to be first in line. I'd rather buy you, my cat, than keep you."

She saw red. She saw a pinwheel of colors explode before her glazed navy-dark eyes. She felt strength in her arms and she felt it flow in volcanic heat through her body. She felt like killing him. She tightened her whole body into one galvanic spring of muscle power, so unexpected that when she heaved herself upwards, bucking like a wild horse, he reeled backward and toppled to the floor.

She scrambled across the mattress to face him, crouching, on the other side of the bed. He lifted himself up slowly, slightly dazed, in awe of her insane strength and determination. She looked like a primitive warrior woman across the span of mattress, her body arched, ready to jump, her night-black hair in a wild tangle around her pale face, her eyes a blazing navy-blue, her mouth drawn back in a snarl. Her fingers curved, ready to attack. There was something uncivilized in her eyes, as if she were looking at the enemy. . . . And she *was* looking at the enemy, the man who wanted to kill her, the man whom she wanted to kill.

The atmosphere steamed with the force of their emotion. He had never wanted her more. Her hate, her disdain, were barbaric. She didn't lie down and let him step over her, and he would have hated it if she had. She was a fighter; she had an unbendable pride, and he wanted to break it. He wanted to snap it in two to show her who was the stronger. Who had the power.

She made a sudden movement, and his body lurched in response. There was no way she could escape. Even if she got out the door, she would have to contend with Ellie. His flinty eyes never left her face. There was no slackening of tension in her; the line of her mouth revealed it clearly even as her face remained impassive and her eyes burned with loathing.

He made a subtle movement forward, and her eyes flickered. He was determined to have her now. Something in his face must have changed because her whole body tightened again, becoming primed to fight him as he kept her relentless gaze pinned to his.

He put one knee on the bed and paused. She immediately moved backward toward the door, reaching out her hand to feel for the doorknob.

"Ellie will chase you right back up, you know," he said conversationally. He had to get her now, otherwise she would be out the door. "Ellie likes to see her guests get their money's worth," he added, goading her, and he could see she didn't know whether to attack him or run. The split second of indecision cost her. He bolted onto the bed and grabbed for her hand — and just grasped it as she made her decision to dash out the door. He pulled her forward, off balance, and onto the bed again, covering her this time with the full length of his rock hard body.

"Now, Kalida . . ." he murmured against her burning face. "And now . . ." His mouth captured hers, and she almost swooned at the sensation of his tongue touching hers again.

She had to harden herself against him immediately, before he stormed her senses and took what she would have willingly given him. She couldn't let him see the yearning in her, and how much she had missed him, how much he had cost her. She didn't even know, despite the churning emotion inside her, whether she would have actually found the strength to run from him. Part of her wanted him still, part of her was still in thrall to lush sensations she knew his body could evoke from her.

To feel him again! Everything in her wanted it, wanted him. Except that staunch part of her with the unending memory of him accusing her of vile things, of sending her away with money in her hand and no hope. Of loving her and abandoning her.

To let him conquer now, in this setting, with Ellie gloating downstairs, was a mockery of everything she had felt for him. He wanted a whore, she thought, her anger building now, as he slowly and expertly explored her mouth in that sensually familiar way, he would get a whore. A woman paid to lie on her back and let a man have his way with her. Just like Charlotte said. And then she would collect the goodies. And that would be the end of that.

And still, it was hard not to respond as his hand began its enticing trail along the soft lines of her body. Hard to withhold her pleasure when his fingers began caressing her breasts and sliding downward to rediscover the treasure there. Hard to quell the little murmurs and excited moans that would encourage him and let him know she loved what he was doing.

But she did it; she lay still as a rock and let him play with her, kiss her, feel every inch of her body, strip away the ridiculous nightgown, turn her this way and that to better touch her buttocks, her thighs. It was lovely just to lay back and participate minimally. Lovely to feel his frustration building at her neutrality, delightful to know her plan was working even as her body screamed for the release she was not going to allow it to have.

God it was formidable, the task of restraining herself from responding to him. She felt herself shaking with the force of it, almost crying at her own nonfulfillment.

She didn't care. She was determined that he would see his dollars had not bought very much. She held that thought in her mind as he finally parted her thighs and slipped his hard length into her pulsating body. And she had to hold the edges of the bed to keep herself from meeting his frenzied thrusts, to hold everything back, to think of anything else she could in order not to think about the luscious sensations that he evoked with each stroke.

She opened her eyes once, and the naked emotion in his face made her cringe with guilt and triumph. She couldn't bear it, she thought. And at that, she was more generous than he: She would never have denied him anything, no matter what he had pushed her to. And now he *had* pushed her to the point where she had to make the choice. And she made it. She made it. And she would make it again.

And his body thrust against hers unwillingly, and with one swooping lunge, he collapsed against her. "Bitch, bitch, bitch," he hissed in a terrible whisper against her ear. "You stupid bitch, you . . ." He levered himself up with one sudden movement, disgusted and ready to strangle her. "You goddamned whore . . ." He groped for his clothing blindly.

"What did you expect?" she asked softly, snidely, propping herself on her elbows to watch him, knowing that her pose might tempt him, wanting to tempt him so she could not give him what he wanted all over again.

He looked up at her as he bent over to reach for his shirt, and his charcoal-darkened eyes flamed with an ugly light. She looked pagan and desirable all over again, and her firm mouth was curved into a snide little smile that he wanted violently to crush away. She was totally untouched, unmoved by what had just happened. She hated him that much. She was right. What *did* he expect?

"My money's worth," he answered abruptly, sliding his muscular arms into his shirtsleeves. He leaned over her reclining body, the edges of his shirt brushing against her breasts. "But I expect the management will remedy that," he added, crushing her lips under his savagely. She responded almost involuntarily, and he pulled away after a long moment. "Not too jaded — yet," he commented sardonically, calmly buttoning his shirt and tucking it in his pants. "But I think I will leave it to others to teach you your place, Kalida-cat. A variety of experience will enlighten you properly. And, of course, you've had a bounty-full already, haven't you?"

He walked away from the bed, turning his back on her enticing body, remembering she had chosen to come here, remembering the eagerness of Mr. Humas, remembering Jake Danton's gun; remembering her wanton body, eager for his tutelage. Or had she already been primed by someone else? Now he would never be sure, and he was

381

ready to walk away from it. Now, without looking back. The only thing that imprisoned her was her own wanton greediness. He didn't need her. He wouldn't need her.

She watched him walk resolutely out the door and close it firmly behind him, and she fell back on the bed, dazed.

I could have had another night with him, her numbed body screamed. Another night of sensation and culmination to store against the barreness of the nights to come. You whore, you let him walk away and you gave him nothing, just like you were the whore that Ellie is going to make you into. Why did you do that? *Why?*

But she knew the answer: because he had no trust, because with the overwhelming loving, he had no trust, and he still didn't believe her, about anything. And she couldn't allow herself to believe in him.

Eighteen

"What did you do with that beautiful man last night to make him request you again tonight?" Charlotte demanded as she opened the door with Kalida's breakfast tray. "My gracious, he gave Ellie money for you even though he was in an awful rage. What *happened?*"

"Exactly what you described," Kalida said, stunned. Deuce had given Ellie more money? Deuce reserved her for tonight? He wanted a replay of their sensual war? He was crazy; she would refuse to see him. She would jump out the window.

"You must have *something,*" Charlotte muttered. "That man was out of his mind with anger, and I don't know if he was madder at Ellie or you."

Kalida shifted her covers so that she could reach for a biscuit and a cup of coffee. She felt old this morning, ragged, without hope. It was obvious she had to escape Ellie and forget about ever seeing her father again. All she had done was allow herself to be entwined in more traps, more situations over which she had no control. She took a deep breath and a deep sip of the hot black liquid as Charlotte made herself comfortable at the foot of the bed. "He said," she went on suddenly, "that he'd better not find any more Mr. Humases in your room. He said if you told him Ellie foisted anyone else on you, he'd kill her. That's what he said," she added at Kalida's disbelieving look. "Where do you know that man from?"

"I've known him a long time," Kalida answered noncommittally. Too long, too fast, too far with him. Even now, he thought he owned her. Damn him. She eyed the window consideringly. Ellie had said it was bolted from the outside. There was some kind of screening over it, fastened from the outside. If she broke the window, she would have to cut the screening somehow.

"Ooh," Charlotte murmured, looking around as Kalida's mind seemed to have gone elsewhere. "You had some to-do in here with him. I'd better send Bonita up to get rid of all this glass. What went *on?*" Her eyes were wide with avid curiosity.

"I didn't want to entertain him," Kalida said ironically, taking in the extent of the broken objects that littered the floor. One of those shards would cut a screen.

"You can't refuse to do that," Charlotte said seriously. "He paid a *lot* of money."

"And he'll pay a lot more," Kalida muttered under her breath. "I have to get dressed, Charlotte. Is there any chance Ellie would let me out if I promise not to try to run off?"

"Probably not; her mind is real set about you. She's in a rare simmer about that man last night, and she's brooding over your daddy's not returning to look for you. She's one angry lady," Charlotte answered honestly. "But she sure liked the size and color of those bills that man gave her; she said it almost made up for the rest."

She got up, and took Kalida's tray, and left her, being

384

careful to lock the door behind her.

And that takes care of the amount of sympathy she has for me, Kalida thought ruefully. And I've had enough sitting and feeling sorry for myself and damning Deuce Cavender. It's time to *do* something.

By the time Bonita came upstairs to sweep away the mess, she had dressed in her canvas skirt and shirtwaist, had secreted one long shard of glass from the framed lithograph that was crumpled on the floor, and was standing by the mirror brushing out her crackling inky hair, her expression neutral, her eyes hooded so as not to reveal their electric blue gaze that would have immediately alerted Bonita something was up.

Ellie hated her, she thought, watching Bonita in the mirror as she took one last look around before removing herself, without a word, and locking the door carefully behind her. Ellie hated her because she, Kalida, had taken Hal Ryland from her and had caused her to be rejected by Deuce. Ellie hated her father now, for abandoning her and not keeping whatever promises he had made to her. Ellie would want to humiliate her, Kalida, in any vicious way that occurred to her.

Kalida wondered what made Ellie think that she would just sit in that room and take it? She had even played with the idea of trying to overpower Bonita or Charlotte the next time either of them appeared, but she thought that might prove to be useless. There were still men in the house, men beholden to Ellie, who wouldn't hesitate to attack her at Ellie's word. And apart from that, she had no idea of the configuration of the house, so escape other than through the front door seemed impossible right now. Although, she considered, she might question Charlotte about it. And appear meek and cooperative to lull Ellie's suspicions.

Oh, but Ellie must know her better than that, after the time she had spent with her. Still, the situation was one that would cow many women; why *not* Kalida Ryland?

The explosive sound of a shotgun rocked her out of her reverie. It was in the house! Outside? She ran to the window, but there was no undue commotion out there. Another shot! She turned, her back against the cold glass. Silence followed. A long silence, with no explanations forthcoming. No one came. Nothing happened. Kalida sat alone with her thoughts after a while, wondering who had been shot and why, considering the window and the position of her upstairs room, and whether she could risk breaking it and jumping out.

She pushed the question of the shots out of her mind. They weren't germane to her situation. Finding some way to escape became the paramount question in her mind.

She watched the sun set out the window. Deuce would be here soon if he meant what he said to Ellie. Ellie did not try to force anyone else on her. Ellie provided her meals and left her alone. What more could she want?

She wanted the window more accessible. It had begun to look to her, after a whole day's staring at it, like a prison bar. She couldn't mitigate the noise when she broke it, she couldn't be sure she wouldn't be cut to pieces as she climbed out of it, and she had to contend with a drop of at least ten feet after she slashed the screen.

Damn.

Darkness fell. Bonita brought her dinner. Deuce did not come.

She turned up the gaslight and considered again whether to attack Charlotte and try for the front door. It seemed a lot easier than jumping out a window. After all, what could Ellie's cohorts do to her but put her back in the damned room if she were caught?

Her ears caught the faint rattle of the key in the door. Very faint, almost stealthy. She darted behind the door, so it would hide her when it opened, and listened. Whoever was turning that key did not want anyone to know he was gaining entrance to Kalida's room.

The tumblers clicked and the door swung open slowly, slowly . . . Not Deuce, Kalida thought wildly; he wouldn't be sneaking in. Mr. Humas, thwarted by his rejection, coming to seek his brand of restitution? She pressed herself against the wall as a heavy figure slid into the room and his soft voice whispered, "Kalida?"

Oh my God! "Papa!" She pushed the door closed quickly. "Papa!"

They stared at each other, he holding his arm awkwardly, she her heart pounding with the unexpected absurdity of it.

"Ellie shot me," he explained in a low, embarrassed voice.

"Ellie *shot* you?" she repeated, incredulous. The gunshots! *"What* are you doing here?"

"I came for you, of course," he said as she drew him to the bed and examined his arm. He had tended to it as best he could and brushed away her concern with a sweeping gesture of his good arm. "Ellie thought I took too long."

"Yes, you did," she said tartly. "I thought you were hundreds of miles from here; I never expected to see you again."

His pale blue eyes looked hurt. "Well, I would have been if things had gone right for you and Deuce."

"They didn't," Kalida told him sharply.

"So I hear," he said, but his pointed gaze rested on her as if it were her fault. She couldn't believe him! "Tell me what happened, maybe we can salvage it."

"Are you crazy?" she cried. The man *was* crazy; he fully expected that now she was going to participate in some wild scheme in the hopes of ressurrecting her father's chances of pulling off his fantastical scheme!

"What happened," she said grittily, pacing to the other side of the room, "is that Deuce believes I'm in league with you, and the whole trade you made was a setup for you to pull off this wild plan. What the hell are you doing here?"

"Look, I've been hanging out all day, after Ellie chased me off with her rifle; you forget I know this house very well. There are lots of places to hide, and a back entrance to which, even though Ellie has it guarded right well, I was able to gain entrance—because I needed to see you. You've got to go back to Deuce."

"*WHAT?*" She couldn't believe her ears. Her father hadn't come to rescue her, he had come to persuade her to do *him* a favor. Not that she wanted to be saved by *him* any longer. The man was out solely for himself. He didn't care a whit about her. He had his eye on the easy gain, the big chance. Her father. The scoundrel, just as Deuce had said.

She walked away from him. She couldn't believe that all his plans had come down to her somehow saving him once again.

"You'd better tell me everything," she said finally. There was no point in not knowing now. Deuce had probably been smart to back his investment in her father's cattle by giving him a mortgage on the Ryland ranchland. After all, hadn't he made a point of telling her he had always known what her father was like?

She didn't know the man at all.

He began hesitantly. "Basically, I found I didn't like ranching."

"That's good. After all these years . . . Papa . . ." She was running out of patience with him now.

"I didn't like it, and I thought the best way to keep on going without relinquishing my partners, was to get that share of Deuce's syndicate. Because then you see he'd do most of the work, and we'd all rake in the money."

There was a sinking feeling in her stomach. She sank onto the other end of the bed and watched his face as he detailed the rest.

"He's always been in love with you, Kalida, believe me. Probably since the day you shot him and ran off with Malca under his nose. He really loved that. He's always wanted you. So I thought I could use that. He never broached it that way, and as I told you, the conversation we had about it was not so direct as my saying I'd convince you to have him if he'd give me a share of the syndicate. But that's what it came down to. And I believe what I told you: It was a better opportunity for you than it was for me, especially because I always thought you had deep hidden feelings for him too."

"Well, they're still deep and they're still buried," Kalida said sarcastically. "He thought it was a bit too handy that the house happened to burn down in the midst of this. He thought you did it."

"And you thought he did it," her father countered, reminding her of her own words.

"I guess I did. I don't know who to believe now," she said slowly.

"It doesn't matter," her father said. "The minute it happened, and then Deuce whisked us to Sweetland and offered to buy the herd and you, I saw my opportunity to escape the whole shebang lock, stock, and barrel. I'd take his offer on the cattle, I'd mortgage the land to him, and I'd live off the proceeds. I never even thought about stealing the cattle back until you mentioned he was bringing them down sooner than I'd anticipated."

"Oh my God," she whispered. But how could she have known?

"See, with all the rustling going on, I just thought he might assume the thieves were at work again. I *never* thought he would blame you and think you were a blind."

"Well he did," she interpolated in a heavy voice, "and

he sent me packing. He's got pride, Deuce does, and I tramped on it just a bit before you pulled your vanishing act, and that was the end of that."

"But how did you wind up here?"

"Ellie thought this was the first place you'd come looking for me. We needed each other, she said. I had nowhere to go, and she wanted to get hold of you. Which she did, right and proper, didn't she?"

"She never wants to see me again, but that's of no moment. When I tell her my plans, she'll forget about you like a shot."

"Really," Kalida said sardonically. "So what are these famous plans?"

"Deuce has got private detectives out ransacking the county to find evidence of who stole the Santa Linaria bulls — and looking for me, particularly. And the herd. I *had* to spirit them away before he branded them, you understand."

"Where are they?" she asked curiously. "Where does a fugitive hide five hundred head of cattle?"

"There's a remote little canyon hard by the Crazy Mountains; I got them there, and I've got to get them to Virginia City. So you've got to convince Deuce to call off his men."

"Tell me just how I'm supposed to do that? Ellie's got me locked up and Deuce feels like killing me on sight."

"No, honey, he won't. He loves you, Kalida."

"He loves being King of Sweetland."

"Yes, well, that he is. I'll take care of Ellie. All I want is the chance to drive the herd down to Virginia City — with Ellie, mind you; there's a buyer. And we'll take the money and live off the proceeds. We'll never come back to Montana again, I promise you. I have had quite enough of this godforsaken place. And I know you love it. And you love Deuce. Now, Kalida, consider. We'll 'arrange' an escape for you, and you get back to Sweetland. Tell him

390

Ellie kept you against your will. . . ."

"He didn't believe that," Kalida interrupted harshly.

"Tell him *I* kept you against your will. . . ."

"He'd send a posse out after you."

"Yes. I guess he would. Tell him you escaped. Tell him—"

"I don't know what I would tell him; anything I would say would either betray you or him. How can I do that?"

Her father looked at her meaningfully. His eyes were hard, his face drawn. It was the same face that commanded her obedience about the question of marrying Deuce at the beginning. He wanted it. It was his last chance. He wouldn't beg, but he was commanding her obedience once again. He couldn't do anything to make her obey, but she would have to live with her conscience. And who could bear the betrayal better—him or Deuce?

She turned away from him. She didn't know him any more. But she did not want him to spend his remaining years in jail. The more she thought about it, the more it seemed he was taking his own punishment on himself if he meant to include Ellie in his plans. They deserved each other. *She* would make his life a living hell.

All she cared about was escape; the rest could take care of itself.

"All right, Papa," she said. "I'll do what you want."

Joe Slim's news wasn't any too good either. He saw Deuce riding up slowly into the valley that separated the Ryland rangeland from Sweetland, and he shivered with apprehension. Deuce had been a bastard lately, and he wasn't too happy to be the bearer of bad tidings. But it was his job. He was foreman now; he directed the operation. He had chosen which men to station at the Godown pasture. He was responsible.

But as Deuce drew abreast of him, he could see he had

already divined what Joe wanted to say. His face was set in a way Joe didn't like, with new hard lines etching either side of his mouth. "They got another one." It was a statement, and Joe nodded.

"Damn hell, I just can't figure out who the hell is going around thieving one or two bulls at a time like this. And how the hell did they find Godown anyway?"

"Don't know," Joe said, shaking his head. "I'd of sworn we had them boxed in as sweet as a railroad car."

"One of our men is passing information somewhere," Deuce snarled. "Damn him, whoever he is, when I get my hands on him. We're down ten percent because of this. I'm losing money, and I have to adjust the syndicate payout because of it, damn it; blast it. Joe, you've got to get a line on who's giving out information. The men last night, you handpicked them. You question them. You find out something."

Joe nodded. He didn't like the way Deuce was looking at him. He didn't like anything that was going on around Sweetland these days.

Neither did Deuce; as he slowly moved away from Joe to check up at Morgan field, he was feeling as if he didn't give a shit about any of it. And he knew what it was. Goddamned Kalida, in his mind, and in his blood, and he couldn't stop thinking about her inert body under his the night before.

To be in love with a bitching whore like that; he marveled at how she had duped him. Ardelle had never liked her. But his aunt had said, and he had seen it, that she was willing to make the effort to welcome her and teach her how to run Sweetland. And Ardelle had detailed very graphically all of Kalida's hoydenish little tricks she had played during her stay. Ardelle just washed her hands of Kalida Ryland.

"Blood tells," Ardelle had said to him. "Look at who her father is—the biggest huckster you'll ever want to meet. You're well rid of her."

He wished he felt that way. He wished his groin didn't tighten whenever he thought of her gorgeous response to him, her beautiful wanton body, her hands that had just been learning to please him . . . Or did she know that already and had she just been pretending?

He just couldn't convince himself that she had been pretending. She had been a virgin when she came to Sweetland after the fire. *He* had shown her what her body was meant for. *He* had been the first to elicit those glittering spasms from her. God, and he remembered every last one of those sumptuous culminations. She was a sensual animal. Born for him. Meant for him. And he had determined this so long ago that it was in his blood and impossible to exorcise.

He still wanted her.

He pushed his mount slowly over the ragged back fields of the Ryland ranch, the pasture that Hal Ryland had never developed because it was becoming increasingly clear that he had never intended to ranch a minute longer than he had to. Deuce knew, in spite of her father and whatever she might or might not have done with Jake and at Ellie Dean's, that he still wanted her. It was unimaginable that she would not be a part of his life when he had wanted that for so long.

And yet . . .

That was why he had paid Ellie so much money—to keep her safe for one more night, and perhaps another until he could figure out how to save her. Ellie knew he would come after her if she abrogated her promise. She knew it. There was no possible way she could mistake his feelings last night.

He didn't rest any easier because of it. Kalida didn't want his help now, and he was further hampered by this new wrinkle of another theft, just when he thought the Linaria were safe for this season.

He rambled through Morgan field, barely aware of anything that was going on, and then back to the house. He hated the summer, as it didn't impose any work. The summer just entailed caretaking.

And then there was Prestina with her reproachful eyes, ever since he had forced Kalida to leave. It was obvious she did not agree with Ardelle's assessment. But Prestina was a romantic. And it wasn't his family that had engendered that in her, unless it was Camilla's seemingly successful marriage that she looked to, rather than his parents'. He supposed that he was a romantic too, that he wanted to believe there was someone who could share the rigors of ranch life and build a dynasty and not fall to pieces in the process. He had thought that woman was Kalida.

He knew that woman was Kalida.

There was no changing that: She was what she was, what he had always perceived in her, the perfect complement to himself, the exact opposite of his fluttery sickly mother and the pampered, self-centered Camilla, who now lived on some great estate on the moors in England.

Kalida was of the earth, as dazzling as the sky, as hot as the sun. God and God again, he had to get her back to Sweetland somehow.

Her father's plan was simple and rather ironic, Kalida thought. He was going to occupy Ellie's attention and Kalida was going to break the window and escape. He would approach Ellie as late at night as possible, and Kalida was to have no doubt of his ability to charm Ellie and make her listen to him. So therefore, he would knock twice on her door at about eleven-thirty, and she should prepare then to make her escape.

"Why don't you just give me some money and let me walk out the door?" she asked him caustically.

He looked horrified. "Ellie can't have an inkling that I've even spoken to you or seen you. And she's got someone guarding the whole house. And I don't have any money to give you. So you'll have to do it this way, Kalida. And that's the only time when the street is fairly noisy because of the saloon across the way, and the noise you make won't be all that obvious."

"What if I kill myself on the drop?" she said, curious as to what his response would be.

He waved her question away. "You wouldn't let me down," he said with a downright surety that made her want to smack him. "It's all up to you, Kalida." He smiled at her brightly, his eyes as innocent as the blue sky, confident now of her cooperation.

And so now she waited for the signal at the door. The hours crept by at an alarmingly sluggish pace.

She figured her father had left her about eight o'clock, but where he was concealing himself was anyone's guess. He would wait until Lorena and Charlotte were suitably occupied, and then he would creep back up to her room, knock on the door, and then accost Ellie and make his peace with her.

It was almost funny; he wanted her to do what Deuce had thought *she* had done for *him*. She choked back a strangled laugh. The whole damned situation was too damned amusing for words.

She whirled as she heard a hard rapping at her door.

And waited.

The signal!

They had even planned what she would use to crack the window—the leg of a chair. And she was to take her time. If she hurried, she would lose her nerve and spoil everything.

Not likely, she thought, her mind clearing miraculously and a cool, calm purpose descending over her. Not likely in the least. She would foil the lot of them. She would get away on her own terms, and her father and Ellie could go hang.

She picked up the chair—a small wooden side chair that had been pushed next to the bureau—and walked to the window.

It was very dark outside; she would punch the legs of that chair right into the darkness. Fitting, she thought, and swing the chair dead center into the window pane.

The glass shattered instantly, but not with the loud impact she had been expecting; the screening muffled it and the shards fell against the screen. Carefully and slowly she picked them away one at a time, removing the last little piece from the window frame as well.

And then she stood still and listened.

Nothing.

She picked up one of the larger shards of glass and pushed it against the screen. Nothing happened. The screen was a fine wire mesh; glass wouldn't cut it. Her hopes sank. What would?

The chair! She could push the chair legs against the framing, probably enough to loosen it. Her desperation lent her an uncommon strength as she lifted the chair again and poised its legs against the screen frame. With a tremendous trust, she heaved the legs against the wood. And again, and again.

Nothing moved. And again. And again. A creak. Another shove. She couldn't lose her control now. She had to take it slow. Slower. It was going to work. It *was* working. Another push. And another. It was giving. The frame was giving, she felt it loosening, the nails pulling from the window casement. Good, good, slowly now, with patience. Assume no one was watching, that no one had heard the noise.

Assume her father was pleading with Ellie and that she was so intent on making him pay for his perfidy she wasn't even thinking about what Kalida Ryland might be doing.

Slowly now . . .

She put all her strength behind this last push, and with an aching creak, the screen angled out from the window and fell, with a resounding little crash, onto the ground below.

Her heart was pounding like a drum, her hands shaking violently. She closed her eyes and took several deep breaths. The way was clear. Almost. She put her hands on the windowsill and looked down. A ten-foot drop.

Her father was insane to think she could just jump out. She needed . . . what? Don't panic, she told herself. Sheets. She could tie the sheets, slide down the sheets. Wouldn't someone notice a woman dangling from a sheet out of Ellie's house in the middle of the night? She was getting hysterical. Her nerveness fingers grabbed at the sheets and covers. Not much to work with. A couple of pillow cases, two sheets, a thick quilted cover . . .

She knotted the pillow cases together and tied them to the foot of the bed closest to the window, and then the two sheets to the pillow cases. Good, she told herself, her nervousness escalating by the second; now move the bed to the window. God, it was heavy. What if she strained herself pushing it?

What a fitting ending to her father's schemes!

The bedframe moved, grudgingly, as if it were trying to prevent her from taking the last precarious step, and she managed, with some difficulty, to jam it up right against the window.

The next thing . . . the next thing . . . She threw the rope sheet out the window. It looked dazzling white to her in the darkness. Darkness . . . darkness . . .

She whirled and doused the gaslight, and then ran back to the window. The sheet dangled, looking impossibly fragile. It could never support her weight, she thought frantically. Time suddenly was speeding by. She had no idea how much time she had spent in these machinations. She only knew that now — or never — she had to climb over the windowsill and hope that the length of two thin sheets would bear the bulk of her body long enough for her to attain a height from which she could, with some safety, jump to the ground.

The other alternative was unthinkable. And time was passing. She jerked hard on the sheet and it pulled firmly against the bed. Now or never. She climbed onto the sill and looked down. And turned her back. She couldn't look, and she had to thrust the strength of the muscles in her arms — pathetic arms at best, she thought wryly, grasping the sheet and swinging herself out of the window.

There was nothing to grasp onto, and she felt like she was falling into thin air. And then her hands pulled and grasped desperately, involuntarily, and the headlong slide of her body stopped abruptly, and she dangled crazily over the ground for the space of time it took to gather her addled wits together.

She was out, successfully; she hadn't fallen. She had only to get down those few more feet and then she could drop down — and run. It seemed to her that her hands acted independently of her body. Her hands knew to release their clawing hold just that little bit, experimenting, so that her body dropped downward again, sickeningly but with some control. She thought her heart would beat right out of her chest. She thought she would hang there forever. And then her hands let go again and she slid downward; they grasped, she stopped, they released the sheet again, she dropped; they grabbed the sheet again, and then she heard an appalling little sound — a tear, as her weight pulled the much-laundered fabric to its limit.

She let go and dropped, falling with a nauseating thud onto dirt, feeling as though every bone in her body had been jolted out of place and the breath knocked out of her.

She looked up. The sheet still dangled, looking ghostly white and ominous.

She couldn't stay there. Painfully, she got herself to her feet, limped around the corner of the house, and began to run.

Nineteen

She never quite remembered what happened next. She thought maybe, somewhere in the shelter of a woodshed or a barn, she might have passed out. Or fallen asleep from the sheer exhaustion of executing her escape and her fraught nerves. She woke up very early in the morning, when it was gray and dank outside, and she was cold. She thought the cold had awakened her, as well as her overwhelming hunger.

The light was just enough for her to take stock of herself and determine she did not exactly look presentable. Her shirt was dusty and torn on one shoulder, her skirt was covered with dirt, her inky hair was a wild tangle of knots, and she knew her face must be smudged and scraped. Altogether an unprepossessing picture who couldn't hope to cajole anyone out of anything.

She hadn't the faintest idea what she was going to do next. Presumably her father had made Ellie reasonably happy this night. Perhaps Ellie hadn't yet discovered that she had escaped.

She felt so weary and trapped. It seemed as though one way out led to a different pitfall, a different direction she had to go in order to untangle herself, and that proved to be just another snare.

What to do? Where to go?

She wondered if it wouldn't be a bad idea to do what her father expected. She could return to Sweetland, and she could . . . try to entice Deuce so that her father could make good his escape. Throw herself on his mercy, rather.

The sardonic idea appealed to her. After all, what could he do to her other than throw her off Sweetland once again?

Could she take that?

Supposing he actually listened to her.

Oh really, and when had he done that before? He wouldn't believe her.

She felt like the wind had been taken out of her. She watched the sun come up, and her stomach growled. At the very least, Prestina would feed her, she thought. She'd have to get there somehow. A horse. A wagon. Something. She might faint before she did. It really seemed like the only thing she could do.

She got painfully to her feet and began walking.

Ardelle was sitting on the porch, feeling extremely pleased with herself. Everything was fine. Deuce was in the fields; Kalida and that whore Ellie Dean were long gone. Everything seemed ordered exactly as she liked it. She was her own mistress, with no uppity bitches with plans to take her place at Sweetland. She was in control, and there was no one to poke a nose into her business.

She did not count Prestina, who hovered around her with a faint air of concern. Prestina was family. Prestina was like having a safe, secure wall surrounding her.

Nothing could touch her now. She felt powerful because something that had seemed a reversal had turned out to be a blessing, and she laid it to the fact that the Rylands were now out of Deuce's life and, concurrently, hers.

She looked out benignly over the broad fields of Sweetland and leapt up as she saw their peace disrupted by a hard-driving rider. Not Deuce. Not anyone she expected. Not anyone she could possibly want to see.

And certainly not Kalida Ryland, who was coming toward her across the fields at breakneck speed. She almost toppled off her mount as she pulled him to a quivering halt.

Ardelle stood as still as a statue, mustering her reserves, quelling her temper. "What do *you* want?" she finally demanded ungraciously.

"I must see Deuce," Kalida panted, sliding off the mangy horse she had commandeered earlier that morning. A simple task, right from an unlocked barn, when everyone was still asleep; her shame was incalculable, but she had to.

"Well, you mustn't," Ardelle contradicted her. "And you won't because he certainly doesn't want to see you. So now you will kindly remount and leave."

Her hostility was palpable, and Kalida recoiled.

"He'll see me," she said harshly. "Tell him."

"I can't and he won't. And you can just leave. We don't want you here." Ardelle turned to go back into the house, and Kalida's question stopped her.

"Why?"

"Deuce doesn't want you here," Ardelle repeated.

"Let him tell me," Kalida countered, trying to buy time. She *had* to see Deuce. "I'll go to him. Where is he?"

Ardelle considered for a moment, and then whirled back to her. "He's gone away. And he wouldn't want to see you, don't you understand that? It would be better for you if you would just go. And stay away."

"Maybe," Kalida said cannily, wondering at her insistence, knowing how much Ardelle disliked her, "it's you who wants me to go away, not Deuce."

Ardelle's face hardened. "I do; I thought I had gotten

402

rid of you."

Kalida's glazed cobalt eyes widened at this bald statement, but she didn't have the strength to assess just what Ardelle meant by it. "Tell me where Deuce is, I'll go find him."

"Really, Kalida—" God, Kalida was so tired of that contemptuous "really, Kalida" of Ardelle's, but she repeated it. "Really, Kalida, I would think you would understand you are not welcome here, and you would just leave as graciously as possible."

"I haven't got the energy," Kalida muttered, but Ardelle did not hear her. She had wheeled away and was disappearing into the house. Kalida stared after her, utterly numbed by her callous treatment.

She just couldn't face climbing onto that horse again and the jolting ride back to Bozeman. And the time. The time it would take . . .

"Miss Kalida." She knew that soft voice. She looked up to see Prestina motioning to her from around the corner of the old house. Gingerly, Kalida walked the horse over to her and let Prestina's warm embrace enfold her for a brief, revivifying moment. "You need Mr. Deuce?"

"Desperately," Kalida whispered.

"He is with the Linaria. No one knows where. Do you need to eat?"

"Please."

"Come, we go around the back, and quietly; Miss Ardelle need not know."

And then she waited ever so patiently in the loft of the barn at her old homestead. It seemed the most reasonable thing to do. Ardelle was still thumping angrily around the house, finally coming into the kitchen and catching Prestina feeding Kalida, which caused her to have a tantrum.

But Ardelle felt betrayed. Prestina was family; Prestina was there to cosset Cavenders, not Rylands. Prestina had sided with those who were no longer welcome at Sweetland.

Prestina was totally bewildered. She had sent Kalida off with a canteen and a basket of food, with instructions to wait, since she could not return to town today, nor did she want to. And Prestina would tell Deuce—whenever that might be—about Ardelle's strange humor and how she had turned Kalida out once again.

Kalida was, in reality, relieved to be alone and far away from everyone. She needed to think, to understand Ardelle's animosity, to decide what to say to Deuce. . . . What if it came down to begging money from him? she wondered. What if he truly meant everything he said? But then, why would he have paid Ellie to reserve her time the next night after the godawful evening he had spent with her? No, she was reckoning he had some vestige of feeling left for her, as she did for him, and that he would help her once she told him everything she knew.

The peace of the homestead was restful after the evening and morning she had spent. It was a relief to feel comfortable, full, free, and unencumbered of other people's machinations.

She didn't understand anything. Weeks and weeks ago, Deuce had been adamant about marrying her. And then suddenly she had been the pawn in a game between her father and him. And then she had tried to discourage his interest by making herself into the kind of woman Ardelle said he distinctly did not want.

But her instincts had said differently, even as she went about convincing Ardelle that it was not so. Ardelle had no reason to hate her so much. She had never known before the incident with Jake that Ardelle wanted the same thing she did—to get her off of Sweetland. In fact, she herself was doing a nice job of showing everyone how she felt about the whole thing. So why would Ardelle be so adamant suddenly? What did she mean, "I thought I had gotten rid of you"?

Kalida's head whirled. Had Ardelle misdirected her from the beginning for her own purposes? And then when Kalida went straight ahead and behaved outrageously, it must have thrown all her plans out of whack.

Kalida groaned; more plans involving her that she had never had an inkling of. Ardelle never meant to be her friend. It must have killed Ardelle to watch her doing the very things that Deuce would have wanted her to do, that he really would have expected her to do. Why wouldn't she have wanted Kalida at Sweetland?

There was something she was not understanding. Ardelle hated her; that much had become very obvious. But Ardelle had welcomed her, had taken her in hand and instructed her as to what Deuce expected. It was Kalida's own defiant nature that had caused her to flout Ardelle in the hopes of earning her bad opinion so she would convince Deuce to get rid of her.

But it seemed like Ardelle hadn't needed convincing. Ardelle seemed to never have wanted her there in the first place.

But why? She hardly knew Ardelle before she came to Sweetland. And since she herself had played directly into Ardelle's hands, why would her animosity be so intense, so abrupt and dismissive *now?*

Because she knew Deuce still wanted her? Did he? Could he? After everything that had happened? *And* Ardelle's expressed negative opinion?

Ardelle did not want Kalida on Sweetland. That was the conclusion she came to abruptly. But she couldn't figure out why. Ardelle had intimated that when—and if—Deuce married her, she would leave. But it didn't look like she had any intention to—now.

She still didn't understand. It was like a puzzle, with a

405

piece missing. Perhaps Deuce had the information that was lacking.

She heard her name being called, and a weight lifted off her shoulders. He had come.

He walked in the barn door and his body cast a long shadow deep into the recesses of the stalls.

And then he called her name again, and she knew Deuce hadn't come for her. Someone else had. And, as she sought desperately for someplace to hide, she wondered frantically how he had known.

Never had Prestina seen Deuce in such an uproar.

"You are telling me that Ardelle just sent her away — again?" he repeated harshly, his whole body tightening at the thought that she had come back of her own volition and Ardelle had banished her — for what reason he couldn't begin to guess. It was crazy.

"Miss Ardelle has been wrought up, Mr. Deuce. You know. She was very upset Miss Kalida had come back. She did not want her here, and so we arranged she would stay and wait for you in the barn of her old homestead. I do not know why Miss Ardelle chased her away. I do not understand it. But I do not understand much of what has happened," she added pointedly, her liquid eyes accusing him.

"Neither do I," he growled. "Where is Ardelle?"

"She has gone out, I do not know where, but she was riding."

"What?! But she never rides anymore."

"She was riding," Prestina said firmly.

"All right," Deuce said brusquely; he didn't have time to figure it out now. "I'll go and get Kalida. Ardelle can't refuse her sanctuary when I am in the house."

Prestina nodded. "Please, Mr. Deuce, you will listen to Miss Kalida. You have not heard what she has to say, only what your eyes interpret."

Deuce paused with one foot in the stirrup and swung around to look at her. "What do you mean?"

"I mean your heart too knows what is the truth. Now you must listen with your mind. Go to her now, Mr. Deuce. She waits you."

He rode fast, but it seemed to him that Prestina's words echoed in every hoofbeat. He already knew the truth; he had only to hear her words. By God, he was desperate to hear her words, he thought, as the miles raced by, seemingly so slowly. Kalida. The horse's hooves sounded her name, beating as fast as his heart as he finally came in sight of the stone markers of the Ryland property.

Kalida, as he wound through the fields and up the drive to the house and the barn. Kalida, as he dismounted at the barn doors and thrust his way inside.

To emptiness.

Intense, gray emptiness. And the sinking feeling she had played him for a fool once again.

She lay bound hand and foot on the cold dirt floor of an abandoned line shack on the furthestmost boundary line of Sweetland. It was a one-room shack, with two built-in bunk beds, a ratty, rusty old stove that provided heat and cooking facilities, a tilted table with one foot slightly shorter than the other three, three crates that were used as chairs set around it, some cracked dishes on top of it, and a dresser in the corner that was falling to pieces. On it a guttering kerosene lamp threw dim, eerie light. On the furthest wall there was a dilapidated box that served as a cupboard. Sitting in it were tins of tomatoes, coffee, vegetables, dried fruit. On top of the stove a coffee pot simmered, sending a warm aroma through the dank atmosphere of the shack.

On one of the beds Jake Danton hunkered, a rifle

across his knees, utterly entranced by the sight of Kalida helpless on the floor.

She hadn't spoken. For some reason, she sensed she would be in worse trouble if she said a word. Jake was just looking for a reason to exercise his power over her. Her lungs were sore from screaming anyway; as he stalked her in the loft, she had prayed that Deuce *was* coming, that he would arrive in time and hear her. But he hadn't come, and there was nowhere to hide, and Jake's pursuit was inexorable until he finally shot at her to show he meant business.

She didn't even ask questions. He had tied her, gagged her, lifted her onto her horse, taken her to this godforsaken shack, removed the gag when he had set her in the corner on the floor, and she had not opened her mouth. Her blue gaze said everything she had to say — her contempt, her anger, her pride, her determination not to be cowed by him.

He read it all there, as he made the coffee, lit the stove, and sat back on the bed with his rifle to watch her squirm.

But she didn't squirm. He could not intimidate her by the look in his flaming eyes or the motion of his rifle or the way he had her helpless and at his mercy. He hated her in those brief first moments that he perceived all of this, and then it didn't matter to him. He had the gun, he had the might as long as it was in his hand, and she would have to do whatever he wanted.

He waited for her to speak, to ask questions, to beg. She said nothing.

He poured himself some coffee finally, holding it close, letting its heat penetrate his body, its warmth heat his hands and his emotions. And he sipped, looking at her over the rim of his cup, daring her to ask for some. Which she didn't. She closed her eyes to avoid looking at him altogether, and he thought at that moment he might kill her.

But he had to wait. And when he had apprehended her, he had been eager to wait because he now had his chance with her. Even though her molten blue eyes told him she would not willingly do what he wanted, he now knew he could make her. He looked forward to making her. And since no one knew her whereabouts, he had all the time in the world to make her.

He waved the rifle at her, wanting to see fear in her face. She spat at him.

He threw down the rifle and crouched over her, pulling her hair so that her head fell back and she could look him directly in the eye. Her teeth nipped at his upper arm as he yanked her inky hair so tightly she felt like he would pull a whole hank of it right from her scalp. He slapped her and she went for one of his fingers, barely missing it with her biting teeth.

"You bitch, so high and mighty," he growled, his hand going for her neck, encircling it, his fingers constricting just enough to let her know who had control of her. Her blazing eyes did not flinch, and he felt like beating her to make her grovel and bend to his superior strength.

Her bound legs lifted suddenly and whacked him sideways on his thigh. His face turned murderous as the heel of her boot bruised his hip, and his fingers tightened and lifted her chin so she could see him more clearly. See him more clearly and know . . . And he didn't care if he never got to enjoy her luscious wanton body now. He would enjoy making her pay for all the trouble she had caused and for the beating Deuce Cavender had given him — over her, over the slut bitch tease whore. . . .

"JAKE!!"

The voice that roared from the doorway was the last one Kalida expected to hear — ever.

Ardelle.

She choked as his constricting fingers released her

409

throat and he stood up slowly, shaking away the obsessive sensation of wanting to destroy her. He turned to Ardelle and said familiarly, "It's about time you got here."

"So you found her where I told you? Good." The mean little smile on Ardelle's lips was chilling.

For the first time, Kalida felt scared. Ardelle. And Jake. She shook her head to clear her brain. Nothing made sense. Why the devil would Ardelle feel she had to kidnap her? And what was Jake still doing on Sweetland?

Ardelle turned her attention to Kalida. "You are the most interfering bitch — even when you don't know it. I wish to hell you had just gone away and stayed away, Kalida. Really, things would have been much simpler if you had."

"Truly," Kalida agreed sardonically, wondering why Ardelle had sent Jake after her and what she intended to do with her. Her surmise was not positive.

"Too late now," Ardelle said, accepting a tin cup of coffee from Jake and seating herself on one of the bunks while he made himself comfortable on the other. "So here she is," Ardelle said to Jake.

Jake said, "I'll take care of her. I have an old score to settle with her."

Ardelle nodded. "Fine. But not here. You'll have to get her away from here. I can't take the chance Deuce might come looking for her if that lousy Prestina tells him she came to the ranch today. Joe Slim may have seen her too, I don't know. He's rather preoccupied by the fact that Deuce is about to accuse him of rustling."

Jake cocked an inquiring eyebrow at her, and then they both laughed, an unpleasant sound that made Kalida shiver.

"Maybe it's time we copped out," he said tentatively.

"Maybe," Ardelle agreed cryptically. "But not before we tend to Kalida. Really" — she turned back to Kalida with that hateful preface that made Kalida want to smack her—"if you had just stayed away after Deuce got rid of you . . . It's really all your fault for coming back."

Lovely; her father thought it was all her fault for allowing Deuce to send her away. She was crunched between the two of them and did not even know the reasons why. "How?" she demanded suddenly. "How is everything my fault? Why don't you explain what is going on, since you're probably going to kill me anyway?"

"If I do explain," Ardelle said ominously, "I *will* have to kill you. Unless you're a better actress than I thought, and you've made all the connections already."

"Tell her," Jake said. "Tell her; we don't have to kill her. I'll keep her. For a while. And by the time I leave her, we'll be so far away nothing can touch us anyway. Tell her."

Ardelle stood up and walked toward Kalida, and Kalida's eyes widened: no limp, no hobbling. Her back and her gait were as straight and firm as Kalida's own.

"Really, Kalida; I was sure you had noticed on a number of occasions that I didn't have my cane or that I was walking without infirmity. On the steps that night, when we were bringing you your clothes? Out in the garden with Ellie? No? When you saw me meeting Jake on the drive? You didn't think I knew you were watching? I was damned mad when you stole my ruse, Kalida, and then rather happy about it when I realized everyone's attention would be focused on you. Too bad Deuce wanted you instead of some meek little town girl who wouldn't poke her nose all around Sweetland and discover what I was doing."

Kalida's darkening eyes narrowed, trying to fit the pieces together as Ardelle talked. She didn't quite get it yet, except that Ardelle had been pretending all these years to be lame. And Ardelle didn't want anyone to know her business. What business? "What *were* you doing?" she asked softly.

411

"Stealing cattle, of course," Ardelle said, and everything clicked. Of course . . . of course . . . Hadn't she heard Deuce say again and again that someone on Sweetland must be giving away information? And who else intimately knew Deuce's movements? Who had demanded to know every moment of his schedule every day? Who kept the account books? Dear God. "The Linaria," she whispered, in sudden comprehension.

Ardelle nodded, complimenting her deduction. "The very reason for the whole thing. Every other hit was a blind, designed to draw attention away from the piecemeal decimation of the herd. I wanted a good stock of bulls, and that was all. They're worth a fortune, you know, and with the other stock, I can breed my own now. So you see . . ."

Oh yes, Kalida saw. Who would suspect infirm Ardelle? Who would suspect a woman? Who would even conceive of her having ambitions in that direction?

But why?

"I don't see," Kalida prompted. "Why?"

"Why? Why? Don't you know the years I spent caring for my brother. And do you know what he left me in the end? The wherewithal to be his son's pensioner in my old age. He gave me nothing but a place at Sweetland should I wish to have it — not a share, not a piece, not money, not a life. Just a bed in a room in his son's house. And I wouldn't take charity from Deuce, Kalida. I rather suspect you wouldn't either, were you in the same position. But I wanted to do something; I wanted revenge, and I wanted independence.

"And just at that time, Deuce began experimenting with crossbreeding, the result of which were the Linaria. And I thought if I could siphon off some of the growing herd, a little at a time, I could build a future for myself away from Sweetland.

"So I had a convenient little accident — yes, I see by

412

your face you are acquainted with that kind of ploy, eh Kalida—and I pretended to willingly stay and take care of the house, and when Jake came, we discovered we had similar interests and we went into a partnership.

"It was he who suggested that we begin raiding surrounding ranches periodically to draw attention away from the Linaria thefts and to build our herd. It was brilliant, just brilliant. No one could catch us because we always knew when the stockmen's patrol was riding.

"And then Deuce decided he was going to give your father a share in the syndicate in order to get you. Well, I knew what you were like, Kalida. You're not a homebody. You'd be out in the cow chips every day; you'd be in the account books and the tally books, the breeding books. You would eventually have found irregularities. You would have seen me without my cane or riding, as you did the day of the calf drive, and Deuce would then tell you I never ride because of my injury, except in dire emergencies. . . . Well, the odds were against my getting away with anything else while you were in the house.

"And Deuce would have you. About as much as you pretended not to want him. Really, Kalida. But even that would not have been enough to stop him, you see. And actually, it might have been amusing to keep watching us work at cross-purposes, Kalida, but I needed to convince him that you weren't worthy—and quickly. I needed something that would destroy his trust in you. So I suggested to Jake that perhaps there might be a situation or a time he could put you in a compromising position in Deuce's eyes. He said he would be happy to. I didn't know how happy—then. And it worked beautifully. How fortunate for me that over and above *that,* your father had the good sense to steal his cattle back. A stroke of genius, Kalida. I really commend him for that. Especially because it cemented Deuce's feeling of distrust for you."

"I'll tell him," Kalida murmured cuttingly. This was so

incredible. "If only you'd just left things alone . . ." she started to say.

"Really, Kalida, how could I take the chance?"

"How many of Deuce's men were in on this?" Kalida asked curiously.

"Four others," Ardelle said airily, as if this were nothing. "And now you know everything. Do you feel the better for it? Or do you feel threatened by it? You see what I meant about your unholy curiosity, Kalida. Something would have piqued it, and you would have been after me like a hound. I promise you, I read the situation correctly, and there was only one thing for me to do. And now it's all worked out perfectly, because Jake got to you before Deuce could. And now *I* have the power to make you go away forever."

The import of her words struck Kalida like a blow. Ardelle had just pronounced her death sentence in the most conversational tone possible.

Twenty

It all came down to power, Kalida thought wearily, who had control over whom. And right now it was Jake who had the power over her, and she had no idea what he intended. Ardelle had gone in order to waylay Deuce and calm his suspicions. Everything seemed to be working against her, particularly the gleam in Jake's eye. Jake liked seeing her like this. Jake seemed to feel this gave him some kind of edge over her, that her helplessness would make her correspondingly weak. Jake didn't know her at all.

But she watched him warily as he paced the room, his bulk and his shadow on the wall making him seem suddenly larger than life. He carried his rifle almost as though it were an extension of his arm. There was an edginess about him; he couldn't quite make up his mind what to do about her. He didn't want to kill her, she perceived. Yet. He wanted something else from her—the something she had promised to give him on the riverbank that afternoon that now seemed years ago.

Yes, his eyes glittered with that speculative light that was so dangerous. She couldn't play with him this time, and she had no idea what his demands would be.

But he must be thinking, she reasoned, that he could

force her to do whatever he wanted. Her gorge rose at the thought, but to defy him, though that was her first instinct, might be the worst mistake she could make. She couldn't let herself panic. Nor could she try to talk him out of anything. Her only weapon was him—to use him and what he wanted to her own ends. If only she had an inkling . . .

Or maybe she did. The way he looked at her with that cunning, supercilious little sneer . . . He still remembered the afternoon by the stream. He still thought she was a tease who liked to show off her body.

"What are you going to do with me?" she said finally in as neutral a tone as possible.

"Play with you, of course," Jake said lightly, sneeringly, meaningfully to her. Her heart plummeted; she had surmised his state of mind correctly. She gathered her wits. She had to get away from him, although trussed up as she was now, the idea of that seemed ludicrous. Although she thought her feet might be possible. Jake had tied the boots, with one loop around her calves, and she could move her feet. But she could not get purchase against anything solid to pull. Yet. The crates around the table might do, would have to do since the table had no stretcher. If she could get on her feet. . . .

"What can you mean by that?" she asked archly, her mind a fury of possibilities.

"We haven't nearly finished what we began," Jake said slowly, painstakingly. He wanted to make sure she was in no doubt what he wanted. He had the night to fulfill his desire. Tomorrow . . . Ardelle would come early, and tomorrow he could begin his future.

"You have the gun," she said flatly.

"Oh, but Kalida, I'm sure I don't need to coerce you. If you were honest about it, you would admit that day on roundup you were just aching to do what I made you do by the stream."

416

"But now," Kalida interrupted with a goading sweetness in her voice, "you don't have to make me do anything. You can do it yourself."

He looked at her strangely, as if this permutation had never occurred to him. Like he was turning it over in his mind and picturing it, and what it might make him feel. And then he shook his head. "No, no, that wouldn't be the same."

"But my hands are tied," she said plaintively, with a dawning hope, awed by the fact that her cooperation was really and truly what he wanted. She supposed she could have thought of worse things to do to save her life than undressing before this unprincipled thief who looked like he was salivating at the thought. But his eyes scared her. His eyes told her he took all of this very seriously. Too seriously for her own comfort, her own safety. He had not hinted before, or now, of wanting anything of a sexual nature from her. But that didn't mean . . . She shuddered at the thought. Whatever it meant, she couldn't see herself going that far. She would goad him into shooting her first. She would.

"Yes," he repeated thoughtfully. "Your hands are tied."

"And you have the gun," she added helpfully, hoping that would convince him to release her hands. She never would have believed how impotent a person could feel without the use of his hands. She prayed he would untie her hands, as her lightning cobalt gaze swept the room surreptitiously, seeking something she could use as a weapon if her hands were free. The coffee pot! The still-simmering hot coffee pot.

Jake got up from the bunk and came to squat down beside her. He rested the rifle on his knees as he reached forward to lift her chin so he could look into her deliberately bland cobalt gaze. His own eyes took on a menacing glare, and he shook his head again. "No, I'm not going to untie you, Kalida. I just will have to forgo the delights of watching you expose your body." His tone of voice was adamant; she hadn't deceived him for one moment. His and Ardelle's plans were more important than his desire to see her fulfill his daydreams.

She felt frantic as he levered himself upward and turned back to the bunk. Almost involuntarily her feet jutted out to trip him, and he fell with a curse and a violent thud.

And then he didn't move.

Oh my God, Kalida thought, her eyes widening. Awkwardly, she shifted her body forward to get a better look at him. He had hit his head on one of the crates; there was blood on his forehead and he lay supernaturally still.

Oh my God. He could regain consciousness at any minute, she thought frantically, trying to decide what to do next. Her legs! She wriggled and snaked her body sideways so she could avoid him and come closer to one of the crates. Then she lay down on the floor, with her fear-glazed eyes still riveted on Jake, and lifted her tied legs onto the crate, moving her body forward until her boots were dangling over the edge. She maneuvered the crate against her bottom, bent her knees, and aligned the edge of her boots against the edge of the crate. And then she flexed her knees so that the rim of the crate pushed her boots forward and she could slide her feet — with no little difficulty — out of them.

The rope around her calves tangled around her feet, and she kicked at it impatiently until it finally shimmied off.

Jake lay still, his blood staining his shirt and flowing onto the dirt floor, which hungrily absorbed it.

She couldn't believe he was still out cold. She had to get calm. She had only accomplished the first step in escaping. The next was to find something to cut the rope from her hands. It was too much to hope there might be a knife in the cupboard, she thought wryly, as she tried, backward, to open the doors and search it.

Jake stirred.

Panic overwhelmed her, and she froze, paralyzed by the inadequacy of dealing with him with no hands. Her frantic eyes lit on the coffee pot again, and she edged over to it, turning around so that her hands could get a grasp on the handle, which was uncomfortably hot. She took it and walked sideways around Jake's body, which was starting to stretch its way out of the cramped position in which he had fallen. He mumbled her name and lifted his head weakly.

Kalida took a deep breath and knelt down next to his head so that her body was side by side with his, and her hands holding the coffee pot were above his head.

"Kalida? . . ." His voice was hoarse, groggy. For fully one long second she had a guilty feeling of sympathy for him. And then her body twisted and she rammed the coffee pot against his head.

And dropped it, looking away as she saw his limbs go limp.

Her heart was pounding wildly and she couldn't calm herself down. He could have grabbed her and subdued her just then if he had had just an ounce more strength. He could have killed her if he had been angry enough.

Had she killed him?

She turned to look at him finally and was sickened by what she had done. Coffee stained his shirt and hair and dripped down from his collar. His face was scalded from the heat of the pot, and a bluish lump had already developed on his forehead.

She didn't know if he were dead or alive.

She had to get out of there. Slowly she got off her knees, and then back down on them. Jake might have a knife. Jake might . . . She recoiled at the thought of touching him, but she had to. She had to do it backward, too, by feel, rummaging through his pockets, her hands spastically groping to feel an edge of hard metal.

And nothing.

She collapsed wearily against the table. She was almost ready to give up. She could lie there until daylight, and then get out and start walking. That was one easy solution. But Ardelle could be gone by then. Ardelle would have won. She would thwart Ardelle, she thought, or die in the attempt. The resolution gave her strength and she climbed onto her feet, searching the shack once again for something sharp—something dull even, she didn't care—just something she could use to work against the rope that tied her hands.

It seemed hopeless.

And then a burnished gleam caught her eye in the corner by the cupboard. She scrambled onto the floor and began digging frantically in the dirt, her back bent at an injurious angle and her thigh muscles screaming at the unjust pressure of her whole body weight pulling on them.

"Damn!" she screamed, as her fingers found what she surmised was there—an empty tin that Jake, or some long-ago range rider, had buried there instead of in a refuse pile outside the house. Maybe it had been snowing or . . . Who cared? Her frenzied fingers ripped off the circular top as she shifted to her knees and began turning it to feel the sharpness of the edge and position it at exactly the right angle.

And she cut herself. She felt it, and she ignored it. Damn her wrists that didn't bend inward far enough. She could only use her thumb and forefinger, not nearly enough grasp to be efficient, but all she could do. She might be at this all night, she thought hysterically. She might cut her wrists and bleed to death.

Oh no, she wasn't going to die this night, she resolved, working steadily away at the rope with the sharp-edged circle of tin.

But after a while it seemed like hours had passed, and

then it could have been days in her mind as time began to blur and she felt the rope fraying strand by strand, and her hand cramping strand by strand. She switched to the other hand, which was weaker and therefore less efficient — and slower — and she sliced that rope apart, strand by strand, until she felt her hands would fall off, and then suddenly, thankfully, she could wriggle her numbed hands free, dropping the tin in the dirt next to Jake's inert body.

She grabbed her boots and slid into them, snatching up Jake's rifle almost as an afterthought. Then without consciously considering what she was going to do next, she ran for the door and flung it open.

Ardelle was standing there.

Kalida reacted instinctively, with all desire for self-preservation propelling her arms, lifting them with the rifle butt end out, ramming it right into Ardelle's midriff. Watching her go down on the ground as if everything were moving slowly and out of time.

And then suddenly Ardelle's voice broke the silence of the night as Kalida ran for Jake's horse, which was tethered right in front of the shack. "You bloody bitch!" Ardelle screamed, levering herself upright with a huge effort.

Kalida's nerveless fingers unwound the reins from the hitching bar, and she swung onto the horse. The horse disliked the unfamiliar weight, and as she guided him out, he bucked her, almost sending her into the dust. Behind her, she could hear Ardelle making for her own mount, and her urgent hands wrenched on the reins to gain control of the unruly animal.

He reared backward one more time before her commanding thighs pressed him forward. And just in time. Ardelle was right behind her, screaming imprecations into the night.

Kalida gave the horse its head and let him run. She had no idea where he would go; she only wanted distance between herself and Ardelle. Distance. Crouched low over the horse's neck, hanging onto the rifle and the reins with one desperate grasp. The horse felt her fear. And he was well-rested and eager. He spurted forward like a racing horse and Kalida let him go.

The hoofbeats on her heels receded, and after a while, she thought they had veered off. She surmised Ardelle might have gone back to the shack to tend to Jake.

But what if she hadn't? What if she were going back to Sweetland?

I've got to get to Sweetland before her, she thought in the same moment. But how? It was dead dark, and only the damned horse knew where he was going. She didn't know. She thought she might look for some landmark, something familiar as a guide back to Deuce. But in the dark every tree, every fence looked the same; every tree look menacing, every shadow looked as if it were alive. Only the horse's motion could save her, and she hung onto him as if her life depended on it.

It did.

Ardelle knew she was free. Ardelle would not rest now until she was dead because Kalida knew all about her.

She was locked in a race with Ardelle to see who could reach Deuce first and convince him of the truth. *Her* truth. God, how deadly. *Who* would he believe — assuming she herself could even make it to Sweetland sometime tonight?

Calm yourself. Think! she told herself harshly. Ardelle had obviously just arrived at the shack when Kalida broke out. That meant she had been riding for at least an hour before to even get there.

Which meant her mount couldn't possibly sustain the pace that Kalida's horse was going.

But she was lost; she was sure the horse was running

wild. It would take time to ascertain her direction, time to find her way to Sweetland.

No matter where she was, she thought, she ought to keep on going. Just keep on going—away from the Ardelles of the world, and men like her father, like Jake, like Deuce.

She felt the horse's muscles constricting, and his head lift up as if he were scenting the air. She had a sense of a closeness, a containment, and then she perceived the bulk of a building ahead of her.

She yanked at the reins excitedly. The horse pulled up and veered to the left, galloping down another hundred yards or so before she managed to halt him.

It was incredible, she thought; she never would have guessed this would happen given all her circumstances being out of her control.

The horse had brought her straight back to Sweetland.

Had she returned before Ardelle? There was no way to tell without actually going into the house. If Ardelle were back, she would already have turned out her mount, and if it were true she never rode except in emergencies, she would already have changed out of her dusty clothes. She would . . .

Kalida flattened her shaking body against the wall adjacent to the back entrance to Sweetland as she heard voices. In the entrance corridor. Deuce!

"Where the devil have you been?"

His voice was muffled; he must be near the stairwell to the second floor. Talking to . . . Ardelle. Her voice floated downwards loud and clear. "I've been here all the time, Deuce, in my room. Why?"

Damn her, Kalida thought, gripping the rifle. How was she going to counter her lies? She hadn't even planned how she would confront Ardelle. Or what she would say to convince Deuce *she* was telling the truth.

She heard his heavy footfall treading upward; he was going to talk to Ardelle. She took a deep breath. If *she* could make it up the stairs, she might be able to hide in his room before he got there.

The thought moved her to action, and stealthily, she nudged open the back door and slipped into the hallway.

A kerosene bracket lamp sent its long shadowy fingers inching down the dark hallway to touch her. She gripped the rifle tighter, made her way to the stairs, and looked up. No sound of voices. Her heart started pounding again. Slowly, step by step, her back against the wall, she proceeded up the steps.

The silence was ghastly, almost threatening in the way she felt that just the slightest noise would cause her to scream and do something drastic.

There was no sign of Prestina, no hum of voices as she edged past Ardelle's room. And then as her hand touched the doorknob to Deuce's room, his loud roar broke from Ardelle's bedroom: "Goddamn it, Ardelle!"

The words were so loud and so close, it seemed to Kalida, that she almost collapsed from the force of his anger. Quickly, she let herself into Deuce's room and leaned her body against the closed door, quaking with fear and trepidation.

Damn it, she thought, *I* have the damned gun. And I know how to use it. What can they do to me? She put her ear against the crack of the door.

She heard Deuce. And his voice was getting louder. He must have left Ardelle's room and was coming to his own.

She did the first thing she could think of as his voice came closer and closer, every word loud and clear.

"Damn it, Ardelle, I still do not understand, and I don't want to understand, because what you're saying makes no goddamned sense."

"I swear to you . . ." Ardelle's voice now, coming behind his, conciliatory, slightly anxious. But of course she did not know Kalida would hear her. ". . . she ran off with Jake Danton."

"I don't believe you."

"He was hanging out at that old line shack back of the property, near the Haskins' line. And looking for his chance, Deuce. Honestly. You must believe me. Everything you felt about that incident was right. Your instincts were right. Kalida never belonged at Sweetland."

"Go to hell." His last words before he opened the door and was greeted by the sight of Kalida, dust, dirt, and blood smeared, sitting in the middle of his bed, her rifle cocked and aimed directly at his heart.

Twenty-one

She smiled unpleasantly and waved the rifle at him and Ardelle. "Please come in and tell me more about this abortive elopement with Jake Danton."

Deuce stalked in cautiously, his mind a powder keg of emotions.

"You too, Ardelle," Kalida ordered. "I'll shoot if you try to move." She was gratified to see Ardelle chose to bluff her way through this confrontation. She sent Kalida a meaningful look as she hobbled into the room and elaborately seated herself in the upholstered rocker.

Deuce closed the door and leaned against it, his mind clear of everything but one thought: Kalida was in his bed again. His flinty gray eyes narrowed as he watched, then they slowly smoked to flaming charcoal. She had never looked so beautiful to him, even with her smudged face, blood-stained wrinkled clothes, her inky hair in its usual tangle, and her eyes burning molten blue as she kept them—and the rifle—riveted on Ardelle.

"Betrayed Jake already, did you?" Ardelle said, her voice insincere with sympathy. "I expect you had nowhere else to run to. Maybe you thought Deuce or I would give you some money. Maybe we will," she added darkly, "just to be rid of you."

Deuce folded his arms across his chest as he sent Ardelle a speaking gray look. Ardelle raised her eyebrows and turned her fiery sherry gaze to Kalida.

Kalida opened her mouth to say something scathing—and thought the better of it just in time. She had to keep her wits about her now, if at no other time. Emotional outbursts would not refute Ardelle's nasty insinuations. If Deuce were to believe *her*, she would have state the facts as plainly and unemotionally as possible. She could see already, as her mind leapt ahead to how it would sound, that what she would say would damn her more than it would support her story. If she would be allowed to tell it.

Nonetheless, she shifted her navy-darkened gaze to Deuce and said flatly, "Jake Danton is lying unconscious, possibly dead, in that line shack."

"You were there," Deuce said, his voice as level as hers.

"I—" The falter cost her. His eyes closed to her. "I was there," she admitted finally. "I knocked him out."

"You see?" Ardelle said, as if what Kalida said utterly condemned her.

"You were at the shack with Jake," Deuce said suddenly, still watching her in that curious suspended way.

"He *forced* me," Kalida said, hoping to convince him by the baldness of her words and seeing, with a sinking heart, that he looked skeptical.

"That," Ardelle interpolated, "is a familiar story. I wouldn't be surprised if she says that every time about every man she has ever dealt with. Isn't that the story she told about what happened on the roundup?" She turned to look at Kalida. "Really, Kalida. I don't blame you. It's so much easier on the conscience that way."

Kalida gripped the rifle, her anger and her feeling of being cornered almost getting the better of her. She could kill Ardelle right now, right where she sat, and it would do her no good to quiet that snidely sneering face. No good at all. Deuce plainly disbelieved her.

As Ardelle's words reverberated through the room, Kalida quickly went through in her mind what she had wanted to tell Deuce. It sounded absurd: Her father had arranged her escape. She had stolen a horse. Ardelle had chased her away. She'd hidden in the loft of the barn at the old homestead. Jake had abducted her. She had fought him, tripped him, knocked him out. Raced Ardelle to the Sweetland — for what? Only to be trapped again by the patent irrationally of everything that had happened to her.

Ardelle was right: She could make her, Kalida, go away forever. She looked over at Deuce, who was staring at her from under hooded coal-hard eyes. What was he thinking?

Probably just what Ardelle wanted him to.

"Is that where you went after you left here?" he asked suddenly, harshly. He didn't know what to make of her contradictory statements. She hadn't offered any explanation whatsoever yet, and he did not like the way she was looking at him with those blazing navy eyes.

"No," she said slowly, thoughtfully, swinging her gaze back to Ardelle. "I went exactly where you might have guessed I would go — where Ardelle herself surmised I would go and sent Jake to find me."

Ardelle flashed her a contemptuous look. "Really, Kalida . . ."

And Deuce's expression didn't change one jot. "*Ardelle* surmised?" he asked evenly, not showing just how disconcerted he was by the fact she would use anything at hand to embroider the truth. God, he wished she hadn't dragged Ardelle into her story. He was willing to believe almost anything she told him to explain what she had done. But not deliberately using Ardelle.

Kalida could almost feel him wavering. He wanted to give her a chance. But not if she shot off wild accusations about Ardelle. If only he knew the half of it, she thought wryly; and he would—soon. She had nothing to lose now by tossing out her allegations. Ardelle would deny them, they'd give her some money, and that would be the end of her. At this point, she couldn't even seduce Deuce into believing her.

"Ardelle sent Jake," she reiterated firmly. "Who else knew I was going there but Prestina, who had promised to tell only *you*? How else would Jake have known? And why was he still on Sweetland, tell me that, when you supposedly fired him? And that line shack. That place is godforsaken. I'm willing to bet the only one who knew about it besides you was Ardelle. Not Jake. Jake wouldn't have had time to explore the boundaries. Wouldn't have cared to, I wouldn't think. You haven't run cattle there for years. Think about it, Deuce. She doesn't want me here. Jake is still here. I wind up back here, claiming Jake abducted me on the heels of her story that I ran off with him. Why would I have, if I came here for help to begin with? Ask her why she hates me so much. Ask *her* why Jake is still hanging around." She stopped at the blankness of his expression. It *was* no use. She couldn't accuse Ardelle flat out to him. It would sound insane. She had to prove it somehow.

Prove it somehow.

Ardelle was not infirm, she thought. She had only to make Ardelle drop her cane and run.

"You think it doesn't make sense, don't you?" she said to Deuce, her mind furiously busy trying to figure out what to do to expose Ardelle. As long as she kept talking, as long as her accusations sounded like fairy tales . . .

"No," he said, "it doesn't make sense."

Kalida looked at Ardelle, her eyes glinting steely blue. "There *is* a reason that makes sense," she said slowly, and Ardelle chuckled.

"This is more entertaining than a theatrical show in town," she said to Deuce lightly. "Do go on, Kalida, your imagination is extraordinary."

Kalida smiled at her and slid off the bed to walk around to where Ardelle was sitting, all the while aware that Deuce was watching her intently, watching his aunt, and not making a move to stop either of them. Not, thank heaven, chasing her out of the house. Yet.

"Ardelle was at the line shack, you know," she said to Deuce. "You may wonder how that is possible. *I* certainly didn't expect to see her when Jake brought me there. He tied me up and brought me there. Uncomfortable ride, too," she added, nudging Ardelle's smooth white cheek with the nose of the rifle. "She can walk, Deuce. She's always been able to walk. And to ride. It was a better cover for her to pretend not to though. But she was there, and she gave Jake tacit permission to do with me whatever he liked—at least tonight—and she was willing to talk about the reasons why. Weren't you, Ardelle?"

"Perfectly extraordinary," Ardelle murmured, rocking back and forth, hoping the movement covered her growing agitation. She had to try to bluff her way out now, and she wasn't at all sure Deuce would believe either of them.

"So now she's in league with Jake?" Deuce questioned with a sardonic edge to his voice.

"For a long time, apparently," Kalida said, moving away, willing him to believe just that little much she was telling him. She couldn't bear to look at him in that moment. There was no way to convince him other than to force Ardelle to become mobile, but even that did not prove she was a thief and in cahoots with Jake.

"Monstrous lie," Ardelle muttered.

Kalida whirled on them. "You're so good at denial and lies yourself," she hissed at Ardelle. "Deny you've been stealing the Linaria—and with Jake's help."

The room fell dead silent.

Ardelle said nothing, just stared at Deuce and shrugged helplessly.

Kalida turned away again. Stupid chance to take. It sounded insane. *She* sounded insane. Her best chance was to dive out the damned window again and run as fast and as far as she could get, just as she had thought before she came back here tonight. Deuce would never trust her. The outcome didn't matter. Ardelle had won, and she knew it.

Ardelle rocked herself back and forth complacently, sparing a snide little covert smile for Kalida, as if to say, How could he buy that? Really, Kalida.

His face was impassive, his eyes closed as he leaned his muscular body against the door; as if he were blocking the way out—but whose way out, Kalida wondered, as she watched him assessing her words. And she knew she didn't want not have to prove to him what she had said was the truth. She wanted him to believe it because he believed in her. But how was it possible? Ardelle was his aunt, family, and Kalida was the daughter of a schemer who had stolen from him.

How hopeless could it be?

"Utterly ridiculous," Ardelle said suddenly, impatient to hear Deuce's reaction to Kalida's accusation. He couldn't entertain it, she thought, even for a second. It sounded crazy. She had counted on it sounding crazy, impossible.

Deuce said nothing.

Kalida's heart fell to her feet. There was no telling what he was thinking, except she could almost scent his negative emotion against her.

"What some people won't do," Ardelle said in an

undertone, shaking her head as if in compassion, as if to say Kalida had no choice; he couldn't have expected her to ask for mercy. And he knew by now she was full of guile. He *must* know that.

Kalida raised the rifle once again, at the disdainful note in Ardelle's voice. Damn her, Ardelle was *not* going to get away with this, even if it meant that she, Kalida, would be sent away from Sweetland forever. Her feelings for Deuce hardly entered into it anymore. Her feelings for revenge were paramount, almost vital in their intensity.

What would convince Deuce? she wondered as she eyed his tall muscular body leaning against the door. He was still motionless, impassive. Was he waiting? For what? For which one to speak, for which one to trip herself up?

"Deuce, this is—I can't sit here and listen to this anymore. Why don't you just give her some money—enough to take her to Miles City. That's the place for her," Ardelle said into the bleak silence. "I just can't stay here a minute longer and listen to her."

"I haven't said anything—yet," Kalida countered harshly. "But don't think I'm not going to." Now or never, she thought.

"Say away," Ardelle invited, sitting back in the chair, that chippy little smile in place, her eyes burning dark red fire in challenge. The chit can't hurt *me,* she thought complacently. But the scene was taking on the aspect of her worst nightmares, when she had actually imagined Kalida confronting her after having discovered the truth. But then, she had never thought Kalida would be spirited enough to fight Jake. To hear him tell it, Kalida wanted him, would be happy for a chance with him. And he would have taken her with him, she knew. *He* never would have killed Kalida. *She* should have done it herself, damned girl.

She waited, noting that Deuce's hooded eyes were focused on Kalida. And the damned gun. What could

Kalida say that would damn her and not sound deranged?

"When Ardelle told me," Kalida began in a nonchalant conversational tone, "that she had been stealing the Linaria one by one systematically over the last few years, it was like everything fell into place."

"Your *father* was probably stealing them one by one over the past few years," Ardelle interjected nastily. "That's how she knows details, Deuce. That's how she knows anything."

Kalida's face hardened. It was a good ploy, she thought; excellent. A lot could be blamed on her father's greed. Too damned much. But not this, she vowed, and turned back to Deuce. "She knew where you were every minute of the day. She knew where the herd was, when you were moving it, when the patrol would be on night watch. When you'd be away from the ranch. And she did the account books; she told me so herself. She wanted a piece of Sweetland, pure and simple, because your father apparently left her nothing in gratitude for her years of nursing him. So she thought she'd build herself a little herd, piecemeal, with *your* prime stock. That's what *she* told me," she added, as she detected the merest flicker of a muscle movement in his jaw.

"She was scared to death of your interest in me," she went on, "because she knew I was no homebody. That I'd been involved with Father's business, and I probably would want to be involved in yours. And if I started looking at numbers and breeding forms . . . Well, she needed to discourage your interest in me. She tried teaching me to be a lady, and I was hardly cooperative in that respect. But then there was Jake, her partner, interested in me already for his own reasons, eager to help her dishonor me for still others. Anyway, she said they occasionally hit other syndicate members to make it look like a band of thieves was operating in this area. She said four of your men have a cut. She told me all of this herself, out at the line shack."

"Really, Kalida," said Ardelle, standing up. "Deuce, this girl should be institutionalized. Do you realize that if her father had the guts and the wherewithal to take his herd back from you, it could have been him taking the Linaria also? What better deal for him! A little at a time, not too greedy, crossbreed a few at a time, and eventually, he gets ready to make his big move. Fortunately, fate took a hand. Don't you see how perfect it is that Kalida accuses me, but *she* herself knows *every* detail of how it was done? Was her father not on patrol with you? Did he not know all your comings and goings—as a neighbor? Did he not bribe you with Kalida when he wanted into the syndicate?

"And we know why, don't we? Kalida was to be his informant, to get him out of trouble if you should ever discover the reality of what he *really* had been doing." She hobbled across the floor and patted the rifle head. "A good try, Kalida, but as you can see, Deuce and I do know the truth. You're a liar and a cheat, possibly a thief, and we're well rid of you. Now, do excuse me. These bedtime stories have made me excessively tired." She motioned for Deuce to move from the doorway.

The gall, Kalida thought angrily, lifting the rifle and taking aim at her. She had nothing to lose now anyway; Ardelle had very successfully circumvented the truth with her artful lies. At best now, she could satisfy her own growing blood lust; she could shoot at least one of Ardelle's lies out from under her and prove to Deuce that one thing at least was the truth.

He made no move to stop her. His eyes flashed as he stood aside to let Ardelle open the door.

His eyes . . . He wasn't going to prevent her from stopping Ardelle from leaving the room. Why? Because . . . something of what she had said made sense?

She pulled the trigger before Ardelle was out the door,

and her cane shattered in two pieces. "Run, Ardelle," she hissed, "because I'll kill you if you don't." Another shot, aimed just over Ardelle's head, ricocheted through the hallway. "Run, Ardelle, I don't care what happens now; you've taken everything away from me." She blasted the floor behind Ardelle's skirt.

And Ardelle ran. She heard the cold-blooded note in Kalida's voice; Kalida didn't care now. She had lost Deuce, her father, Jake. She had nothing. She could have nothing in jail as easily as anywhere else. And she would have her revenge. Ardelle would not be the instrument of her revenge. She ran.

She dashed down the dark hallway as Kalida's bullets made a path directly behind her. An excellent shot, Kalida, she remembered thinking fleetingly. She could have lifted that gun another inch and crippled her forever. In a blur, she saw Prestina's frightened face peering at her from behind her bedroom door.

A bullet smashed into the newel post at the top of the stairs, an inch in front of Ardelle. Startled, she stumbled and tried to catch herself on the spindles of the banister—fragile spindles; the momentum and weight of her body pulled the very one she grasped right out of its socket and she tumbled down the stairs with it, landing with a sickening thud at the bottom.

Kalida dropped the gun in horror. "Oh my God," she moaned, crouching at the top of the steps. "Oh my God . . ." She felt strong arms lift her and cradle her against pulsating warmth. How could he hold her like that, with Ardelle unconscious at the bottom of the steps?

And he held her, so close, so tight; it was a homecoming, his holding her like that. He believed her. She started crying, as much from shock as relief. He believed *her*. And for just that one moment, Ardelle had ceased to matter.

* * *

It was incredible the difference a couple of days could make, Kalida thought, as she stepped into the parlor of Ellie's house to wait for Deuce.

It had been two days, but it seemed longer since they had brought Ardelle into Bozeman in the buckboard, unconscious but still alive, after driving at breakneck speed all night.

And one day since the doctor had pronounced her well enough to travel, although she was permanently crippled by her unfortunate fall.

A day since she and Deuce had sought Ellie Dean, only to find that Ellie had disappeared in the middle of the night several days ago with some gentleman or the other, Charlotte said, leaving the house once again in hers and Lorena's hands.

A day since she had slept, she thought wearily, dragging herself up to one of the rooms that Charlotte had offered her for the duration of her stay in Bozeman. It was a room very similar to the one she had occupied earlier, as sumptuously furnished, with the same kind of little china knickknacks strewn all around and pretentious lithographs on the wall.

She needed a week to assimilate everything that had happened. Explanations came later, Deuce said. They had their whole life for explanations, he said. *He* knew everything anyway now, about Ardelle and the thefts. She had yet to tell him about her father, but at this stage, she was sure he would say he didn't care. Her father was apparently gone for good and had taken Ellie with him to live off the spoils of his ill-gotten gains.

She would probably never see him again, she thought, and strangely, she felt only an affectionate exasperation for all he had put her through.

Ardelle was being sent to Deuce's sister in England, who apparently had enough servants to care for her now that she really must cope with being permanently disabled. But for now, Deuce had requested that Ardelle be present in Ellie's parlor this afternoon. And Kalida, "well rested," he had specified, "and dressed like a woman, please, for a change."

That request rankled, but since she was hot, tired, and grubby, needed a bath and to refresh herself totally, she willingly let Charlotte lend her a plain blue dress and had complied with Deuce's wishes only so far as to wear it. Her freshly washed midnight hair was brushed to a glossy cascade down her back, and her cobalt eyes sparked with a curious anticipation as she called to Ardelle, who was slumped in an invalid chair, staring out the bay window at the vigorous movement of the street.

"I'm glad you're here," Kalida said bustling in, hardly wanting to talk to Ardelle at all, let alone try to be pleasant to her. "Deuce was adamant that you be present this afternoon."

"What for?" Ardelle growled, wheeling the chair around viciously.

Kalida shrugged. "Perhaps a little going-away party," she suggested. Ardelle spat and whipped her chair back to the window.

Kalida smiled to herself. Everything was fine, and everything was not. She hadn't seen Deuce since they had heard the final verdict about Ardelle from the doctor and he had sent her back to Ellie's house with his set of instructions.

She didn't know why she still felt guilty, as if everything were her fault. And why she still felt trapped.

The door burst open and Deuce strode in, with a strange kindly-looking man in tow.

"What's this?" Kalida demanded briskly.

"The minister," Deuce said flatly, his flinty eyes flaring as he looked at her, daring her to run away from this reality. "The *minister*, Ardelle," he added harshly, for emphasis, turning his stone-gray gaze to his aunt who had whisked herself around at his announcement and was staring malevolently at the stranger.

"It's your mistake," she shrugged finally.

"Really," Kalida said, a lick of anger grazing her body, "*who* were you thinking of marrying?"

"Kalida . . ." Impatience now in his voice, his eyes hardening to rock-gray at the way her body stiffened.

"Charlotte perhaps?" Kalida asked sweetly. "Have you been having a liaison with her all these years just like my father had with Ellie? I'm so happy for you; she'll be right glad to be legitimized . . ."

"Kalida . . ." A growl this time, brooking no nonsense, and still she raced headlong ahead, fiery with resentment at his high-handedness.

"Not Charlotte. Lorena? Both of them? Oh my, Deuce . . . Strange no one can recall your asking any of those good ladies to marry you. . . ."

"The hell I didn't," he exploded, thumping his hand down on the nearest table with a force that nearly collapsed it.

"And rescinded it, as I recall," Kalida hissed, "so surely it can't be little old *me*." She turned and stalked out of the room, nearly in tears, but she swore she would never let him see her crying. God, and she wanted that more than life—his love, his trust, his commitment—but how could he do that to her, just assume it was what she wanted and never *ask* her? After *all* that had happened. It wasn't *right*. And it wasn't right that he hadn't allowed her to explain. How could he want her to marry him without hearing her side of what had happened? It was too big a reversal, that; she couldn't in conscience have said yes to a ceremony on those grounds. She *couldn't*.

But as she climbed the steps slowly to her room, she wished she had. What damned difference did it make anyway? He believed her about Ardelle; what did it

438

matter what he thought now about her father and Jake? He still wanted to marry her; wasn't that enough?

She never heard footsteps behind her on the stairs, and she screamed as she was suddenly lifted bodily upwards and hauled over one muscular shoulder by two huge capable hands.

"Deuce . . . damn you!" she shouted, grabbing his shirt, his hair, pulling, kicking him, wriggling so violently she almost threw them both off balance.

"Kalida . . . damn you," he echoed harshly, his voice rough with something she couldn't define. He smacked her bottom without mercy, and then slid his hand down her leg and under her skirt as he made his way briskly to her room.

He kicked open the door and looked around. "Lots of good ammunition for throwing in here," he commented caustically, dumping her as inelegantly as possible on the bed. "Can I get you something?" He bowed sardonically.

She struggled to sit up as he depressed one side of the bed with his weight. "Don't bother," he advised her, watching with amusement as she checked her upward movement.

"You arrogant bastard," she hissed at him.

"You predictable bitch," he countered grimly. "I swear, Kalida, there really is only one way to keep you in line. I knew it months ago, and I just let it go right out of my mind with all these other distracting goings-on." He leaned over her and covered her mouth ruthlessly with his own.

She wrenched away. "You don't have to marry me for *that*," she muttered nastily, feeling as if she wanted to gouge her fingers into his ribs. He had no right to be so potently and righteously *there*, where she wanted him, with the answers that she wanted from him just when she did not want him.

"What should I marry you for?" he whispered, shifting

his weight onto his arms and fitting his body against hers.

"You don't have to marry me at all," she suggested kindly, turning her head away from him.

"You're right," he agreed cheerfully, pushing her down on the bed. "Absolutely right." His mouth hovered over hers, and the look in his smoky gray eyes singed her. "But I will." He licked her resistant lips as she struggled helplessly beneath his weight. "Anyway," he added softly, to punctuate the point before biting her reluctant lips apart to command her capitulation.

"Deuce . . ."

"Do you have to?"

"I don't understand."

"Yes you do." He delved into her mouth fiercely now, then pulled away, with the softness of her lips imprinted on his. "Yes you do," he reiterated in the softest of voices. "I've waited a long time, and I don't give a damn about anything right now, Kalida, except keeping you forever."

She was drowning, carried away by his surging words, words he would not have said days ago, things he did not believe days ago. She didn't care; they could sort it all out another time. Her hungry body demanded she respond to him.

"Oh God, but Deuce, everybody gets away. . . ." she cried. "Ardelle, my father, Jake; they all get away."

"Not everyone," Deuce whispered, his eyes darkening to flaming charcoal as his lips met hers.

And now, and now . . . Words conveyed no meaning. The motion of his hands held all the meaning in the world. How they touched her and aroused her, pausing here, sliding there, gently unfastening, unbuttoning, caressing. And her own hands, audacious with her own suppressed need, her feelings multiplied uncontrollably by the horror of having thought she would never have him again. She would never have believed how much she yearned to feel all the hard planes of his body, to learn

440

each and every angle and hollow, every long beguiling line that led to the one inexorable, incredible part of him that she desired the most.

And she loved having him reduced to wanton need by the very caresses of her torrid fingers, loved the elemental sense of laying naked next to him, her long bare legs entwined with his, her hands stroking his body, her tongue stroking his in the same tempestuous rhythm. And she loved his hands exploring her body in just the same way, sliding over each curve as though he had never felt it before, holding her breasts and caressing each ripe nipple to a stiff turgid peak of pleasure.

And then the long, honey-hot moment before he shifted himself over her, poised at her velvet cleft, seeking her demand in the heat of her tongue, entering her then with one luscious thrust of pure molten sensation that elicited a long, satisfying satin sigh from deep in her throat. How could she live without *this?*

"Kalida." He breathed her name in that same urgent voice she knew. "Kalida. No one else can have this," he whispered against her lips. "No one else will ever make you feel this. And you know it, Kalida. You know it."

"I know," she murmured, savoring the moment, and her understanding. She felt infinitely connected to him by every pore of her skin, by the words she had uttered, by the fact that she loved him. Her whole body quivered as she admitted the thought into her consciousness at last.

The dimension this acknowledgement added to her feeling was indescribable. The possessiveness she felt suddenly, the sense of the strength of his being within her, driving his need within her, answering hers wholly and fully with every ounce of that virile male strength of his, potent, surging, indomitably *hers*. The insatiable wild joy of knowing he desired *her* now, meaningful beyond anything between them so far. She loved him.

And he sensed that spurt of fire in her. Something had

changed, had ignited her ardor to a fever pitch. He intense response sent him soaring. Her body demanded all of him. Her hands explored all of him, every muscle every hollow of his body, learning where to gently squeeze, where to stroke, feeling and holding his buttock in a way that excited her still more.

He plunged into her satin-moist sheath with short, quick ravishing strokes. He felt her body tighten beneath him, spreading, unfurling then to feel each voluptuous thrust to its utmost, bracing her feet against the back of his knees to give her body purchase to move with each sultry thrust.

The gush of sensation was intense, tantalizing at first, each lavish stroke compelling her to reach still further and wider for all he had to give. And she opened her pliant body to him, demanding even more, submitting to his passion, letting it propel her into a sumptuous spiral of sensation, riding with it, letting it carry her endlessly upward until the very peak of her endurance, when it crackled into an eruption of spuming sparkles that danced all over her skin like molten fingers.

He held her tightly, rocking her body against his as he nestled deep within her. "I love you, Kalida," he whispered as he took every subtle movement of her body deep into his consciousness. "I've loved you since you were fifteen." He moved gently, tentatively, testing her readiness to receive him. "And you knew it," he added in concert with his first driving thrust. "You knew it, you knew it. . . ." He buried the words in her mouth, feeling for her provocative tongue as his body went wild with the sense of her beneath him. He plunged vigorously into her sultry core, consuming her essence, seeking her elusive femininity with every ounce of strength he possessed. She would be his, she *would;* nothing else mattered, nothing.

And then he heard the words. "Now . . ." A breath in the air between them, in rhythm with his thrusts, "Now

. . now . . ." And . . . "Now . . ." And with her demanding words resonating through his whole body, he gave one last churning surge and spewed his seed deep within her.

She curled herself against him, feeling his warm arms surround her and the wetness of his body sticking to hers. They lay still a very long time. She didn't know how long.

Time seemed meaningless. Nothing was urgent. He loved her.

"I love you," she murmured.

"I know."

She could feel his smile as his chin rested against her tangled inky hair. "Brute, and you put me through so much."

"You didn't know."

"Maybe I knew," she admitted huskily. "Deuce, why did you let me go after Ardelle?"

"Not now, Kalida."

"Now; I have to know. I *have* to." She felt his arms tighten around her, as if what he would say would be something she wouldn't like. And she didn't.

"You said she could walk. And I thought, if you could take it—badly as you did—so could she. And if she were faking, everything you accused her of made logical sense. So I let you prove it."

She felt his smile again, and she slapped him on the thigh.

"Kalida, I wanted you to prove it. You proved it. And that's all I'm going to talk about it. Now."

"I hate you." She didn't move, and his hands cupped her breasts gently.

"But you will marry me."

She recoiled from the resonant *male* surety of that statement.

"Maybe," she said saucily, twisting her body around sinuously, *"you'll* marry me."

"Thank you," he said huskily, "I accept your proposal. And soon, please, because that poor patient minister is still waiting for us downstairs. But not," he added, as he shifted her body so that she was beneath him once again feeling the evidence of his desire for her, "just yet."

LOVE'S BRIGHTEST STARS SHINE
WITH ZEBRA BOOKS!

CATALINA'S CARESS (2202, $3.95)
by Sylvie F. Sommerfield

Catalina Carrington was determined to buy her riverboat back from the handsome gambler who'd beaten her brother at cards. But when dashing Marc Copeland named his price—three days as his mistress—Catalina swore she'd never meet his terms . . . even as she imagined the rapture a night in his arms would bring!

BELOVED EMBRACE (2135, $3.95)
by Cassie Edwards

Leana Rutherford was terrified when the ship carrying her family from New York to Texas was attacked by savage pirates. But when she gazed upon the bold sea-bandit Brandon Seton, Leana longed to share the ecstasy she was sure sure his passionate caress would ignite!

ELUSIVE SWAN (2061, $3.95)
by Sylvie F. Sommerfield

Just one glance from the handsome stranger in the dockside tavern in boisterous St. Augustine made Arianne tremble with excitement. But the innocent young woman was already running from one man . . . and no matter how fiercely the flames of desire burned within her, Arianne dared not submit to another!

SAVAGE PARADISE (1985, $3.95)
by Cassie Edwards

Marianna Fowler detested the desolate wilderness of the unsettled Montana Territory. But once the hot-blooded Chippewa brave Lone Hawk saved her life, the spirited young beauty wished never to leave, longing to experience the fire of the handsome warrior's passionate embrace!

MOONLIT MAGIC (1941, $3.95)
by Sylvie F. Sommerfield

When she found the slick railroad negotiator Trace Cord trespassing on her property and bathing in her river, innocent Jenny Graham could barely contain her rage. But when she saw how the setting sun gilded Trace's magnificent physique, Jenny's seething fury was transformed into burning desire!

Available wherever paperbacks are sold, or order direct from the Publisher. Send cover price plus 50¢ per copy for mailing and handling to Zebra Books, Dept. 2271, 475 Park Avenue South, New York, N.Y. 10016. Residents of New York, New Jersey and Pennsylvania must include sales tax. DO NOT SEND CASH.